"Books can have teeth. A whole mouthful of them. The Pallbearers Club has a whole lifetime of them."—Stephen Graham Jones, New York Times bestselling author of The Only Good Indians

"Any new book by Paul Tremblay makes me sit up straight. Part of the joy is not knowing what to expect from each new story."—Adam Nevill, author of The Ritual and No One Gets Out Alive

"The most beautiful and heartbreaking funeral I've been to in a long time, The Pallbearers Club is melancholy, funny, and very cruel, but you won't regret carrying this coffin."—Grady Hendrix, New York Times bestselling author of The Final Girl Support Group

"Replete with the trademark brilliant characterisation, intricate switchback plotting and general weirdness you get with a Paul Tremblay novel, Art and Mercy's friendship—and bickering over what may or may not be a vampire story—will haunt you long after the last page."—A. G. Slatter, award-winning author of All the Murmuring Bones

"An extraordinary novel. This book is fun, warm, sad, and most of all, profoundly humane: it subverts horror tropes and real-life certainties in one go. I loved it and I need to shout it in the streets."—Francesco Dimitri, author of The Book of Hidden Things and Never the Wind

"Brilliant, profound, moving and shocking, held together in a delightfully unique and intriguing narrative structure that will tell you truths... or lies... but probably both."—Tim Lebbon, New York Times bestselling author of The Silence

"A ... and something quietly beckons us to look deeper."—Eric LaRocca, author of Things Have Gotten Worse Since We Last Spoke and Other Misfortunes

"This is horror at its most heartfelt, horror that confirms our fears and flaws, the insecurities that we carry with us from our formative years." —Priya Sharma, the award-winning author of Ormeshadow

"Tremblay at his most audacious best. It's such a sneaky mindblower! It'll burrow deep inside you, and by the end, you'll be wondering if the room you're sitting in, the people you're talking with, or even your own memory, are real. This book is horror's answer to Nabokov's Pale Fire."—Sarah Langan, acclaimed author of Good Neighbours

"The Pallbearers Club constructs a maze of uncanny ambiguity and disquiet—a Nabokovian labyrinth that sustains its mystery past the point few writers but Paul Tremblay would risk."—Ramsey Campbell

"A new novel from Paul Tremblay is always cause for celebration. The Pallbearers Club has it all—growth and decay, metatextual playfulness and earnest terror, dark hilarity and deep melancholy."—Karen Russell, author of Swamplandia and Orange World

Also by Paul Tremblay and available From Titan Books

Disappearance at Devil's Rock
A Head Full of Ghosts
The Cabin at the End of the World
Growing Things and Other Stories
Survivor Song
The Little Sleep and No Sleep Til Wonderland Omnibus

THE PALLBEARERS CLUB

~~A MEMOIR~~
A NOVEL

~~BY ART BARBARA~~
BY PAUL TREMBLAY

TITAN BOOKS

The Pallbearers Club
Print edition ISBN: 9781789099003
E-book edition ISBN: 9781789099010

Published by Titan Books
A division of Titan Publishing Group Ltd
144 Southwark Street, London SE1 0UP
www.titanbooks.com

First edition: July 2022
10 9 8 7 6 5 4 3 2 1

Grateful acknowledgment is made to Bob Mould for permission to
reprint an excerpt from "Thirty Dozen Roses" (written by Bob Mould),
courtesy of Granary Music © 2019.

This is a work of fiction. All of the characters, organizations, and events
portrayed in this novel are either products of the author's imagination or
are used fictitiously. Any resemblance to actual persons, living or dead
(except for satirical purposes), is entirely coincidental.

A CIP catalogue record for this title is available from the British Library.

Printed and bound in the United Kingdom by CPI Group (UK) Ltd, Croydon,
CR0 4YY.

For Lisa, Cole, and Emma

Who are they?

Maybe out of everything I thought I knew, there was nothing I was more wrong about than my own life story.

—Sara Gran, *Claire DeWitt and the Bohemian Highway*

So some of him lived but the most of him died.

—Rudyard Kipling, "The Vampire"

The swollen hollow of my wobbly heart.

—Bob Mould, "Thirty Dozen Roses"

IF I TOLD YOU

(2007)

I am not Art Barbara.

That's not my birth name. But at the risk of contradicting myself within the first few lines of a memoir, I *am* Art Barbara.

Imagine my personage, the whole of me (I prefer that phrase to "spirit" or "soul") exists in Plato's World of Forms. That me, the one slicked in the amber of Greek philosophy, is Art Barbara. Sorry, Mom and Dad, the name you assigned was a valiant effort, but it does not sum up who I was, who I am, or who I will become.

Art Barbara is bold, declarative, striking, and upon first hearing it spoken your brow furrows, head tilts, and mouth smirks. Admit it; your face is in thrall and acting on its own. You might know a Barbara or even an Art, but you haven't met, nor do you know, Art Barbara.

However, the initial "Oh" upon the shores of appellatory discovery soon gives way to incredulousness, to there-must-be-some-mistake. Let's be honest, here (and you have my promise I will always be painfully honest) the name tries too hard. It is more than a little ridiculous, shading toward pathetic (a word derived from the Greek *pathos*, of course), particularly when spoken with a Boston or Rhode Island accent as the coterie of *r*'s disappear into obnoxiously long *ah*'s. Even without the accent, there's a slant-rhyme clunkiness to the first two syllables, or three if you insist upon pronouncing Barbara as *Bar-bar-ah* as opposed to the shortened *Bar'bra*. Regardless, the combination of the first two syllables, the *Art-Bar*, forces the speaker to comply, to slow down and enunciate the harsh coupling before dumping an auditory body into the dark water of *r*'s and *a*'s. I make no claim to be an expert of phonesthetics (the study of inherent pleasantness of the sound of words, according to Wikipedia), but clearly Art Barbara is no *cellar door*.

I saw the name written on the bathroom wall of Club Babyhead, spring of 1991. The letters were capitalized, angular slashes of neon-green ink; a cave painting glowing in the lovely darkness of the early 1990s. I have never forgotten it. And by the end of this memoir, neither will you.

Isn't time strange? Time is not linear but a deck of cards that is continuously shuffled.

I will change all names to protect the innocent and not-so. I will take great care to choose the names appropriately. As astounding and beyond-belief the goings-on to be detailed are, the names will be the only fictions.

Beyond the act of communication, sharing my story and experience and life, exploring fear and fate and the supernatural (for lack of a better word) and the unknown universe big and small, vulnerable confessions, and base gossip (Truman Capote and the nonfiction novel this is not), perhaps a lame excuse or two for lifelong disappointments and why I am and where I will be, the purpose is hope. Hope that one reader or one thousand and one readers might empathize with the "why" behind the poor decisions I made, make, and most certainly will make.

I assume you intended for me to find this. Maybe that's a lot for me to assume. Maybe it's not. I mean, you left it on your cluttered desk with a literal yellow bow tied around the manuscript. Holy shit, I bet I'll have a lot to say about this book based on the opening chapter.

Art Barbara. Jesus, dude.

I promise my commentary will be as honest as you are claiming to be. That sentence by itself makes it sound like I am already accusing you of lying. I don't mean to. We've had our ups and downs, but I've always considered you to be one of my dearest, oldest friends, and I hope you feel similarly.

Frankly, I'm a little scared to read more, to find out what you really think of me.

Based on the title, I don't think it's vanity to assume I'll play a large role in this, um, memoir.

Memory is a fucked-up thing, especially as time passes, stretches, and yawns. Your comparison of time to a shuffled deck of cards comes close to the truth, or a truth. I think time is better represented as a house of cards, an unimaginably large castle of cards, one in which rooms and entire wings collapse and are endlessly rebuilt. Those collapsed rooms and wings hold memories, both personal and collective. That card house is forever haunted by the lost memories and by the ones that are retained but changed.

Sorry, I know this is your book, not mine.

It occurs to me if our memories of certain events differ, that doesn't necessarily mean one or both of us are lying, certainly not lying on purpose.

I'll attempt to keep my comments solely to after each chapter. I will read and comment as I go without skipping ahead. I can't promise that I won't mark stuff up within the manuscript though. As you know, I've always been a bit impulsive.

Looking forward to reading what name you'll give me, Mr. Art Barbara.

NEW DAY RISING

(October 1988)

A chapter in which a club's hero rises, or at the very least, raises a shaky hand.

A-House was one of three wings attached to the main building of Beverly High School and it telescoped out, as vast and empty as the cold universe. A yellow hall pass clutched in my sweaty adolescent hand granted permission to go to the AV room so I could assist with the morning announcements broadcast on our closed-circuit Panther TV. As a senior who regularly achieved honor roll, I'd earned "senior privileges," which included the ability to traverse the campus during homeroom and free periods without need of a pass. My asking for a pass from my calculus teacher, Mr. Langan (a kind if not awkward middle-aged man who wore sweater vests and an Abraham Lincoln–style beard) represented the kind of student I was; skittish, afraid, desperate for approval of any kind.

I ghosted past rows of lockers dangling their bulbous locks. Most of me ached to turn around, to return to homeroom, to give up on this foolish idea, to forget it ever occurred to me. There was another part that realized this was a Robert Frost path-choosing moment. If I went through with my plan, this smallest AV step for humankind, my life would be irrevocably changed. By the time I swung open the creaking metal door of the AV room, my resolve leaked away, literalized as flop sweat.

Ian, one of two Panthers newscasters, he of the swimmer's shoulders and beer-keg leer, greeted me with "Hey, it's Artie the one-man party."

[Note: Ian did not say that. As we've discussed, my name was not Art. I will not break in like this again to point out other, minor factual name discrepancies. It's enough for you to know Ian was the kind of chud who would've said that if my name were Art. What he did call me wasn't my real name either. He called me Bones. I had always been the skinniest, most slight kid in my class, and at that AV moment in time I weighed a scant one hundred and forty pounds. Most of my male classmates called me by that nickname, which I never had the option of approving when it was pinned to me at age eleven along with another kid's fist to my big nose. (I fought back, but all that earned was another, bigger kid's fist to the stomach.) At ages seventeen and eighteen, the nickname was uttered with tradition if not endearment, certainly with less intentional cruelty, but it was there in the name's history, so I will not use nor refer to it again. We will stick with Art to the end.]

The other newscaster, Shauna, gave me a wave and a slightly puzzled tilt of the head as she buzzed around the small studio, handing out photocopies of the morning's announcements to the producers, to Ian (slouched behind the news desk, a combo of James Dean and a pile of dirty laundry) and the camera operator. She wore the high-school equivalent of a business suit, her black blazer with shoulder pads of a size somewhere between a football player and David Byrne's *Stop Making Sense* suit. Shauna and I were in the same calculus, English, and French classes and she had always been cordial if not coolly competitive. She had the third-highest grade point average in our graduating class of three hundred and twenty-four. I was number nineteen, one of only two boys in the top twenty, which told you all you needed to know about my male classmates.

Shauna asked, not unkindly, why I was there. I told her I had an announcement about a new club.

She said "Okay" about ten times while scribbling on her announcements sheet, and said (to herself, I assumed), "I can talk about it between the student council and powderpuff football sign-up." Then, to me: "Got it, Art."

"Oh. Thanks, but, well, because it's a new club and as the founder and president I think I need to make the announcement myself, and, um, Mr. Tobin said that I could do it."

Shauna smiled but her eyes moistened, as though on the verge of you-can't-do-this-to-me tears. Before I could say sorry, she said, "We have five minutes to air, do you know what you're going to say and how you're going to say it, and when it might be best suited for airing?"

I shrugged, offered something mostly committal. She shoved me into the adjacent secondary studio, an isolation chamber encased in thick windows so no one could hear me scream.

The announcements began when they were supposed to. They were piped through a small box of a speaker perched above the door of my studio. Ian and Shauna sounded trapped in a tin can, but I was the one sardined in here with barely enough room for me (standing, no chair), a tripod, and a bored underclassman lurking behind a camera.

Instead of practicing what I was going to say while awaiting the go signal, I uttered a silent mantra in my head: *This is so you can get into college.* My guidance counselor, Mr. Brugués (he of the novelty fish ties, walrus-thick '70s mustache, overstarched dress shirts, and brown-bag lunches that were always open and left half-eaten on his desk), said my grades were great but I didn't have any extracurricular activities. No sports, no student council, no clubs, no volunteer work outside of school. My lack of well-roundedness as a student was, well, a lack, and, to quote, "lessened my college acceptance prospects." Panic set in as soon as he said it. Now that my chance to finally flee these people and this town was within sight, I was desperate to get into a school that wasn't Salem State or North Shore Community College (not that anything was wrong with those schools—well, their proximity to my house was wrong with those schools).

I stood in front of the camera, trapped under a mini spotlight that might as well have been a heat lamp from the cafeteria. This was the last place in the world I wanted to be, and I normally spent most of my school days trying to not be seen.

See me:

I was six feet tall, having grown six inches in the prior eighteen months. The rapid height gain exacerbated my scoliosis. The condition had been discovered later than it should've, as I somehow slipped through the cracks of the embarrassing annual scoliosis checks during gym class. The checks consisted of a line of boys with their shirts off (my head down, wishing I were invisible, my arms matchsticking across my chest), and after a properly lengthy time of mortification I was in front of a disinterested school nurse holding a school-issued clipboard. I bent over to touch my toes, so skinny that my vertebrae stuck up through my skin like the back plates of Godzilla, and the nurse's cold hand fish-slapped onto my right shoulder blade, her audible "hmmm" and "you look a little off" (me being *a little off* was her diagnosis) and then she told me to switch to carrying my bookbag with my left shoulder. Since being diagnosed eighteen months prior, I attended physical therapy sessions and slept in a hard-plastic-and-metal-framed back brace at night (the doctor had never insisted I wear it to school, knowing I would not), which improved the curvature in my lower spine, but not in the upper region between my shoulder blades where scoliosis was most difficult to correct, where the curve to the right measured thirty-five degrees. The prospect of spinal fusion surgery loomed if the curvature increased in my upper spine. I wore baggy enough clothes so other people wouldn't notice the encroaching kyphosis, my curling into myself. No one at school commented on my back, and I never told any of them about it. Maybe no one noticed the burgeoning hunchback because of my other unpleasant physical attributes. We've already discussed my ectomorphic build (or lack of build). Additionally, my skin was a raw and angry map of acne. Archipelagos of pimple volcanoes regularly erupted on my face and my back and chest. That no one would ever see my back and chest was a small consolation. Of course, now, on announcement morning, I had a new Mount Washington red nodule, its craggy peak above my right nostril.

In the secondary studio, I sweated under the interrogation lamp. The kid behind the camera breathed too loudly, sucking up all the air. Where was the goddamn go signal? Was Shauna going to purposefully dump me from the announcements, like I was a never-been Z-list celebrity in the talk-show green room, bumped for an animal act that went too long? I'd be trapped standing in this tiny soundproof room forever.

The speaker above the door cut out. The light on the front of the camera pointed at my head finally burned red. I took a deep breath. And I spoke.

"Hi, for those of you who don't know me, my name is Art Barbara, I'm a senior, and I'm starting a new club. It's called the Pallbearers Club. We'll volunteer at local funeral homes to be attendees and pallbearers at funerary services for homeless people or for elderly who have outlived family members and won't have many or any mourners show up. I've already called Stephens Funeral Home on Cabot Street and they would love to have our, um, help."

I glanced to my right, out the studio window. Ian looked smug, bemused, and disgusted, or *smusegusted*. Shauna manically spun her hands in front of her, which I assumed was a wrap-it-up gesture. But I was not ready to wrap it up. I'd just started talking.

"I know it sounds a little scary or weird, but we'd be doing a great service for the community, and um, for the people who died, of course, even if they don't know it. It's still a very nice thing to do. It would look good on a college application too. Mr. Brugués told me it would. We'd mainly attend services on the weekends. And um—"

Shauna was at the window and banging on it with hammer fists. A crack spidered through the soundproof glass.

"Yeah, I guess that's it. If you're interested, keep an eye out for flyers I'll post around school, or just find me to learn more.

My homeroom is A-113, or you can leave a message for me in the front office, or if you forget my name, leave a note addressed to the Pallbearers Club. Thank you. Back to you, Shauna and Ian. Um, go Panthers."

I like your use of "chud" though an editor or copyeditor might be confused.

This chapter is a little "woe is me," don't you think? I'm not judging and I'm not belittling your school-aged experience nor your state of mental health, but by way of perspective, you have white cis-male privilege, did not grow up in poverty, and you did not suffer tragedies during childhood, none that I'm aware of anyway. Apologies if there are revelations to come regarding the latter.

I get it, though. Kids/teens are confused and cruel and then they generally become confused and cruel adults. The emotional scars you described, the type so many of us wear and conceal, are the crucible in which we are formed, especially if we dwell on such things. I hope the act of writing this finally purged some of this poison. However, given everything that happened since you wrote this chapter, I guess that it did not.

For what it's worth, I do not remember the you from that age as being a hopelessly ugly duckling. If you were, your appalling lack of self-confidence and self-awareness did not help. I do not blame you, but it's a point of fact.

I'm not saying this very well, but the person who is cruelest/hardest on you is almost always the person looking into the mirror. We never see a reflection of ourselves in the mirror, do we?

Sorry, I sound like a self-help guru. I always wanted to help you. I tried to help you. I truly did.

None of what I've read so far is a surprise. I recognized what you needed the first time I saw you and your hunched back.

Sorry, bad joke.

SOMETHING I LEARNED TODAY

(November 1988)

A chapter in which we introduce the dead.

Did you really write up minutes?
I hope you're joking . . .

The Pallbearers Club Meeting Minutes

Opening: The meeting was called to order by Art Barbara. Wednesday, November 5th, 2:37 P.M. It was held outside of Mr. Brugués's office. He offered us a sandwich bag half-filled with pretzel sticks.

Present: All current/initial members. Art Barbara, Cayla Friedman, Eddie Patrick.

Approval of Agenda, Approval of Minutes: Two votes to zero. Eddie Patrick abstained from voting. He said it was dumb.

Business from Previous Meeting: None. This is our first meeting.

New Business: We will be pallbearers/attendees at a small service for a homeless woman. Her name hasn't been shared with the club yet.

Additions to Agenda: After a brief period allowing for motions (none were brought forth), Art Barbara was elected president, vice president, and secretary. One person probably shouldn't hold all three offices at once, but as pointed out by Cayla Friedman there are no bylaws preventing such a result. Perhaps a topic for future meetings.

Adjournment: Meeting ended when Eddie Patrick pretended to choke on pretzel sticks and insisted Cayla Friedman perform the Heimlich Maneuver on him. She declined. Next meeting is at the Stephens Funeral Home, Saturday, 9:00 A.M., which is thirty minutes prior to the start of the 9:30 A.M. service to be held within the funeral home.

Minutes submitted by: Art Barbara

Minutes approved by: Art Barbara

[I submitted the minutes along with my college applications to Bates and Middlebury Colleges as an attempt to appear both creative and disciplined. I did not get into either school. The 2007 me is still salty about it.]

You deserved not to get in

I pulled my parents' beat-up blue station wagon into Stephens Funeral Home at 8:45 A.M. I hated being late. As vast as the night ocean, the parking lot funneled me toward a hearse parked under a trellis-lined awning shading the home's main entrance. Set back a considerable distance from busy Cabot Street, the converted colonial house was painted white with black trim, the official colors of a New England funeral home. I do not know anything about architecture, but let's call it Colonial Gothic. At three-stories in height, the mournful manor lurched and sprawled at the edges of the well-manicured lot.

The funeral director, Mr. Stephens, stood outside the entrance smoking a cigarette. He was my height but easily outweighed me by one hundred pounds. A balding, middle-aged Black man, Mr.

Stephens wore an immaculate navy-blue pinstripe suit adorned with a maroon tie. His wide glasses, each lens could be used as a birdbath, claimed most of his face.

"That is a fine suit you have on, young man." His voice was a growl in a puff of smoke, yet each syllable carefully enunciated, as though he'd practiced what he was going to say. "Did you wear it to your first communion?"

"Um, no?" My white dress-shirt cuffs mushroomed out of the too-short, blue blazer sleeves. I covered my right wrist with my left hand, but that exposed the left cuff. I tugged and fussed at the sleeves.

Mr. Stephens laughed warmly, and I couldn't help but join him. (There's a difference between a bully's laugh and one that offers commiseration, one that recognizes if not shared experience, then a common frailty. Detecting that difference is instinctual for some, while others learn it only after repeated hard lessons.)

He said, "Don't mind me, you are dressed handsomely. Art Barbara, I presume?" He stubbed out his cigarette on the bottom of a shoe and wrapped the remnant into a kerchief, which he pocketed. "I'm Philip Stephens. I'm grateful for your volunteering and hope this is the beginning of a continued community-service partnership."

He ushered me inside and gave a tour of the first floor. The rooms were impeccable but static. Not the same static of a museum, where one at least could imagine the exhibits representing the living, breathing past and present. This place's static was entropic. Closed coffins surrounded by brightly colored flowers and wreaths occupied half the rooms.

The floors were a dark-stained hardwood and the walls an off-white, shading toward a melancholy sunrise color. That phrase stuck with me as Mr. Stephens said the name of one of the rooms was in fact *Melancholy Sunrise*. Other named rooms included *Moonlight Forest* and the more abstract *Midnight Wish*.

I asked, "Do you tell the guests the names of the rooms?"

"No, the guests are dead."

"Oh, I meant the visitors, then."

We returned to the front entrance, went outside, and waited under the awning for the arrival of my fellow clubmates. I smiled inwardly at the thought of having clubmates.

Mr. Stephens fished out his cigarette stub from his pocket, quickly restored its cylindrical shape, and lit it again. "You don't smoke, do you, Art? A wonderful, terrible habit. Don't start unless you intend to see it through to the end."

I laughed politely, and itchingly eager to share something personal, I confessed that I'd never been inside a funeral home before and the only funeral mass I ever attended was when I was four years old, for a great-uncle. Uncle Heck. Short for Hector of course. I had no memory of his funeral, but I remembered him letting me grab his nose with my tiny hands. My parents and other family members frequently told me that was what I always did to Uncle Heck when he was alive, so it was possible my memory was a staged, mental reenactment of what they told me. How could I know the difference?

Mr. Stephens ignored my weighty contemplation of the nature of memory and said, "To have never been in a funeral home, I don't know if you are fortunate or not. The law of averages tends to catch up with us all."

Mr. Stephens wasn't nearly as friendly with Cayla and Eddie as he was with me. (Perhaps he sensed I needed kindness more than they did. Perhaps he was annoyed by how loosely Eddie's skinny black tie hung around his neck, and that Cayla—while wearing a respectful black dress—loudly chewed bubble gum.)

He led the Pallbearers Club up a set of wide stairs to a viewing room on the second floor. The room was much smaller than the ones downstairs. I wanted to ask if this room had a name, or perhaps suggest one (*Mourners' Pantry*, given its smallness?) but the proper moment had passed. An open casket was set against the far wall.

The club moved as one as we entered and flowed left, tracing the perimeter, sticking to the wall opposite the coffin. Speaking as president of the club, we were having second, third, and fourth thoughts about our being here and about our club's charter and mission statement.

Mr. Stephens told us the woman's name was Kathleen Blanchet and she had died from complications associated with untreated tuberculosis. She was a former resident of the Shore House (a local homeless shelter), and an anonymous donor paid for her viewing and service. He didn't know if shelter residents would be attending, though an invitation had been extended. We might be the only attendees. We were to wait for Father Wanderly to arrive and lead a brief prayer service. Mr. Stephens did not ask if we had any questions. He told us he was going downstairs to make a few phone calls, but he would return shortly. He pointed out where the restrooms were on the second floor, "if you must use them." His footfalls echoed as though he descended a staircase of infinite depth.

Eddie exhaled, didn't look anyone in the face, and said, "Guy's a Chester" (as in, Chester the Molester). During the first month of my freshman year, Eddie sat behind me in English and kicked my thighs and jammed a foot in my lower back. He threat-whispered about how he was going to kick my ass using typically '80s homophobic vocabulary. My defense was that of a baby rabbit in tall grass: I didn't turn around, didn't say anything, didn't move. One day, unrelated to his tormenting of me, the teacher threw him out of class for swearing at her and sent him to the principal's office. I honestly don't remember if he swore or not. The next day in class I spun around to face him as he sat down, him and his big stupid face and perma-flushed cheeks, and before he could snarl something at me, I babbled that I would tell the principal he didn't swear if he needed me to. His weasely eyes dilated (not softened, there was never to be any softening), he nodded, and the flush in his cheeks tuned a few hues lighter from war red. A peace achieved, <u>but at what cost to my soul?</u>

You have always been a soul spendthrift.

"This is so weird," Cayla said. She was in one of my honors classes, ran cross-country, was a cashier at Star Market (where I worked too), and liked to draw and paint. She was friendly to all at school, but her comfortableness within her own skin made her off-putting to the rest of us maladjusted teenagers. She often joked she was from *the* Jewish family of Beverly.

Eddie and Cayla had yet to confide in me why they had joined our esoteric club, beyond expressing a similar desire to accrue extracurricular activities that would most assuredly lead to future successes in life. It really didn't matter to me *why* they joined. Because of our shared honorable endeavor I hoped we would be friends forever (cue an '80s-movie montage of carefree madcap adventures while we learned to accept each other's differences).

[Note: We would not do any of that. But I did think so in that instant.]

Eddie turned and walked backward toward the casket. His smirk was too eager to mask his social ineptitude with cruelty. He said, "Five bucks and I'll stick my pinky up her nose."

Cayla dug into her shoulder bag and pulled out a five, calling his bluff. Eddie declined with a shrug and a brief collapse of his shoulders.

The three of us stood before the padded kneeler set by the coffin. We were close enough to each other to hold hands. We were holding hands, metaphorically speaking. We psychically supported each other as we prepared to participate in a time-honored, vital social ritual. And we stared at the body of Kathleen Blanchet.

One half of the coffin lid was open, and her torso was visible from the waist up. Her skin stretched tightly across her brow and wide forehead, which tapered into a dried-out, autumn field of brown stalks of hair. Her cheeks had caved in, and her eyelids spanned precariously across sinkholes. She was desiccated, a dried-out insect. How long had she been dead? The heavy-handed application of foundation makeup did not add health, weight, or life to her face. She did not look like someone sleeping peacefully, nor did she look like an uncanny, waxy mannequin. The coffin was too big for her, and she receded into the plush lining. She wore a prim, long-sleeved navy-blue dress. Her hands were folded over her stomach, and her fingers and wrists were skinnier than mine. I hid my hands behind my back, afraid I was seeing a future snapshot of my own grotesquely thin corpse. My initial spark of discovery at witnessing life's most final, physical mystery was extinguished. I wondered how old she was. Twenties? Early thirties? What had it felt like when her heart stopped beating? Did she register the last thump? Did consciousness cease with a final darkness or was there darkness first, then a sensation of ebbing away, of falling, or was it a lessening into becoming nothing, which wasn't a becoming, then? You couldn't *become* nothing, could you? Whatever the nature of the transition (from living to dead), it was something no one could describe because there was no one around who had fully experienced it. I knew that was trite, but why didn't we talk about this more? How was it not part of our constant, daily discourse? How was *this* a natural thing? How was this allowed and tolerated, never mind celebrated? I wanted to know what had happened to her and I wanted to know her story even though the ending had been spoiled. How could any of our stories mean anything when we knew the inevitable end? I didn't want to be there anymore and didn't want to look at her anymore. But I still looked. I memorized her face, the whorls and folds in her right ear, the lines that were there in her skin and the lines that weren't there but should've been. The longer I stared the more I expected her eyes to open. Her eyelids would audibly and dustily creak and crinkle open. I saw it happening, and they revealed two empty sockets, or maybe her eyes had gone white, a terrible white like the rolled eyes of an attacking shark or swollen spider eggs ready to hatch, and the worst part was I'd feel them seeing me. They'd always see me. And I was the baby rabbit again, and if I didn't move maybe I'd avoid the gaze. I was barely breathing, holding my breath, trying to save it, like a miser hoarding coins. I looked left and right to my clubmates, trying to break out of the spell, but spells could only be broken with the right words. Should I ask if either of them had seen a dead body before? For as awful as seeing her body was, there remained an I'm-getting-away-with-something feeling, a not-quite-schadenfreude sense of *Thank God I'm not you and you are not me and when we leave this building we'll talk louder and laugh harder and run faster and whistle past all the graveyards.*

Eddie flipped the padded kneeler up and down with the toe of his scuffed shoe. He nudged me and said, "How'd you come up with the idea for this freak club? You wanna be an undertaker or something? You look like you could be one. All you need is a creepy hat."

"There's a club like this near San Francisco. I saw it on the news." I didn't admit to watching teen news on the kids' cable network, Nickelodeon.

"And you thought, 'Wow, that sounds fucking neato.'"

I looked to Cayla, like she was going to answer for me. She walked away from us and the coffin. I said, "I wanted something that would stand out on a college application." I left out *So I can get into a school far away from here and far away from you, Eddie, and all the other fucking Eddies.*

Cayla removed her black banana clip and adjusted her hair. She said, "Oh, this is going to stand out." She laughed and covered her mouth, which made her laugh harder.

I wondered if Cayla was here because she decided to make me her social charity case. Upon seeing the morning announcement, she figured no one would join my club and I would be embarrassed/crushed/hurt and so she attended the first meeting and when Eddie was the only other kid who showed up, she had to stick it out (because, come on, *Eddie*) as an unspoken favor to poor, outcast me. If any of that was a mitochondrion in one cell of the truth organism, I loved her and hated me for it.

Father Wanderly (white, early middle-aged, and as short, svelte, and fastidious as a plastic groom atop a wedding cake; he told us to call him "Father W.") and Mr. Stephens were all business as they entered the room along with two other men in black suits, presumably employees at the funeral home, who did not introduce themselves.

After we signed a blank page of a guest book, Father W. took his place at the head of the coffin. We moved back and formed a semicircle facing the priest. He read a prayer from his leather-bound book. We said "Amen" when instructed to do so. Mr. Stephens said his amens the loudest. Cayla was second loudest. Yes, I inventoried the volumes. I mumbled, which was more than what Eddie was doing, or not doing. Maybe Eddie had suffered abuse or tragedy and the anger oozing from his pores was how he coped, and he had joined the club to confront the pain and emotions he'd never been able to properly process. Or maybe he was an unrepentant dick with nothing better to do.

Father W. sprinkled holy water on Kathleen and the coffin. We said "Amen" one last time. Mr. Stephens closed the lid. There was one lonely wreath of flowers hanging via a metal stand by the foot of the coffin. A yellow sash across the donut-hole middle silently demanded PEACE.

Mr. Stephens ascended to the center of the semicircle and addressed the gathered as though there were dozens more of us in the room. "Thank you for the good word, Father W., and for your implacable grace." The father was already halfway out of the room, strutting like John Travolta in *Saturday Night Fever*. He acknowledged receipt of thanks with a little bow and a jaunty salute of his left hand. He was halfway down the stairs before Mr. Stephens continued. "Thus concludes this morning's service for Kathleen Blanchet. Thank you for being a part of our intimate gathering. Though we are few, the grief shared is divided, and the joy of celebrating her life is multiplied. May she finally be at peace and may you go in peace." He bowed his head, holding the pose.

The two men in black suits left the room, one following closely behind the other. The Pallbearers Club was confused. We looked at one another. The president, of course, should speak for the group. I was reluctant to bother Mr. Stephens, who appeared to be having some sort of moment, but better I asked than Eddie, so I said, "Excuse me, Mr. Stephens. Those were, um, beautiful words, but is that it? Are we done?"

Mr. Stephens animated and clapped me on the back hard enough that I stumbled a few steps away to disperse the transferal of energy and momentum. He said, "Not quite, my friend. It's time you three bear the pall, as it were."

"Huh?" Eddie said. At least he was succinct and to the point.

"We need to you help haul her to the hearse."

"I'm stronger than I look."

I didn't say that, but I shouted it in my head.

The two men in suits were at the foot of the coffin, taking the brunt of the weight, leading us slowly downstairs, while holding their end up higher in an attempt to keep the coffin as level as possible. Cayla and I were in the middle, with Mr. Stephens and Eddie the anchors by the head.

Eddie said, "Is she gonna slosh around inside if we tilt too much?"

Cayla leaked a small, involuntary "Yuck."

Mr. Stephens named the parts of the casket as we huffed and groaned our way down the stairs. "You saw the pillow box, of course. The interior frame of the lid is called the flange. The cover is the bridge. The apron on the inside, when viewing, the part folded over the crown is the overlay—"

The coffin was heavy but not unmanageable. I tried to catch Cayla's eye and act like this was no big deal, that I could do it one-handed if I wanted to. She puffed out her cheeks, blowing out a spout of air, in what I assumed was a this-is-hard-work gesture. I nodded and shrugged. Well, I couldn't shrug, as my shoulders were bearing a considerable load.

"At the far end, or the foot-end, is the fishtail, the ogee, corner, and tip—"

It was more than a little bizarre to think that I'd got up this morning, showered, eaten a bowl of Honeycomb cereal, put on my "best" clothes, and now I helped carry an ornate box containing a body, or a person, or an unperson. I thought about Eddie's question regarding her possible movement inside the coffin and I listened and felt for little thuds or thumps, a light but longing tapping. I tried not to think about her opening her eyes again. More than halfway down the stairs and the silver-colored handle was getting slick, but I couldn't let go and wipe my hands. As though in panic response, my temperature spiked and every inch of clothing on my body dampened. My chest was heavy and tight.

"Those plates where the handles are attached are lugs or ears, and the handle itself held in place by the arms. Odd, or perhaps fitting, the exterior has so much body nomenclature."

We made it off the stairs and walked through the front door, but the cargo mass had somehow increased. Maybe my leverage position in the middle had meant the people in front and back shouldered most of the lifting burden while going down the stairs, but now that the weight was evenly distributed my arms and legs quivered and I was not getting enough air.

Cayla asked, "Are you okay?"

I didn't look at her or at anyone else. "I'm fine."

I was not fine. My vision blurred and uninterpretable inkblots encroached at the edges. My head filled with damp peat and moss, and my ears rang as I sank into the bog of myself. Was I going to faint? I tried to blink everything away and I took deep, noisy breaths as my feet shuffled through the swampy blacktop to the hearse, finally the hearse.

The two men loaded their end in the back and onto rollers, and the coffin glided into place, its length receding into the interior darkness of the shrouded vehicle.

No longer clutching the coffin handle, I backed away and was instantly revivified. My vision cleared and chest wasn't heavy anymore. I clapped my hands once and giggled, relieved that I was not going to pass out, or die. At least, not in that moment.

Everyone else stared at me. I said, "Piece of cake, right? What?"

One of men in black suits said, "You look blue," and the other added, "More greenish. Like he's seasick."

Mr. Stephens wrapped an arm around my shoulder, engulfing me, and I wanted to cry.

Eddie said, "It wasn't that heavy. Eat a fucking sandwich sometime, you rail."

I wriggled out from Mr. Stephens's embrace. "It wasn't too heavy for me. I don't know what happened. I was fine, it was easy, and then, I don't know, I just got light-headed. Or more like, heavy-headed."

Mr. Stephens said, "You did perfectly well. It was an emotional ceremony and upon seeing a body for the first time some people have delayed physiological responses. I've seen it many times."

[Note: 2007 me knows Mr. Stephens's "delayed physiological responses" was an unknowing (on his part) clue to what had happened to me and to what would happen, the type of clue the universe mockingly provides.]

One of the men in black suits apparated at my side with a plastic cup of water. I begrudgingly accepted it. As I sipped, everyone's focus and attention shifted away from me.

Cayla asked Mr. Stephens if he would write her a college recommendation and handed him an envelope (no idea where she had kept it hidden) with her academic record and list of extracurricular activities.

Eddie ripped off his tie, wrapped it around his forehead like he was a parking-lot Rambo, and skulked off toward his car chuckling to himself. Even though I knew he was chuckling at me, there was nothing sadder than a person laughing by themselves.

The other man in a black suit rooted through a brown paper bag and offered me half of his ham sandwich, slathered in radioactive yellow mustard. I hated mustard.

I wished I had passed out or died.

I don't remember the first dead person I saw. Is that strange? Has it been so long that I can't remember? That memory wing in my house of cards must've collapsed and been replaced ages ago. I think whoever it was I saw was very old. I can summon faces of elderly family members who passed, but not of them in their caskets. I'm thankful for that, frankly. I must've seen a dead person when I was quite young, and I'm sure it made an impression on me. I'd be a monster otherwise, right? Although, our Western culture's reaction to death and dying is totally fucked up. There are other countries—so I hear—where death isn't taboo, isn't something to hide or send shuffling off into the bleak, white corridors of hospitals and nursing homes. I say that and it sounds nice, but like you I am but a widget and cog within our capitalist, consumerist, puritanical culture. I'll admit it: death freaks me out.

I do vividly remember the first wake I ever attended. I don't think I ever told you and I don't like talking about it. My mom died when I was young. She doesn't count as my first viewed dead person because her casket was kept mercifully closed—at least, it was closed when I was around. How she died was a cruel whisper passed among congregants, as though fearful what had happened to Mom would happen to them soon. An older cousin told me Mom dried up and blew away, so I imagined she was a pile of dust in her coffin. I didn't like that at all. I tried to replace the gray, ash-like dust with a pile of fallen but brightly colored leaves instead. I still have nightmares of being at her wake. Nothing overtly frightening happens, but the horror is in simply being there again, feeling the renewed feeling of wrongness; a sad, angry, powerless feeling as I stare at her small coffin buried in bright, shining flowers because horror is a full-color thing.

It is wonderful hearing the voice of "Mr. Stephens" again. I've always had a soft spot for him in my heart.

I do not understand what you are getting at with your almost fainting while carrying the casket and Mr. Stephens's comment as a supposed clue from the universe.

BOOKS ABOUT UFOS

(November 1988)

A chapter in which I make a strange friend. *You're strange*

Ten days after the club's maiden voyage and it was Tuesday afternoon. Mom was home from the bank (she was a part-time teller), Dad was still at work (he supervised the mail room at the United Shoe factory), and I was in the TV room. That was what we called it—not a living room, family room, sitting room, or even a parlor. (Names are important. You'll see.) Like every and any other day after school I watched MTV alone, hoping they played older Def Leppard videos and not the lame "Pour Some Sugar on Me" for the billionth time, and I played my Walkman cassette player until a better video came on. Or I watched a movie on HBO I'd already seen. Or I watched *M*A*S*H* reruns or *Cheers*, and if it was *Cheers*, I took odd local pride in the show set in Boston as Mom had been born there, raised in public housing the government arranged for World War II veterans and their families. Or I wasn't embedded in the TV room and, instead, I was in the dining room, lying on the floor, flat on my back, my head tented between the stereo speakers, listening to Scorpions and Creedence Clearwater Revival records and I imagined I was onstage, singing and playing the guitar, and everyone in the audience was there to see me, and frankly, they were all very impressed and thought I was an important, admirable person.

When the phone rang, I was doing any one of the things described above. Mom answered and after a hushed exchange she curled around from the kitchen into the TV room, or if I was lost between the stereo speakers, she glided through the dining room and kicked my splayed feet.

"What?"

Mom was tall, a scant twenty-one years older than me, and had dark short hair (not Annie Lennox "Sweet Dreams Are Made of This" short, but close). The stretched-out phone cord trailed behind her with plenty of slack. One hand cupped the receiver. Her eyes were windows thrown open on the first warm spring day and her smile was a porch door.

"Art, it's for you"—a pause because it was never for me—"and it's a girl."

I tried to play it off like I expected the call.

Mom repeatedly asked "Who is she?," and perhaps in her head she sounded like a supportive friend or peer, not a mother yearning for her son to have friends, never mind a girlfriend. Instead of nonchalant cool my shrugs communicated *I have no clue, what do I say, what do I do?* judging by Mom's avalanching smile and her "You want me to ask her name?"

I grabbed the phone. Mom receded into the kitchen as though a wave swept her out with the tide. She buoyed in the periphery.

"Hi. Hello?" I groaned, as yes, I said both "hi" and "hello."

"Hey there. Is this Art Barbara?"

Whomever she was, she was not a classmate; it was less I didn't recognize her voice in five words than what it was she said. Would a teen who didn't know me and wasn't making fun of me use my first and last name like that?

I said, "Yeah. This is him, or, um, me. Can I ask who's calling?"

"Sure."

Silence.

She added, "I said you can ask."

"Oh, okay. Um, who's calling?"

"Jesus. My name is <u>Mercy</u> and I saw the flyer about your club at the library."

Mercy. Seriously?

My flyer had ensnared a potential member and would surely accrue more to the service of the dead! Prior to the call, the club had one (me) or maybe two members. Cayla had been noncommittal about attending a second service this coming weekend. Eddie had been demonstrably committal about his never going again. Whenever he saw me in school, he called me the Undertaker and pretended to faint under the weight of his book bag. I understood that he caricatured my coffin carry, but at least, if the non-reaction reaction of bystanders could be interpreted, no one else knew what the hell he was prattling on about. Regardless, with the betterment of the club in mind, I gestaltedly removed him from our masthead.

Mercy continued. "I also saw the flyer on the front windows of the White Hen Pantry, Beverly House of Pizza, Super Sub, the post office, stapled to telephone poles on Rantoul Street, taped to mailboxes—I don't think that's legal, by the way—a tornado of them swirled around the Burger King parking lot, and I watched seagulls fight over one at Dane Street Beach."

She was definitely not in high school. Maybe a college student. Maybe someone's mom? I no longer anticipated her becoming a future club member. She had likely anger-dialed to lodge a complaint about my carpet-bombing the town with flyers.

I said, "Yeah, sorry, I put up one hundred and twenty-three of them yesterday."

"How precise. So, is this club legit?"

"Legit?"

"Is the club and the flyer for real or is it a joke? I honestly can't tell."

"Yes, the club is real. It's, like, *so* real. We attended a service not this Saturday but the one before, and Mr. Stephens wants us back this—"

"I ask because the Pallbearers Club stencil on the flyer looks like the logo of a cheesy hair metal band, like something a bored kid doodles in their algebra class."

I chafed at the comparison to a doodle. I had spent more than an hour on design, getting it just right. I had used slash-drawn power letters. Like a mountaineer's flag planted on an impossible peak, a small but unimpeachable "the" perched atop of the Pallbearers "P." "Club," not an afterthought but the uppercut punch after a left-right combo, dangled off the end of the word and it didn't care what you thought of its reckless boldness.

I said, "I wanted the flyer to be cool and attention-grabbing."

"You're one for two. At best. But I'm in. Let me know where and when."

Mr. Stephens admitted to being pleased Eddie was no longer a member of the club, saying, "He was a cloud that hung over your honorable venture." He was not pleased, however, that our newest member was late. He declared the service would begin in fifteen minutes with or without her. He, Cayla, and I continued our vigil in the funeral home's front foyer.

Mr. Stephens asked, "Can you be a club if you number only two members?"

"Art is still working on the bylaws," Cayla said. I couldn't tell if she was being commiserative with me or conspiratorial with him. Either or any of the ways, I didn't care and was thankful she was here, even if this service was to be her last.

"I do love a thorough set of bylaws—" An unlit cigarette stuck to Mr. Stephens's lower lip. It bobbed in rhythm with his jaw, the baton of a symphony conductor. "Though you cease being a club at two. You're a partnership. The Pallbearers Partnership."

Cayla snorted a hard laugh at this.

I stopped myself from asking if either of them thought college admissions boards would look less favorably upon an extracurricular partnership. I said, "No. We're a club. Mercy will be here."

"One can hope."

Outside, a click and a low-volume, high-pitched whine of a small mechanism, its whirr ended with a second click. Mr. Stephens yanked open the front door. A rush of air filled the vacuum, swiping the cigarette off his lip, but he caught it deftly.

Mercy Brown had her back to us as she faced the hearse. She turned leisurely, revealing a cubic Polaroid instant camera held in one hand and a developing photo with the other. She asked, "Do we get to ride in that later?"

Mr. Stephens said, "If we're fortunate, we all will eventually."

Mercy walked inside (Mr. Stephens holding the door open), breezing between us to the staircase. She placed the photo on one of the stairs and said, "It's still developing."

"You must be Mercy. Thank you for coming, but I would've preferred you arrived more than twenty minutes ago."

She idly adjusted her shouldered canvas bag. "I'm sorry, and it won't happen again."

Mercy wore an oversized green army jacket that was too long in the sleeves, the cuffs swollen by her rolling them over. Punk band pins and patches decorated the coat's chest and shoulders. Blocky combat boots weighed down her feet, their green-laced tops disappearing under her pegged jeans. Her face was round and pale, boxed in by shoulder-length light-brown hair that hung loosely, a style in stark contrast to the big-hair '80s. Aside from the lack of hairspray and makeup, her appearance was otherwise not remarkable. (I do not mean that in a judgy, beauty-standards way, though I would grant that might be impossible for me to guarantee despite my sincerest ongoing efforts.) <u>Let me try again.</u>   Please do.

Mercy was neither tall nor short. She was not skinny (like me) and was not obese. She had no scars, no birthmarks, her face had symmetry but not so symmetrical as to be unnatural, and her facial features were in proportion with the size of her head. I would never describe her (or anyone) as plain because I don't know what *plain* means. Maybe the best way to describe her is as follows: she looked like someone who would get declarative-sentenced with "I've met you before." As such her age was undeterminable. She could easily fit within a ten- or even twenty-year range, whereas I looked much younger than my seventeen years old. If she told me then that she was nineteen or twenty-nine or even thirty-nine or any number between, I would not have been shocked.

Mr. Stephens asked, "What school do you attend?"

"North Shore Community College. Part-time." Mercy nodded at me and asked, "Art?"

"Yes, hi, thanks for coming. So, you're a photographer? Our club could definitely—"

She snapped a picture of me. Momentarily flash blinded, I rubbed my eyes, pre-mortified, wondering how many of the splotchy blemishes on my face would show on film.

"If you mean one who takes photographs at this moment in time, then yes." Mercy returned to the stairs, dropped the new photo on one of the treads, and slid her first photo (presumably of the hearse) into her bag. "You two move closer and I get a two-for-one."

Cayla and Mr. Stephens obeyed without protest or a demand of explanation. They even struck poses: Cayla crossed her arms over her chest and jutted out a hip; Mr. Stephens gripped his chin, miming deep thought, and arched one eyebrow.

"You guys are stars. Art, stay away from your picture. I got your good side."

I froze in mid-sidle toward the stairs. In my head I was already grinding the picture of me under my heel and saying, *Oops, sorry, I was going upstairs to use the bathroom and I'm such a klutz.* Instead, I swiveled and turned and pivoted, longing to believe in a good side and display it.

Mercy passed the milky, developing photo to Cayla and asked Mr. Stephens, "Can I hang up my coat somewhere?"

Mr. Stephens directed Mercy to a foyer closet. Cayla shook the exposed negative, impatient for the result.

Mercy said, "No, don't shake it. You'll cause the image to separate or form little blobs." She hung up her coat as she explained that newer, instant film wasn't wet, didn't need to dry. Mercy renewed her grip on the camera and re-shouldered her bag. She plucked the snapshot away from Cayla, who held it inches from her face as though inspecting a jewel.

"It's not done developing yet," Cayla said.

"That's okay." Mercy returned to the base of the stairs, quickly swapping the photo with the shot of me. "Art, your eyes are closed and mouth is open."

I didn't ask to see it. She banished the photo into the darkroom of her bag.

Mr. Stephens said, "You're more than welcome to stow your photos and gear."

"I'd prefer not to."

He added, "While I wouldn't say you are inappropriately dressed, Mercy, I wonder if you don't happen to have a dress or pair of slacks in that shoulder bag."

Cayla and I were wearing the same clothes we wore two weeks ago. Mr. Stephens waved a palm-up hand in our direction. We were the models of dressing appropriately, though his hand was disappointed in us too; it was a look-what-I-have-to-work-with hand.

Mercy said, "A black sweater with no holes is as good as I get."

"Fair enough, and I am not throwing fashion stones in anyone's direction. As long as you're comfortable, I'm grateful for your presence." Mr. Stephens wheeled on a squeaking leather shoe and led us through a curling hallway to a viewing room, the one named *Midnight Wish*.

Cayla latched on to my arm and yanked me back, allowing the others to go ahead. Mercy snapped pictures of the walls and ceiling, each flash a bit of lightning, foretelling larger storms to come. She dropped the grayed developing photos onto empty chairs.

Cayla whispered, "Do you know her?" I hesitated to answer, partly because her stage whisper echoed. "How'd she know about the club—oh, was it your flyers?"

"Yes, I mean, no. I mean, I sent a flyer but she's a friend of my cousin. Jennifer. Graduated in '85. She's a senior in college, up at Bates." (Why do we think added details makes something sound less like a lie?)

Cayla gave me a naked, unprotected, or unvarnished look, less *I'm on to you* than *Oh, now I know who you are.* "And what's her deal with the pictures?"

"I don't know—"

Mr. Stephens called us into the room.

The new and improved Pallbearers Club gathered by the casket, behind which was an assortment of potted plants, not flowers. Inside the gunmetal-gray coffin was an old, dead man wearing a cream-colored burial suit. He was bald but for cotton-candy tufts of white cumulonimbusing the horizon of his Jurassic ears. Jaundiced wallpaper skin displayed a complex pattern of liver spots on his forehead. His hands were a pile of sticks and stones. While my head buzzed with fascination and an urge to flee the room, I was not nearly as affected (mentally or physically) at the viewing of his body as I had been by Kathleen Blanchet's, and I was not sure why. Perhaps this was what I always imagined a dead body would look like. And I did appreciate his suit; it read as cheerful to me.

I snuck a look at Mercy and Cayla, both shuttered inside their own heads, and I was reminded we are always alone.

So gloomy!

Mr. Stephens cleared his throat and announced the ceremony was about to begin. The club dropped a few steps back from the coffin and into Mr. Stephens's orbit. He nodded at each of us. We returned our own volley of nods. He pulled out a letter from inside his jacket and almost as an afterthought, he told me to stop slouching.

I wanted to smart-aleck back at him that I'd straighten my crooked spine if I could. Instead, I mumbled, "Sorry," and I faux-unslouched, briefly lifting onto my toes before sinking back to my regular, defensive posture. I conceded he was probably correct in his accusation, though, as I was suddenly feeling extra slouchy, like I was actively shrinking, or shriveling. Which was fine by me. Although my blazer was still two sizes too small, I ached to disappear into its billows.

Mr. Stephens said, "At the request of the deceased, the brief ceremony consists solely of the following reading. The gentleman we are seeing off this afternoon is Mr. Tom Jones. He died ninety-two years young." Mr. Stephens levered his giant glasses off his face and onto his forehead. He squintily read from a single sheet of paper. "Life and death have taken turns being cruel to Mr. Jones. His beloved wife and partner, Linda, died in 1966 of colon cancer and their daughter, Donna, died four years ago due to the same insufferable, greedy illness. Despite having his heart shattered twice, Mr. Jones stubbornly if not foolishly went on living. If hope is believing there will be one more moment of joy, then despair is knowing there was a final one—"

A click, flash, and whir. Mercy snapped a photo of Mr. Jones's body.

"He specified no photography during the ceremony," Mr. Stephens said, without missing a beat.

Mercy said, "You're making that up."

"I am not." He flashed the typed page at Mercy but did not hold it out long enough for it to be read.

"Mmm-hmm." She plunked the photo onto the kneeler.

Mr. Stephens continued reading. "Mr. Jones is survived by everyone else, however none of those people are immediate family members. Someone must always finish last. Mr. Jones wishes to specify he was named after the eponymous protagonist of the farcical novel published in 1749. While he enjoyed the impishly handsome Albert Finney's performance in the film, he thought the screenplay was a bit too bawdy. If anyone would care to respond, please do so now."

I stammered something about his being at peace.

Cayla said, "I hope he's with Linda and Donna."

"I liked Albert Finney in *Wolfen*," Mercy said.

* * *

> I might have said that to you at some point, but not at the end of the ceremony. You make me sound like an uncaring asshole.

We ferried the casket to the hearse, a winding trip that went smoothly if not quickly as we didn't have to contend with lugging the deceased down any stairs. Once the coffin glided down the tracked gullet of the hearse and the rear door closed, I cracked my knuckles and rolled my neck like a preening weightlifter, making a show of how little physical exertion was expended.

The hearse driver still asked if I was okay and offered me half of his mustard-slathered sandwich. I told the man I was fine, and I didn't want or need his sandwich, or a cup of water, thank you.

Cayla drifted away into the parking lot with a barely audible "Bye." She moved too quickly for me to ask for a ride, or to do so without being a self-conscious, awkward dweeb.

I asked Mr. Stephens if I could use the phone and he told me there was one in a small office opposite the entrance of *Melancholy Sunrise*. I headed back into the funeral home, pausing briefly in the foyer, trying to remember if I'd find the *Sunrise* to the right or left.

"I can give you a lift," Mercy said, all but shouting into my ear.

Startled, I spun until I completed two circles. But she was not behind me. The front door was closed. I was in the foyer by myself.

I sputtered unconnected syllables until I mustered a weak "Sorry, what?"

She didn't answer, nor did anyone else. Was Mercy checking out the other rooms by herself? After all, she had been late and never got the tour from Mr. Stephens. But if she was exploring, wouldn't I hear her camera going off? What would stop her from taking photos now? No, she had said she can give me a lift. Maybe she was attempting to trick me into searching for her and she was hiding, pressed flat against a wall, or she crouched in a corner, creeping in a shadowed spot near a closed coffin and then she'd jump out and take a picture of the scared-shitless me. I'd only been exposed to her for about fifteen minutes, but I thought she was fully capable of doing something like that. Enough time passed that I questioned what I'd heard, or how I'd heard it. Was it possible she was outside and walking to her car because I didn't answer her in time? I couldn't get rid of the image of her hiding on me, and my thoughts

Lift?
Did I step
out of a
hardboiled
detective
novel?

turned to mercury in the quiet of the funeral home, its mortal hum of silence, a frequency I couldn't hear and instead felt in my tightening chest and tingling scalp. Okay, maybe I didn't need to find the phone and I'd just walk home. No need to get all worked up, get all fuzzy again. Did Mr. Stephens leave or was he still out front? I'd go find him, say thank you, tell him, "Yeah I called but no one answered. No big deal. No, really—"

To my right, Mercy backed out of the foyer closet, wrestling her coat away from bulky wooden hangers, two of which clattered to the floor. Deadpan, she said, "Monster in there. Wouldn't let me go."

"D-Did you get a picture of it?" A good line, but there was no commitment in the delivery.

"Not this time." She looked away as she climbed into her coat, suddenly pensive, mourning the missed shot.

I edged away, toward the front door, and rattled it open. "Yeah, okay, well, thanks again for coming, and um—"

"Do you want a ride or not?"

[*2012 me:* I wonder if this is another one of near infinite life-path-choosing moments. One that at the time seems the smallest, least impactful, most forgettable, but is in fact the opposite. The problem with those kinds of moments is they're impossible to recognize in situ, and when excavating the self in retrospect, you pick at the lost and irreparable moments that might be false positives because you can't be sure if this was a moment where everything changed, where everything to come after was written but for the minor details. Regardless, you keep digging. I have spent years digging into this moment in the foyer. Maybe if I told her I didn't need a ride she would've quit the Pallbearers Club and I would've never seen her again and my life from that point would become someone else's. This is not regret, as there's not remorse, not exactly. A wish of foreknowledge, perhaps.]

[*2017 me:* In giving one last read-through before I abandon the manuscript, I continue mining the cavernous pit into which I was led, and I'm in so deep I no longer see any light and there's only more digging.]

Mercy's car was a beat-up early Datsun, standard transmission, an orange box on wheels, but it had a tape deck. Music clanged to life along with the car's engine.

Dueling vocals screamed to be heard over a din of tinny, fuzzed-out guitar and a rolling, jackhammer drumbeat. Underneath the high-treble blast a pistoning bass was the groundwater, a low rumor of order. The overloaded speakers crackled and hissed.

Mercy turned left out of the parking lot, whacked me on the shoulder, and said, "What do you think?"

"Of what?"

"This band."

I couldn't parse the lyrics. There was no heroic guitar soloing. No chorus with slick background vocals. Zero production value. It was as though someone broke into their rehearsal space (I imagined a musty, low-ceilinged basement) and dropped a mono-channel tape recorder in the middle of the floor, and because of the analog recording intrusion the band played louder, faster, angrier. Hints of melody surfaced and imploded, only to ooze back later, and then the song abruptly finished, crashed, and it was the end of the speakers and the tape player and the Datsun and maybe the rest of the world because it was all too much. Then the next song exploded. My initial response: I didn't like it. It was too much. The emotion and lack of control was dangerous, too painfully confessional, and I wanted to hide from its rawness, but I couldn't stop listening.

I said, "They're okay, I guess."

Mercy turned down the volume and smirked at me. "Better than Def Leppard."

My face turned into a tomato. I wouldn't have been more embarrassed if she walked into my bedroom and saw all my stuffed animals. "Who says I like them?"

"You look like someone who listens to Def Leppard." *That was mean of me.*

"What does someone who listens to Def Leppard look like?" *Even though it*

"You." *was true.*

"What, like my face and hair or my clothes? These aren't my regular clothes."

"What are your regular clothes?"

"Jeans, sweatshirt or sweater, not that different from yours."

"I notice you haven't denied your Leppard allegiance."

"I—I don't like their new record at all, but their older stuff, before they got super popular, is still good."

"Fair enough."

Two air fresheners shaped like pine trees dangling off the rearview mirror couldn't fully mask a damp, skunky smell. Her window was half-open (and not level), and heat blasted through the air vents. She had to leave the heat on, otherwise the engine would melt down. "Total nuke show," she said.

Her shoulder bag was in my lap and under my hands. I snaked one hand out to roll down my window a crack. The forced hot air wasn't oppressive, but it was soporific.

Mercy said, "Your cousin Jen says hi, by the way. She's doing well but can't wait to leave Maine. Or maybe she'll stay and grow weed in the woods."

Was she a mind reader? The Def Leppard bit was one thing, but how did she know about Jen? Though my strait-laced (as far as I knew) cousin never struck me as the weed type. Weed type? Christ, I was ridiculous.

Mercy didn't say anything else, waiting me out, or waiting for me to figure it out. And oh, yeah.

I said, "You heard me tell Cayla you knew my cousin, right? Sorry, I just—"

"Don't worry about it. I get it."

How could she get it or get me when I sure as hell didn't? I worried she thought I lied to Cayla because I was embarrassed to have her, a stranger, in the club, which, fine, was slightly true. I wasn't embarrassed by her per se, more that I was unable to get other classmates or "friends" to participate and I had no other recourse but to invite a stranger to join, and voilà, Mercy was suddenly a friend of my cousin.

Eager to change the subject, I asked, "Can I see the pictures you took?"

"Yeah. Hold on." She plucked her bag away from me and deposited it on her own lap. She rifled through it with both hands while presumably pinning her knees against the underside of the steering wheel to keep us on the road. She passed the stacked pictures across to me. "Be careful not to touch the exposed film. I'm picky about my photos."

Not yet confident enough to try out a joke about how not-careful the photos had been left in her bag or how not-careful she was about hands on the steering wheel, I said, "Got it."

The photo of me was on top. I was caught in mid-cringe next to the stairwell banister, sporting a goofy non-smile. The camera flash bleached my craggy, lunar-surface face. I ostracized the shot to the bottom of the stack, and I quickly fanned through the set. No one picture was remarkable in terms of composition (though I was far from an expert) other than the photo of Tom Jones lying in repose. The colors were soft, and the image blurred the farther the eye moved away from the subject, which was of course his body. This was the last photograph anyone would ever take of the man. How many other people would see this photo other than Mercy and me? How many of those people would know his name? This square document of finality in my hand swelled a sudden wave of sadness. A futile gesture born from the optimism and cynicism of youth, I committed his photo and name to memory.

I asked, "What's with the pictures? Are they for a class or something?"

"I'm on the lookout for evidence."

Was she joking? My joke/truth radar was nascent at best, but the reading I got was *truth*. I asked, "Evidence of what?"

"I can't tell you yet." Again, the needle pointed to *truth*. "If you must know, I'm looking for aliens and UFOs. They're everywhere."

Okay, that read as bullshit. Maybe. I said, "Fine, don't tell me," and I not-so-nonchalantly shuffled through the photos again while birdily twitching glances at her.

Mercy said, "You're too easy. I take pictures because I like taking pictures, and I use them to make collages or mess around with double exposures and other artsy stuff."

"I'm *Art*-sy."

"I'm sure you are."

"No, I mean that I'm—"

"Art. You don't have to explain bad jokes." She said it with an almost laugh, which was good enough for me.

I reset the stack of photos. "I knew you didn't believe in UFOs."

"Maybe I do. Depends on the day. I love the show *In Search of . . .* though."

"Yeah, me too. Best theme song ever."

"Agreed."

Mercy kicked up the volume in time for a blasting chorus referencing UFOs, and the rest of the ride passed in companionable silence. She pulled up onto the curbless sidewalk in front of my house, a small three-bedroom colonial-style, the rooms tightly packed into 1,500 square feet of living space. Neighboring homes huddled in close, keeping an eye on us. A crabapple tree and a young pine about as tall as I was flanked the short walk to the front door.

I gave the pictures back to Mercy and thanked her for the ride. She stowed the photos and Frisbeed the bag into the backseat as I spluttered through saying I'd call to let her know when the next Pallbearers Club meeting was.

Twisted in her seat, one arm behind the headrest, she eyed me for a length of time enough for me to consider what it was

I'd said in addition to all possible other things I might then say. I couldn't hold her stare, but I also couldn't look away. The car's heat billowed around my head along with the sweet, dizzying tang of antifreeze. For the first time since the funeral home, I thought about how unnerved (or frightened, I should probably admit that I was frightened) I was when I thought Mercy was hiding in the moments before she emerged from the coat closet. I was now convinced that whatever she'd say next she'd say without moving her mouth and I'd hear it as coming from behind me and feel its black-hole mass over my shoulder. As I was about to be sucked into the gravity-hungry event horizon, she ejected the cassette from the tape deck.

"I don't do meetings. Tell me when I need to show up at the funeral home and I'll be there. I can pick you up, too, if you want," she said.

"Okay. Right. Thanks."

She tossed the tape into my midsection as I crawled out of the bucket passenger seat. "Hey, you can have this. Give it a good listen."

"Oh, thanks. That's, um, that's very cool. Are you sure?"

"No big deal. It's a copy of a copy. I'll make another one."

The cassette was a TDK brand. I similarly used blank tapes to record my records so I could listen to them on my Walkman. This cassette was framed by black plastic with a clear middle, a window to the two spools of audio tape. There were no stickers, and nothing was written on the cassette to identify the band or albums contained therein.

As I inspected the tape, flipping it over and back, and after I shut the passenger door with a hip, which meant I shouldn't have heard her as clearly as I did (I'm not sure if my memory can be fully trusted here), she said, "You're gonna like it. Trust me," and it sounded as loud and as right behind me as her "I can give you a lift," from the funeral home.

No shit.

From inside my house, I watched Mercy drive away (me hiding behind a curtain) before I re-inspected the tape's inscrutableness. I forced myself to wait before jamming it into my Walkman and the music into my earholes, as though to prove to Mercy I was not in any rush to listen to the recording more closely. After giving my parents a one- or two-sentence report on how the service went and somewhat successfully deflecting questions on who gave me a ride home, I prepared my typical lunch of champions: a stack of cracker and peanut butter mini-sandwiches and a glass of Coke. The tape was in the Walkman and puffy orange headphones pillowed my ears before I finished eating. I rewound Side A to the beginning and pressed Play. The opening drums of Hüsker Dü's record *New Day Rising* kicked in. Forty-one minutes later I rewound to the start and pressed Play again.

Lost in my third listen, Mom tapped me on the shoulder. Phone call. It was Mercy, though she never identified herself.

"I told you you'd like it."

Click.

I spent the rest of the afternoon and evening listening to the tape.

Never had I previously been the stereotypical late-sleeping teen, but the next morning I remained in bed until 1 P.M. Easily a new personal record for sleeping in. Dad came into my room and yelled at me to get up and not sleep the whole day away. Despite the extra rest I was not refreshed. I was so crushingly exhausted, I asked for his help to take off the bulky back brace I wore overnight. Then I was late for my four-hour bagboy shift at Star Market, and when I got home, I was luggage and spent the rest of the night on the TV-room couch. Mom worried I was sick, but I was back to my disappointing self the next morning.

"I'm not sure if my memory can be fully trusted here."

Is this really a memoir? I'm no expert on publishing categories, genres, descriptions, etc. but this reads like creative nonfiction, or a creative nonfiction memoir. That's a thing, yes? It's not a criticism but more a pointed observation: this book, more times than not, reads like fiction. The quoted conversations especially. If you're quoting in a memoir, aren't you implying those exact words were said? Maybe I'm being too literal.

That aside, there is no way you remember all these conversations as presented, is there? I shouldn't presume your memory works like mine, or like anyone else's. I sure as hell don't remember our exact conversations from almost thirty years ago. Or, I suppose, that's not wholly accurate. I remember our many and varied conversations, and I cherish most of them, but what I remember is the information shared with a vague sense of when and where it happened. I do not remember our talks as exact quotes with an accompanying nuanced give-and-take. Not sure why that line about me asking if you wanted a lift really sticks out as something I would never have said, but it bothers me.

Eh, I guess it's not a big deal—yes I doth protest too much. My portrayal in these pages—at least in this introduction to, ahem, "Mercy"—stings a little, cuts too close to the heart. I come off as aloof, strange, and kinda mean, and socially awkward, too, different than your shade of awkwardness, of course, in which you wallow and celebrate. I always encouraged you to not care what other people think about you as a blanket social survival philosophy, but valued friends are not included in that "other people" category. I cared and care deeply what you think of me.

Even though you have me saying and doing things

there's no way I said or did at the time or in the manner you described, I cannot rightly claim you're inaccurate in how I pushed you around initially. I am sorry for that, but, frankly, it was necessary. It's complicated.

This was a long chapter. You might consider splitting it up. A few more thoughts, going in order:

I was right about Def Leppard. The Pallbearers Club logo on your flyer was essentially the same as DL's, so it didn't take ESP to figure out you were a fan.

I'm weary and leery and all the -earies as to why you gave me the name Mercy Brown.

I did not take a photo of Tom Jones's body during the ceremony. I took it well before we started.

I did not hide in the coat closet. Even if I wanted to, I couldn't fit, too small and too many other coats. You tiptoed into the foyer—already freaked out, scared to be in the funeral home by yourself—and I called out my offer of a ride, and maybe, yeah, I called out too loudly. You jumped out of your skin, nearly levitating. But there was no ventriloquism—no thanks, those dummies are freaky—and no me creeping out of the closet to scare you. You did a good enough job scaring yourself.

Who is the imagined audience for this book, by the way? Nonfiction writers need to be able to answer that question. Is this a story about overcoming or succumbing?

Based on the date you give on the first page and in a section in this chapter, I assume you started writing this in 2007. Then, later, your 2012-voice and 2017-voice interjections are quite different tonally. The present-day 2017-you commentary is concerning.

I am not a path. I am your friend.

I loved that old Datsun. I miss making tapes too. Streaming playlists are not the same. I want a physical artifact in my hands. Yes, I am an old person.

I don't remember ever joking/saying I took photos because I was hunting for mysterious evidence. I don't mean this to be a fact-checking, refutative read, but this is supposed to be nonfiction after all.

Rereading our exchange in the car I think you wanted to work in a reference to UFOs so you could name the chapter the way you did. I only now notice the chapters are named after Hüsker Dü songs. Awwww. It's endearing, and also, given you're pushing fifty years old, maybe a wee bit pathetic. "Pathetic" isn't the right word—it's too strong—but I'm using it. And no shame meant toward you, or solely you. I don't know how else to describe a level of fandom in which one attaches a sizable measure of value, pride, and self-worth via the act of being a fan. I am not excluding myself from this. I still wear my old green jacket with band pins and patches. If I were to title this part of my commentary like your chapters, I'd call it "Dead Set on Destruction," so I could be the Grant Hart to your Bob Mould, because as we flail into the decaying teeth of the twenty-first century, most of us communicate our neuroses, narcissisms, and tribalisms via T-shirt alliances, Instagram tags, and "well actually" subtweets. I don't know why I'm being so judgy. Maybe I see too much of myself in you, and when I see it, I want to invalidate it because it makes me sad, and I don't know exactly why.

I do proudly take credit for introducing Hüsker Dü and punk music to you. I like to think I saved you from following

Def Leppard into the Matchbox Twentys and Imagine Dragonses of the world. There lies madness. So fine, I was an important path in your life. You should be happy you took it. And I am glad to be but a humble branch.

Not sure why the last paragraph is about you being tired after our time hanging out. I'd cut it.

FLIP YOUR WIG

(Fall 1988–Winter 1989)

A chapter in which my high school life takes
multiple turns.

*You are so heady. I don't even
know what that means.*

This was a heady time for young Art.

Perhaps the headiest. Well, that's an overstatement. It's a partially
heady time, the best for which any of us can hope.

The week after Tom Jones's service, Cayla quit the club. Her
leaving was not a shock, but I was disappointed. She told me she never
planned on being in the club for the long haul and she was weirded out
by Mercy shooting all those photos at the funeral home. I appreciated
Cayla's promptness and candor and I was grateful she had been
there at the start, and really, the club wouldn't have happened if she
had not joined. There was no way I would've gone through with any
of it if the club was Eddie and me. I didn't tell her the above, but
standing in front of my locker, I thanked her and offered a formal
handshake hand. She laughed, pumped my arm up and down once,
and said, "Pleasure doing business with you, Mr. Barbara."

Let's press the Fast-Forward double arrows on this tape.

I didn't make and distribute more flyers and I didn't recruit
other classmates for the Pallbearers Club. I was satisfied with a
club of two. Most every Saturday morning Mercy picked me up
and we helped with services at the funeral home. Mr. Stephens
tolerated her photography if she showed up early and adhered to

his pre-ceremony-photos-only policy. After, we hit McDonald's or Super Sub (never Nick's Roast Beef, which was the main hangout area of Beverly High School students), and we drove around listening to and talking about music. She dubbed more tapes for me; never mixes, always full albums. Ramones, Bad Religion, Black Flag, the Slits, Dead Kennedys, the Damned, Blondie, Bad Brains, Patti Smith, the Minutemen, Siouxsie and the Banshees, Buzzcocks, X-Ray Spex, Fishbone, Mission of Burma, Joy Division, and many more. I liked some bands better than others, but every band was daring, challenging, and unlike anything played on local radio or MTV. This music was a new prism through which I viewed the world; a thrilling secret, and for the first time in my life I was in the know. Chords vibrated on a wavelength that fused me to the music and together we were bigger than a shouted chorus and together we were as small as a promise and for those two-to-three glorious minutes of song duration, we were the same. That was not to say I'd found where I belonged, whatever that meant. Compared to the spandex and pyrotechnics of rock and hair-metal bands I previously worshipped, punk was honest and real (not that there wasn't any posing going on, myself included). The scene was still unattainable to skinny old me, but a different kind of unattainable. Music was performed and made by gods, after all, but I had new ones now. Hüsker Dü remained my favorite and I quickly burned through their catalog, their early hardcore records were as thrilling and revolutionary as their mutation into melodic/outsider post-punk and power pop. In an extra notebook at home, I filled pages writing out the lyrics to their double-album *Zen Arcade* as I listened, pretending the loose concept about a kid who ran away from home and into an even scarier world was about me. In the song "Newest Industry" I found a truly cathartic expression of my dying-in-a-nuclear-war fears and flash-of-atomic-light-nightmares I collected throughout the terrible and terrifying '80s. Of course, as cursed as I was, the band had already broken up in December 1987. I purchased most of the other Hüsker albums at the Record Rack, a small downtown store that Mercy and I ended up hitting after our fries-and-soda lunches. The inside was shaped like a shoebox with two thin walking aisles staked out by rows of record bins. Cassettes filled one wall. Band pins, patches, and posters wallpapered the opposite wall. I snapped up all the Hüsker Dü pins they had. I bought other pins, too, including bands I hadn't yet heard if the pin looked cool. But I didn't have a suitable jacket on which the pins would be the proper accoutrement. My blue zip-up knockoff <u>Members Only</u> coat and *You so fancy* my as-puffy-as-a-life-preserver winter anorak were both big pin nopes. Rides home at the end of our Saturdays often ended with Mercy playfully prodding me to radically change my look, starting with a <u>leather jacket.</u>   *Like the Fonz. Is that reference old enough for you?*

I guffawed at the thought, seeing myself through the eyes of others (and if I'm being honest, myself) as being even more slumped and ridiculous-looking, the opposite of the jacket's promise of timeless, defiant cool. She insisted she wasn't joking and that us punks didn't care what other people thought we looked like and that was kind of the point. I asked her why she didn't have one and she said she wouldn't wear dead animal hide. I pointed at her leather Doc Martens, and she curled her lip at me. What I really wanted was a jacket like Mercy's. I could maybe pull that off (probably not), but I couldn't be that pitiable. Or I could, but I chose not to. I told her what I needed was a punk starter kit, and start slow, maybe cut a hole or two into my jeans, see how it went from there. Figuring a jean jacket was a workable compromise between leather and her army jacket, I did the unpunk thing of asking Mom to get me one for Xmas. Excited that I was showing even the slightest interest in fashion, she obliged and sent me to the mall with fifty bucks to pick it out myself. I won't detail the amount of angst and indecision that went into the choice. Suffice to say I purchased a severely acid-washed jean jacket with no hint of its original hue. It was too big for me, but I didn't mind being loose within the bleached denim. I handed the jacket over to Mom when I got home, and she promptly wrapped it and put it under the Christmas tree. On Xmas morning (upon seeing the jacket again, with new holiday eyes, I wondered if it was somehow a mistake, because I couldn't enjoy a fleeting moment of happiness without an undercurrent of self-inflicted dread), I ritualistically arranged my pins on the lapels. I wore the jacket around the house before we left for my grandparents' house, breaking it and the look in. I did not dare go to school with the jacket on, but I wore it on weekends, an inapposite outer shell covering my funeral-home finery. When Mercy saw me in the jacket for the first time, she didn't hesitate to give her approval. Well, she said "Rad" in a mocking way, but she was not mocking me. Her "rad" was self- and culture-mocking.

Umm . . . sure.

We relegated our hangouts to after funeral services. We did not see each other on weekdays. The Sundays after the Pallbearers Club outings were hangover-like crashes (not that I'd experienced a hangover yet). I slept well past noon and could barely muster the energy later in the day to go to work or to do homework or my back-strengthening and stretching exercises.

As fun and transformative as our Saturdays were (the solemn funeral services notwithstanding, which is an odd thing to say, but they quickly became somber background precursors to the rest of the day; how quickly I got used to death), my weekdays were as dreary. No one at school (beyond Eddie) was outwardly or obviously cruel to me, but I metamorphosed into the boy who wasn't there, or was less there than he had been previously. During lunch or before class started, kids gossiped about who's going out with whom and whose parents wouldn't be home the next weekend and, as the calendar turned to December, what colleges everyone were applying to. I was the hole in the donut of the conversation happening around me. Sure, I was still a fellow member of the soon-to-be-hallowed class of '89, and oh weren't we having the time of our lives, yeah?, and I laughed and feigned interest and surprise like a good donut hole should, but no one asked me about the club or what I did with Mercy on the weekend or where I was applying or if I did my calculus homework. Even the brainy kids (of which I was a member) froze me out. Cayla said hi to me in the hallways, but we didn't run into each other often, and in the one class we shared she sat on the opposite side of the room.

Elsewhere in the less-heady portion of these months, my scoliosis took an unexpectedly severe turn for the worse. (Yeah, I'm sorry, and I won't pun again.)   I kinda like that one

After school on Tuesdays and Thursdays I trekked from the high school to Beverly Hospital for physical therapy appointments. My therapist was young and affable, and she offered the space to me if I ever wanted to come in on non-appointment days to weight train or work out on my own. (I didn't.) As the fall progressed into early winter, neither my flexibility nor strength improved. Frustrated, the therapist told me I was regressing, and she saw it in my curling posture when I entered the room. I wanted to say I always walked into a place like a question mark. To punctuate her point, she pushed and pried at my shoulders like she was opening a bear trap. On the verge of tears, I assured her that I kept up with my exercises, that I was doing the best I could. Either hearing the quaver in my voice or clocking my downturned, brimming eyes, she softened and said she knew I was working hard and it would pay off. Both suitably embarrassed, we barely spoke for the rest of the appointment, in which she attempted to summon enough irresistible force to stretch the immovable object. I had told her the truth about my working hard. For over an hour daily I sweated through the various exercises until my legs and torso quivered. I spent more hours at home squeezed into the iron maiden (not the band) back brace too; putting it on right after   Run to
dinner instead of waiting until before I went to bed. The main part   the hills
of the brace was hard plastic molded to the shape of my torso from hipbone to collarbone. Mom or Dad tightened the contraption with three Velcro straps beyond my reach. If I got lazy and didn't first corset myself in an itchy, hot, gauze-like body sock that in theory padded the brace, red sores erupted above my hipbones. Wearing the constricting brace exacerbated and irritated the acne on my back and chest. Piloting my arms through the brace's designated slots without pinching my armpits was a leveling-up video game

I lost more times than not. Twin metal bars rooted at the height of my shoulder blades spindled into a contiguous halo ringing my neck. With the brace on, I moved through the house like a barge in a narrow canal, and getting into bed, finding a sleeping position where the metal halo did not garrote my neck required the patience of a monk and PhD levels of pillow engineering. I'd been wearing this goddamned torture device almost every night for eighteen months, and, as it turned out, it was all for naught. On the same dreary January day the feckless George H. W. Bush was inaugurated, I had a follow-up appointment with my local orthopedic doctor. D-day for me and my sea serpent backbone. The doctor had bad news. While the brace and exercises corrected the issue in my lower spine, the curve in my upper spine had increased a jaw-dropping eight degrees since he'd seen me in September. For context, in the sixth months prior to my September appointment, my degree measurements had held steady. The doctor was at a loss to explain the rapid increase beyond the "you're still growing" catchall, and he admitted he'd never seen this dramatic a change in such a short span of time. Mom mentioned how exhausted I'd been on Sundays now, as though in explanation (which, in retrospect, it was). The doctor, unmoved by Mom's non sequitur, said that I was still growing, which meant the curve/kyphosis would continue to worsen and, if unchecked, I'd curl into myself and important stuff like internal organs wouldn't have any room in my hammocking chest. We had known addressing the upper spine with physical therapy and a back brace did not have nearly the success rate as similar treatment for the lower spine. Because the brace was no longer effective and due to the severity of future complications, the doctor recommended I undergo a spinal fusion. He gave us a name of a surgeon who was tops in his field (aren't they all?) at Boston Children's Hospital. Two weeks later we drove into Boston, my parents periodically asking "How are you doing, bud?" or "You doing okay, honey?" and otherwise they didn't talk. I burrowed in the backseat with my Walkman, listening to *Zen Arcade* at full volume. Upon arrival, the hospital loomed as large

Wait, what are you getting at?

as a castle. There were more X-rays, and the pictures of me without my skin were shocking, stills from a black-and-white horror movie called *The Incredible Kyphosising Creature*. Aside from film of my torso in rear and portrait views, they x-rayed my left wrist and hand, and based on the growth-plate imaging the doctor determined my bone age was that of a typical thirteen-year-old (gee, thanks?), which meant I was indeed still growing. My surgeon, Dr. Seward, was soft-spoken but direct. He outlined the broad strokes of the procedure: a whopping two-thirds of my vertebrae would be fused together using bone scraped away from my ischium (hipbone), and metal Harrington rods were to be attached as scaffolding to hold my straightened spine in place while the fused bone hardened. The fusion wouldn't be fully healed for one year, at which point the metal rods were no longer necessary, but they would be left inside unless there were complications. If successful, my spine would be rooted within its proper path. With the benefit of the rods, I would be walking within a week post-surgery and able to attend college in the fall, though I had to avoid contact and strenuous exercise for a full year. As with any major spinal surgery in which the vertebrae were being manipulated, there was a remote chance of paralysis if the spinal cord was somehow damaged, however that "outlier of risk" (his words) was far outweighed by the benefits and the dire long-term health consequences of not having the fusion. We set a surgery date for six days after my high school graduation in June. And as a delightful denouement to the appointment, Dr. Seward told us he suspected I had the connective tissue disorder Marfan syndrome, given the scoliosis; my ectomorphic build with unusually long limbs, fingers, and toes; double-jointedness (a misnomer, but was catchier than saying abnormally flexible joints); my high arched palate (which had to be widened before my braces); and flat feet. As a precaution, he ordered an echocardiogram for three weeks prior to the surgery to test for heart murmurs and/or signs of aortic enlargement, the latter being the more catastrophic symptom, which meant death. The death symptom.

My takeaway from all this? I was fated to be freakishly skinny (and soon to be freakishly tall) with a heart that might pop like a zit.

The good news was that I no longer had to wear the back brace. Score!

The following Saturday, on the aimless drive around Beverly with Mercy, I told her about the impending surgery, but not the Marfan's, as that possibility made me feel more fragile than I already felt. I joked that I'd be like the Terminator, living tissue surrounding my metal endoskeleton. It was a relief to tell someone other than a family member about the fusion. The date was far enough away that it would never happen, but when it did, I would have a friend who would support my recovery, even if it were from afar. She commiserated and said that it sucked but I'd be fine and imagine how tall I'd be after, "You'll be the tallest Terminator, the T-Tall-1989 or something," and she promised to visit me when recovering and bring me new music.

I said a simple "Thank you." I didn't tell her what she said meant a lot, but I hoped it was in there crouching between the two words.

Then, after a beat, she made an odd joke. "We need to get our Renfield straightened out."

"Renfield?"

"Wasn't that guy all hunched over? No, wait. Igor, then." She waved a hand as though swatting a fly. "Same diff."

There are some big-ass paragraphs here. I don't mind them, but others might. Maybe I should read more memoirs before making comments like that, but not knowing hasn't stopped me from giving an opinion before. It's the American way! I'm tempted to quote lyrics I'm sure you already know by heart from "In a Free Land"—one of the Hüskers' finest moments.

I could read about your love of music all day, every day. Do any of us love music—or anything else—as much as we loved it when we were young(er)? In the earlier chapters, despite my criticisms, I'll now admit you captured my tired cynicism well upon meeting me. Maybe you couldn't tell how much I enjoyed listening to albums with you. Your unbridled joy at the discovery was intoxicating. I couldn't get enough of it, so I kept happily feeding you and feeding off you.

Like last chapter, I don't think you need the bit about your hangover Sundays. What does that add or tell the reader other than our Saturday jaunts tuckered you out? And then your mom brings it up at the doc appointment, plus your ominous parenthetical hint at explanation . . . of what? I haven't figured it out yet. I probably won't like it.

For all my complaining about how people don't remember generic conversations from their past, especially ones that are decades lost, I do remember the morning you told me about the impending back surgery. You started right in before I pulled away from the sidewalk in front of your place. I'd never heard you talk so fast and so much, weirdly breathless about the whole thing. Wanting to have your back straightened/healed isn't weird, of course. That's not what I mean. There was something else there and it was tied to your bottomless-pitted self-esteem. Your exuberance in telling me all the gory details was less about you having something new to tell me, something out of the ordinary, and was more that somehow this crazy major surgery would in and of itself transform you into a special or remarkable person, instead of the life-altering procedure being something you'd have to overcome on the journey of continued remarkableness. Huh? How's that for masturbatory memoir indulgence and two-bit analysis? Goddamn it, it's your fault I sound like a New Age guru again. So fuck you very much for that.

You did talk about the Marfan's stuff that morning, and I made heartless jokes about your ticker. I remember your Terminator joke too. You incorrectly said "exoskeleton." I didn't correct you because I didn't want to be that person.

The Renfield quip is utter bullshit. Ignoring the casual, comfortable cruelty of a jab at your surgical expense, I would've known Renfield wasn't famously hunchbacked. I was the horror fan before you were, remember? Or at the very least, that character wouldn't be my go-to. Igor, fine, maybe, though Quasimodo is the easiest and obvious reference point. And now that I've googled your "Dr. Seward" name choice—he's a character in Stoker's <u>Dracula</u>, as if you didn't know—I'm getting the sinking suspicion you're using our relationship to construct a metaphor—or allegory, I often confuse the two—that I do not appreciate. No, sir, I don't like it.

FOLKLORE

(March 1989)

A chapter with a lion in which Mercy pretends to be ~~or becomes (you get to choose by the end of this book)~~ a vampire to help me with my homework *I cleaned that up for you.*

In my senior elective class, *New England: A Local History*, Mrs. Danforth assigned a research project. We students were to find a lesser-known event (something we had not studied in the course) tucked within the nooks of New England's history on which to write a five- to seven-page, properly cited paper. Despite the chorus of groans, wails, and laments that she was no longer our favorite teacher, she encouraged us to be creative and have fun. Then she supervillained a laugh in our faces. I was instantly in a semi-panic over the assignment.

Later that week, the Pallbearers Club served a closed-casket ceremony for a John Doe who froze to death in his encampment along the tracks between the Montserrat and Pride's Crossing train stations. After the decidedly non-celebratory service, Mercy and I attempted to rally our spirits, picking up food, and at my suggestion (I said something lame about a *punk picnic*), going to Lynch Park. The temperature was warm enough to remind us spring might grudgingly return to the region one last time, but cold enough that the large grass park with its two rocky beaches and a rose garden was deserted but for a few people walking dogs, Invisible Manned inside knitted hats and long, collar-up overcoats.

We entered the garden, passing between brick pillars adorned with stone plaques. Mercy read the engraved warning aloud: "'Whosoever enters here let him Beware'" and "'For he shall nevermore escape nor be free of my spell.'" We followed a short brick walkway carving through dead grass and passed under skeletonized tree branches. The hibernating rose garden opened before us and we continued down a small set of stairs and perched on the not-quite-twin marble lion statues. With lions safely beneath us, we greased our hands with overly fried chicken fingers.

I said, "Maybe I should write my stupid paper on this rose garden."

Mercy loosened a noise that was less apathetic than a grunt, so I told her about the assignment and how I was freaking out because I had no idea what I was going to write about.

She responded as though waiting for me to broach this very topic. *Ugh!* "You could write about my namesake. She's a New England vampire."

I heard her wrong and started in about how two students were already writing about victims of the Salem Witch Trials.

"I didn't say anything about witches. I said a vampire. Not the movie kind either. And she's from Rhode Island. Not Salem. Everyone's sick of Salem." Mercy launched into a story I'd never heard before yet was also familiar. It was great and awful and scary in the way all folktales about dying young were great and awful and scary.

I said, "Where did you hear all that? That sounds amazing but..."

"But what."

"I need to be able to cite sources and—"

"What, you think I made it up?"

"No, but—"

Mercy said "But" again, at the same time as me, and louder, swamping my "but."

"I thought, I don't know... it's one of those oral-tradition kind of things."

"It's settled. You will write your paper on this, and I'll help you find sources. Next weekend we'll road trip."

The Pallbearers Club had the next Saturday off from the funeral home, so the plan was to get an earlier start on our ninety-minute drive to Providence. When Mercy screeched to a stop out front, I bounded from the house wearing my acid-washed jean jacket, of course, and a pair of acid-washed jeans. In my possession, a waxy bag of honey-dipped donuts, a spiral-bound notebook, two pens spiderwebbed in the tight metal coil, and the emotional baggage of another soul-sucking week of high school, one that prominently featured am-I-going-to-ask-anyone-to-the-prom-or-pretend-the-prom-doesn't-exist anxieties.

The donuts were an offering Mercy refused, telling me she'd be all right. She didn't look all right. Purple dusked under her eyes, and she sagged and listed in the bucket seat. For the first time in months, I wondered how much older she was than me.

She pawed around her ashtray, emerging with a roach pinched between two fingers. She asked, "Do you want the last hit before we go?" She had occasionally smoked weed on our drives around Beverly and had offered to share once. I'd declined and, I'm proud to say, had resisted an urge to detail a nonexistent asthma or blather on about the time my mother had let me try one of her cigarettes when I was seven and how I'd coughed until I'd puked. (Despite everything else, I do credit Mercy for <u>making me marginally less pathetic.</u>)   *You're welcome.*

I said, "No, thanks," and clipped my seat belt, which was all but useless as it held no tension, as slack as a Mr. Congeniality sash.

"You sure?"

"Yeah."

She popped the roach into her mouth and swallowed.

<u>"You can eat the roach?"</u>   *"Renfield" should eat it.*

"Some of us do." She reached into the backseat, retrieved her Polaroid, took a picture of me, and returned the camera from whence it came with the photo sticking out from the base. "It's been a while since I shot you. And you're vibing this morning." She wiggled spooky-vibe fingers at me.

I thought about asking (again) what she did with the photos, specifically, the ones of me. Were her community college classmates and teacher clucking and tutting at some wall-sized impressionistic collage filled with images of my goofy mug? E-fucking-gads. I didn't ask because Mercy seemed a bit off, and I didn't want to risk souring the road trip before we'd even shoved off, so I said, "I'll try not to get any vibing on the car seat."

"You better, that shit doesn't come out."

I ate both donuts before we reached I-95 south, and consequently I wasn't feeling all that great. The mix of cold air leaking through the cracked windows and the antifreeze and heat ozone from the vents wasn't helping. Mercy had perked up, though, almost as soon as we'd left my house, and talked about the music scene in Providence.

Once my queasy stomach settled and the cold air/heat ratio found a tolerable equilibrium, I tried to get Mercy talking about herself. The more time we spent together it seemed the less I knew about her, which made me even more self-conscious and reluctant to ask personal questions. What kind of lousy friend was I for not knowing the Mercy basics at this point? Sure, she was evasive, and my already fuzzy head seemed to get fuzzier whenever we hung out, and at this point in our relationship I still worked and worried the wording and tone of what I said and what I would say later, terrified of scaring her off. It was possible she'd already told me all sorts of personal details (even the silly ephemera, the stuff most of us are only remembered for: Favorite color? Dog person or cat person? Coke or Pepsi? Pickles or no pickles?) and I'd blanked because I was hopelessly lost inside myself. Now we had all this time ahead of us in the car and I was determined to learn something beyond eccentric instant photography and punk music.

"How is school going?"

"Fine."

"How many classes are you taking?"

"Too many."

"Right. Did you do anything cool during the week?"

I made you
fuzzy wuzzy?

"The usual."

"Where do you work again?"

"I don't want to talk about work on the weekend."

"Oh, sure. Um, where did you grow up?"

"You taking notes over there?" Mercy sighed. "Rhode Island. We're going to my ancestral home. I'll introduce you to the family, then bury you in the basement and grow flowers from your corpse."

"You'd only get wallflowers."

Mercy laughed. It was rare to get anything more than a smirk from her, so I reveled in it, attempting awful pile-on jokes that weren't funny but were in that moment. It loosened her up enough to give me the following information: Orange, obviously; Dogs, but they didn't like her; Dr Pepper (blucky); and dill pickles (the monster).

When we hit Providence, Mercy showed me where her favorite music club, the Living Room, was. She idled on Promenade Street, and I jumped out to peer into the darkened windows and run my hands over posters from past and upcoming shows. As excited as I was to see the vaunted club, it was disappointing to find notices for shitty, cheesy bands like Extreme next to Living Colour and the Ramones. Even more of a bummer, I'd hoped against hope to see the promo for the 1987, November 11 Hüsker Dü show, as the band broke up exactly one month later.

Mercy said, "Punk is dead. You missed it. Bad luck, man. Long live punk." She said it like she attended Bowery shows in 1976. It pissed me off because she was right, even if I aspired to fake it in a lifelong way.

From there we detoured through the Financial District, a square of blocks hemmed between the Kennedy Plaza bus terminal, Johnson & Wales University and Weybosset Street, the dilapidated Civic Center, and the library on Washington and Empire Streets. An unsettlingly vacant cityscape, almost no one lived downtown, and the denizens generally fled the area once regular work hours ended.

At the sight of the expansive library's ornate main entrance of three arches held up by towering columns, I despaired, thinking we'd never find the sources I needed for my paper on the other Mercy Brown, a New England Vampire (I was still working out a title). We navigated the library interior and found the microfiche machine on which we would search almost a century of *Providence Journal* newspapers.

Mercy left me to scroll through the early 1890s, not quite sure what I was looking for, other than Mercy's name. The days and weeks blurred, the greenish tint of the microphotographed newspapers blended text and photos. After the initial rush of potential discovery, I got distracted reading headlines about horsecar accidents, the first electric streetcars, and odd personal histories detailed in death notices, all those forgotten struggles and lives summed up in a quirky paragraph. Would anyone ever go looking for Julia Walton, who, at age seventy, died after a six-month illness, no occupation listed, but devoted her life to acts of charity that were described as "spontaneous acts of a kindly heart"? Perhaps, like I did, someone might stumble upon her paragraph hidden within thousands of images imprinted upon a roll of microfiche, which was housed within the haystack of one library, or another hypothetical someone might find themselves walking through one of the hundreds of disused graveyards, marked by crumbling stone or rusted fences, that pocked the New England landscape and amble by her weathered gravestone (if it was indeed still intact) melting into the dirt. In either scenario there would be no recognition of who Julia was, which was our fate. The erasure of familial and cultural memory of any one individual was simply a function of time. My being so starkly reminded of the yawning void awaiting me was unmooring and left me feeling detached from what had been to that point a fun afternoon. If I'd said any of this to Mercy, she'd rightly accuse me of leaving punk for goth and tell me to go listen to Bauhaus.

I kept scrolling and found no vampires. The machine was getting hot and smelled of burnt licorice, so I shut it off to give it a break.

Mercy appeared behind me and dropped a book titled *A Clutch of Vampires* in my lap. The cover featured a lurid font and a pencil sketch of a vampire wearing a billowing cape casting a mountainous shadow as it approached a cluster of lonely headstones. The illustration was more playful than sinister. The book detailed a host of folkloric tales of New England vampires, including a chapter on Mercy Brown.

Bumping me and my rolling chair aside, Mercy hunched over the microfiche, turned it on, spun the knobs expertly, the pages whirring by, pausing briefly (too briefly for my eyes) to scan the date, before landing with an "Aha" and a vindicated pointer finger aimed at the viewing screen.

The front page of the March 19, 1892, issue of the *Journal* had this as a headline:

EXHUMED THE BODIES
TESTING A HORRIBLE SUPERSTITION IN THE TOWN OF EXETER

Bodies from the dead relatives taken from their graves
They had all died of consumption, and the belief was that live flesh and blood would be found that fed upon the bodies of the living.

We (or Mercy) quickly found two more articles detailing the same event on the twentieth and twenty-first. It was as though she knew they were there and left me to hunt for them on my own first, so I'd feel like I'd worked hard. I paid for photocopies of the articles and copies of the relevant pages from the one book Mercy found. Still one source short of the five required, we left anyway and spent the afternoon on the east side of Providence over by Brown University, browsing through the record stores In Your Ear and Tom's Tracks on Thayer Street.

On the ride home, Mercy suggested a way to write the paper, as Mrs. Danforth had encouraged our getting "creative" with it. Maybe it would make up for being one source short.

I can't believe you saved this. But I'm glad you did. Look how good it came out! We had a good time sometimes. Most of the time!

INTERVIEW WITH MERCY BROWN, A NEW ENGLAND VAMPIRE
by Art Barbara

ART: At the end of this, I hope you'll disclose how you're still among the living.

MERCY: I'm not alive. Or am I?

ART: Quite! Do you mind if I record this?

MERCY: My voice won't record because I'm a vampire.

ART: Really? Is that true?

MERCY: No. Go ahead, record.

ART: Who were your parents and how many siblings did you have?

MERCY: My parents were George T. Brown and Mary Eliza Brown, and I had five brothers and sisters.

ART: And you lived in . . .

MERCY: You forgot to phrase it as a question. We lived in Exeter, a small town about twenty-five miles south of Providence. We farmed corn in the impossible, rocky soil, raised assorted dairy animals. Life was hard. When humanity foolishly transitioned from hunting/gathering to an agrarian-based society, that's when we became a miserable, or more miserable species, doomed to suffer from hunger and want.

ART: Sure. Who in your family was the first to die and when?

MERCY: My mother died in December of 1883.

ART: How did she die?

MERCY: Consumption. The wasting illness.

ART: Which is what we now know as tuberculosis, a bacterial infection of the lungs. It has killed millions of people worldwide and was especially deadly during the 1700s and 1800s when it was by far the leading cause of death in the northeast. Even now there are antibiotic-restraint strains.

MERCY: Consumption is more descriptive than tuberculosis. The sufferer is wracked by painful coughs, usually at night when they try to sleep, and their faces drain of color except for their cheeks that go a blood red. They lose their appetite and weight, become gaunt, emaciated, eyes sink into their skulls, like they're being consumed from within. We all lived in fear of the disease because it ran through families and whole towns like wildfire. No one knew where it came from or how you got it, never mind how to cure it. Some people lingered for years with it, like my brother, and it would hide, like a hibernating bear, only to come roaring back. Or in my case, it could be a secret that you carried because you didn't have any symptoms, but you still had it inside and you spread it without knowing. Such an evil thing.

ART: Your poor family suffered another tragedy shortly after your mother passed away, correct?

MERCY: My older sister, Mary Olive, died from consumption seven months after we lost my mother. Mary was twenty. Older than me by nine years, she was like a second mom to me because my mom was usually too busy on the farm. Everyone loved Mary and even though neighbors were afraid to be near my family and catch our illness, they came out to see Mary off. She knew she was dying and had picked the hymn everyone sang at her own funeral. Her voice was missing and would've been the most beautiful. When I was little, she sang to me until I fell asleep. She was the only one in the family I didn't mind calling me Lena—but never Mercy Lena. I miss her terribly.

ART: Can you describe the years after Mary died, but before you and your brother fell ill?

MERCY: We set ourselves to the grim work of going on. What else could we do? My father further devoted himself to sustaining the farm. He remained kind, but distant, with a haunted look, as though he was continually witnessing fresh horrors. Some neighbors helped looking after us kids, but Dad leaned on my brother Edwin to run the household. He grew into being as big and strong as a horse.

ART: Then Edwin fell ill.

MERCY: Yes, a few years after Mary Olive died, Edwin started losing strength and color, and he had that awful cough at night, a hollow, hopeless sound that rattled the wooden boards in my bedroom. Every tickle in my throat filled me with terror that I had it too. It was simply a matter of time before I became sick, but each night I prayed, asking God if I could have one more day before the coughs and fever kicked in. And the next night I'd again pray for one more good day, and the same prayer again the night after and the night after. Just one more day, please.

At wits' end, Dad sent Edwin to Colorado, the thinking being the mountain air would help him, that the air here was foul, or fouled, and it was what made him and Mom and Mary sick. He did go into a kind of remission on occasion, but it always returned. He came back home, looking like a very sick old man in the fall of 1891. I was sick by then, too, but unlike Edwin who suffered with it for years, I declined quickly.

ART: Can you talk about what it felt like?

MERCY: What it felt like? It felt like dying.

ART: Right, sorry.

MERCY: On those worst December nights sweat poured off my head even though I was freezing, and I coughed with lungs made of stained glass. When December became January, Mary Olive came to see me. I could see only her silhouette and she was smaller than she was in life. She had become as little and creeping as a child and her hair had grown flowing and wild as though it hadn't been cut for all the years since she was gone. But then her child-shape changed, flowed, didn't hold, and she was something else entirely. I was afraid and I couldn't speak her name and I couldn't move as she wormed up onto my bed and sat on my chest. She was as heavy as the boulders we couldn't move from our fields. Even though I was so scared I wanted to say hi, tell her I missed her, but I couldn't breathe. Mary leaned close so we were both lost in the forest of her hair. Then her hair moved and waved on its own, forming inky clouds that hid her face. There was a rattle in my chest, and I knew she had come back to listen to my purr and to take it away with her, and that's when I felt oddly light, like a feather wanting or willing a breeze to lift it away. This was all right because I knew she loved me even though she wouldn't sing for me anymore.

ART: You died in January of 1892. Edwin continued to get sicker, and then your neighbors approached your father with an outlandish idea of what was happening to Edwin.

MERCY: They said one of us three Brown women were coming back at night and eating the living tissue and blood of Edwin. Always the women's fault.

ART: Did your father believe them?

MERCY: No, he didn't. He wasn't superstitious or religious, and he wanted to be left alone, but his grief and fervent neighbors wore him down. He eventually gave permission for all three of our bodies to be exhumed and examined.

ART: Right, on March 17, 1892. Why exhume the bodies? What proof of you being a vampire were they looking for?

MERCY: To be clear, no one ever uttered the word "vampire" until after the *Providence Journal* reported what happened.

ART: My apologies.

MERCY: Just let me tell it. The locals exhumed my mother and Mary Olive first. My mother was essentially a skeleton. Mary's body was in a similar state of decomposition, though her skin formed a tight leather around her bones and her hair had continued growing, forming a dark, dusty wreath around her head. They found me turned around, facedown in the grave, which caused a gasp or two. Some of the gathered argued I'd turned over after being buried— which was a sign—while others said I'd been buried that way to prevent my returning, in accordance with local superstition.

ART: Which was it?

MERCY: Can't say I remember, sorry. And stop interrupting. When Dr. Metcalf examined my body, he found my heart and liver to be full of blood, which he said was a natural occurrence given the timeline of decomposition. But according to the locals, my blood-filled heart was proof of their greatest fears, that at night I'd been feeding off Edwin. With the doctor and my father—I can't imagine what my father was thinking, what this spectacle must've done to him—and sickly Edwin, barely with the strength to stand on his own power, all looking on, the gathered burned my heart and liver atop a stone. Once the organs were no more than ashes, Edwin drank a tonic with the ashes mixed in. That was supposed to stop my nocturnal visitations and cure him of his affliction.

ART: Did it stop your nocturnal visitations? Was he cured?

MERCY: Edwin died two months later. And of my remaining family, only my father and youngest sibling survived into the new century.

ART: The *Providence Journal* ran their first disapproving story about the ritual on March 19, 1892, calling it a "barbaric superstition" and criticized the lack of education and the amount of ignorance in the rural communities of New England.

MERCY: They were right to be skeptical, but I have sympathy for the people of Exeter too. They did what they did because they were afraid and wanted the horror to stop. When people become desperate, it's human nature to assign blame to someone.

ART: Yours wasn't the sole case of exhumation and suspected vampirism in New England in the nineteenth century. Interestingly, in the documented cases I found referenced, all focused on curing or stopping the suspected vampire and none of them posited how people became vampires in the first place. Circling back to the beginning of this where you said you were indeed a vampire, I want to know how . . .

MERCY: I didn't say I was a vampire.

ART: I can play the tape back for you if you'd like.

MERCY: No need. I said, "My voice won't record because I'm a vampire." And you asked if that was true. And I said, "No, go ahead and record." You assumed my no was an answer to the recording question, when it could've easily meant I wasn't telling the truth about me being a vampire.

ART: Are you a vampire then? I mean, how do you explain your being here, burnt-up heart and all, almost a century later?

MERCY: Meh, maybe, I guess, or not, whatever. But I can tell you this unassailable truth: I don't believe in the supernatural.

ART: You don't believe in the supernatural?

MERCY: Nope.

ART: But the unexplained—

MERCY: The unexplained means it just hasn't been explained yet.

ART: I guess that's one way of looking at it.

MERCY: You're looking a little peaked, Art. <u>Are you feeling okay?</u>

Muhahahaha!

I appreciated the help Mercy had given me on the paper, though I was puzzled by her insistence of having last say on the edits before I submitted it. I wanted to change the last part to make it clear Mercy admitted to being a vampire. She insisted that her answers and the confusing ambiguity/mystery remain, word for word.

I got a B- on the paper. Mrs. Danforth docked points because there wasn't enough history in my history paper, but I aced the creativity aspect of the assignment and she encouraged me to submit to the school's literary magazine. I didn't take her suggestion. The most creative aspects of the paper weren't mine. Mercy had come up with, seemingly on the spot, the personal details, descriptions, and the bit about Mary Olive sitting on her chest at night, no reference of which appeared in my sources. While I had no problem using her impromptu answer in my history paper, I wouldn't have felt right about submitting her work as mine to the lit magazine. And I was disappointed in the grade. By disappointed I mean my brain worked overtime churning out worst-case scenarios, including but not limited to a college retracting my acceptance because of an improperly sourced B-.

Three weeks later, I received my acceptance letters to the University of New Hampshire and Providence College, neither of which was revoked. I chose Providence.

Four weeks later, the Pallbearers Club attended its final funeral.

Man, you should've submitted the paper to the lit magazine with me listed as your coauthor. That's some good stuff I gave you. I recall you wanted to cut the bit about the Mary Olive sitting on Mercy's chest thing as it strayed too far into invention/supposition. Oh, the irony now, with my banging on about your creative ornamentation, shall we say, within this book. Aren't you glad you kept that part in though? That's some creepy-and-sad gold right there, my friend. We've collaborated well.

I've been thinking about my differing recollections of many of the events here and how the observer effect applies to writing a memoir. The writer typically constructs conclusions, or anti-conclusions, through analyzing recollections and reflections, which are refracted via a predetermined level of candor. Hell, I just did it with that sentence. I meant to come stronger with the word "honesty," but I softened the blow with "candor" instead. A memoirist could, if they so desired, write a set of different books while re-observing the same autobiographical material. But would it be the same material after being so heavily observed within the prior memoir?

I do wonder how purposefully you changed, embellished, and muddied details, or maybe you don't know how much fictionalizing is occurring subconsciously—like you and your supposed fuzzy head whenever I was around. I've brought up your impossible recall of detailed dialogue earlier, but should we apply the same scrutiny to your painstaking depiction of the seventeen-year-old you's emotional life? Does the adult you, the one who knows what is going to happen next to that kid, truly remember how you felt at seventeen? Is that kid forever trapped inside you, as easy to recall as the name of your first pet? All memoirs must trade in emotional ventriloquism; it's part and parcel of a memoir's allure. I'm more interested in the answer to this: Is it fair to young Art to be so harshly judged by someone who's had decades to craft his responses?

Sorry to ramble. I'm putting off moving onto the next chapter because I know it won't end well for either of us. Poor us.

One last thing re: Goth. Dude, it's like you read my mind. For someone who claims he doesn't want to be remembered after he's gone, you sure do spill a lot of ink on the subject. You'd make the worst kind of immortal.

IT'S NOT FUNNY ANYMORE

(May 1989)

A chapter in which a blob, a dinner, an attempted
break-in, and not-a-jacket change everything

Dramarama!

It was as though Mercy knew we were driving to the last wake we'd
attend together.

A few minutes before we pulled into Stephens's parking lot, Mercy
said, "Hey, remember the first time I showed up at the funeral home? To
be honest, my plan was to check it out, see what kind of curio show it
was. I mean, sorry, your flyers were a bit much—"

"You mean awesome."

"Yeah, totally. So, I showed up to take some photos and that was
gonna be my only time. I thought it would be all I needed. But then,
you know, it was kind of nice. Morbid and odd and creepy, but nice."

Afraid where this was going or not going, I blurted out, "And you
met me and wanted to turn me into a punk."

"There's still some work to do there. Turned into something
anyway."

"Bite me."

"None of the other ceremonies hit me like that first one though."
She paused, and as she savored her wistfulness, an unbidden
image from my first ceremony (the one with Eddie and Cayla) of
the wilted body of Kathleen Blanchet developed in my head like one

of Mercy's Polaroids. She added, "And that bit from the letter Tom Jones wrote, that was his name, right?"

I nodded yes.

She said, "Hope is believing there'll be another moment of joy, and despair is knowing there won't be one more. That has stuck with me. The kind of thing you forget about until you remember it. Like last night, I was in the BK drive-thru and I never usually get fast food unless I'm with you because you're such a picky eater—"

"Hey!"

"And I was behind some asshole in a pickup that needed a new exhaust, and that's when I randomly thought about Jones and the line about hope and despair, and I was like, What am I doing here? And by the time I got to the window I was almost in tears. Happy or sad or both happy-sad, sad-happy? I don't know. I was also kinda high."

"You ate the roach?"

"I ate the roach. With a large Coke and fries." Mercy parked in her usual spot.

I asked, "You okay?"

"Fine and/or dandy."

[Note: It's clear to me now she was trying to tell me something with her maudlin-ness, but I didn't pick up on it then.]

I don't mean this in a Fight Club/split-personality way. I'm real, obviously. But you're making up so much of the content of our chats.

The morning's start at the funeral home went according to script. The dearly deceased was a peanut of a woman in her mid-nineties. Thirty minutes before the start of the service Mercy shot her photos and Mr. Stephens commented upon my slouching and the hearse driver offered me half of his cinnamon bun, and later, if I wanted, half of his chicken salad sandwich.

A grandson was to be the lone family member in attendance. He arrived five minutes before the visiting hour began. Almost six and a half feet tall, his oblong head dripped feathery brown and gray hair that curled and cowlicked, framing his broad forehead, his prominent nose a flag in the middle of his face. A patchy beard attempted to fill

I don't know how much of this Mercy is me and how much is you.

in his cheeks and define his chin. Thick-lensed bifocals fun-house-mirrored his light-colored eyes. A tan suit draped over his gaunt frame as though he were made of wire hangers. If I were to judge by his frail, wan appearance, I would've guessed he was in his sixties, but he had to be younger. He tottered and stooped through the foyer toward us as though grief was a city built upon his back.

Being newly preoccupied with my maybe-Marfan-syndrome diagnosis, I couldn't help but wonder if this man had it, if I was looking at my bleak future, and if his timid heart was already as large as an elephant's.

His hand swallowed mine in a gentle handshake. He responded to my "I'm sorry for your loss" with closed eyes, a bowed head, and a whispered "Thank you." He shook Mercy's hand as well before slouching into the viewing room and engaging Mr. Stephens in hushed conversation.

Mercy whispered, "He kinda looks like you as an older dude."

"Shut up."

"I knew you were thinking it, so I couldn't help myself, sorry. You will not look like him as an older dude. Okay? I promise."

I made a mental note, at the very least, to never own a tan suit.

Mercy said, "Something's not right with him. I should take his picture." Her camera remained in her bag as we joined the others.

The grandson did not engage us in conversation during the visiting hour, nor did he speak on behalf of his grandmother when asked by Father W. He did require, however, that the Pallbearers Club serve the ceremony graveside. This was news to us, and I think to Mr. Stephens, too, as he apologized for not giving us notice sooner.

Mercy and I were third in a three-vehicle funeral procession. While driving she sifted through the pond of cassettes pooled in the center console and threw on the Jim Carroll Band's "People Who Died." (If you've never heard the tune, think *The Gashlycrumb Tinies* as sung by a sneering junkie punk poet.) The song jangled into life somewhere in the middle, at the part about Tony who apparently didn't fly and suffered the consequences foretold by the title. I pressed rewind. We briefly argued about why one always had to start a song

The song fits the motif, but I never owned a Jim Carroll Band tape. Is this subtle foreshadowing/you admitting to something?

at the beginning. She begrudgingly agreed, but to punish me for my rare victory, she insisted we listened to the song (the kind you only needed to hear once to appreciate) twice more before we arrived at the cemetery.

A liar of a cloudless blue sky pushed the temperature into the seventies, and thanks to the Datsun's blasting heat I was already sweating through my pallbearer garb before stepping onto the sprinkler-wet cemetery grass. Mercy told me to take off my blazer, but ever the professional, I endured.

The dead grandmother's final journey was a short one, and the club shepherded her casket ten steps from the hearse to her resting place. A stainless-steel (according to Mr. Stephens, who never missed an opportunity to fill in the details, perhaps hoping one of the club members would pursue the funerary arts as a career) lowering device framed the rectangular grave. We stepped onto a mat of artificial grass, and beneath the green carpet some sort of planking wobbled under my feet. I avoided looking into the grave because if I didn't look at it, I wouldn't get sucked in.

With the casket cradled between two horizontal straps attached to the shiny arms of the lowering device, the club retreated behind the grandson, Father W., and the hearse driver. Aside from funeral home employees and us volunteers, there were no other attendees. I hoped that my presence counted for something in someone's ledger, but I worried it was a selfish hope, so I did my best to honor the woman and her grandson by standing as reverently as a sweaty humpbacked boy could.

After the brief, impersonal ceremony comprised of a few biblical readings, the grandson placed flowers on the casket. Mr. Stephens released the device's hand brake, and the casket sank into the grave. (Note: I wanted to write "yawning pit" but that's a bit of a melodramatic cliché, and if taken literally, implies the grave was expanding, which it was not.)

The moment the ceremony ended, Mercy dashed to the Datsun, leaving me trapped with Mr. Stephens and Father W.

Mr. Stephens explained how the casket rested on bumpers a few inches above the earthen bottom, which allowed them to easily retrieve the lowering straps. When he paused to breathe between sentences, Father W. jumped in, asking if my parents were Catholic. They were, sort of. *Sort of* because they were lapsed Catholics. Before the full family lapsing began in earnest, I'd made it to my first confession in second grade. Unsurprisingly, my first and only confession did not go well, as I lied about lying to a teacher who had accused me of purposefully spilling hand soap on the boys' room floor. I didn't spill the soap on the floor, although, apparently, in the eyes of my teacher, I acted guilty and embarrassed as though I did, so it became this paradox of lies that neither me nor the confessional priest could follow, and I was eventually absolved of my sin(s) by his exhaustion.

Lying about lies. How are we supposed to trust you?

Mr. Stephens wedged back into the three-way conversation, dissecting the lowering device, showing me the gears and hand crank that reset the unit. Then Father W. parried and asked if I would consider studying theology at Providence College as a possible step toward the seminary. Mr. Stephens and Father W. shared a raucous laugh at the ridiculousness of it all, though I think their notions of what was ridiculous were not the same. Father W. clapped my back and said he thought priesthood would suit me, which I took as a total dig and a dire forecast of a dearth of future romantic opportunities.

Ha! Will you stop. You were not *that* pathetic.

Already a bit punch drunk by the time I wobbled back to the Datsun, Mercy pulled me into the car. I recoiled and flailed into the passenger seat like a vacuum cleaner's power cord.

"Look at this! I won't say anything else until you tell me what you see." Her too-cool-for-school affect gone, replaced by a stranger, UFO-eyed manic Mercy. An unsure laugh leaked out of me. She grabbed two fistfuls of my lapels and ragdolled me in the seat. "I'm serious! No fucking around—"

"Okay, okay. Jeez."

"Hold out your hands." She had a photo pinched between two fingers. "Make sure you don't touch the film part, and hold it right..."

She hectored instructions all but requiring I wear protective gloves and deposited the photo into my compliant hands.

At first blush, it was her standard photo of the open casket and the deceased in repose, similar composition and camera angle. blue But there was a ~~green~~ blob on the film, and it hovered over the dead woman's chest, blotting out part of the open lid and the floral wreaths in the background. The blob was oblong, and its borders were porous, the color diffuse.

"Do you see it?"

I said, "It's a thumbprint, right? You touched the photo while it was still developing."

"No, why would I do that?"

"I meant by accident. Didn't think you did it on purpose."

"Not my thumb. I know how to handle film."

"Well, I didn't touch it! M-Maybe Mr. Stephens or someone else picked it up, moved it from wherever you left it to develop. The kneeler, right? That's where you usually leave your pictures, but I didn't see this one there. I mean, I didn't notice. I swear that's not my thumb! I didn't touch it—" I kept babbling and I sounded unequivocally thumbprint guilty, and this was like when my second-grade teacher thought I'd purposefully spilled hand soap on the bathroom floor because I acted like I had even though I hadn't. Well, I didn't press my thumb on Mercy's developing photo either. In both cases, I perseverated on my accusers being convinced I was the culprit, and then I couldn't stop thinking *What if I did it? What if it was me?* and I saw myself doing the things I hadn't done because I couldn't (and still can't) stop making worst-case scenarios real in my head.

"Art! Stop. I'm not blaming you or Mr. Stephens or me. No one put their thumb on the picture, okay? Jesus. That's not why I wanted you to look at it. Relax. You're okay, no one touched it."

"Oh. Really?" I inspected the photo closer. There were no telltale swoops and swirls of a fingerprint, but the distortion or discoloration still looked to be the shape of a thumb pad. She had to be messing with me. I fought the urge to measure the blob against my thumb and

I wondered how Mercy would react if I asked her to hold hers up to the photo.

She asked, "You know what this is then, right?"

"You're sure it's not a thumbprint? Because it looks like one to me. Not mine, but—"

"Fucking yes, I'm sure."

"So, what am I looking at then?"

"It's evidence. Proof."

"Of what?" I flashed to our first day together in the Datsun and her I'm-looking-for-evidence answer to my what's-with-the-photos question, an answer I'd long assumed was a joke.

"I can't believe you're not getting this right away."

I asked, "Someone shook the photo, like they're not supposed to?"

"I said no one touched it!"

"Okay, then, holy fuck. . . . Aliens? Leonard Nimoy's head? I don't know what you're getting at. Stop yelling at me!"

She snatched the photo away and sighed. Could one's life be measured in the collective spent oxygen of sighs one received? Christ, I hoped not. "We spent a whole day in Providence researching this shit, and you don't see it. Love ya, Art, but you're so goddamn oblivious about what's going on around you sometimes." Mercy sighed protractedly again, which really wasn't very fair.

I shrugged and said, "Sorry?"

Employing the condescending tone of someone who believes something in which no one else believes, she explained the image on the photograph was evidence that the deceased was a New England folklore kind of vampire, like Mercy Brown, and she listed more names, some of which I recognized from the campy vampire book we'd found at the Providence Library.

She pointed at the photo and said, "Hovering blue lights just like this have been sighted over the graves of suspected vampires."

"But it's green."

"Dude, it's blue." She hid the photo back inside her bag. I wasn't worthy to view it anymore. "Because I got the blue orb"—not a ~~green~~

You are so not getting the last word on the color.

blob—"on film it means that the old woman is actively feeding, and likely on her grandson. I mean, look at him."

The grieving man was a scarecrow at the foot of his grandmother's grave. His arms hung loosely at his sides, hands neither clasped in prayer nor folded expectantly in front of his waist.

Mercy said, "He's fading away in front of our eyes. Didn't you hear that miserable cough of his?"

"Yeah," I said, but I lied. I never heard him. Now a gagging, expectorating urge balled in my throat, but I swallowed, wrestled it down.

"Did Stephens tell you how this guy's grandmother died? Two-berk-you-low-sis." She pantomimed hand gestures along with the syllables. I only understood her held up fingers for "two" and her pointing at me for "you." "Or how about we call it consumption for tradition's sake? These poor people almost exclusively feed on loved ones or the ones closest to them. It's what families and friends do, right? Maybe they can't control it and they aren't even aware they're doing it. That's the most horrible part, I think."

I side-eyed Mercy, hard, and tried a smirky laugh to get her to crack. She was crackless. There was no way she believed this, was there? This had to be a joke, but unlike her practically infinite digs at my expense, all of which were uttered with a deadpan style and a dryness arid enough to drop the dewpoint, now she emoted. Vacillating between anger and passion, she was invested. She was credulous.

"I've been researching this shit forever. How'd you think I knew about Mercy Brown and where to find sources for your paper? This photo, this proof"—she paused and patted her bag—"is why I've been taking shots of almost everyone I meet and it's why I joined the club."

The Datsun's engine was now running, and with the heat geysering through the vents and me still in my stupid blazer and my top shirt button buttoned and tie fat-knotted and pressed against my Adam's apple I roasted in my own juices. Slumped and melted into my seat, I couldn't breathe, and purple splotches did their

you're-about-to-pass-out amoeba dance at the edges of my vision.
I clumsily pawed at the window handle.

Mercy said, "Keep the window up. I don't want anyone to hear us."

"I'm so hot I'm gonna die." I rolled down the glass, then stuck my
head out the window like a panting dog.

"You're not going to die now. Maybe later. You never know."

Mercy shifted into gear and crawled us away from the gravesite. I
got one more look at the grandson as he walked to his car. And
he got one more look at me. I wanted to warn him about what
might happen, to any of us, to all of us, but I didn't have the words.
I still don't.

"Do you want to know what you and I are doing tonight, my
sweaty friend?"

Ooh, cliffhanger!

I asked for the tenth time, "So what are we going to do between now
and later?"

Now: late afternoon, parked at Hospital Point and sitting on a
waist-high rock wall, overlooking the ocean, the ocean breeze in my
face while I methodically worked through a pack of Nerds candy.

Later: roughly between ten P.M. and midnight depending on
my curfew, we were going to return to the cemetery and observe the
grandmother's grave and watch for more blue orbs/blobs (I preferred
blob to orb) and other signs.

"Ugh. What do you want to do?" Mercy looked across the bay
to Salem and held out a gimme hand. I dotted her palm with grape-
flavored sugar rocks. I didn't give her any watermelon from the
other compartment of the box, even though she had bought me the
pack. I was a hopeless Nerds miser and a bad friend.

"It doesn't matter to me," I said.

"Nope. You make the choice for once. What do you want to do?"

We were both cranky and on edge without being able to explain
why. It was as though we were splitting a pizza of our bad moods.

"Okay. I want to go home and change my clothes," I said. "Then,

I don't know, maybe get food and go to the movies, see *Amityville* part whatever."

She hopped off the rock wall. "If you don't want to go tonight, that's fine, my feelings won't be hurt, you just have to tell me . . ." She was agitated, but for a change I didn't think she was agitated with me. She wanted to back out of the cemetery trip, yet couldn't admit it to me, or to herself.

Nah, I was agitated with you and your Nerds hoarding.

"No, I do," I said. "I just don't want to be wearing my TPC clothes anymore."

"TPC?"

"The Pallbearers Club."

Mercy leaned over the rock wall and made faux retching and puking sounds.

We didn't talk on the ride to my house. Mercy played the latest Ramones record *Brain Drain*, which, sorry to say, was one of their more forgettable (everyone's a critic) efforts, aside from the song "Pet Sematary." The lyrics were at first blush funny and a comic-book retelling of the Stephen King book and film, yet the chorus lament of not wanting to come back to relive one's life drips honest metaphysical dread.

Mercy pulled into the end of my driveway instead of idling in front of the house. I asked her if she wanted a drink or needed anything. She said she didn't. I told her she was welcome to come inside and wait, but also, I wouldn't be long. I darted out of the car and to the house without looking behind me to see if Mercy followed, or, as an equal possibility, to see if the Datsun pulled out of the driveway without me.

I opened the front door and shouted into the depths of my house, "I'm changing and going back out!" From the kitchen Mom responded with a confused sort of yodel and I leapt up the stairs two at a time to my second-floor bedroom. While shedding clothes, I kept an ear out for Mercy's car horn. I didn't have time for a shower, so I washed my face, quickly scanning the craggy terrain for impending Vesuvius whiteheads, and wiped my armpits with a washcloth. Back in my room I penciled into jean shorts but then I couldn't find my

Memoir as "Pet Sematary." Author buries old life but relives it anew in the pages. Or do you bring up the song solely because of our ill-fated boneyard boondoggle?

one plain black T-shirt that fit me okay. With each passing T-shirtless second, the Mercy-is-waiting bomb clock ticked in my head as loud as a bouncing basketball. There was in fact a basketball bouncing, outside, in the backyard. Dad was outside, too, and he said, "Hey, nice shot. You're a pro," and giggled his goof's laugh.

You as the monster in the maze of this book. Important detail. Verbing the noun might distract the reader.

Oh no. I threw on a green Boston Celtics 1986 champs T-shirt that was too small and <u>minotaured</u> through the house to the back door.

Mom sat on the stairs, smoking a cigarette. Mercy, her green coat still on despite the warm late afternoon, shot a jumper from fifteen feet. A jumper by name only as she didn't really jump, and instead more <u>shot-putted the ball to the hoop, but it went in.</u> Dad cackled like a madman.

I'm shocked you're not writing me as a Teen Wolf–like hoop star, vamping out to dunk on everyone. Tearing off your dad's head to use as a basketball.

Dad said, "There he is. Larry Bird." (I groaned inwardly, and outwardly too.) "Let's play a quick game. Come on, Patty, you too."

Mom and I hemmed and hawed, suggesting HORSE instead, as she didn't want to get sweaty, and that dinner was almost ready.

Mercy said, "Me and Mr. Barbara versus you two. One game to eleven. And we're gonna win." Dad gave her a high-five.

We played on that patch of lumpen, frost-heaved blacktop, where footing was dicey at best. Dad, instantly in coach mode, reminded us players to watch out for the tire ruts and other more random sink spots in the pavement. Also, you had to be careful driving to the hoop because the rim and backboard hung off an old dilapidated garage and the plywood-boarded-up doors bowed out at the bottom and nibbled at your ankles if you got too close. I was not athletic in the classical sense (or any of the senses) but I had a deadly outside shot thanks to countless hours spent shooting by myself. I scored our first five buckets in a blink with jumpers and quick two-dribble pull-ups over Dad. He and I were the same height, but my arms were longer so I could extend and shoot over him. He took it easy on me that afternoon, not bullying me down in the post like he normally would. When the double-teams started coming my way (highly illegal ones in which Dad or Mercy or both would grab my arm or shirt), I dished to Mom, who had starred for her high school team twenty years prior, and she didn't miss from ten feet in.

I'll admit that I was happy (shooting lights-out helped), until Mercy accepted a stay-for-dinner invite. Then it was back to doom. Doom, doom, doomy doom doom.

While Mercy was in the bathroom washing up, my parents barraged me with a lightning round of questions to field, deflect, and face-palm, most of which were variations on the are-you-taking-her-to-the-prom theme. Dinner was beefaroni; elbow pasta, ground beef, store-bought (usually Ragú) red sauce. A staple in the house because it was one of the few meals I would eat in large quantities. My mercurial eating habits were a main topic of discourse. Mom dutifully listed all the things I wouldn't eat, her sharpness of tone increasing with each enumeration as though finally freeing herself of a crushing burden. My mortification is presented below as a French existential-hell play:

LE MANGEUR DIFFICILE
(or, The Picky Eater)

MOM: He won't use ketchup—

MERCY: Ketchup, wow.

MOM: Mayo, mustard, relish—

MERCY: Yeah, the no-condiments thing. He says it's why he never gets a burger when we go to Micky D's. He always orders fries and chicken McNuggets.

MOM: What kid won't eat McDonald's burgers besides mine?

ART: Okay, Mom. Stop. I eat burgers. Just not those ones.

MOM: No pickles. Doesn't like the flavor of coffee. The only vegetable he eats is corn—

ART: Ma, I eat carrots.

MOM: Only if they're not cooked. He doesn't eat anything. It's why he's so skinny. He doesn't even like bread.

ART: I like bread fine. I just won't eat PB&Js anymore.
I overdosed on them as a kid.

MOM: When he was little, I had to trick him into eating fried
fish by calling it Fried French.

MERCY: Amazing!

ART: All right! That's enough!

MOM: Art has always been so sensitive. Can't let anything roll
off his back.

Art stabs himself in eye with a fork.

*The others briefly acknowledge his agony with polite
yet aloof applause before continuing their discussion.*

While Mom cruelly sat in food judgment (note: She was
quick to take offense and a world champion grudge holder, but I
admired her bluntness, righteousness, and unwavering loyalty. You
knew where you stood with Mom; there was no bullshitting her.
The older I get, the more I wish I were like her.), Dad was equally
embarrassing. He changed the focus of dinner conversation to
his favorite topic, him. Despite an utter void of climb-the-ladder
ambition in his work life (that does not equate to saying he wasn't
diligent, and his is an employment philosophy I've followed)
he never met a social spotlight he didn't like. He always had to be
the center of attention, the storyteller, made more cringy for me
because he <u>reveled in a glorified self-deprecation</u> that reflected a Sounds
manic narcissism, one working to reshape everything and everyone familiar . . .
into his ever-narrowing worldview. Aye, but there's the rub: he was
dynamic, charming, witty, and engaging, especially compared to
his awkward, *sensitive* son.

Mercy did not escape my parents' attention. She remained
evasive, though politely so, and did not divulge personal details

beyond her growing up in rural Rhode Island and her part-time enrollment at North Shore Community College. At the latter, Dad said, "An older woman, all right!" and while I died fifty-nine deaths, he gave me his signature hey-it's-just-a-joke, openmouthed, head-nodding, silent pantomime of laughter, like he was one of Jim Henson's Muppets. (And God help me, as an adult, I do the same damn Muppet act sometimes.)

After dinner Mercy asked to snap a picture of my parents, telling them it was for her photography class. Mom protested with her too-usual "I look horrible" until we told her she didn't (which was the truth), then she staged the photo so Mercy would get her good side. Dad puffed out his chest and hammed it up. Mercy took two photos and gave them one that Dad magneted to the fridge while the image was still lost in a gray chemical fog. I wondered if he'd eventually find two of Mercy's thumbprints over their heads. Dad offered to shoot a picture of Mercy and me, boasting of his photography skills, but Mercy lied, claiming she was out of film. I would take my first picture of Mercy later that night.

Dun-dun-dun!

It was dark out and long past time to leave. Staying any longer would've put us in danger of being forced to re-create the dinner-table scene from *Texas Chainsaw Massacre* with the horror of the card game Whist replacing the casual cannibalism. My parents followed the two of us to the front door, telling us to be careful, to have fun, to be good, emptying the quiver of parental cliché phrases that they hardly got to use. Dad even snuck in a tousle of my hair before I closed the door behind us, but we finally escaped, me clutching a sandwich baggie of homemade chocolate chip cookies.

Safe within the Datsun, Mercy said, "They're fun."

"Yeah, a barrel of fun. Why'd you take their picture?"

"You know why." Mercy lit a joint and wordlessly offered it to me. It was all I could do not to admonish her for sparking up in the driveway. My parents likely had all four eyes pressed against the front door's windows.

"Did you find any *proof* in their picture?" I was brazenly

dismissive for someone who'd interrogatedly admitted he didn't like PB&Js.

"Yup." Cloud of smoke in my face. "They're aliens." Shift into first gear.

Thus, inauspiciously, began the first of the strangest nights of my life. *I will read the next section from between my fingers. Please don't write what I think you're going to write.*

It was still a couple of hours before our planned cemetery siege. The Record Rack was closed for the night. By the time we rolled into the lot of the local chain record store Strawberries, we had fifteen minutes to browse. We didn't go to the mall. We didn't go to the movies. We drove around.

For dramatic purposes, I'd love to write that I remember Mercy as being sullen, maudlin, spewing forth ominous, portentous quips. But in the hour-plus we spent in the car before we hit the cemetery, we were us; silly, both generous and self-important, continuing to construct the shared grammar of our friendship while still futilely clutching to personal secrets and lies.

That said, she did smoke a shit-ton of weed, enough that I had a slight secondhand buzz. *Dude, you were a chimney that night.*

Central Cemetery's gates on Hale and Lothrop Streets were closed and locked, the wrought iron bowed and misshapen from its battles with the living. Before I could dust off my hands at the whole late-night grave-watching enterprise, Mercy said she knew a better spot for us to ghoul inside. Snaking her car along the fenced perimeter, she turned onto the less-traveled Butman Street, and she pulled over, parking on the grassy shoulder between two other locked cemetery gates. I questioned whether we should park so near where we were sneaking in and suggested we park closer to the library a few blocks away. Mercy said she was too high to walk.

We sat in the car and the engine knocked and ticked as it cooled. The row of homes huddled across the street watched us, their windows ghostly glimmering. Mercy took two more freediving inhales from a stubby joint that had once been as long as my pointer finger and she reiterated we were to watch for a blue light, a ball of fire, hovering above the grandmother's grave. We were also to note if the grave dirt was already sunken in. She said, "We can't use lack of vegetative growth on the grave as a sign yet. They just threw down some seed today, yeah? Or wait, I don't remember if they saved the sod to roll it back on. If there is grass and it's all yellow and dried up, then that's a sign too. A big one."

I wanted to ask: *A sign of what?* to further press the case for my unbelieving state, but I didn't. Treading in the quiet possibility of the moonless night, I wasn't in an unbelieving state, already creeped out at the thought of traipsing around the graveyard. Also, rule-follower Art was nauseously nervous about getting caught. My good name and all that. So punk.

She said, "One of the strongest signs are sprouts, like vines, growing without light way down, under and sometimes into the casket. We can't check that out now, obviously." She swallowed the roach and hiccupped. "Maybe next time." She ejected from the car without warning and slammed the door shut. Dogs barked their domesticated alarms and there I was, dome-lighted in the Datsun's interior like a horror movie's first victim.

I whispered, "What are you doing? We have to be quiet," and I crept out of the car.

Mercy didn't go far, a few crow-hops beyond the grille, and she pressed up against the chest-high wrought-iron fence. "This spot is as good as any." She didn't whisper. She projected. She orated as though we were in a theater in the round.

I shushed her. She shushed me back.

I joined her at the fence, my head surveying in every direction.

She said, "We just hop on over. Right here."

On the other side of the fence, inches beyond our feet were a clear patch of grassy turf and a sapling tree within an arm's length. To our left and right, thin, weathered headstones crowded. Where we stood was the only spot we could jump the fence without landing on crooked granite teeth. Maybe her parking here wasn't so random. Had she scouted out this place earlier? But when? Had she snuck into this graveyard before?

She said, again nearly shouting, "You first, Spider-Man." Across the street, dogs tattled on us again. This was a horrible, terrible, no-good idea.

"Why are you being so loud? You're gonna get us caught."

"Relax, no one around here cares." She acted like Quint (she did have the matching green jacket) in the movie *Jaws*, who by the end of the film had self-sabotaged his way to getting him and his boat eaten by Bruce the shark. "If you need help getting over, I can give you ten fingers."

Farewell and adieu.

"I don't need help," said by no one who ever meant it.

The skinny, vertical iron rod posts were four inches apart and tapered to sharp points at their tips. One horizontal bar flossed across the posts about half a foot from the top. The footholds weren't great, but the fence was short enough I figured I'd able to jump and anchor my left sneaker on the horizontal bar, then push, lift, and swing my right leg over along with the rest of my body, like a not-so-high jumper, while grabbing a tree branch for balance and leverage.

I wrapped my hands around the cold metal rods and yo-yoed up and down on my toes. I was less worried about the climb than I was about being by myself on the other side of the graveyard fence.

"Limbering up?"

I took off my jean jacket and tossed it to Mercy. The buttons and pins clicked chitinously.

My planned choreography started off, well, on the wrong foot. It was a longer stretch to reach a sneaker toe onto the horizontal bar than I anticipated. I bounced back off the fence once, saying, "Testing it out," before Mercy could offer a boost again. There was no way I would let her feel how light I was. On the second try, I went for speed and momentum to raise me up and over. Left foot on the horizontal bar, I jumped and pulled and got my right foot on top of the pointed rods, but I was losing this game of *Twister*, my body too tightly compact and with no center of gravity, I teetered. I didn't think I could jump safely to the ground now. It wasn't so much the height as I feared my left foot/ankle would get caught or clip the top and spill me over headfirst. I decided to push off and up with both feet and make a mad lunge for a tree branch to help swing me over. I had a fistful of branch and thought I'd cleared the fence, but my left foot did clip the fence. I braced for full-on impalement and/or crashing onto my head. Then my legs somehow elevated. It had to be momentum from the fall or a quirk of panicked memory, but I swear I felt them, well, float. They didn't go weightless, not exactly. It was more my legs lifted, or were lifted, up and away, freed from the fence's top. The night seesawed and my outstretched fingers tickled grass instead of tree leaves, but I didn't crash to the ground. I hung upside down, held aloft by my snagged, and now ripped, jean shorts.

Mercy said, "Another, more obvious sign of a vampire. Hanging there like a bat." My view of her feet and legs were prison-barred by the fence.

Cue the old man in an unbuttoned and untucked flannel (still a few years away from those shirts being popularized as the grunge-rock uniform) from the neighborhood with a flashlight. "Hey, what are you kids doing out here?"

Mercy said, "Zoinks."

The old man added that if we tried anything funny, he'd send his wife the flashlight signal for her to call the cops. Mercy assured the man I was done trying for funny.

While acknowledging someone who was more confident in themselves might've reveled in the absurd late-night act of dangling by one's shorts from a cemetery fence, I will not dwell on the multiverse of humiliations here, including but not limited to: Mercy and the old man origami-ing my legs, manipulating my shorts, wondering aloud if they needed to cut them off; Mercy joking about the jaws of life; the denim gashing open from left mid-thigh to crotch; me spilling floppily onto the ground like a dead octopus; my torn shorts now a flasher's trench coat showing off tighty whiteys and a burning-red scrape on my inner thigh; my hands covering my shame while having to convince them that I didn't need to wait for the old man to return with a stepladder and wishing for a grave to open beneath me or for one of Mercy's vampires to instantly drain me into a blissfully unconscious husk; the reclimb with shaking legs; the two of them instructing and encouraging me like parents cajoling a cautious toddler, their arms outstretched to grab and catch me, their high-fives once my feet landed on their side of the fence, and their shared, commiserative "Didn't think we'd get him over."

I took my jacket back from Mercy, tied it around my waist, skulked back to the car, and hermit-crabbed into the passenger seat. Mercy kept on talking and laughing with the guy for a few more minutes. Tired of waiting, I beeped the horn at them. They jumped, but also broke up into gales of laughter, holding each other up like two drunks at the end of an epic bender. He finally left, but not before knocking on the Datsun hood until I looked at him and his thumbs-up.

Mercy ambled over to the passenger side. I expected her to break me down and build me back up, to come at me with (deserved) jokes and then a pep talk about not giving up or giving in and the night was far from over and we would still do what we'd came here to do. My *nope* to that would be resolute. I was resolved. I wasn't going to budge. I was a barnacle. I was a rock. I was an island. I was a goddamned Simon & Garfunkel song or whatever moveless thing I needed to be because I was not going into the cemetery.

To my surprise, Mercy dangled her keys through my open window and said, "I'm way too stoned to take you home right now. You drive."

With my hands on the wheel at two and ten and my jacket mossed over my lap, I drove. Proud to say I didn't stall once despite my lack of experience driving a stick. From the passenger seat, Mercy offered no commentary on my ill-fated fence jump, not that I wanted to talk about it. Though who knows, maybe I could've laughed it off, maybe there's another dimension where we looked at each other and cracked up and then we drove off into the night in search of definitively meaningless adventures. I couldn't tell if she shrugged off the pratfall for my benefit, knowing how hard I was on myself, or if my not-quite-midnight dangle so lessened her opinion of me she couldn't even proffer faux hey-no-big-deals.

However, Mercy was far from quiet; she soliloquized. I don't think it mattered to her if I was listening or taking her seriously. She was working something out for herself and talked in circles that broke apart, the arcs shrapneling into Euclidean space, and through it all, an underlying desperation within the uncertainty. The gist/summary of her spieling: What bothered her the most about the New England vampire was that there was no description or supposition within folklore as to how someone like the woman we buried or Mercy Brown or anyone else whose body was harvested from the stony, unforgiving soil of this region, became a vampire. Within the margins of history there was plenty in the record regarding grief-laden, distraught exhumation and burnt-heart cures. But no mention anywhere of how or why any of them became vampires. It was as though people were vampires by effect, not by cause. At one point, Mercy pounded the dashboard like Khrushchev (sans shoe): "I want a reason. I want an origin. I want how someone becomes one, even if it's stupid and lame and supernatural." Did the transformation occur after death? Did they become one while living? She thought the latter was more likely, that maybe there was a strain of tuberculosis that acted like the regular one, but then didn't fully activate until the person's organs started failing and shutting down, sending them into a deathlike state, but not fully dead. (Here, I quoted/referenced the film [I had yet to read the Goldman book] *The Princess Bride*, "They're mostly dead?") But if vampirism was a virus, it wasn't all that virulent. It didn't spread or behave like a typical virus, as not everyone in the family who succumbed to consumption and had been significantly exposed to the vampire became one as far as she could tell. Which, she acknowledged, was the long way of saying the vampire's victims weren't necessarily transforming into new vampires; they were just dying. Even though I didn't say anything, Mercy said, "I know you're thinking, 'Doesn't it have to be supernatural?' How else would the vampire be able to suck the life out of a loved one while lying in their grave? Just because we don't understand the process doesn't mean it's supernatural. But fine, let's go down that vampire rabbit hole." She didn't take us there directly, though, not without a brief detour about how God wasn't an individual but was the universe itself, and its language was the laws of nature and we would be forever striving to learn its parts of speech. With all that as a caveat, she said a vampire as supernatural creature or phenomenon implied the existence of pure evil (I wasn't sure why that had to be the case, but I wasn't going to argue it), particularly if we were to view this within the puritanical New England folklore setting. She saw three supernatural possibilities (keeping in mind there was no record of vampires simply making more vampires), each of which she rejected. The first, and silliest, was one became a vampire because they communed with the devil, did the moonwalk together in the night woods, drank the devil's milkshake, etc. Dismissed out of hand because if it were that easy to extend your life and become a vampire, everyone would do it. (Maybe I was high too because that made total sense to me then. But who would choose to suck life from the grave?) Option two: the vampire must've committed some unpardonable sin, one that tainted and marked their soul. For believers of any type of religion or spiritualism this option works better than the first because of the more universal notion of karmic balance or godly meted justice, and it was more difficult to dismiss as what could any one of us possibly know about what truly dwelled inside another's heart, but by all accounts, the people accused of being New England vampires were hardworking farmers, cherished and charitable loved ones, all-around upstanding members of their communities. They didn't deserve to have that happen to them. (Does anyone?) Third, and *almost* the most horrific option, was a decidedly Calvinist vampire, someone who hadn't done anything terrible in life beyond being born and being predestined to be a life-sucking monster. Vampire as Job: the infinitely cruel God fucking with people for the sake of fucking with them. I interrupted and asked what the most horrific option was. She said, "I already told you. It's more

[margin note:] You make me sound like a bizarro Jehovah's Witness. Cut me some slack. I was high as a kite.

[margin note:] I can't believe I let you drive.

[margin note:] Hmm.

horrifying that there is no reason, even if the reason was malicious divine whimsy. Doomed to grieve and suffer and propagate more of the same, the vampire is effect without cause. More unknowable than what existed before the Big Bang." I pointed out that physicists might one day figure that out. She said, "Yeah, but they might not, and that's exactly my point. There must be a why; the why must exist. It's there, but we may never learn it. I don't get it. I hate it. It's not fair and I'm tired. Tired of not knowing."

"Wow, you're really high."

"I'm high on you, Art." She pulled another joint from an endless jacket pocket, lit it, clicked on the cassette player, and raged along with Black Flag's "What I See." Six and a half minutes (or three songs) later, I pulled onto the sidewalk in front of my place and shut off the car. Mercy beat out the drum intro of "Gimme Gimme Gimme" on her lap and a cappellaed the first verse. Since she was now, presumably, higher than a weather balloon, I asked if she wanted to come inside, have a glass of water or soda before she went home. She nodded.

The light perched above my front door was on, so too most of the downstairs lights, judging by the voyeuristic glow from the bay windows. I had no idea if either or both of my parents were waiting up for me. I assumed they were but hoped they weren't because they would insist on talking to us and I'd have to it's-not-what-it-looks-like explain the tied jacket and torn shorts, which would result in my excruciating death by embarrassment at the hand of blunt-force innuendo jokes from Dad. Also, Mercy and I clouding into the house reeking like weed, her eyes as red as a demon's, would be an issue.

"How about you stay here, and I'll bring out drinks. It's a nice night to not be interrogated by my parents."

"Can I crash at your place?" Mercy looked out her window as she asked. Her non-look I remember vividly, as it was so out of character. She normally tractor-beamed me into eye contact whenever one of us spoke. It was as though by swapping seats in the Datsun, we swapped roles. She said, "Couch or floor is fine. All I need is a pillow and a blanket."

"Yeah, sure. Are you okay?"

Her head pointed out the opened window, gazing perhaps at the fluttering pink petals of the crabapple blooms or at a winking star the size of a rice grain, she said, "I'm fine, just tired, fuzzy. My place is a bit of a drive from here. Something I probably should avoid in my current state."

My head was clouded, too, but anxiety burned through the mist as we marched up the front steps. I opened the door wide and into the brightly lit first floor. I braced for the initial swarm of *Hi, honey* and *Did you have a good time?*, but by some minor miracle, Mom and Dad were upstairs and in bed. (Unbeknownst to me at the time, and I found this out almost twenty-five years after this night, my parents had their own party when we were out. The two of them, dutiful ex–flower children of the '60s, smoked their own secret stash of weed, drank wine, fooled around [ew], and fell asleep.)

We waded through the dining room and to the kitchen for a glass of water. After turning down my offer of finding a horror movie on cable, Mercy said she probably should turn in. I led her into the TV room, which had a closet-sized half-bathroom, and offered the pullout couch. She collapsed onto it without waiting for the bed transformation, which was probably just as well; the mattress barely papered the jabby springs and metal bars. I gathered her a pillow and a thin blue blanket that might've been older than I was. Once she was settled, I closed the glass French doors and went upstairs. I left a note on the floor outside my parents' bedroom. The note: "Mercy isn't feeling well and is sleeping on the couch. Dad, if you get up early don't wake her and don't bug her. Maybe get us donuts."

I washed my thigh scratch with a facecloth, brushed my teeth, and Gollumed to my room, leaving the upstairs hallway light on and my bedroom door open to keep an ear out for Mercy. The hall light wouldn't help my hearing, of course, but I was still casually (let's call it) afraid of the dark, or afraid of what could be hidden, what couldn't be seen, and what might be seen. The hallway light was a nightly battle waged with my parents and it remained on until one of them invariably woke to shut it off. My room was a messy cave off the second-floor landing, across from a waist-high banister and mouth of the staircase. After initially trying to sleep with the stairs in view, I flipped over, the blanket pulled up to the cliff of my eyes. The blanket was the flimsiest form of sleep protection. I've always dreaded the act of going to sleep, not for fear I wouldn't wake but instead that I *would* wake and be woefully, perilously, self-loathingly, odiously, heuristically, irrevocably unprepared for the new and banal terrors that awaited. I fell asleep facing a wall.

I awoke centuries later in the blankness of total void. I could not move, and I did not want to move. This was not a dream. There was nothing else and I was nothing else but my aged, coagulated thoughts, pestle-and-mortared by time into a thinning, gritted incoherence and inchoate loss, and I wanted the nothingness, wanted to be snuffed out not only from now but from having ever been, wanted to be freed from the tyranny of regret, pain, fear, memory, and hope. Until. Until the gears of my stubborn body reflexively turned and sparking arcs of back pain bubbled up through the foetid bog of my psyche. As I returned to myself, there was constricting pressure on my chest from a mass pressing me into the mattress. My lungs flattened and clamped shut. I shook my head slowly, which set off a beehive headache, and the heaviness on my chest became heavier, and I thought my worst nightmare had come true; a nuclear bomb had reduced my house to rubble, and I was trapped under the collapsed ceiling and my shorting-out head Giger-counted the encroaching radiation poisoning. Aided by a fear-adrenaline rush, I thrashed in bed and the weight lifted away. I gasped and sat up and, in the nano-instant before opening my eyes, there was a splooshing thud on my floor, followed by a ratlike patter descending the stairs to the first floor. I kicked the covers off and swung my legs out of bed, feet to the floor, and even in my newly awake haze and heart-pounding, hyperventilating fear and misery, I worried about my feet's exposure to what might be reaching for them from under the bed. The hallway light was off, so I couldn't see anything in the hallway or on the stairs.

This is a little much.

It was 1:19 A.M. I remember the time because the digital clock on the nightstand was all angry red numbers, skyscraper tall and brutalist. Once I got my breathing under control, I ventured into the hallway and turned on the light. I stood at the banister and listened to the noiseless downstairs. My headache remained a low hum and my mouth was dry and tasted acidic, as though I'd thrown up a little in my mouth. Most alarmingly, a sharp pain rooted between my shoulder blades and ivied into my neck. Rolling either shoulder or my neck was eye-watering agony, so too any attempt at straightening my posture. My only relief came from curling forward and holding an insectlike pose. Had I slept on it wrong or pulled a muscle in the throes of my nightmare? I'd already decided what I'd experienced was a nightmare as every one of us does and must do in the middle of the night. Otherwise, how could we go on in the face of awe and terror?

I crept downstairs. The kitchen light was on, though I didn't remember if I'd left it on. After a half glass of water and two Tylenol, I stretched and flexed my shoulders, but the pain intensified, and I worried I'd somehow injured myself more seriously. After a brief interior dialogue in which I told myself there wasn't any reason for me to look in on Mercy, I scuttled the short walk to the TV room anyway. One of the French doors was pressed permanently shut by the television cabinet, but the other was open. I hovered in the doorway, a dead-of-night Quasimodo with no bell to ring. Silver moonlight smoked through the orderly row of windows of the back wall above the couch on which Mercy splayed. Her green blanket was rolled, twisted, and tentacled around and between her limbs and bunched on her torso. I was struck by how there wasn't enough room on the narrow couch for her to have tossed and turned and sleep-rolled herself into such a cat's cradle. Plus, the blue blanket I'd given her had been discarded and pooled on the floor. Wait, where did the green one come from?

Have you ever looked at someone or something in weak light, if there was such a thing, or different light, though the word "different" didn't cover it by a long shot, perhaps ineffable was closer, or more utilitarianly as light you were not used to, or light that existed to display its own reality and you might assume the unrepeatable, sui generis wavelengths were quantum imps playing tricks on you, the unsuspecting, the unwilling, the unbelieving, and you knew all this but you still couldn't unsee what you saw?

From my vantage within the wide doorframe boundary, my confusion at the number of blankets momentarily forgotten, Mercy's face was not her face. My legs carried me into the room autonomically, acting as dilating pupils, bringing me physically closer to better focus the image. As I approached, I realized I was wrong; it was Mercy's face but withered. Her cheeks had sunken into concave pits, so too her eyes, the skin stretched tight but also wrinkled at the sharpened corners. The wrinkles were not because of age; she didn't necessarily look older, but instead was husked out, used up, dried out, corpsed. Too shocked to feel concern for her well-being (If *Is she sick?* and *What is wrong with her?* were questions I considered, they quickly sank to the bottom of my after-midnight mind), I tranced in dreamlike thrall, moving closer still, to within arm's reach, and my initial observation of her face not being her face was both right and wrong. Her face was also Kathleen Blanchet's face, the deceased woman I helped serve at the inaugural meeting of the Pallbearers Club. This was no mere hey-I-saw-someone-at-the-mall-who-looked-just-like-you doppelgänger resemblance. This was a reveal. This was revelation. Had I been able to blink my eyes and transport back to the first October morning in the funeral home, this was the face that would've greeted me. Mercy and Kathleen were the same person. (At the writing of this almost a quarter of century later, I am as sure of that equivalence as I was in the ruinous moment of discovery. Though in mornings after and the years between, as you will see, I allowed for skepticism, possibility, and rationalization. But not anymore.) *This is fucking RIDICULOUS.*

Mercy twitched her left arm over her head, landing it on the couch's armrest. At her movement imagine me as a cartoon cat

Thanks, bro.

I fixed the title page for you with angry cross-outs.

frightened out of eight of his nine lives. Mercy remained asleep or whatever state she was in. Coiled around her wrist and elbow, the blanket rippled as though caught in a breeze. There was no fucking breeze. The blanket pulsed like exposed musculature made of a glistening, convoluted network of connective and vascular tissues. And it flexed and it squeezed, fluidly readjusting its hold and position. Mercy gasped, releasing a quick, high-pressure tire leak of air, and I froze, a mantid fiend curled above her. I tried whispering her name but only pushed up dust. The bulk of the blanket remained bunched on her chest. Swirled within the mass of this impossible external heart (I don't know how else to better describe it), there was a human face. I can't state the following strongly enough. This was not a case of seeing something that wasn't there; not a magic-eye poster trick, not an optical-illusion face Freuded onto clouds or tree bark or wheat fields or rock piles or the leering shadow on your bedroom wall or your divinely inspired morning piece of browned toast. Perhaps what I saw was closer to the fake faces of skate fish and stingrays, where on their underbellies their aquatic mouths and black-dot nares created their uncannily emotionless smiley faces. I make no claims that the thing ensnaring Mercy's limbs and rooted on her chest was human, only that it exhibited a human face. Ageless and, somehow, clearly adult, its eyes had lids and its eyes were eyes (iris, pupil, sclera), and it had defined cheeks and brows. A nose shark-finned above a small, partially opened slit of a mouth. And it looked at me with an expression so matter-of-fact, so ho-hum in its indifference as to be the most malign, baleful look I'd ever received. Were this face to pop up in the middle of a nightmare, say, inside a hole in a wall of a neglected old house you'd never been to but in the dream it was your house, your home, you would be frightened beyond reason or measure, and the worst part would be knowing you would see it again in the next nightmare and in all the ones after that and then finally in the interior eternity before you closed your eyes for the final time.

The thing's flagella turned liquid and reshaped and re-formed as Mercy twitched, and that goddamned face blinked its eyes and its lips wriggled into shapes of soundless, impossible words. I gasped and covered my ears and I stumbled backward and my feet shoelaced together, crashing me to the floor ass first. From the lower vantage, the moonlight wasn't as bright or as silver and as a result (or unrelated, I don't know, I don't know anything) Mercy's face was hers again, and the thing on her chest was her green jacket she'd decided at some point to use as a blanket. She stirred at my landing on the floor but did not wake.

Despite the horror of it all, I sat blinking and turning my head, attempting to wrest the prior vision back into existence. I clambered onto my feet and like a shimmering heat mirage on an endless highway, Mercy transformed into Kathleen Blanchet's corpse and the jacket was not a jacket but an anti-heart, one that strained to inflate and relaxed into its deflate, and fucking hell the face's expression altered slightly (an arched brow, a narrowing of the eyelids) to communicate that I had its attention. Its lips writhed with a speed that was so unremittingly awful, involuntary whimpers, moans, and glottal chokes bubbled from my throat.

With the modest shortest-term goal of leaning against the wall, I reeled to my right, and as I did so I kicked Mercy's shoulder bag, clanking it off the baseboard heater. Simultaneous to my movement, the TV room darkened, though not entirely, as a wispy cloud must've tissue-papered in front of the moon. In this darker dark, Mercy was not Kathleen but looked like a younger version of herself, a teenager like me, and perhaps this was the singular lie of the light that evening, or maybe it was a distant truth I wasn't ready to confront. Either or any of the ways, I decided two things: I would wait for the cloud to pass, and I needed proof (that single inviolable, irrefutable, elusive syllable); Mercy's version of proof.

I bent and rooted through her bag and pulled out her camera. That she hadn't woken yet given my floor crater, heater clang, bag rifling, and various exclamations was, I grant you, improbable, narratively speaking. Though, given my back was killing me and my headache throbbed like a mini DJ was inside my gray matter thrumming the

WHAT THE FUCK ARE YOU TALKING ABOUT??????

not-so-soothing industrial stylings of Ministry, maybe her not yet waking was very much purposeful.

Regardless, I knew I would only get one shot, so I waited and watched with the camera held up to my face. Through the square viewfinder, the room brightened and dimmed as moonlight waves crashed and receded, but the horrific vision did not return and all the pieces I thought fit together no longer matched, but then I remembered the photo of the woman we buried and its hovering, green maybe-it-wasn't-a-thumbprint blob, and how maybe the idea was to take a picture when nothing obvious was there or happening, and of course, that was how the inexplicable worked, like it had rules to follow too. With no plan beyond applying pressure with my digit, I pressed the shutter button.

The flash went atomic white, detonating the whirring, porcine-like camera screech, and Mercy sat up like a stepped-on rake before I had even pulled the photo out of the camera. I said, "I'm sorry," I think, or I wanted to, but I was already backing away, and the room had gone pitch-dark, maybe because of the camera flash, maybe not, and Mercy was an amorphous shape sitting on the couch and I couldn't see her face, and while still backing away her jacket rolled off her. It didn't roll and formlessly parachute like a sweatshirt you shed when it's too hot. The shadowed form of the jacket stretched and taffied toward the floor. Instead of a wet thud on impact was the clacking of her punk-band pins, unless it was something else that was clacking, or chittering.

I turned and ran, slow out of the blocks, clipping the closed French door with my left shoulder. As I foaled through the living room toward the front of the house and the stairs, I didn't dare look behind me. I didn't have to, because Mercy joined the chase. I heard and felt her closing in with that evolutionary extra sense, a holdover from when the earliest of us were on the plains fleeing from all manner of beast. If this were simply a nightmare I would've slowed down, been stuck in the quicksand of the dream, but I ran faster and took the stairs two or three at a time. Mercy was right there, her fingertips stretching for the collar of my shirt, the hair on the back of my head curled away. I missed a step and stumbled as I hit the second-floor landing, but I used the momentum to pitch me forward into a head-first dive across the narrow hallway. I skidded on my belly and chest into my bedroom. Blinking away tears of pain, I crabbed around on hands and knees and flung my bedroom door shut and turned the lock in the center of the doorknob, the kind you had to pinch between your fingers and turn right, like that delicate mechanism would keep any monsters out of my room. Instead of sitting with my back against the door, I stood and groped along the wall for the overhead light switch. I hesitated when I found it, afraid to see what was waiting in there with me, or for me, that my own bedroom would be the trap all along like I always feared it would be.

I squinted and blinked in the light, and the menagerie of menacing creatures were the slumping clothes piles and kicked-off bedcovers. The locked doorknob rattled as it reluctantly refused to turn. The door creaked, too, as though Mercy pressed herself against it. She whispered my name and told me to open the door, and her whispers ricocheted and echoed in my Humpty Dumpty head.

I said, "Leave me alone," and retreated to my bed. There was nowhere else to go.

Her whispering stopped. The door creaked, though this time it was more like a sigh after a heavy load had been lifted. Mercy tried the knob one more time and mumbled, "Fuck me." (I hate to pull you out of the moment here, but her saying "Fuck me," and saying it like anyone of us would say to themselves when something went awry, is a small, humorous [at first blush] detail that makes everything else that happened before it seem more true, because it is true. If I were making this all up, I'd have her say something more obviously threatening or frightening. Don't let my self-awareness here truth-dissuade you. This isn't an I-know-that-you-know-that-I-know kind of thing. Could I have misheard her? Maybe. But that possibly is as remote as Gilligan's Island. And the thing of it is, her forlorn and very human declared exasperation makes everything that happened and will happen more frightening and sadder.)

Mercy slid a square slip of paper under the door and flippered it side to side. And *fuck me*, it was a Polaroid photo. I futilely patted the bed mattress and scanned the floor for the picture I took and had had in my hand at some point during my maddest of dashes while knowing, of course, that the pic (my *proof*) was currently tonguing under the door. As much as I wanted to see it, I wasn't going to leave my bed; the floor was lava.

I said, "Leave me alone."

Mercy retracted the photo from under the door and clomped down the stairs. Was she going back to the couch? Hiding somewhere downstairs? Was my locked door enough to protect me if I ever fell asleep? What about my parents? Did I need to do something to save them? I wanted to cry because I didn't know what to do. After a few breathless minutes of silence, my back pain, somewhat forgotten in the excitement and terror, insisted I pay attention to it.

Sundial slow, I eased out of bed and slothed to my bedroom closet. Inside there weren't any monsters or Narnias, just my back brace, the personless shell I'd filled with so many of my worst hours. Dusty from its banishing, I dragged the brace out of the closet and wriggled into its unforgiving mold. Maybe it would make my back feel better and the hard-plastic chest plate would protect me if something or Mercy herself were to sit on my chest. And maybe this sounds totally fucked up, a part of me felt like I'd failed this night somehow, that I must've done something wrong for everything to have happened the way it did, so I deserved to wear the brace another night.

As I struggled to keep from sobbing too loudly and as I strapped myself into the brace, I might've heard the front door quietly open and shut. I left the light on, and my bedroom door stayed locked. I was unable to stack my pillows right so that the brace's metal halo wouldn't bite into my neck, and I might've heard the Datsun engine sputtering and coughing and drifting away.

I said, again, "Leave me alone," though I don't think I meant it.

I had to walk away after reading this chapter. I walked for hours. Do I have to enumerate the ways in which this has gone plummeting off the rails?

Okay. You're clearly writing a novel, not a memoir. *Deep breath* In that spirit, I've decided to be flattered a character based on me gets a starring role. BUT—plus all the buts in the world—let's go through this chapter's unveracity somewhat briefly, just to be on the record.

The photo: After the funeral I essentially admitted to you, without coming right out and saying it, I had smooshed my thumb on the photo of the dead woman while it developed. Pretending the blobbed film represented the woman's ghoulish leanings was a fun, silly game, one you were totally in on. At least, I'd thought so. And fucking hell it was a blue blob on the photo, not green. Not even close to green. People have reported seeing blue lights or orbs over Mercy's and others' graves. Are you not going to mention the slew of other New England vamps who were dug up in the late 1700s and 1800s? And it's always blue blobs. Not green ones. Though now with the entirety of this chapter ringing in my head, I'm guessing you described the thumb blob as green so my green jacket could transform into . . . what . . . some sort of parasitic monster thingy that's part of me? At some point within the NOVEL you'll have to explain what that was, dude, even if your Arty explanation is, "I confess I smoked weed that night and it might've been laced with angel dust or something." And you DID smoke that night, two different times. The first time after dinner with your parents, which I'm guessing was your first time ever. You didn't tell me that. But, come on, you didn't have to. I'm willing to give you the benefit of the doubt and assume you being high was why you stumbled over the top of the cemetery fence. I still don't get how you, Mr. Floaty Legs, managed to get your shorts caught without impaling yourself on the sharp metal pikes. Lucky fella. Yeah, that batch of weed was way strong, and more than probably had some extra chemical enhancements. My bad?

The second time you smoked was after the graveyard while we idled in your driveway. You were so freaked out about having to talk your parents about my staying over I thought another hit might take your edge off. In hindsight, that didn't work out so great. You were a freaking puddle, and you drank half a liter of Coke straight from the bottle, crushed a large bag of potato chips, and then I had to coax you out of spending the night curled up on the floor under the kitchen table. You were using the empty chip bag as a pillow. Crinkly. Then an hour or so later, I woke up with you in my room, leaning against the wall, holding my camera, and snapping a pervy picture of me while I slept on the couch. Then you ran away with it. I mean, what was that all about? You can't blame all of it on being stoned out of your gourd. So, yeah, shooting that picture was not cool, and it was why I didn't call you or seek you out until after your back surgery.

The rest of this chapter? Jesus, man. The idea that you were going to sell/publish this as a memoir is batshit insane.

In a memoir the writer finds meaning in the meaningless, purpose within the inexplicable unpredictable machinations of the universe. In addition, within the course of the memoir bad things happen without warning, without provocation, without conforming to narrative structure or arc. To wit, I enjoyed the bit with your parents and the French play is funny and clever, and was very memoiry. But, duuuuude, suspension of disbelief as it pertains to the supernatural isn't something a memoir is built for, you know?

As a novel, this book can work. Maybe. But fiction isn't real life and generally must in some way fulfill expectations of rising action and arc and cause and effect and reason and blah, blah, blah. Fiction can't be too real either, can't mirror reality's cruel capriciousness too closely, otherwise most readers won't buy in.

So right now, you're stuck with one foot in each form, there, Arty. You should pick and stick with the novel. I will say this is surprisingly well written for someone who didn't study writing formally. I don't mean that as a shot, I just didn't know you had this in you. Whatever this ends up being, at least it won't have had the life sucked out of it—see what I did there?—by workshops and writing teachers.

A few more observations/questions for you before I take another long walk. And yeah, a smoke, okay?

What is my character's motivation for shooting the Polaroid photos? It's there in the text, but I think it's somewhat hidden, so you likely haven't spelled it out enough for some readers, especially the I-just-want-to-know-what-happens reader. I'm not judging. Much. Anyway, let's talk this out. So, I tell you on the day we met I was looking for proof, which sort of maybe played out in the most recent chapter, though the readers don't know if that woman with the blue blob photo was some kind of supernatural entity that, for the sake of clarity, fine, we'll call a vampire. Ergo, my motivation for taking all the photos, particularly if I'm the 1890s Mercy Brown—though that doesn't yet make sense, as Mercy's heart was removed and burnt, and hence, cured, yeah? Maybe I'm a different person, one to be revealed later in the NOVEL?—was that I was hunting to find someone else who was a vampire like me. Right? It fits the loneliness/loner/didn't-fit-in theme of the book. You didn't fit in, and neither did I, and we both desperately wanted to. Readers are suckers for that kind of story because deep down inside none of us believe we belong. We fear we are imposters doomed to a life of imposting. Sorry, I couldn't resist aping your writing style.

Let's go back to the first funeral, where I was "Kathleen Blanchet," dead by all appearances. Hopefully, somehow, my mouth and eyes weren't sewn up and my body not full of formaldehyde and the rest of the funerary chemicals as that would've made it, um, difficult for me to return from the grave, so, yeah, you probably don't want to mention any of that in the NOVEL. So, I was there, in the coffin, because . . . I'd given up on my life-plus-extra-life? I was ready, if not for the big sleep, then a little one? THEN I found you, or you found me. As you carried my casket was when you first described yourself as growing weak and back-painy and fuzzy headed, and now we are to presume your assorted physical sufferings were because I had a sip of your soul/life/whatever. Also, I recognized in you a kindred spirit, someone equally alone, so I decided to postpone my dirt nap, return to the land of the living, punk out, and get a fuller feed on you, and . . . I don't know yet and will have to read more of this NOVEL, I suppose.

I get it. You can't answer everything at the end of the first-ish act. But! What I and your more astute readers already know/figured out: while you and I hung out, I was on a Holy-grail-like hunt for photographic proof of more vampires. Beyond long-ago friends and family being dead and beyond being literally starved for companionship, I was afraid of being the only vampire in the world (or New England?), afraid that I was existentially alone. Which explains my rant about wanting to know the why and how of vampires.

But what about you, Art? That's the question a reader is going to be asking throughout the book. How reliable a character are you in all this? If the reader pays close attention, they'll find you've coded that YOU are the real monster here. Yeah, there are the Renfield and eating-roaches references, which are cute winks and nods, but, man, that bit about you being a minotaur wasn't some off-the-cuff, throwaway bit of descriptor, even if one were to argue the author didn't consciously intend a monstrous confession. That your subconscious ratted you out is even more damning/powerful. And the proof is this line: "I froze, a mantid fiend curled above her." That's dropped amid dense pages about how scared you were and how scary I was supposed to be. But in that line, you admitted you were the monster. YOU were the gaunt, pale, long-fingered, Count Orlock from Murnau's silent Nosferatu in that moment and maybe in the rest of the moments to come after.

Put that in your weed pipe and smoke it.

59 TIMES THE PAIN

(May–June 1989)

A chapter in which I keep my own blood, <u>a heart is found</u> <u>to be broken,</u> then surgery and a home visit.

You don't have to beat us over the head with the heart riffs.

The morning after the sleepover, with my back brace re-hidden in the closet and my torn jean shorts Jimmy Hoffa-ed at the bottom of a garbage barrel in the garage, I endured jokes, winks, and pats on the back from Dad. Mom was more direct during our cornucopic donut brunch, saying she hoped I was smart enough to use protection and you couldn't be too careful these days. She otherwise didn't perseverate on the prior evening, didn't ask where Mercy and I went or what we did. I think she sensed I was upset, that something was off. I didn't share details, as much as I might've wanted to. I told them nothing had happened as I set about the task of making myself believe that nothing had happened. It was easy to do in the light of morning: all that <u>secondhand smoke I'd inhaled</u> *Eye roll* had to have affected me, plus that terrible I-can't-breathe nightmare further messed with my head, and I wasn't feeling well, and the weirdness in the TV room including seeing a face (face? what face?) in a jacket and seeing Mercy dead and desiccated was all a trick of the light.

[If you, reader, pause here and are honest with yourself, you know how easy it is to cobble together the truth you want, particularly when you are young, confused, and lonely.]

I did not allow myself to dwell on that night and its implications, ramifications, repercussions, or insinuations, but the part I was unable to dismiss or compartmentalize was Mercy chasing after me for the photo I shot of her and the "Fuck me" she said outside my bedroom door. Those two words ended the weekly ritual of my calling to provide an update on the upcoming Pallbearers Club weekend itinerary. Mercy did not call me either.

I phoned Mr. Stephens and told him that with prom (not that I was going to prom; I did ask Cayla but knowing she already had a date, so it wasn't a real ask, not an ask that risked hope for a yes) and graduation, all the weekends were filling up with high school senior shenanigans and bacchanalia, sure to result in friendships and memories to last a lifetime, and I'd scheduled my back surgery six days after graduation, all of which meant that the Pallbearers Club was going on an extended hiatus. I couldn't bring myself to say the club was no more. Mr. Stephens thanked me for my volunteer service and proffered that if I needed a summer job or if the college thing didn't work out, he'd be happy to have me in his employ. He flourished with "We'll always save a space for you here at the funeral home," which was sweet, but also a little creepy.

On the late afternoon of Beverly High School's senior prom that I didn't attend (did I tell you that already, that I didn't go to the prom? So many years later it seems ridiculous to bring up, but also, <u>what about prom, Art?</u>), I donated a pint of blood, my sixth pint in twelve weeks. Well, I wasn't really donating. More like I put my blood in storage because I was going to reuse it later. Dr. Seward wanted me to have my own blood for transfusion instead of someone else's.

The final bit of pre-surgery preparation was the echocardiogram Dr. Seward ordered because of the possible Marfan syndrome diagnosis. That procedure wasn't as needly as the blood donation. I lay on an exam table membraned with crinkly white paper. The tech slathered a cold, clear gel on the sonic wand, the knobbed

Will anyone get a <u>Pretty in Pink</u> reference?

head of which she firmly pressed against my bare chest, paying no mind to avoid my galaxy of acne, and I swear at times she jammed the wand underneath my sternum. A small black-and-white screen broadcasted Doppler ultrasound images of my beating heart. The tech pointed out ventricles, arteries, and the aorta. Then, as instructed, I rolled onto my left side, facing away from the screen, my face inches from a wall. What would show on the monitor now that I couldn't see it? Maybe there was a face hidden within the digital swirls that only I might recognize. The tech said we were going to listen to my heart and turned the volume to eleven. The sound wasn't a thump-thump of a stethoscope or an ear to someone's chest. It was organic, wet, and grainy, undulous. More like a glup-glup. My heart was a flopping fish, which seemed kind of appropriate. We kept listening as the tech stabbed the wand around, back-alleying it between my ribs, until she said, "Huh." My swimmy heart glup-gluped along and I asked if there was something wrong. She said, "No?" with a requisite and confidence-draining pause, and then, "But I did find a little something." With the caveat that she was not a cardiologist and could not officially offer diagnosis, she said it appeared I had a slight heart murmur caused by mitral valve prolapse. The aforenamed valves weren't closing properly, so when the heart pumped, the valves, or flaps, collapsed into the left atrium, then a small amount of blood that was supposed to be pumped away, leaked back into the ventricle. It was a common condition, and for most sufferers their health wasn't appreciably affected, but the heart would need to be monitored over time for other complications. She said, "I'll slow down the audio and you can hear a little swish of regurgitated blood." I didn't want to hear the regurgitated swish.

On the follow up appointment with Dr. Seward, he said mitral valve prolapse was a symptom typical in patients with connective tissue disorders, including Marfan syndrome. While my heart murmur was mild, he recommended I undergo an echocardiogram annually to keep a sonic eye out for aortic enlargement, which could lead to fatal dissection or detachment when the heart was stressed. Surely, something to look forward to down the road.

Two weeks before my uncurled-spine day, I moped around the house with nothing to do, as I'd quit my job at the supermarket. My parents didn't hassle me about the time off. They had a better idea of what I was in for post-surgery than I did, but they didn't let on. When I wasn't listening to music or shooting hoops by myself in the backyard, I orbited the kitchen telephone, picking it up randomly, listening to the dial tone, then hanging up. The initial pickup-and-hang-ups were me struggling with the urge to call Mercy, but then it became this thing where I imagined I lifted the phone off the cradle at the precise moment Mercy called me, and all she'd hear on her end was a busy signal and she'd either get frustrated or maybe think that I'd moved on, found another friend, maybe even the register guy at the Record Rack and he and I were doing totally cool punk stuff, which I knew didn't make sense that she'd equate a busy tone with me not being on the phone and out doing totally cool punk stuff with someone else, but don't harsh my daydream mellow.

I was surprised you didn't call to apologize to me.

The first Sunday in June was graduation. It was blisteringly hot out and three hundred plus grads herded into the middle of the football field. The PA system sucked, so all the speeches were accompanied by Sonic Youth—esque feedback and distortion. I skittered across the stage to the most tepid of perfunctory applause, or *tepfunctory* applause: the passionless, percolatory clapping of damp, sweaty hands by a crowd pummeled numb and nearly drooling from pomp-and-circumstance boredom. After the tossing of mortarboards, kids who wouldn't deign speak to me in the hallways slapped my back or chucked my shoulder and wished me luck in college, telling me that I would do great, would be a big success. I didn't run into Cayla to wish her the best, but that walking troglodytic row of exclamation points, Ian, shouted, "Artie the one-man partyyyyyy!" across the width of the field, and that toolbag sociopath-without-the-charm Eddie Patrick, true to his inveterate dickishness, said, "Have fun at dead-people school," and as usual, the worst part, the one that made me hate myself almost as much as him, was his self-satisfied laugh at the punchline (me) to the joke that would never get old. I wish I could write that I said "Fuck you" through gritted teeth to everyone who deserved it and even those who might not have, but the best I can do is to express that sentiment in writing now.

Maybe the above paragraph is an ungenerous memory or reflects me being ungenerous in interpreting the memory for you. Or one more: I'm filling a yawning gap in memory with a narrative curated to what I know or believe to be true now.

Time continued to speed up on me (as it does), and five days later, I'd somehow arrived at the early evening before my back surgery. Dad was out picking up pizza, a last-meal kind of gesture, and Mom was in her bedroom packing. My parents planned to spend the next three days at a hotel near the hospital. I'd packed a bag earlier, but Mom went through and took most of the stuff out, somberly saying the hospital requested I not bring more than I needed and I wouldn't need more than one set of clothes to change into for when I was discharged. Not getting it, I mumbled something about having to wear the same stupid T-shirt for my entire weeklong stay. Mom patted my shoulder, lightly, and said that I'd be in hospital garb the whole time. That was an "Oh" moment. After months of simultaneously obsessing on the abstract concept of surgery and choosing not to think about the surgery itself, my sagging, deflated knapsack was a sting of the soon-to-be-reality I was not in the least prepared for.

The phone rang, the kind of ring that made everything else stop, go quiet. I shouted upstairs, "Don't answer it, Mom!"

She shouted from her room, "Why? What if it's important?"

In an attempt to stall her from answering because there was no way she wouldn't, as it could be the doctor or someone at the hospital even though I knew it wasn't, I shouted back, "What kind of important?"

"What are you talking about?" The phone rang two more times, bringing us to three rings.

I yelled, "It's not important," which negated my previously shouted question. I stood next to the kitchen wall phone, my hand on the receiver, and it rang a fourth time. Would I answer it and listen only, or say hello, or pick up and hang up in one motion?

The phone stopped ringing. My hand buzzed with aftershocks, anticipating another vibrating ring that didn't happen. Mom came downstairs, frantic, saying, "Dammit, Art. We missed it. Shit. Should I call the hospital just in case?" Then she asked again, "What if it was important?"

I shrugged. I sure as hell didn't know. And Mercy didn't call back.

It wasn't me that called.
Okay, maybe it was.

We were up well before the sun the next morning. Dad asked that I not listen to my Walkman on the ride into Boston so we could talk. I complied, leaving the headset dangling on my neck, but I don't recall anyone talking much. Dad commented on how light the traffic was as we crossed the nightmarish Tobin Bridge's upper deck, more than one hundred and fifty feet above the Mystic River. Mom said we all should've stayed in the hotel last night instead of having to rush around this early, the last line in an argument to which I hadn't been privy. The rest of the ride into the city was candy apple gray.

Once we arrived at the hospital, a valet took my parents' car and hid it so I couldn't change my mind, be my own hero, attempt a madcap escape. Unlike the usual thirty-plus minutes of waiting rooms we endured with our prior hospital visits and appointments, I immediately checked in and a staff member braceleted my wrist with a plastic band imprinted with the data of my identity so while under sedation they wouldn't lose me. Minutes later, I was alone in a dressing room where I had to take everything off, including my underwear, and wrap myself in two gowns that were too short in length and too big in width. This was the moment pre-surgery in which I was the most scared, partly because everything of mine was stripped away and now I was alone, truly alone with myself in the moments before I was to be zippered open and changed.

Then I sat in the pre-op waiting area, but the wait wasn't long. Dr. Seward emerged from between swinging doors adjacent to a nurse's station. He was already gowned and capped, and it made him appear small. He promised my parents they would take good care of me. He asked me how I was feeling. I said, "Okay." He said, "I'll see you inside." In my head I repeated and tweaked the phrase like a mantra: *I'll see you inside. I'll see your insides.* And yes, I was afraid and nervous, but also, this was thrilling. I was going to emerge from the surgery physically transformed. Maybe not quite a butterfly poking through a chrysalis, but my kyphotic, cowering body would be radically altered/reconstructed by this time tomorrow. It might not be enough (it would never be enough), but I hoped it might be.

A nurse led me and my parents through those swinging doors into the brightest hallway, then into a large room partitioned by white curtains. I climbed onto a hospital bed; the top half raised so I could sit up. The nurse inserted a needle/port into my left hand, which hurt like hell, burning as it truffled through my skin. The IV saline solution rushed in cold. Mom squeezed my other hand as I hissed out air. She said, "You're doing great," wide-eyed with a *How did we get here?* look.

I wondered if anyone else besides family members would spare a thought for me on this day. The reality was, only one other person knew about the surgery. That night in my house with Mercy seemed so impossible and far away, and I wished I'd called her, and I also vowed to never call her again.

A team of nurses swarmed, unlocking the bed's wheels and attaching an oximeter to my finger along with various other contraptions tethered to beeping monitors. The anesthesiologist said, "Okay, Art. We're ready for you. You're going to do awesome."

For as often as the sentiment was expressed, what was I going to have to do? I assumed the act of spinal surgery was passive on my part.

She inserted a syringe of the knockout drug into a port on the IV bag. She said, "Your parents will be here with you until you go to sleep, okay? Once I press the plunger it'll happen fast. Ready?"

"How long until I'm unconscious?"

"You'll be out before you count to five."

"One."

Most of us like to think we're wired with a factory-installed inner clock. It doesn't keep the time of day necessarily; it more accurately measures time elapsed. We believe this despite a Kraken of evidence to the contrary. Our head clocks are often the Salvador Dalí melting kind. Which, ironically, is closer to the truth of time.

I mention the above in the context of my waking, or my first memory of waking, post-surgery with my metal Harrington rods bone-spackled into place. Thanks to morphine and whatever other drugs rowing merrily down my bloodstream, I couldn't open my eyes when I returned to myself. To be blunt and to the point: man, my back fucking hurt like nothing else I'd felt before. The pain dove deep, agony units measured in fathoms and Mariana trenches. Something must've gone wrong; a rod or two must've unmoored and now skewered and <u>Hellraisered</u> my rent flesh. Holy shit, was my entire week in the hospital going to be like this? No one properly warned me. Had I known, I would've stuck it out with my question-mark existence.

Verbing a Clive Barker movie. You are a monster.

Voices of nurses and doctors ricocheted around my amorphous room, though I knew I was the amorphous one and not the room, and then the owners of the voices moved me, changed my bed position, turned me onto a side, yet with my eyes still closed, I couldn't tell which side I was on or facing, but there was a fire, a conflagration splitting my skin and muscles apart. I whimpered and, in my head, I asked them not to move me or touch me, and they were sorry, but I had to turn and rotate and be split apart at my new seams again and again. Eventually I'd pass out, but when I would wake again, the pain was there, tapping an impatient foot. The sole comfort was passing time. And based on the number of times I thought I'd been asleep and then awake, I tabulated multiple days had passed since my Monday-morning surgery. I hoped I was sleeping through the worst of it and when I next opened my eyes it would be Friday, or Thursday, or Wednesday evening at the very least.

When the stones of my eyelids finally rolled away, I was in a private room and the ceiling seemed especially high from the valley floor of my bed. The walls were a light sky-blue. Mom was seated next to my bed and Dad stood by the tall windows (and now, in this memory, they are both young and beautiful in the blue room). I asked them what day and time it was.

A resurrection riff?

It was Tuesday morning, a little after 9 A.M. I'd only been out of surgery for twelve hours. A one-thousand-page novel titled *Despair* (not the Nabokov novel) might come close to capturing my domitable spirit that sunny Tuesday morn in June.

I will not dwell on the rest of my stay in the hospital, one that included conflicting shame and arousal during sponge baths, the body-horror removal of the catheter, my first quivering steps across the divide of linoleum to the bathroom, a midweek overdose of morphine that turned my lips and speech purple and brought on the random appearance of a Dr. Blah Blah Blah (him I never saw before or since) and his syringe full of narcotic-offsetting lava he shot into my arm and my instant soaking sweats and full-body convulsions and weakly plaintive "what's happening?" Morse-coding through chatterbox teeth and my passing out in a fish-bowled roomful of medics holding me down with looks that at least shared in my terror, which I could've done without, although later, waking refreshed with an oxygen mask face-hugging me was a kind of nirvana (not the band; *Nevermind* was still two years away).

Almost ODing on pain meds. Foreshadowing, right?

Pre–spinal fusion, I was six feet and weighed one hundred forty begrudging pounds. Upon my vainglorious return home from the hospital, I marionetted through the front door of my house a humpless and hunchless six-three (and the late bloomer I was, I would grow one more inch in the following year). Sweet! But because I gained height, I had to lose somewhere else. Like a body conservation-of-mass thing. On my first day home, I tipped (well, given how not-heavy I was, there was no tipping) the scale at a scant one hundred twenty-five pounds.

[For holy-fuck-you-were-skin-and-bones reference, at the writing and editing of this book, I am six-four and roughly two hundred pounds.]

The first three days post-surgery I wasn't allowed to eat anything but broth and Jell-O, and I followed that up with four days of bird-pecking at hospital food, ergo the loss of weight I could ill afford to lose. Now home, in theory I could eat whatever I wanted and would gain the weight back and more, but my hoped- and yearned-for physical transformation was at hand (I'd dared imagine myself post-surgery as tall, handsome, winsome, and all the -somes) and the new me was a barely walking skeleton. My collarbones were so prominent, you could hook a clothes hanger on them. Luckily, I was still in a tremendous amount of pain (even with the Percocet), which helped take my mind off my emaciated visage.

My parents set up the TV room as my nesting/healing area. Mom moved the wooden rocking chair in from the living room, jammed it into a corner so it couldn't rock, and padded the seat with towels. I would spend a considerable amount of the summer of '89 rooted in the splintery wooden behemoth.

That first week home, I was whizzy on pain meds. Mom stayed home and the only visitors were family, and they didn't stay to chat for very long. There were no phone calls for me and I didn't make any. I watched a lot of cable TV and picked my way through a book about Thor Heyerdahl's homemade raft ride thousands of miles to Easter Island. I still associate that week with drifting through the Pacific alongside Thor on the *Kon-Tiki*. I took two showers a day to help my back shed the last of the butterfly-winged Steri-Strips. I didn't have the range of motion to rotate my torso enough to display the entirety of my nearly spine-length scar within the small window of the medicine cabinet mirror. What I did see was thick and red, as was the smirking mouth above my right hip, the site at which the doctor harvested bone to be reassigned to my spine. After the showers and scar inspection, I'd step on the scale. Not only was I not gaining weight, by the end of the first week home, I was down to one hundred twenty pounds. I didn't tell Mom, as she would've panicked, which wouldn't have been unreasonable. As it was, she asked me every hour on the hour if I wanted ice cream or a shake or if there was anything special I wanted her to cook or bake. I didn't, so I wasn't eating much besides cereal and peanut butter slathered on Ritz crackers. I finally gave in to her offer of French toast the night before she returned to working at the bank.

The first morning I was home alone I foolishly started reading Stephen King's *It*. After inhaling the famous opening chapter in which Pennywise sweet-talks poor little Georgie (who was my younger cousin Danny in my head) into his sewer doom, I apoplectically quit and returned the beat-up paperback to the bookshelf in the living room, spine facing in, so *It* wouldn't seem me when I walked by on my way to the kitchen. I would've been on what's-that-noise edge anyway, given my physically and emotionally vulnerable state, but the book catalyzed my level of freaked-the-fuck-out to DEFCON 1. I became my own ghost, Art the Friendly-When-Given-the-Opportunity Ghost, haunting my own house, or more accurately, frightened by my own haunted house as I drifted around the first floor listening until I heard the sounds for which I listened. There was plenty to hear. Because my parents left their bedroom door open upstairs in the morning, it slammed shut as the heat of the day increased and coastal breezes gusted (that was my working theory, not that I investigated). There were more noises, sources unidentifiable, coming from other rooms; sharp knocks, low rumbles that started but didn't finish, what sounded like footfalls on the floors in other rooms, and worst of all, noises from the basement. Even in the light of day the basement was a nightmare factory made of steep wooden stairs, spiderwebs, exposed beams and wires and dangling lightbulbs, stone foundation that sweated and wept water and shadows, slab floors dusty enough they might as well have been earthen, a bulkhead escape hatch to the driveway, and a crawlspace at the far end, under the kitchen. It was too easy to imagine something (something with a face, *the* face) slithering on the basement floor or worming through the crawlspace. Prior to lunch, I walked through the dining room to the kitchen, avoiding even looking at the basement door (and who's the asshole that designs a house with a basement door in the dining room, in the middle of the goddamn house, anyway?), and I heard a languid groan on the basement steps, a weight settling or readying for a spring-loaded leap. It took every ounce of mousy courage I had to work the basement door's flimsy hook and latch into place without making any jangling sounds.

When Mom came home that afternoon, I was dozing in my chair. She insisted I get up and follow her into the kitchen, a glass of Coke the carrot at the end of the stick. She detoured in the dining room, circling the table that was primarily used for homework, card games, and the stacking of clean laundry piles, and stopped in front of the basement door. She asked why it was latched. My don't-know shrug cost me a jagged lightning strike of pain down the middle of my back. She must've seen my wince, or maybe she didn't like how zoned out I was because she asked me to walk the length of the room and back. She asked me to do it again. I obeyed.

"You have to stop walking like that."

"Walking like how?" I asked.

"Walking like you're going to break."

Powered by indignation of the exposed, of the found-out, I said, "You want me to do cartwheels?"

"I'm not saying it to hurt you, Art. I want you to get better. For one, you're holding your head tilted to the side, and you need to hold it up, high, regular, to strengthen the muscles, or—"

"It'll get stuck like that?" I was pissed because she was right.

"You aren't swinging your arms when you walk, not even letting them hang loosely. Do you notice you're cradling them? I know your back hurts and it's going to hurt for a while but it's two weeks after surgery and the doctor says he wants you up and about and walking as normally as possible." As she spoke, there were creaks descending on the basement stairs, and I think Mom heard it too because she flashed her eyes to the door, which she unlatched with a flick of a finger, as though on a dare. "And you have to eat more too. Way more." She walked into the kitchen, opened a can of Chef Boyardee beef ravioli with our clunky, mercurial electric can opener, and warmed it briefly in a small, squat saucepan. The preservatives-filled ravs left a radioactive orange stain around my mouth that didn't so much wash away as melt under my skin.

The next day, I left the family stereo on, playing a stack of records one after the other; the monolith cabinet speakers sentineled in the dining room, their backs stiff against the wall only a few feet from the basement door. I didn't want to hear the noises in the house I wasn't supposed to hear, and I wanted the whatever it was (critter, settling house, Pennywise, or you-know-who) making the noises to ~Santa?~ hear the music. Because music meant I was healing, I had returned ~Oscar the~ to myself, I was doing fine, I wasn't afraid, I was living life, being me, a ~Grouch?~ new and improved me, I wasn't in pain, not living in fear, not existing for existence's sake, not walking like I might break, not walking like I was simply waiting for and accepting the inevitable horrors to be (I still walk like that sometimes). The house and basement had their considerable rebuttal during the brief silences between one record finishing, the needle whirlpooling to the record's center, the tonearm lifting and retracting, the next record falling on top of the mini stack of used records on the platter, and the arm carefully bowing until the needle made contact.

Maybe an hour or so before Mom was due to come home, I got sloppy as the haunted-house DJ and fell asleep in the rocking chair, a sleep too heavy for dreams and for remembering what it was I was supposed to do. As I clambered into waking, Living Colour's Side 2 of

Vivid finished up with Corey Glover's screams and a sample of a somber news broadcast punctuated by a gunshot. Then silence, one too thick, and it made it hard to think and it made it hard to breathe and I blinked and waited and pleaded for the next song until I remembered that was the last record in the queue. There was no more room on the platter for records and I forgot to be vigilant, to be ready to swap the spent disks out with minimal auditory interruption. This was bad. I turned the TV on at full volume to make up for the lack of music, but the set's tinny built-in mono speaker wasn't enough to fill the house. Not even close.

I stumbled into the living room, then the dining room, and a full-throated rusty screech and floor-tremoring clang in the basement filled the musicless void. Was that the bulkhead opening and closing? I was beyond scared, yes, but I could function because I was furious with myself; whatever was to happen would be my fault for letting the music end. I triple-checked the basement latch and I moved a dining-room table chair in front of the door. Jamming the seat back under the doorknob sparked flames between my shoulder blades. I sprint-walked the short distance to the turntable stationed on the other side of the wall in the foyer. A sliding, sandpapery rasp in the basement mimicked my first-floor movement and progress. Not thinking clearly, I removed the spent albums instead of just restacking the same ones, and let them drip to the floor until the platter was an empty spinning circle.

In the basement a foot clapped on the bottom step, the one that was loose and sagged like a wannabe letter *u*, and the rickety handrail ricketed, then a second stair clap, this one louder and closer, then a third.

I cued up the closest record within reach, Side 1 of Hüsker Dü's *Warehouse: Songs and Stories*. I gathered other records from the leaf pile scattered around the stereo stand and pancake-stacked them on the spindle as the opening riff of "These Important Years" buzzed.

Heavy feet on the basement stairs continued toward the summit. I mumbled, "Okay, the music is back on, you can stop, you can go away," and stood under the doorjamb between rooms.

"Art! Hey, Art, it's fucking dark down here. Is there a light switch you can hit for me? Never mind. Found it. Jesus," Mercy said, her voice muffled behind the basement door.

I didn't answer her, but I turned down the volume until the music was a mist around my feet and ankles.

She said, "I thought this was your least favorite Hüsker album."

It was true. *Warehouse* was their breakup album; essentially two different bands alternated songs, sounding like parents presenting their grievances and arguments, not to each other but to their child, explaining why they had to split up. Instantly defensive despite my terror, I had the urge to shout that just because it was my least favorite it didn't mean I didn't like it.

I shuffle-stepped into the living room, my head titled slightly to the right, cradling my arms, the tips of my long fingers lightly pressed to my forearms.

The basement door rattled in the frame. The worthless dining-room chair slid out from under the doorknob and tumbled to the side.

"You're walking like you're going to break," Mercy said.

"What did you say?"

"I'm not trying to weird you out—"

"By breaking into my basement?"

"Fair point. I'm not reading your mind or anything like that. I was down here yesterday and I heard your mom say you were walking like you were going to break. I mean, ouch, Mom, but she's right, you know. And—"

I interrupted her again. It was easier to interrupt her when she was behind a door. "Wait, wait, wait. You were down there, in my basement? Fucking yesterday?"

"There's a shit-ton of cereal boxes down here, dude. Yeah, I was down here yesterday." *Seriously, it was a wonder you didn't shit*

Light was dawning on my marble head. "Was yesterday the only *Frosted Flakes* day you were down there?" *and Froot Loops.*

"No." Pause. "I'm here today, aren't I?"

"How many other days have you been in the basement?"

Avoid regional colloquialisms involving the small coastal town of Marblehead.

"I can't and won't lie to you, Art." She didn't say anything else, didn't add to the basement-break-in sum.

"Were you down there last week too? You were, weren't you?" Now I knew she had been in the house during my dizzy, lethargic, lifeless first week home, where instead of healing and gaining weight my battery charge continued to drain.

"Yeah, sure. I mean, I wasn't always in the basement, to be fair. I peeked through the windows from outside too. Might've ducked into your kitchen once when you were napping. I wanted to see how you were doing and eat one of the peanut-butter cookies your mom made. So good. But you're missing the point, Art."

"I'm sure you'll tell me."

"Look at you with your new-height attitude."

"Shut up."

"No, seriously, please, give me and give the world more of that. Anyway, the point is you need to stop walking around like you will break. It's not just a now thing either. You walked like that before your surgery."

I slapped the door with an open hand, which was dumber than dumb, and pain solar flared from my center.

"That's the spirit."

"Go away."

"Art, listen. Yes, you feel terrible, and you look terrible now. Like a goddamn corpse. I told you I won't ever lie. And I'm not being cruel or mean, but you need to hear it now, and not just from your mom. You need to hear it from a friend—"

That hurt then, "Oh, you're a friend?"

and it hurts now "You will feel and look a hell of a lot better eventually, and sooner

reading it. than you think. But right now, Art, man. Not good. And you need to do something about it."

"I need to do something about it? I need to do something about it?" I screamed the question into the closed door twice. The latch hook quivered in the expectorated frequency. "I'm like this now because of you!" I waited for her to be indignant, to protest, to laugh, to make fun of how ridiculous I was being. She didn't say anything. I wanted to let everything out, talk about how at the first Pallbearers Club funeral I felt dizzy and weak and sapped of strength when I was carrying Kathleen Blanchet's coffin, how every Sunday after being with Mercy I'd feel the same way, totally wiped out, and how my scoliosis had stabilized until I met her and how the curve impossibly worsened in the few months that we'd hung out together, and I wanted to talk about sleepover night and me waking with a weight on my chest and how it felt like I was going to die and I felt like I wanted to die, and I wanted to tell her what I saw and who I saw when I went downstairs and talk about my week and a half home since the hospital and how I'd kept getting thinner and weaker not wanting to live like this, and how I knew it was all because of her, because she was Mercy, *the* Mercy Brown.

The doorknob turned and the basement door leavened from between the doorjamb, straining against the latch. The skin around my incision itched and throbbed.

Mercy finally said, "I'm sorry I didn't come see you sooner, Art. I truly am. And I only want you to get better. That's why I'm here. Let me help you. Will you open the door?" She pushed against the door. The latch held.

"Please don't come in." It hurt to say that. I didn't understand it then, nor do I understand it at the writing of this book. There was always so much hurt.

"Yeah, okay. But before I go, you know you'll get better, right? Healthier, stronger if you let yourself?"

I nodded (unclear if she could see or sense my nodding), afraid I might say something traitorous.

"Will you tell me one thing, Art? I need to know you'll be different now. The same you, always, please always you, but also— different. Better or worse, who the fuck knows what that means according to whatever bullshit value system that might be applied other than your own. I'm not doing a good job, here. Fuck it. Look. You need to tell me you won't continue to hide yourself, that you'll try to be who you imagine yourself as being. I want to know if you'll take actual fucking risks to be that person and still like that person when you fail and when you succeed. I want you to tell me you're not going to be the same scared, woe-is-me kid who hides in his head. Please tell me you won't float along with everyone else through the drunk and stupid numbing bliss of college and then zombie into a middle- or upper-class job you won't care about because you need to pay student loans and then pay all the other loans to come. After all we've done, tell me you won't pretend you're happy and you won't pretend you can't do what you want to do even if you aren't entirely sure what that is. Can you tell me that?"

I didn't answer. How could I make any empty promises about the opaque future? How could anyone?

"All right. I'll leave you alone now, Art."

I unlatched and opened the basement door.

I am a lot of things, but a liar is not one.

Mercy had lied about flipping on the light switch because there was only darkness. I glimpsed movement, maybe a showing of eyes and teeth, two sets of each, but I cannot be certain that my imagination wasn't filling in details to simplify the vastness. There was no hiding from this, no closing the door that was opened. Then there was a flash of light and a high-pitched squeal. The door slammed shut, and I honestly cannot remember if I shut it.

I relatched the lock, apologizing to Mercy in my head, making doomed promises, as though there were any other kind. I listened and did not hear her weight shifting on the stairs. I knocked on my own basement door and said, "Mercy? Are you still there? If you're gonna stay on the stairs, should I leave out a plate of peanut butter cookies and put on the Ramones?" I meant it as a joke, one of the most desperate kind.

Outside the house, the metal bulkhead doors gonged closed. I pivoted to the open window on my right. Mercy dusted off her jacket as she walked down the driveway. I yelled after her, but she didn't stop. She turned and disappeared onto Echo Avenue. I waited for her Datsun to putter by, but it didn't.

Alone again. I turned off the stereo and the television. The house was quiet. I trudged upstairs to my bedroom and then back downstairs. I walked laps around the first floor, increasing my pace until I was out of breath, and while my back ached, the soreness wasn't wholly unpleasant. After the exercise, I was hungry for what felt like the first time in memory, and I made two English muffins, slathered each in peanut butter, and chased them with a full glass of whole milk.

Instead of resuming what would become a daily routine/workout of walking around the house, I returned to the basement door and opened it. The stairwell light was on. A box of Frosted Flakes totemed on the stairs, like a giant Easter Island statue head, one tread below the dining room floor and my feet. A Polaroid photo was jammed underneath the cardboard folds of the cereal box top. The picture hadn't fully developed, yet within the gray square of film I could make out my body's outline, haloed by the basement door frame. The angle of the photo was from the same sunken vantage as the cereal box, as though Tony the Tiger had snapped the pic.

Mom came home from work and found me in the rocking chair, staring at the Polaroid.

She asked what I was holding. I gave it to her without explanation.

"What is it? What am I looking at?" She held the photo close to her face, briefly, before banishing it away at arm's length.

I say, "It's me. Standing at the top of the basement stairs."

"I don't see it."

"Well, I don't know what to tell you. It's me."

"I guess I can see it. A little. Why is everything gray and washed out?"

"The photo never fully developed."

"Was it a mistake or is it supposed to be one of those artsy photos?" Mom acknowledged her pun with a faltering, unsure smile. Like son like mother.

"I think both."

"How are you feeling? What do you want for dinner?" Sometime during those earliest days after my return from the hospital, Mom had

[handwritten note:] There's no way your mom knew she was punning with "artsy," because your real name isn't Art. Do you think of yourself as Art now?

Is this Artception?

taken to tacking on another question right after the *How are you feeling?* to leave me an easy out to not have to answer it. Mom was as scarred as I was by the surgery summer, and she would continue couching or seeding questions about my well-being in the same manner for years that silted into sediment.

I ignored her first question but precipitately answered the second. "Can we get a pizza? I'm starving."

Likely due to the quirks of that old camera, the last picture in the pack always came out "undeveloped," as you described. Always. Nothing foreboding or metaphoric or supernatural about it. You know that, of course.

Fine, we've already established this is fiction, but just in fucking case the life-sucking vampire bit doesn't tip off an editor/agent/whomever to this book's fictionness, I again want the following on record, even if it makes me sound like the doth-protest-too-much neurotic mess I might be: Not only did I constantly complain to you about the wasted picture in every pack—that film was goddamn expensive!—I frequently stuck the camera in your face, shot the last/lost photo, then blamed you for breaking the camera with your face, which was a silly "dad joke"—in today's parlance—and you laughed and knew I wasn't serious. There's no mention of this last-photo-in-the-pack bit anywhere in your text despite your featuring my camera prominently while taking every other opportunity to self-denigrate your physical appearance. I would say "how odd" if I didn't think the omission was purposeful and in service to your novel's storyline. If I sound pissed, it's because this scene out of all the scenes in the book so far is the one that strikes the hurtiest nerve. How you write about the sinister nature of the photo and cereal box leaps off the page. I—your friend and poor, besmirched, and betrodden beta reader—left those gifts as my olive branch to you. It was an apology, Art. I was being the bigger person. I figured you'd find the Flakes and mucked-up photo, recognize it as a playful callback to the joke of my always using the last pic in the pack on your mug, and then you'd have a warm, rueful laugh and realize it was my way of saying sorry for breaking into your basement, which I admit, was all kinds of weird and wrong, one of those wrongs that became impossible to admit because it was so far afield.

But hey, both of us were stupid kids, and we were both all kinds of weird and wrong back then, weren't we? Clearly, that's why we hit it off so well.

I was so convinced that after finding the photo you'd call me later that day or night, I waited by the phone for a few hours. Or a few minutes, at least. But you didn't call. And not to put too fine a point on it, that bummed me the fuck out. I'm only human, after all.

In retrospect, and reading our exchange all these years later, I think I was probably too harsh with you, given how emotionally and physically vulnerable you were post-surgery. I was honest, though, and did not exaggerate how rough you looked. If anything, you are underselling how thin you were after your surgery, guy. Seriously. It was scary and hard to watch from the basement and sometimes from the backyard, through the TV room's windows. And not for nothing, I don't know how it took you that long to find me in your house, not that you actually found me. I got sick of waiting to be discovered so I stomped around, and when that didn't work, I knocked on the basement door and called out to you. That's not exactly finding me. How could you not hear me rattling around that whole week? How did you not smell the weed? Yeah, I smoked in your basement. I'm not proud of myself on that count.

Regardless, you didn't call me. So, I didn't call either. Neither of us blinked in that standoff. When we did finally blink, how many years had passed before our paths crossed again? Too many. Way too many.

Before I continue reading your book, I'm going to drop this here: For this novel to work better, maybe you should change my character name. "Mercy" is fun, but I think it's too on the nose. Also, the use of the name might lead to a plot issue: how is THE Mercy Brown a punk Polaroid devotee when her heart was burned and its ashes consumed? You wrote in the intro that you changed all the names, and maybe that's the reason why you're staying away from my REAL first name. If I am really who you say I am, shouldn't you name me to protect others? Maybe you're saving my name as a reveal for later in the story. I get it; you can't give everything away too early. You're smarter than you look, Art Barbara.

Art Barbara. Enjoy: I say that name out loud when I read it. I read it dramatically and I read it with various accents I'm capable of producing. It makes me smile and it makes me think of you, even though you aren't him.

NO RESERVATIONS / BACK FROM SOMEWHERE

(September 1989 to July of 2007, then back and
forth to the years between and 2007)

A chapter in which, frankly, I don't know the best way to
somewhat briefly yet dramatically convey and/or describe
the passing of twenty years, of the invisible years, and
after considerable consideration I land upon using deftly
placed flashbacks [to be presented as unrealistic interview
dialogue] despite knowing said flashbacks are frowned
upon [with, admittedly, good reason most of the time] by the
academia writing syndicate as well as by those who can afford
to pay for the privilege of being taught prescriptive writing
advice, but fuck it, a ~~memoir~~ is all flashback anyway, so we'll   Novel!
all just have to deal, and there's a messed-up and scary piece
of furniture that <u>should've been a clue.</u> This! This is what I meant when
            I encouraged your "new height attitude." You still come off
                a little bit whiny and you're totally rationalizing, but I applaud
                the 'tude here.

I started writing this ~~memoir~~ November 19, 2007. The book's   novel
first two pages were written in one sitting. Go ahead and reread
them. I'll wait. (Waiting.) Aren't they jaunty? The prose brims
with verve, swerve, playfulness, and boils with foolish hope if not
for my improved social and financial lot in life, then for a cracking,
rollicking book. But, let's be honest, there's also a baseless, brazen
bravado, as though I'd assumed writing this would not be difficult,
and there's an obviously manic desperation to make an instant
impression on you, the reader. I have resisted the urge to rewrite
those pages, not because they're perfect but because they are not

perfect, and they represent a truth you might be able to apply to your own life: what has since taken shape, what has since found its own form, is not what I imagined it would be at the beginning.

It has taken me almost five years of writing and rewriting (and I could've spent fifty more) to reach this point in time within the *novel* ~~memoir~~. For Art Barbara, your humble author, these pages are a functioning time machine. Within time-travel narratives, the oft-written-about unintended consequences of jaunting to the past is how the present and future are changed for everyone. Not to worry, reader, you are safe, or as safe as you can be reading a book. This *novel* ~~memoir's~~ butterfly effect will be limited to me however. My past, present, and future are recast with each new paragraph and each edit.

Um, hello? I'm right here.

To wit: I've spent five years (2007 through 2012) reliving one bizarre year in the late 1980s. Have I gained any clarity, some sort of well-worn perspective? Have I become trapped within a period of my life I so longingly wished to escape? A little of both. I do not think this level of introspection is healthy. Further, my mental health is now tethered to the success or failure of this project. *The Pallbearers Club* (title of book, not the club to which it refers) has become my raison d'être, more so than my music, which is unexpected in a sad way that I cannot describe; an unspeakable, eldritch sadness, but one worth exploring in this chapter.

Maybe I should've taken all this energy (for lack of a better term) and done as Mercy once suggested in 2007: write an insufferable, bloated, postapocalyptic vampire series.

Anyway. The next twenty years will wash by in a figurative and narrative blur: I only spent six months (the cost of time, the price of time) writing the following section.

Best of times, worst of times? You're not quite Dickens, there, Arty boy.

[Note: This was the initial opening of this chapter]

Let's hit the double arrow Fast-Forward button, not on the cassette player, but the compact disc digital audio boombox, as we're entering the wrapped-in-flannel 1990s.

Because of my surgery I missed Providence College's freshman orientation weekend at which I would've mined pre-friendships and had the pre-time of my life. I was relegated to the late orientation, two days before all students arrived on campus. My dorm room had a single bed and not a bunkbed like every other room on my floor. My roommate-to-be got off the waiting list at some better school over the summer, so now I had my own room. I would be a freshman without a roommate, no instant companion with whom to share the joys and dramas of living away from home for the first time. A considerable social setback, one that might've overwhelmed me a few short months prior. But I was different now. I wasn't Renfield or Igor anymore (straightened spine!) and I refused to sulk alone in my bell tower, or dorm room. At the sight of the dreary, cramped space with the lonely, single bed, Mom wept and repeatedly said she couldn't believe she was leaving her baby. Dad peppered some proud-of-you-buddy's within his questioning if it was a good idea to wear my black leather jacket to college, where it could easily be stolen or ruined by beer and hijinks. Translation: he thought I looked ridiculous wearing it and he hoped his continued questioning would lead to saving me from myself. When I'd bought the black moto-style jacket with shiny chrome buttons and more zippers than were functionally necessary with my graduation money, it was a commitment to *not* saving me from myself, to making college and the years after that different from my high school existence. If I did in fact (probably) look (more than) kind of ridiculous, I didn't care. And that was me growing into the new, bold Art. If my first night in the dorm was the maiden voyage of new-bold-Art, there was no conclusion to be drawn regarding his success, as there were only two other students in my late-orientation group. Both of whom were friendly enough insofar as they held eye contact when spoken to, but they didn't talk much. Were they intimidated by my rough leather look, or did they wonder why a pale, acned, pipe cleaner of a young man who still didn't need to shave and looked all of thirteen years old would dress like Johnny Ramone (put a long, black-hair wig on me, I bear more than a passing resemblance to Johnny; I have better teeth, but worse skin) while attending the decidedly not-edgy Catholic school Providence College? At the end of our second day and night together, however, I had won the late orienteers over. Louis and Mark. The latter would come to be known as Metal Mark because, obviously, he loved heavy metal. And I was Punk Art. That nickname would stick throughout my three years in college, goosed into its longer life with deft self-promotion.

Groan. You can't give yourself a nickname, dude.

I'm hitting the Stop button here on the boombox (purchased in 1991, weighs almost twenty pounds, and the sucker still works) and the Eject button. I think we need a different CD, because I am attuned to my readers. I hear you: *Where's Mercy, Punk Art? Where the fuck is Mercy?* (I imagine you with a thick Jersey accent, for fun, while assuming you have a certain level of emotional acuity, otherwise you wouldn't be reading a ~~memoir~~. Unless you're a sociopath studying human behavior to become more human-like.)

novel

Fine, we'll skip ahead to more Mercy. Though I'm not crazy about the idea that I'm transforming into my own story's secondary or supporting character. Perhaps it's my lot to be the rhythm guitarist in the punk/post-punk/indie band of life. I did play, briefly, in a band called Life. I quit after two rehearsals because the tyro vocalist insisted we stop playing our instruments in the middle of a song to allow for his free-verse vignettes about Jesus Christ attending, and ironically enjoying, one of the summer's WaterFire events. For the uninitiated, Providence's WaterFire is a mix of festival, performance art, and pagan ritual, free to the public, featuring New Age music and eighty-six anchored braziers (metal thingies that hold burning logs) floating aflame within the rivers that flow through downtown's Waterplace Park. It's a lovely take. In the summer of 2005, I briefly had a side gig captaining one of the Brazier Society WaterFire guest boats until one sweaty August night I bumped (which is almost an exaggeration) one of La Gondola's authentic Venetian gondolas. When "the skilled oarsman practiced in this ancient art" (according

Well, a vampire is supposed to steal your life, yeah?

to La Gondola's website) attempted boarding my vessel to share his practiced displeasure, I retaliated by dumping his sizable oar into the river.

Yes, I know, I'm stalling. I'm stalling because even though my adult years are more recent and more noteworthy in terms of things done (not necessarily accomplished), my memory of them is muddier than the memories of my childhood and teen years and requires a reading-tea-leaves level of interpretation. Our adult years pass so quickly, and for many of us they pass without the obvious markers of time we are provided as children (our first pair of Spider-Man Underoos, kindergarten, Santa isn't real, elementary school, fight(s) with a bully, middle school, first of many crushes, puberty, ~~first kiss,~~ high school, graduation, and all the mini moments between). It's as though my adult years were never really there. And that terrifies me more than anything else that has been detailed in this book so far.

> Just you wait! Sorry, being, um, cheeky
> as I've had a smoke and some wine.

Late July 2007, my band had a gig at AS220, one of the longest-tenured music clubs/art collectives in Providence. We opened in support of Del's Brain Freeze and their seventh 7-inch record. They were a local band named after the region's favorite frozen lemonade purveyors. Think Rocket from the Crypt and Fishbone with punchy choruses of thick Rhode Island accents; an everyone-is-in-on-the-joke kind of band. I'd been in plenty of bands where no one was in on the joke.

My band Antigone was a four-piece; pronounced "anti-gone." I know, believe me, not my doing, and I'd argued long and hard for a hyphen or space (Anti Gone), which would've made for better band logo opportunities. Victor (bass) and Kenny (lead guitar) were our vocalists and an off-and-on-and-off-again couple; their moodiness and interpersonal conflict translated well onstage. If they weren't the most talented musicians, they made up for it as songwriters, their willingness to experiment, and authentic (if unearned) air of disdain. Walter (or Waltah) our unflappable, friendly-as-a-puppy drummer,

> You and
> your band
> logos.

recruited me into the band in the spring of '07. I'd met him a decade before while bartending at Club Babyhead (now Club Hell). He played in almost as many bands as I had, and despite being a lifelong New Englander who'd never been south of DC, he'd been threatening to move to North Carolina for as long as I'd known him.

Prior to that night's gig, I was bullish on the prospects of Antigone. We'd been getting some good press and were in the mix to open for larger acts at Lupo's/The Strand. I'd been part of the local scene for going on fifteen years, which might as well have been fifty years for how often and quickly trends, tastes, and players changed. So, at age thirty-six I was the Socratic grandpa of Providence indie rock. Or to be less generous to myself, maybe I was better described as the Susan Lucci of the scene. Respected (I think?) as the ultimate dues-paying grinder but viewed as a cursed object (the gondola incident didn't help my reputation in that regard), as I was unable to stick with any one band for long nor did any of my bands achieve even momentary success, however that success might be defined.

[An intrusion note from the hell year of 2017: I am cursed and have been so for as long as I can remember, and yeah, fine, most of it is self-inflicted, and maybe you should stop reading this book, as you touristing my life might lead to your own cursing, as it were. A book is a vampire after all. And if that bit makes you think of a Smashing Pumpkins lyric, might I suggest engaging in a juice cleansing, the kind that leaves you rooted to the toilet for a protracted length of time.]

Even in this momentarily frozen post-Napster-and-iPod moment in 2007, Antigone felt like my last kick at the we'll-make-records-and-T-shirts-and-people-will-purchase-them-unironically-and-maybe-we'll-even-play-shows-all-over-the-country can. I'd told myself with every new band that *this was it*, but that phrase once rated more optimism than it did in '07. One way or another, Antigone would be it.

We played a short thirty-minute set bespoke for the party punkers (a throwback crowd if there ever was one; one content to pogo and dance instead of knocking the snot out of one another), who put up with the performative intellectual aloofness of Victor's deadpan reading of the nutrition label off a Del's Frozen Lemonade cup. He was a recent graduate of the prestigious and outrageously expensive RISD, the Rhode Island School of Design, and he had his own apartment in College Hill and no student loans. I still had five years more of loan payments at an elevated interest rate (having defaulted once, almost twice) despite my *not* graduating in 1993.

With both shows over, gear (my Marshall JCM200 and <u>Fender Stratocaster</u>, plus a MXR distortion pedal) stowed in Victor's van, I Slinkyed over to the bar, pleasantly exhausted though my lower back hurt more than usual, particularly for a set that wasn't very long. I'd been suffering from consistent but <u>manageable lower back pain</u> for years by then. Discs are the shock absorbers for the spine, and two-thirds of them were fused together along with my vertebrae, therefore I only had one-third the allotment of functioning discs. And those discs (and the muscles around them) got cranky. The years of performing on stages (or floors in tiny bars and abandoned warehouses) and lugging heavy equipment had taken a toll, along with countless hours standing in clubs watching other bands play, and add to that my medically reckless participation in slam dancing/ moshing during the '90s. (By the by, I've come to loathe that the word "moshing" and the act itself in a post-Nirvana world were hostilely co-opted by frat-house douchebros. To be fair, mindless violence was a dangerous, problematic, and stupidly beautiful part of punk from the beginning. But also, frat-house douchebros.) At least I had enough of a brain to avoid stage diving and crowd surfing, but at the height of six-four (I loved and love my new height), my unsuspecting head was a mountain peak atop the crowd, one the stage divers and crowd surfers invariably crash-landed onto first. The fuckers.

Anyway, I sat at the bar, back turned to hangers-on and revelers, and the stools in my orbit were empty. I was achy and buzzed. My ears rang, and the post-show melancholy I was addicted to kicked in hard so I ordered another beer I didn't need, but it would extend the night a little. After all the practice and preparation and the days of

[handwritten margin notes:]
Same guitar as Bob Mould? Still such a fanboy.

Manageable? How, and using what as painkillers?

what-if-the-place-is-empty/what-if-the-place-is-jammed worries and the want-to-puke nerves moments before playing and the manic don't-fuck-it-up euphoria/panic (new word: *euphoranic*) while playing, the show was over so quickly. They were all over so quickly.

There was a tap on my shoulder; more intimate than a hey-you and more secretive, momentarily protecting the unseen tapper's identity from the unsuspecting tappee. I could go on describing the tap (its rhythm and level of pressure communicating both insouciance and urgency, and the maddening wonder of who might be attached to the digits knocking on my shoulder as though it were a speakeasy's door), but I won't.

I swiveled my stool into a nebula flash. Vulnerable and over-exposed, I mashed the backs of my hands into blinking, malfunctioning eyes, and oh that Polaroid's goddamn <u>Trent Reznorian</u> whir. I hadn't heard her camera in almost twenty years, but I recognized its industrial tones instantly.

[handwritten margin note: Polaroid like a hole.]

"Hey, want a photo of a rock star?" Mercy held up the back of the picture toward my face.

I blinked dumbly (I never have figured out how to blink smartly, consideredly) and I laughed, mainly at myself, and I laughed at how we had arrived at this time and place. I was a drunk's happy to see her, and I said, "Yeah, okay."

She pulled the photo away. "Five bucks."

I held up surrender hands. "I don't have any money. I'm with the band."

She smirked. Hell, she might've even smiled. Her face had always looked like it had just finished and discarded a smile, and you were then forced to share in the dawning sadness over the end of that smile. She said, "I saw that."

"And? What'd you think?"

Mercy glanced at the photo and slipped it into a pocket of her green army jacket. Was it the same coat from twenty years ago? I doubted it, but it could've been. "I dug it. You looked like you belonged up there. Your guitar sound is super fuzzed-out, very Hüsker Dü, of course."

I blushed because I was seen, flattered, and found out, and despite it being a hoary teen-angst sentiment, it was all I ever wanted to hear and hear from her (even if it wasn't true): *You looked like you belonged.* "Aw shucks. That's very nice of you to say. Hell, you look the same. Exactly the same. How's that possible? Except shorter."

"I eat right. But I haven't gotten shorter. You, however, do not look the same."

"That's a good thing, I hope."

"It is. You look great. You should grow your hair out though. And I'm iffy on the goatee."

My hair was almost (not quite) buzzed short, bangs spiked in the front, a mini–Hadrian's Wall. No fauxhawk for this fella. "I don't have a chin, and the scruff provides definition." <u>I didn't tell her that I still had pimple breakouts I</u> wanted to camouflage. Acne, the gift that kept on giving. "And by the way, hi, Mercy." I attempted to stand for a hug, but I was more drunk, more affected by the moment (and by her) than I thought, and a bit dizzy, and my almost stand became a sloppy fall back into the chair. I held out a handshake hand and suppressed a giggle as she pumped my arm up and down once.

No, you did tell me, multiple times, that you had the skin of a fourteen-year-old. I joke-asked if you kept that poor kid's skin hanging in a closet.

"Hi, Art. It has been a while."

"It has. Holy shit it has."

Mercy settled into the swivel chair next to me. "I was hoping I'd see you onstage wearing leather pants and doing Scorpions and Def Leppard covers."

"I wear assless chaps but only during shows on Tuesdays and Thursdays."

"Classy." Mercy downed half of my beer. "I was also hoping to hear you sing. I guess your mic stand was for show."

"You don't want to hear me sing. Too nasally and whiny, which some people can pull off, the kind of bad voice that has character, but not me. You have to settle for my merely competent rhythm guitar."

We fell into an easy conversation about the show, and as she was telling me about her move to Providence at the start of the summer, the dastardly last-call lights came up. Mercy said the night was still young (Sarcasm? Ironic use of cliché? Snark? I could never tell with her.) and she invited me back to her apartment.

I said, "Why not?" multiple times, as though answering my own question with differing inflections.

Bandmates Victor and Kenny were by themselves next to the stage and two acts deep into their usual end-of-the-night argument, so I didn't bother them. I introduced Mercy to Walter, told him I didn't need him to give me a ride home, and joked that if something happened to me tonight, at least he would know who was responsible. Without missing a beat, Mercy added, "No one will find either of us."

I followed Mercy outside to her orange compact car parked across the street. I shouted, "You gotta be fucking kidding me." She still had the Datsun? I wasn't sure why I was so excited by the notion of her apparently undying car. Alas, upon closer inspection I discovered the car's logo hanging crookedly on the trunk as though it were ashamed of us both. It was a Nissan, a Sentra even, late '90s model.

During the ride, "For old times' sake," she cranked the Hüskers' *Warehouse* album. Yeah, that was the record playing in my living room the last time we had talked, but I was instead transported back to all those hours spent sitting in the passenger seat of her Datsun. Despite everything, it felt like a safe place to be.

We drove to the east side and through the historical and affluent College Hill neighborhood full of, well, hills, and colleges (RISD, Brown University). Mercy took a quick I-want-coffee detour down Thayer Street, which was once a vibrant enclave of locally owned clothing stores, hookah rooms, cafés, restaurants, the Avon movie theater, and the wonderful record stores Mercy and I had visited on the day we'd researched Mercy Brown's story at the Providence Library. By '07 a corporate gentrification of a gentrification had fully settled in, including the recent arrivals of Starbucks and Urban Outfitters; the doom had already come to Providence. Nothing was open, so Mercy navigated the narrow colonial streets that were once cobblestoned and lined with encroaching homes and buildings built in the 1700s and 1800s, stacked onto the slopes like rows of teeth. We cruised by the jaundice-yellow Stephen Harris House (featured in H. P. Lovecraft's "The Shunned House," a story I have not read) and shortly thereafter Mercy parked in a postage stamp–lot on Bowen Street. The parking spot itself was probably as much as my North Providence apartment's rent I struggled to make each month. She had a basement studio in a three-story brownstone on the corner of Bowen and Benefit Streets.

We used a basement entrance off Bowen and navigated a small warren to her one-room apartment. Once settled inside Mercy asked if I noticed anything slightly off. I mumbled something about it all looking great to me, but to be honest, my initial impression was that the general layout was odd. A few steps away from the entrance and to my right was an unmade, double-size bed in a wooden frame flush against the drywall lengthwise. A purple partition curtain hung from the ceiling, its bowed rod tracing a quarter-moon around the bed. A bathroom, kitchenette, and office or breakfast nook ran along the exposed brick wall on our left. Dotting that wall, a series of windows followed the slope of the hill the brownstone was built into. Like a reverse dawn-of-humans evolutionary chart, the windows devolved in size and grandeur until the last was a breadbox-size portal near the ceiling. A large blue couch iceberged in the middle of the room. Against the wall across from us was a small television on a stand, flanked by a full bookcase. Otherwise, there was an assortment of lamps, end tables, a coffee table, a dresser, a plush armchair, a locker/armoire, coat rack, and framed photo prints hanging on the walls.

I said, "Hardwood floors. Ain't you fancy."

"You don't see the strange part yet, do you?"

I shrugged and walked into the room, thinking it was a great neighborhood to live in, a nice building, but a wee bit claustrophobic, especially at night. Granted, I had a thing about basements. Really, *we* had a thing about basements.

[Okay, good a place as any to pause because I know you, fearless reader, are thinking, *What are you doing, Art? Why go into her basement, Art, especially now that you are a musician and almost handsome? Why*

Fair assessment of the reader(s).

is she back in your life? Hey, Art, aren't you afraid? I'll answer the last question with I was and I wasn't. I hadn't forgotten about what had happened at my house (and my scoliosis getting worse and feeling dizzy and the chest heaviness and not breathing and all of it), but on this night in 2007 with me standing in the middle of her cavelike apartment, what had happened decades prior felt like a story. Is that

novel

odd to say in a ~~memoir~~ that my past, what I had lived through, felt like a story, a fiction, something that had happened to someone else, a story that had been both embellished and diminished by the passage of time? Well, that night it did. And like any story, I wanted to know what would happen next.]

I leaned against the couch and Mercy said, "Warmer."

"What?"

"You're getting warmer. You must find the strange part of the apartment before we do anything else, and clearly you need help. Love ya, Art, mean it, but you've never been all that observant of your surroundings."

"So mean."

I headed toward the kitchen first (colder) and played along until her colder/warmer designations inexorably led me toward her dresser.

She said, "Now tell me why it's odd."

"I don't know," I said before inspecting it. Farther away from the foot of her bed than it was from the television, the wooden dresser was a creamy white shading toward yellow, though the yellow tint might've been reflected light from the lamps. Likely an older piece, if not an antique; certainly not an-out-of-the-box hunk of particleboard. Solid, squat, and not all that tall, it had four drawers and its top was clear of the usual debris; no dusty knickknacks, loose change, dead batteries, miscellaneous keys, crumpled receipts and pay stubs. (I guess I'm admitting what my dresser top looks like.)

"Well, do you see it yet?"

"The second drawer is missing a knob?"

"True, but that's not it."

"Is it what's inside the drawers? Should I look?"

"No and no. Take a step back and look down."

I did as was instructed and focused on the legs. "Oh, weird. It has bent rollers and probably would mark up your—" What I was seeing caught up to me somewhere in the middle of the sentence, but I didn't stop talking until I was about to say *floors*. Because the rusted rollers would not mark up the floors. The rollers, and the legs they were attached to, hovered about an inch above the hardwood. Was the goddamn thing floating? I bent down and ran my hand in the space between the dresser's front legs and the floor like a stage magician's assistant (look Ma, no strings). Then I pressed one side of my face to the hardwood to get a look at the back legs. Their rollers were not in contact with the floor either.

I scrambled onto my feet, and I might've run out through the front door if Mercy hadn't said, "So freaky, right? The previous tenants had a young kid, and they left their child-proofed dresser behind."

"Oh, okay. Makes sense. No, wait, it doesn't. I don't get it why it's floating."

"They didn't want a wobbly toddler climbing up the drawers and tipping the dresser over onto herself, so they screwed the frame directly into the wall. Try to move it, go ahead. But don't rip it out of the wall, please."

I grabbed the dresser's top, pushed and pulled, and it didn't budge. From this vantage above the dresser, I could see it was indeed flush against the wall. "I still don't get why they'd anchor it so it was an inch off the floor."

"They probably messed up the measurements. Or they were neat freaks and wanted to be able to run a broom or vacuum under the dresser. Or they thought it would be funny as fuck that the next tenant and her friend might obsess over it. Want another beer?"

I did. After she grabbed us each one from her fridge, I sat on the couch, and she claimed the armchair over by the bookcase. She wore a billowy, untucked black T-shirt and jeans. She unlaced her Doc Martens boots and they clunked to the floor as she folded her legs up and onto the chair. We looked each other up and down the way boxers might before the opening bell rings.

My questionable facial hair notwithstanding, I had gone through a considerable physical transformation since we had last spoken. I was four inches taller and weighed two hundred pounds. Mercy might as well have walked directly into this basement studio after leaving my house in June of 1989. Her light-brown hair had no gray that I could see, with the same shoulder-length cut and style she wore in the late '80s. She didn't have any wrinkles or crow's feet around the eyes. I still didn't know how much older she was than me. She could've passed for a woman in her twenties, but she could've also passed for a woman in her late thirties or even early-to-mid-forties. I remember thinking if I'd had a photo from our time together to use as a comparison, I would've noticed how she'd aged. As it was, Mercy was fixed in my mind, as though there was no room for updates or other versions, no room for the newer model, and by newer, I mean older.

Mercy said, "I want to hear everything I missed since we were last together."

"Everything?"

And thus began an interview that lasted until sunrise, not that I would see the sun rising while cloistered within the basement.

[Note: The transcribed interview below has been edited for length and content.]

I can't even. ## INTERVIEW(ED) BY THE VAMPIRE

"Tell me about your educational background, Mr. Barbara, and please include extracurricular activities of note."

You're such a dork.

"I was a mathematics/education major, on track to become a high school math teacher. I can't explain why I would choose that path after so desperately wanting to be free from high school. Maybe it represents a lack of occupational vision; I was good at math, and

I couldn't imagine another job a math person might do. Maybe the choice of major was an act of self-sabotage or self-loathing. You choose! Elsewhere, I made friends easy enough and I fully engaged with the stereotypical college good time. I don't mean to downplay this. In a lot of ways, I blossomed.　　　　　　　**A beautiful flower.**

"For the first time in a wider, general social setting I could be me, or more me, or the me I wanted people to see, the me I wanted to cultivate, the me who wore a leather jacket no matter the season or temperature. And yeah, I felt safe at college, safer than I ever felt in high school. Sophomore year I joined the college radio station, WDOM. My first assignments included remotely producing radio broadcasts of hockey games and programming classical music shows on bleary weekend mornings. Around the time I joined the station, I started hanging out with a guy named Brian. From Long Island, he was more into XTC and the Replacements than the punkier/heavier stuff I liked, but there was common musical ground too. Plus, he played guitar and he played it well. I pestered him into showing me some chords. Though I was far from being a natural guitarist, my long, brachiosaurian fingers fit into the chord shapes easy enough. The summer after sophomore year, I worked long hours at the United Shoe Factory, unloading and loading trucks, stacking wooden pallets, sweeping the floors, and I spent some days on the production lines as a material handler. With my second paycheck I bought a used black Gibson SE and a red mini amp that sounded like someone taking a cheese grater to a metal handrail. When I wasn't working that summer, I holed up in my room and either played Nintendo Tetris or my guitar. Once my left hand was strong enough for barre chords, I figured out how to play most of the Ramones' first two albums. Junior year I became an RA, or resident assistant, in my dorm to help pay tuition. Things were going along well enough by then: I had a primetime Thursday-night radio show, and yeah, Punk Art was my DJ name. Whenever I had a night off from RA duties, I hit the music clubs and recorded interviews with local bands. I'd play those interviews on-air along with one or two of their songs. I made a bit of a name for myself in the local scene that way. When I went home for junior year's winter break, my parents dropped on me that they were getting a divorce, as their marriage was an unbearable slog and had been so for longer than I had been away at school. I was shocked, insofar as I didn't see it coming. Though I never saw anything coming. For years I had assumed my parents' conspicuous unhappiness and emotional distance from each other was the steadying foundation of their relationship. Officially separated that early winter of 1991–1992, they took turns sleeping on the pullout couch and occasionally not sleeping in the house at all. The upshot, there was now a question as to whether they could or would pay for my final year of schooling, and at the very least, they would need more financial help from me. They never flat-out said I wouldn't be able to continue and graduate, but it was heavily implied, as much as a life-changing fiduciary decision could be left to implication. All of which made it easier for the math-teacher-never-to-be to drop out at the end of junior year, join a band, and live on his own in Providence."

"A perfect segue, Mr. Barbara. Could you regale an old friend with your no-doubt-colorful history as a musician? I do hope you'll detail the folly and pathos of your punk Quixotic quest with your many ridiculous and pretentious band names."

You and your pathos. Oy.

"My first band was a four-piece with three older guys who worked at Club Babyhead. Scott, or Scooter, was the band leader (guitar, vocals). He was the mayor of nighttime Providence, as he knew everyone in every club. Carlos was a math grad student at Brown, had a Byzantine sense of humor, and played a bass that was bigger than he was. Our drummer, Phil, a converted Dead Head, fancied himself a semiotician and created a language called ass-speak, the speaker adding or amending 'ass' onto the ends of words. We were the Macedonians, an up-tempo post-punk band with lyrics that ranged from goofy to clever. Think Devo mixed with early R.E.M. or Boston stalwarts Buffalo Tom. I didn't really love the music we played (I wanted to play with more distortion, and faster and louder, always louder), but I learned a lot from those guys. Phil and Carlos let me live at their place summer and fall of 1992, and Scooter got me a door-job at Babyhead and taught me bartending basics. The Macedonians was my longest-tenured band; we lasted about nine months. It was never a thing any of us expected to take off. We didn't play many shows, maybe once or twice a month on average. The band ended like so many do, by inertia. I won't list every band I was in, but lo, a curated sampling: The Brent Underwoods was a pop-punk five-piece (which is too many pieces) that had no members named Brent or Underwood. The pop part was decidedly lacking, and they dismissed me when I balked at providing backing vocal harmonies because the songs contained no discernible harmonies to back. Chin Music emulated Boston hardcore outfits like Tree, Sam Black Church, and Only Living Witness, and we made some inroads in that scene, but the band ceased to exist the night our talented and charismatic lead singer, Derron, tearfully announced he was moving back to Austin to be with his sick mother. A Manuel, Can is the only band with a comma in its name that I've played in. No one got that it was a pun on philosopher Emmanuel Kant's name. Equally as few people got our mix of They Might Be Giants, Kate Bush, and Black Sabbath. Clean was a too-earnest and on-the-nose straight-edge (no alcohol, no drugs) band with a surly bassist who spent half our sets proselytizing to drunken audiences. We played without any distortion (we played 'clean,' get it?), which sounded wrong, as all we did was riff heavy but without the heaviness. They booted me from the band for being too-not straight-edge: I drank caffeinated Cokes before gigs and, fine, maybe a beer or two. Com Rad was a self-styled throwback to early '80s punk with polemic Bad Religion–esque lyrics, and we spent three months raising money for us to go to Seattle to play at the planned protest of the 1999 World Trade Organization Conference. We didn't make our fundraising goal and we blew the money we did raise throwing an unauthorized block party in Pawtucket. Years later

It might be worth noting you were drunk and slurring when you told me this.

we tried for a reunion show to protest the Iraq War but couldn't pull it together because the lead guitarist was lost to Rush Limbaugh talk radio. Should I keep going? There were so many more bands. Carrot Sauce's classified ad wanted a rhythm guitarist who listened to Public Image Limited, Public Enemy, General Public, and Linda Ronstadt. Their music didn't sound like any of those bands/artists, and I lasted thirteen days (my shortest stint). Cross Your Legs aimed to be an obnoxious swagger mix of Dead Kennedys and L7, but our Canadian lead signer apologized for her lyrics after each song. House Hill was full goth and required I dress entirely in black. Each song title was named after famous doomed women in literature. During my last show with them, my guitar was turned down so low in the mix (and the synths were tooth-disintegratingly loud), I pretended to play. Institutional Pasta featured mathy noise rock with science-fiction lyrics delivered either in inflectionless monotone or Gregorian-chant style. They fired me because I wasn't a good enough guitar player, which, I'm afraid, was true. Oh, and how could I leave out Rat Moat? An alternative/indie band, think Sleater-Kinney meets Pavement meets the slacker mope of Dinosaur Jr. Again, not my bag musically, but we were probably the most semi-professional-sounding of the lot. I got kicked out for breaking the band's single rule: no hooking up with your own bandmates. It literally takes two to tango in that scenario, but I was the only one dismissed from the band, and yes, I'm still salty about it."

"If music be the food of love, play on. I believe that's either William Shakespeare or Fred Durst. Regardless, let's pivot or pirouette from music to romance. I am not above prurience, kissing and telling. Art Barbara, lay your love life lore on me."

You think you're so funny.

I'm less upset at my vampirism than this libelous portrayal of my dialogue.

"Christ, really? I don't know if I'm drunk enough. Nah, I probably am. Well, despite my leather jacket and Punk Art moniker, I was still awkward, self-conscious, and devoid of confidence in the romance regard, and lacking the courage to put myself out there, too, it must be said. Isn't it exhausting how often courage is required of us? My first kiss happened when I was twenty years old in the fall of junior year. I asked Nancy (tall and preppy) out on a date after we'd both flirted with each other at a couple of parties. We went to a Tex-Mex place on Thayer Street, and after we browsed Tom's Tracks, where I prattled on too much about Bob Mould's two solo records and first Sugar album. Upon returning to campus, we made out in a dorm stairwell. I remember being relieved that I'd finally kissed someone, but also being underwhelmed, partially because Nancy used a lot of teeth while kissing. She wasn't quite biting my lips or tongue, but she wasn't not biting them either. Too much information? Just you wait. About a month or so before the end of my last year at college, I hooked up with Lucy, who I had been friends with since the start of sophomore year. Lucy was the smartest person I knew, self-effacing, at times charmingly goofy, indefatigable, and the last person to leave the party or bar, and she didn't take shit from anyone, although as the "rock director" of our radio station, she let me get away with my show shenanigans. Her at five-two and me at six-four made us a striking pair. One well-meaning (I think) friend once asked if Lucy, because of the height difference, had to extend her arm over her head when we held hands. Of course, Lucy insisted we walk into Mondo (on-campus café open late-night) that way. She was the first and so-far last person I've said "I love you" to. I said it while explaining why I wasn't coming back to school for senior year. She said "I love you" back to me, both of us crying. We talked about getting an apartment on our own, but that was never really an option, as I had no money (I was crashing on Phil's and Carlos's couch, remember?) and Lucy had already signed on to live in the on-campus apartments. We saw each other over the summer but only when she could make the drive down to Providence from the south shore of Massachusetts, as I had no car. When her academic year started, we were both busy during the times when the other was not, so we saw each other less and less. We didn't fight, and we always had a great time, but it got to a point where being together was a reminder that we'd be apart again and permanently soon enough. Entropy again. She moved to LA after

You mean you're not going to describe her as not-plain and go on for a full page about her plain not-plainness?

graduation and last I heard she was a producer at KROQ. I try not to dwell on what might've been if I went back to school and continued my relationship with Lucy because it bums me out too much. I think it was Emmanuel Kant who said "Happiness is not an ideal of reason, but of imagination." Not sure it applies here. In the years since there have been other relationships, none lasting very long, given the frequency with which people joined and dropped out of the local music and club scene, which, for better or worse, I've been wedded to. I've dated or fooled around with a few bandmates. Jacquie (the lead singer of Cross Your Legs) and I dated during my brief tenure with the band. Things were cool until (goddamn, this is embarrassing, and I can't believe I'm telling you this, but here we are) she came over to my place one afternoon before an evening rehearsal. We were making out on the couch, and she slid her hand inside my shirt and teased and pinched my left nipple, only it wasn't my nipple. My teen-acne had migrated from my face to my back, shoulders, and chest, and I had a large, hard nodule adjacent to my nipple. As she tortured the angry red button (it hurt like fuck), I tried subtly shifting my torso to guide her hand elsewhere, but she was latched on. I was too mortified to take her hand away and breathily say, 'That's not my nipple, try the other one, you'll be pleasantly surprised,' so I pretended to enjoy her ministrations, and that spurred on her enthusiasm until at some point in that yawning stretch of time, she realized what she'd been working over wasn't my nipple. At that point we were both committed to the farce, committed to not embarrassing each other, or maybe it was a bizarre emotional war of attrition, to see who would give in to reality first. We finally finished with quick sex on the couch (with my shirt on), and we drove to rehearsal in silence, like there was a giant zit blemishing the space between us. I quit the band the next morning. Now I'm getting depressed." I stood up and limped around the couch. "Don't mind me, I need to stretch my back out a little. Too much sitting. What time is it anyway?"

"We're almost done, Mr. Barbara. Shall we finish with an accounting of health, as I am concerned about your heart in more than one way?"

"My lower back hurts if I stand too long or sit too long or lay down for too long, so, yeah, it pretty much hurts all the time. Some of that is my fault. I could be taking better care of my back with the stretching and exercises I don't do nearly as frequently as I should. I try not to rely too much on pain and self-medications, but, again, yeah, I should try more frequently than I do. As far as my heart goes, I've been keeping a medical eye on it; well, I was when I had a job with medical insurance, but I haven't had one of those since 2004. I'm overdue for an echocardiogram to make sure my aorta hasn't started hulking out. I'm sure it's fine. It's all fine. I had a scare in 2000 with heart palpitations. One thumping-loud beat, higher up in my chest, as startling as a gunshot, marked the beginning of the event, and the follow-up beat was off-rhythm, quivery, and lower, weaker, like my heart splat-landed on some inner floor. It was such a terrible, powerless sensation, to feel your heart flip-flopping, to be reliant upon this ugly little muscle over which you have no control, to become suddenly and intimately aware of your body as a floundering flesh machine. Whenever palpitations happened, I would both lose my breath and attempt to stop the palpitations and reboot my glitching self by breathing deeply, and if I didn't get lightheaded, I worried that I was, and if my chest felt tight it was likely because of my I-am-going-to-die panic. I had a normal EKG at the hospital, but they sent me home with a monitor that recorded my heartbeats for forty-eight hours. All the tests reported normal electrical activity, function, and measurements, and so they determined the palpitations were benign or a part of my physiology, the latter of which was a bullshit medical phrase for 'eh, we don't know.' The doctor suggested I stop or at least cut down on the caffeine. My former bandmates from Clean would've gleefully said, 'Told you so.' But wait, there's more! In the mid-'90s, roommates and partners complained about my snoring and what they described as terrible gasping noises, like I was drowning on my tongue. They'd ask if I was having nightmares, but I didn't remember having any. Granted, my sleep schedule wasn't all that consistent, given the odd jobs and gigs and late nights, but for two full years I was perpetually exhausted to the point where I was nodding off at bars and restaurants and, more dangerously, when I was behind the wheel of a car. My sleep deteriorated to the point where the sound of my awful gasping breaths woke me up at night, or more terrifyingly, I'd wake while I wasn't breathing and with a boulder on my chest and my airway was a closed fist and I wouldn't be able to breathe until I sat up. After an overnight sleep study, I was diagnosed with sleep apnea: a sleep disorder in which the sleeper's breathing is too shallow or paused. Paused sounds like a polite way to describe not breathing, doesn't it? I tried sleeping with a CPAP (continuous positive airway pressure; I appreciate they worked the word "positive" in there) mask and machine for a few months, and while I wasn't waking as frequently, I remained fatigued, and in follow-up sleep studies my blood oxygen levels dropped too low at night. I didn't fit within the typical age and/or physical demographic of sleep apnea sufferers and the doctors determined that I was, essentially, born with an airway that was too narrow or too small; more genetic fun related to my Marfan's-like connective-tissue disorder. The apnea solution was to literally widen my airway with a tonsillectomy and uvulopalatopharyngoplasty (removal of the uvula and other soft tissue), and they fixed my deviated septum for good measure, like I had a buy-two-procedures-get-one-free coupon. The recovery wasn't pleasant and included an emergency return trip to the hospital when my nose fauceted blood. In the weeks after the surgery, I had to relearn how to drink. If I swallowed too quickly, the liquid would end up shooting out my nose, which happened my first night back at a bar, and let's just say I wasn't very popular for the rest of the evening. My quality of sleep improved, but it wasn't perfect. I don't know how not-perfect, as I haven't been back for a sleep study since the surgery in 1998. If I lay on my back, I sometimes get the not-breathing gasps, so I sleep exclusively on my side. But hey, I'm still among the living and I can't even make fake snoring sounds without my uvula buddy. You're giving me a look. You don't believe me, do you? Really, I have no punching bag at the back of my throat. Want to see?"

"Don't ever show that to me again. Fucking gross, dude."

Earlier, I wrote that what had happened with the Pallbearers Club, Mercy, and everything else in 1988–1989 felt like fiction. While it was a true sentiment when I first stepped into Mercy's basement, it's not true at this point in the writing ~~journey~~ of this ~~memoir~~. That *No. Just no. So not punk.* was the year in which I was most myself, as unpleasant an experience *novel* it often was. Maybe it's more accurate to say that year forged me, or that year was me. If you were to cut me open and climb inside (it's a snug fit) you'd be climbing into that year. Bring your own acid-washed jean jacket. It's the nearly twenty years between basement summit meetings with Mercy I summed up in about ten pages that feels like the fiction, the something that happened to someone else, embellished and diminished by time and by the storyteller. I don't tell you this to explain my behavior. How could anyone truly or fully explain anyone's behavior anyway? I don't tell you this to excuse anything. I tell you this because it's the truth now.

Mercy offered to sleep on the couch and let me have her bed because of my bad back. I refused, bragging I was a couch-surfing champion. She didn't offer twice and joked she'd leave a nightlight on for me, which ended up being the cataracted ceiling lamp in the bathroom. After leaving the bathroom door slightly ajar, she went to bed and shrouded her curtain closed.

I tried sleeping on my left side, which wasn't my usual side, but it was the side I collapsed onto. I should've passed out the moment my head hit the throw pillow. Normally, my superpower was being able to sleep anywhere, anytime, and in any position. Despite my enervation (exacerbated by my inebriated state), the sandman didn't find me. I was hyperaware of the strange surroundings and circumstance; the low hum of the refrigerator was more of a hungry growl and Mercy's sleep breathing fell into a jarring, arrhythmic prog-rock five-eight time signature. The couch cushions sagged under my hip, pinching me into an uncomfortable consummate V. The small knit blanket was too scratchy for my arms, so I reallocated the woolen resource to my jeans-clad legs, but then my upper body was too cold. There was no "just right" for drunk Goldilocks. The sun had come up and turned the room into a faded sepia-and-regret-toned photograph. I got up and snagged my leather jacket to use as a blanket. Upon returning to the rocky socket of the couch, I snuggled, burrowed, and counted the number of sheep it took to knit that stupid blanket on my legs, and finally, I exhaled the I'm-serious-about-sleeping sigh. Then my eyes popped open and locked onto the floating dresser.

Yeah, the missing knob on the second drawer was an ugly pockmark to an otherwise handsome piece, but I couldn't stop eyeballing the empty shadow space between its legs and the floor. As I stared, the amount of space wavered, almost imperceptibly expanding and retracting, and when I blinked the illusion reset. I flipped over onto my other side, but I couldn't sleep with my face so close to couch's puffy seat back. Next, I relocated my head to the other end of the couch, which meant I was closer to the dresser, but I couldn't see it from that sharper angle. Not being able to see the dresser made me think about it more, and I suspected it had to be floating higher off the ground precisely because I wasn't looking at it. And at that point of madness within my involuntary vigil, I decided it was in fact floating and not moored to the wall as Mercy had insisted.

Had I been awake on the couch for an hour, maybe two? I had no idea. I didn't have a watch and there were no wall clocks and even the kitchenette microwave clock wasn't set. I lay there, beyond time and reason, not sleeping, though I must've blacked out at some point as I was suddenly back on the other side of the couch, lying on my left side, facing the dresser but with no memory of having rechanged positions. Maybe I'd dreamed about a relocation upon the couch's tableau. Regardless, I resumed my watch of the dresser and the willowing and winnowing space below its legs. The sound of my breathing became the dresser's breathing.

I'd had enough. I dripped off the couch and to the floor. Avoiding the coffee table, I crawled to the dresser. I slithered and slunk slowly, afraid to wake Mercy. I wanted to fully investigate and confront this, whatever this was, on my own. She was still asleep, as far as I could tell. Her curtain remained closed, and her breathing was deep and unbroken.

When I reached the dresser, I stuck my arm underneath, all the way to the wall, and swished my hand back and forth, disturbing dust bunnies. I grabbed the front legs, pulled down, and then I pushed up. The wheels rattled when I brushed against them, otherwise, there was no movement or give from the stubbornly airborne boudoir furniture.

I sat with my legs crossed and I engaged in another staring contest with the dresser, one in which I blinked first. I opened the bottom drawer. I was reverent and careful to not disturb the contents, which I did not inspect nor itemize. My lone goal while ~Yeah, right.~ in my liminal non-sleep state was to remove the drawers. The wood whispered over the interior rollers until there was a final click of the drawer lifting away, free from its track. I placed the drawer on the floor to the left of the dresser. I plucked out the second and third drawers as one might pick apples from a tree. As I dislodged the final/top drawer, nearing the completion of the partial dresser autopsy, I was no longer concerned about waking Mercy and I didn't bother crafting a just-in-case excuse as to what I was doing.

What was I doing? I needed to see if and where the dresser was or wasn't bolted and screwed into the wall.

It wasn't bright enough in the early-morning room to see much if any detail within the dresser's frame. I ran my hands inside, feeling for holes in the wood, raised screw heads, or even hastily hammered nails. Everything was smooth and immovable. I couldn't even find the screws and dowels holding the frame together, never mind any evidence of wall anchors. I scrabbled back to an end table and retrieved my key chain on which was a guitar-shaped mini flashlight. In its weak, ghostly beam, there was no visual evidence of the dresser having been fastened to the wall. I crouched and contorted, vining my head between wooden slats and into the space reserved for the third drawer. What was I missing? Should I have been afraid? Yes, I probably should've. But I was out-of-my-head angry, especially when I got stuck, my left arm and shoulder pinned, my face centimeters from a side wall. In my struggle to worm free I dropped my flashlight keychain, which cymbal-crashed to the floor and broke. My fingers scratched and scrabbled on the wood and my foul frantic breath reflected off the panel in front of me, and for a century I was unable to climb out of the frame, the wood groaning under my weight. Was the frame retracting, closing around me, squeezing my accordion chest? As I neared the moment when I would cry out unintelligibly for help (and yes, I was very much afraid then), the dresser spit me out.

Lame. And convenient.

If I didn't know any better, I would read this as foreshadowing a live burial.

Are you making a sparkly vampire joke? Now you have me as paranoid as you are.

"Rise, sleepyhead. Shining is optional." Mercy dangled two pizza boxes in my face as though they were smelling salts.

I woke on the floor at the foot of the dresser, lying on my right side, head on a couch pillow, the scratchy blanket spread out under me like an oil slick of sheep, leather jacket draped over my torso. Every muscle and joint in my body had rusted in place and ached as I raised the drawbridge of myself. My mouth tasted of sewage and my head was full of (Philip) glass. A Head Full of Philip Glass. Great band name.

The removed drawers weren't leaning-tower-of-Pisa stacked next to me. They were back in the dresser. I didn't remember replacing them. Did I put them back in the right spots? Was the missing-knob drawer supposed to be in the second or third slot? I wasn't going to admit to anything unless Mercy brought it up. I resisted the urge to nudge the dresser, to take out all the drawers again and look inside, and I instead Swamp Thinged to the kitchenette table.

"What time is it?" I asked.

"A little after five."

"Oops."

"How long were you on the floor?" Mercy poured two glasses of water so I couldn't see a smuggiest smirk on her face, but I heard it.

"I don't remember. The couch ended up being too saggy for my back."

"So, I have a saggy couch."

"No, it's fine. The hard floor was better for me, you know."

"Clearly you are refreshed, limber, and spry."

"Ha and ha. Ow." I twisted and turned, stretching out my lower back, my body creaking on the creaky chair. "Hey, the pizza is from Fellini's, yeah?"

Mercy said it was. Eager to start a conversation that didn't involve the late time of day, floating dressers, stacking drawers, or me being on the floor, I told her I had worked at Fellini's for three years, and that I still made a mean pizza.

"I know you worked there," she said.

"Oh. Did I tell you that last night?"

"No. I walked by once and saw you inside. Red apron, covered in flour, obnoxiously tossing the dough in the air."

"That's not obnoxious."

"It kind of is. Showing off your pizza dexterity."

"Spinning is a totally necessary step in the process."

"Spinning. You're still obnoxious about it."

"Why didn't you come in and say hi? I would've spun you the greatest pizza ever spun."

"You looked busy, the place was jammed, and I was late to where I was going."

"And where was that?"

"I don't remember."

"You don't remember."

"Yeah, do you remember every appointment or errand you had ten years ago?"

"No but—"

"Easy with the third degree then. Enjoy your pizza. I ordered it un-spun."

Our jokey quid pro quo was tonally the same as it was in ye olde days, but it felt different. With the stakes raised, in part due to our adult status and shared, admittedly bizarre history, there was an edge to our sangfroid. More than the one-upmanship, more than spelunking the verbal barbs for real and perceived slights, we waged an unconscious battle to reframe everything that had been done and said all those years before. Maybe that was worth fighting over. One who controls the past controls the present and future. I wanted to ask Mercy more about that night she saw me, but I didn't want to come off as needy, as desirous for her presence within my life. Still. Why didn't she stop by the restaurant some other night? When she walked by was it winter or summer, a weekday or weekend? There was one question that seemed improbable, but I couldn't shake it: Did she walk by on the last night I worked there, the same night I dropped two pizzas and burnt my forearm?

Orwell's 1984. Or a Rage Against the Machine lyric.

Heedless as to whether my hangover stomach would reject the pizza, I inhaled the first slice in all its thin-crusted glory. Emboldened by my second slice, I told Mercy about the night I met Bob Mould of Hüsker Dü. Me and two coworkers from Fellini's hung out by the stage after one of Bob's solo acoustic shows at Lupo's. Eventually he emerged from backstage to chat with us stragglers. Bob was patient and gracious, answering our annoying questions, laughing at jokes that probably weren't funny, and he even put up with autograph requests. The only piece of paper I had on me was my Social Security card. (Yes, in the pre-Internet/identify-theft days, we carried those around in our wallets or purses.) I'd find out later that Bob didn't do autographs and he didn't really autograph this time either. He scribbled a bunch of loops, an infinite string of m's, over my name and government-issued number. I was inordinately pleased, and still am. I mean, how many people have their Social Security card sort of signed by Bob Mould? With the scribbles scribbled, the socially accepted cue had arrived for us to leave him be, but my friend Jim pressed on and invited Bob back to Fellini's, talking it up as the best pizza in Providence. Jim had a say-anything-to-anyone-at-any-time part of his personality, like my father, and it was part of his charm, and yet it made me unfailingly cringe with embarrassment, which was, and is, I fully admit, an ongoing *me* problem. That night though, Jim worked it. I quit mantraing *Stop bugging him, time to go* in my head when Jim seemed to have pushed Bob to the precipice of coming out with us for pizza. Bob even asked where the restaurant was, and he said he knew Wickenden Street well. But he ultimately declined, rightly thinking better of hanging out with us drunken puppy dogs.

"Ah, too bad," Mercy said. "Did you tell him you dumped the poor Scorpions for his band when you were seventeen?"

"Yeah, I told him he should cover 'Rock You Like a Hurricane.'"

"You didn't. But I wish you did. Did you tell him he was the reason why you picked up a guitar?"

"No. And I would never."

"Same old Art. Don't get mad, it's endearing. I mean it. Warms my shriveled heart that you still are who you were. So afraid of the possibility of awkwardness, you hoard it all for yourself."

I was mad and I ate my pizza madly. (It occurs to me now that I've never been more myself than when I was with Mercy. That wasn't a good thing.)

"You're angry," she said. "I can tell by how you're chewing. I'm sorry, I'm being a jerk. But how come you would never tell Bob he was why you started playing music? I'm legitimately curious."

"I didn't want to make our brief conversation about me. And what is he supposed to say to something like that anyway?"

"I'm sure he would've been honored. People like hearing they touched or changed someone's life in some small way."

"Yeah, I guess. I wanted to hang out with him and not be the fanboy."

"Not be the fanboy with an autographed Social Security card."

"Besides, he wasn't *the* reason why I picked up a guitar. Don't get me wrong, he's a huge influence and I emulate his style and sound, the ring of those suspended chords, the emotional high I get from his songs. But there's no singular reason why I play music," I said, which was kind of a lie, and then stammered through the rest. "There's a part of me that plays because it drowns out the noise in my head, or I get to be outside of myself, if that makes any sense. Part of me plays out of spite, to show Eddie Patrick and all the other fuckheads I hated growing up that I can do this thing I'm so passionate about. I know that sounds miserable, because it kind of is, but there's joy in there too. Somewhere. The joy is harder, maybe impossible, to describe, which is probably how it should be. But when the amp is cranked and the roar is a physical thing vibrating my chest in harmony with some inner frequency unique to that moment, I'm suddenly bigger than I am, or even better, I'm as small as an oxygen molecule, letting the waves power through me. Fuck, I don't know. What I'm trying to say is the *why* of anything related to music or art or whatever is always more complicated than a . . . a singular inspiration."

Less inspiring was the greasy bolus of pizza in my stomach that would shortly send me to the bathroom. Even less inspiring, the trilling heart palpitations I had during my spiel. Nothing out of my ordinary, especially when dehydrated, so I wasn't too alarmed. Yet.

I'm glad I stopped spieling there before blurting out that I picked up a guitar because of Mercy. I wouldn't have found the soundtrack to my life without her, and yeah, of course, my love of that music was part of the why I wanted to try making it.

Howeverforever . . .

I played guitar to show Mercy at least I tried, and I continued trying even after I failed (and I would fail some more). I played guitar to show Mercy I wasn't always afraid.

Mercy didn't ask if I wanted to go back to my apartment or be anywhere else. And I didn't tell her that I needed to go home. After eating and cleaning up, we relocated to the couch. I downed a couple of glasses of water and the heart palpitations (mostly) went away. Still, I wasn't feeling well, and it was worse than the usual hangover headache and drag-ass blahs. Her studio apartment was nice, but it was still the basement of a brownstone more than one hundred years old, and the stale, musty, fruited-with-mildew air smogged in my sinuses and tightening chest. Plus eating all that dairy made me phlegmy and congested if you must know. More plus, the double whammy of my barking lower back and a painfully stiff neck with a range of motion approaching zero. My solution was to swallow ibuprofen and switch from water to whiskey.

We sort of watched horror-movie DVDs. To keep from nodding off I tried to get Mercy to give me her story, to share what she'd been up to. She deflected with "Nothing as exciting as being a rock star."

I held up devil-horns hands that had the shakes. Then I asked a long and thoughtful question about her photography, about her pursuing her passion. I got a one-word answer.

Right. You gotta keep me mysterious.

"Hobby," she said.

"How about the camera you used last night. Is it the same Polaroid?"

"Same? Do you mean make, model, type—"

"I mean are you using the same camera you used when I met you?"

"Yes to both. I've kept that camera in working condition. The thing is a pain in the ass to find film cartridges for and they're expensive as fuck, so I only shoot with it on special occasions. Like last night. If you want the photo, by the way, the price remains five bucks. Nonnegotiable."

"Did you take any action shots of the show?"

"Nope. Five bucks."

Because I couldn't move my slept-on-it-wrong neck, I pivot-turned my entire calcified body so I could look directly at Mercy.

She said, "You move like a rusted weathervane."

"The wind is blowing north."

"You stubborn jerk, you should've taken the bed and let me sleep on the couch like I offered."

"Probably. Okay, where's the photo?"

"Five bucks first."

"Don't know if I want a picture of myself that badly."

"You'll want this one."

"Why? You got my good side? I don't have one of those."

"You'll see."

"Is there...ahem...*proof* in my photo? Were you looking for *proof*? Ghostly"—at this I waggled my fingers, which, somehow, were sore too; maybe I'd slept on them wrong as well—"<u>green</u>-blobbed proof?" I laughed as though I truly believed I'd said something ridiculous.

BLUE-
BLOBBED,
YOU
MONSTER!

"I'm always looking for proof, Art," she said. "And I'm looking for five bucks."

I fished out a crumpled twenty from my jeans, the only bill I had, and tossed it to her. "Keep the change for the pizza and whiskey," I said.

Mercy pommel-horsed off the couch but stumbled in her landing. Maybe she was as buzzed as I was. She walked to the coat rack by the front door. This I inferred by sound, as I couldn't swivel my head to watch her. She returned with her canvas bag, which she placed on the coffee table after clearing glasses and a bottle of brown liquid for a landing spot. She made change for my twenty and when I refused to accept it, she threw the money onto my lap. Next, she pulled out the photo, held it up, pinched between forefinger and thumb.

She said, "Part of the transaction requires that you cannot look at it until tomorrow morning. Deal?"

"Do you always have to fuck with me?"

"Yes. It's fun. And the rules are the rules." She extended the photo toward me, but I didn't reach for it. "Don't be a cranky weathervane."

"Who makes the rules?"

"I wish I knew."

I accepted defeat and the condition of ownership. She returned to the coat rack, saying she didn't trust me to not look at it right now, and slipped the picture inside an interior lapel pocket of my leather jacket.

She said, "If I catch you fishing around in there later tonight, I'll remove your spleen and put it in the same jar with your uvula, which I keep in my dresser. Did you find that last night, by the way?"

As she victory-marched back to the couch, the skin on my face and neck and everywhere else flashed red and I attempted to melt between the cushions. Instead of stammering an awkward apology for taking apart her dresser or an equally cringe joke of acknowledgment, I summoned the courage to return us to the basement of my house on Echo Ave with a pointed question.

"Do you remember the last photo you shot of me?" I asked. "Not counting the one you put in my jacket, obviously."

I expected obfuscation and denial. Mercy was direct. "Oh yeah. You were home recovering from surgery, or your first surgery, and I'd snuck into your basement. Man, that was a scary-ass basement." She sat on the couch and continued. "I was, like, halfway up the stairs and trying to talk you into letting me in the house. You were still mad at me, I guess, which was probably fair, and I was still mad at you." She spoke carefully, as though the wrong word or phrase might virus out and infect everything, turn this new basement into my old one. She wasn't lying, but she was leaving stuff out. The most important stuff. "Then you opened the door, and I snapped a picture. You slammed the door shut and I couldn't see and almost bought it going down the stairs. I knew it was wrong that I snuck in there like that, but I thought you'd appreciate the effort. I know that sounds so dumb now. Then I got extra pissed you shut the door in my face and left me in the dark, so I stole a box of Corn Pops off your shelves down there. I think it was Corn Pops. I felt bad about that after."

All I said was "Oh yeah?"

"I knew how you loved your sugary bullshit cereal."

"If you'd taken Honeycomb, I never would've forgiven you."

Mercy said, "My turn to ask the true confessional question. What the hell were you doing creeping on me in my sleep and with my camera the night I crashed at your house? That was fucked-up, Art."

Now I'm a doting elder relative? I'd rather be a vampire.

She sounded sincerely upset and angry, and it was so unexpected and out of character, like your favorite <u>doting elder relative</u> suddenly yelling at you. It threw me for an infinite loop, and I couldn't decide if I should beg for forgiveness or feign innocence, even though I was innocent and there was nothing to feign. Was there? Was I sure of that? (At that moment, I wasn't sure.)

I tried to mimic her matter-of-factness. Instead, I rambled and circumspected. I bent the truth as I (or we) knew it, and I didn't realize it then, but I did so for my own mental self-preservation. An edited gist: "I didn't mean harm with the photo. I didn't mean anything by it. I'd woken up because I couldn't breathe, and it felt like something was sitting on my chest. It was like how my sleep apnea felt years later. Then I went down to the kitchen for some water and thought I'd look in on you. You were on the couch with your jacket over you. Trick of the light, or dark, I guess, but you looked older, too, like, way older. And in the dark your jacket looked like something sitting on your chest. Like in the Mercy Brown story you told me for the history paper, with her sister perched on her chest stealing her breath. When I saw it, or thought I saw it, all I could think to do was to take a picture, for proof right? Stupid, I know, but it didn't feel stupid then. And I ran away when you woke up. Sorry for running."

When I finished Mercy stared at me, blinking intermittently. A camera shutter closing and closing.

I blurted out a statement-question and shrugged with my who-me? palms held up. "Glad we could get all that off our chests?"

We fell into a tears-streaming-can't-breathe laughing fit. After eventually composing ourselves, we shared friendship platitudes. We agreed how stupid and melodramatic we were about the sleepover night and her basement break-in, and we offered generalized apologies, ultimately as meaningless as a handshake greeting because <u>we weren't willing to say what it was exactly we were sorry about</u>—and still, what exactly was I sorry for? Our glasses raised to a retroactive détente.

We played a drinking game through the second horror movie, some shitty slasher. We had to drink whenever there was a fake-out

????? Was I supposed to say sorry for the freaky vampirism?

scare before a kill (drinking for the kill was optional) or a line of dialogue that we both agreed was ludicrous. We were both ludicrous by the time the movie ended.

As Mercy swapped out DVDs she said she had the best idea ever. The next movie in her queue she pulled from a previously unopened, red Netflix rental envelope. It was the '80s campy vampire classic *Fright Night*.

I said, "This is your best idea?"

"Mood setting for my best idea."

"Ever?"

"Ever."

I grumble-protested that if I was still conscious by the end of the movie, the scene where the girlfriend turns into a vampire and reveals gaping great-white-shark jaws and teeth would give me nightmares.

Mercy grabbed me by the shoulders, shook me, and shouted, "Exactly my point!"   *I'm a fun drunk who just wants to help.*

"I'm still waiting for the point."

"Okay, listen. Your band was good and you're really good, Art. You are. I mean that. I'm impressed. You have talent and you clearly worked hard too. I've seen you play with some of your other bands too—"

"What. You did? When?"

"Okay, I saw a lot of your bands, most of them, I think, but forget I said that." She waved her arms, erasing my further attempts at interruption. "Don't think about that part now. Détente, remember?" Mercy raised her glass and took a sip. "Hey, Art, focus, okay? I know you, and you'll hear and get stuck on the worst possible implications of my idea, so I want to be clear. As clear as . . ." She trailed off.

"Crystal," I said.

"No. As clear as, um, invisible wallpaper. Wait, wasn't that the name of one your bands?" She knee-slapped at her own joke. "Sorry. I'm serious. Okay, know going into this best idea that I am not suggesting you give up music. Don't give up playing or making music. That. Is. Not. What. I. Am. Say. Ing…"

"Okay, Christ, just get to it. I wanna drink and watch the movie from between my fingers."

"Listen. My best idea ever. Are you listening? If the playing-in-bands thing doesn't work out the way you want it to, try another creative outlet. Like—and here it comes—writing a vampire novel." She pointed at the screen as the teen watched his neighbor (Chris Sarandon) go all fangy on a woman, and then she pointed at us. "Boom. It's perfect. You could use and embellish what you thought you saw on the sleepover night and weave it in with the Mercy Brown lore I told you. It practically writes itself, man! But look at you. You're not feeling it. I can tell." (I pretended to have passed out, mouth open and drooling.) "All right, fine. I don't think it would be as good, wouldn't speak as much to who *you* are as an artist—"

I came out of my fake blackout and said, "I prefer Art-iste."

"But you could always go in a more commercial direction. Nothing wrong with making money, especially when you don't have much. I'm no publishing expert but think about what's selling now, right? Sparkly vampires and postapocalyptic young adult fiction. So put two and two together, write a trilogy of postapocalyptic vampire books. Boom again. How hard could it be?"

"Christ, you do think my music sucks. Which, fine, probably, but does my music suck that badly?"

"Aha! I knew you'd take my idea that way. I fucking knew it. Didn't I tell you?" She buried her face in a throw pillow and yelled.

I said, "Let me pretend to take your idea seriously for a nanosecond. A vampire novel, really?"

"Are you too cool for vampires? Don't be such a hipster snob. That isn't very punk of you, Art. The first punks, the original ones—and I know I'm being a hipster snob about punk, but shut up—were all about trashy or low culture and used it to sell records. It's okay to like things, Art. Haven't you figured that out yet?"

There's no way I said that. Even if I thought it.

"Hey, relax. I'm clearly not too cool for anything. What makes you think I can write a book? Or write anything anyone would want to read?" Self-pity aside, I was already considering her idea.

"Trying something new creatively could only help recharge your music batteries. Frankly, listening between your lines, you sound worn down, fed up, and cynical about the music scene and your place in it. I want you to be ... fulfilled, Art. Not happy. No one knows what being happy means. I don't know, don't listen to me. I'm kinda drunk."

I didn't argue with her. She was drunk. And yeah, her between-the-lines reading of my disillusionment and disappointment was spot-on. I wasn't going anywhere with music, and worse, I didn't know where I wanted to go with it anymore. My bands weren't making the music I wanted to make. I was going through the motions, like a programmed drum-machine version of a plug-in guitar player. I said, "Maybe I could write a Gen-X memoir about my time in shitty bands."

"That would be cool, but I'm thinking it'd be a tough sell. Readers want plots, plucky do-good characters and inspiring arcs, and tidy, happy endings. They probably don't want to read the music unsuccess story. No offense. Not even if it has vampires. Sorry, I'm bumming you out with this, aren't I. Forget I said any of it."

"When someone says 'forget I said that,' it usually guarantees the opposite."

"See? That's some keen, observational wisdom right there. Thinking like a novelist already."

Was she being serious or was it more fucking with me?

[Now? Now, I'm convinced she was seed planting. Was it an act of braggadocio or ego? Did she want me to write the book because she'd be the star of it? That's part of it, maybe even a big part of it. I keep going back to her obsessive search for photographic "proof," and I keep going back to the sleepover night in 1989, after the graveyard fiasco and before we got to my house, when we drove around and she went on an epic rant about not knowing the why of the vampire. I think she wanted me to write the book because maybe I could somehow stumble upon answers to some of those whys for her. If nothing else,

Dude, I can't even. You're blaming me for this book too? Yes, I made a friendly, what-if suggestion, but it was obviously the throw-away kind.

the act of writing this book would be, for her, a permanent engraved invitation into my life. As aloof and above-it-all as she was (is), Mercy has always been cosmically alone, and she wanted me to be cosmically alone with her.]

I said, "So, what other bands of mine did you see?"

"Shh." She pointed at the TV. "Vampire movie. Maybe you should take notes. Want me to get you a pen?"

On screen Evil Ed cackled at poor Charlie and said, "Oh, you're so cool, Brewster!"

I won't detail the dreams I had that night. No one cares about dreams.

But I'll say this: the dreams were wonderful, and they were terrible, and the terrible parts were what was wonderful, and the wonderful parts were the terror.

I woke in the dark, on my back, openmouthed and gasping. My lungs were bellows, squeezed clean of air underneath a grinding, spurred heel. Pinned flat, I couldn't move. My sputtering heart was an experimental poem. I thought I was dying, that my aorta had burst and my heart hissed gouts of steam and blood. There was a part of me that didn't want to fight, wanted to remain lying down, and was willing to be washed away like a fallen branch in a raging river.

I rolled onto my side without falling off the couch. The thing on my chest was cold and smooth, and as I pushed it to the floor my hands reacted as though it were made of spiderwebs.

I could breathe again, but my heart was still a crazed moth bashing itself into a ceiling light. I sat up, avoiding placing my feet on whatever it was that had been on my chest. I took deep, slow breaths, attempting to reboot instead of totally freaking out.

Scooting to the other end of the couch, I lunged for the end-table lamp, and as I did so, my legs flippered out behind me, kicking the coffee table and toppling it over. The table landed with a heavy thunk, followed by a raindrop patter of tabletop debris. I gathered my feet under me and turned on the lamp. The light barely cut through the murk of the room, but for my light-starved eyes, it was enough to see what I'd brushed off my chest to the floor. Sagging between the couch and prone coffee table was my leather jacket.

My forehead and temples throbbed. My brain had had enough and wanted to break free from its skull prison. My heart resumed keeping proper time, but there was a hot stitch in the left side of my chest. My lower back was weak and loose on its track. The wrong move might send it off the rails.

Shivering even though it was a warm, humid night, I gathered my coat and put it on. I decided it was time to leave, even if it meant walking to my car or directly home despite my legion of physical ailments. After warily eyeing Mercy's shrouded bed on the other side of the room, I reset the coffee table upright. In the table's skeletal shadow, Mercy's canvas bag had toppled and spilled its contents, including her Polaroid camera. I crept and crouched, and like a reverse burglar put the loose change and wallet and everything else back inside and then on the table. Fearing the fall might've broken her camera, I inspected it for cracks and chipped plastic. I briefly entertained taking a dead-of-night, goofy-faced selfie as a functionality test, but the whirring camera would surely wake Mercy. I was not prepared to reenact that scene.

Because you needed what was inside the bottle in your coat pocket.

How about a regular burglar?

As I bent to return the camera to the canvas bag, there was a noise from the corner of the room, near the floating dresser. A click, or a tap, though the descriptor as a singular event wasn't accurate. What I heard was fuller than a solitary note and more like a chorus of synchronized and harmonized occurrences.

I waited for a repeat or an encore and there was only the after-midnight sounds of Mercy's breathing and the hum of the refrigerator. I stood motionless and I listened, and I stared at the dresser. Something was off. Was the drawer with the missing knob in a different slot again? Now it was third from the top, or one above the bottom drawer. My eyes traced the dresser frame down to where the legs and rollers met the hardwood, and I could not identify what was amiss. But everything was amiss, and my heart again stumbled around my chest like a drunk.

The floating dresser was no longer floating. The rusted rollers were flush against the floor.

The pain in my chest hardened into a stone. How had an expected sight (a dresser with legs in contact with the floor) become so deeply upsetting? Did the wall anchors give way, a result of my previous night's autopsy? After all, I had put most of my weight on the frame at times, particularly when my head and shoulders were stuck inside. Did the dresser somehow delay its acquiescence to gravity, and do so that quietly and peacefully? I assumed what I'd heard moments earlier was the floating dresser's equivalent of a tiptoe landing to the hardwood. The distance above the floor had not been substantial, but given the weight of the piece, the landing should've been more jarring and symphonic, not the subtle-as-a-whisper clacking I'd heard. Where was the cracking and tearing of the anchor screws rending from the drywall? Maybe an industrial-strength adhesive was used instead, resulting in the dresser sliding down the wall, but that didn't seem likely. Perhaps the simplest explanation was the dresser hadn't been attached to the wall, had never floated, was never floating. Marooned in the quasi-dark of a one-lit-bulb basement apartment, my shivers werewolfing into full-body tremors, I questioned the events of the previous evening, wondering if they'd happened, if it had all been part of an elaborate dream, or a dream within a dream, and I had now finally awoken in the middle of my first and only night at Mercy's apartment.

I can now say with some authority that a consequence of experiencing the inexplicable is that it recontextualizes everything that has happened and continues to happen. The entirety of your history is as irreal and inescapable as that impossible moment when the uncanny trod upon your life. Later, in the yawning, chasmic aftermath, the banality of the impossible no longer being possible becomes intolerable by comparison. Perhaps that is the truth of all things, as untenable as that is.

Dude. Lighten up. It's a funky dresser.

Angling my head (which, despite the shock[s], hadn't cleared and filled with the static of dread, of the fear of the near future, as if there were any other type of fear) I looked and pleaded for space between the dresser's legs and the floor, and I did not find any. I uprooted and slowly backed away. The camera rattled in my shaking hands, and I waited for the other shoe, as they say, to drop. I didn't have to wait long.

The dresser rose off the floor and hovered in its elevated position. To be clear, it wasn't resting on the floor and then in a blink back where it had hung previously. I watched it lift and traverse a vertical distance. One of the rusted rollers swiveled and turned in lazy airborne circles. Autonomically shuffling backward, my right leg clipped the couch. I stumbled but didn't fall. After a breathless pause, perhaps impatient with my clumsy interruption, the dresser continued its ascent.

Then the coffee table drifted off the floor, taking Mercy's bag as a passenger. To my right, the lamp and the end table knocked into my elbow as it too clambered toward the ceiling. I turned my back on the levitating scene. If I refused to watch, then it wasn't happening. I didn't want to see any more. I couldn't see any more because I was full. There was no more room in my head for madness.

The quality and focus of the light changed as the lamp continued rising behind me. Spotlighted, miles away, was the apartment's door. I would leave. I had to leave. The first step was always the slowest, the most unsure, the most vulnerable, and the stone in my chest splashed into the bottom of a well as I knew something was now behind me. Something with big eyes to see me. More than the sensation of being watched; it was the feeling of being sized-up for predation, a feeling centered not in your brain but rattling within the brittle bones at the base of your exposed neck. I would not turn, and I would not confront. I would run.

My first step didn't land. I lifted off the floor as though there were strings that began inside my toes and the tips of my fingers, and those strands ran up the length of my body, weaving into a thin rope at the crown of my head, and it poked through like the wick of a candle that had been pinched and yanked upward. I moaned a prey animal's elegy and lament that not only was I powerless to save myself, but the final horror and indignity to be suffered through apparently required so little effort to perpetrate.

Behind me, the lamp was at a higher and still increasing elevation. With my right foot stretching, begging for the floor, the lamp lighthoused a beam at Mercy's bed. As though on cue, her curtains parted, the plastic rings from which the purple cloth hung screeched across the bowed rods, and the cloth billowed, fingering into the room, reaching toward me.

There was a pop of the lightbulb mashing into the ceiling and then utter darkness. I was tossed backward. I landed on my un-prepared feet, crumpled onto my right side, and spun and slid across the floor as everything else crash-landed around me. I couldn't see anything, so I wasn't sure of my orientation within the room. I reached out and around for the TV wall or any wall and felt the cold nothing. There was no ambient streetlight sneaking through the windows that should've been on the wall behind me or from the kitchenette wall to my right. For a crazed moment I thought I'd crashed through the basement floor into whatever cavern was beneath. Instinctually, I pressed myself lower to the floor, but I couldn't get lower. I tried not to, but I was breathing so loudly, broadcasting where I was and what state I was in. My shaking limbs rattled the debris I flotsamed against.

Something to my left moved, a soft footfall, then the rough scraping of a wooden drawer pushed aside. My echolocation was off, as the noises sounded both far away and inches from my ears. I said, "Leave me alone." Had those three words ever stopped anyone or anything in this miserable, malignant universe? Another dresser drawer, or perhaps the dresser itself, slammed into a wall. I rolled onto my knees with the camera clutched against my chest.

The camera. I could take a picture, use the flash to find a path to the front door. Click and flash and whir.

Instead of eidetically processing and memorizing the room's layout, my eyes were trained for Mercy, or for any figure or form moving on my left. As I stood there blinking away the flash after-images, did I hear a muzzled sigh of irritation? Fucking hell, I almost apologized for wasting her expensive film.

I didn't see enough to be able to sprint across the room to the front door without a guarantee of my crashing into something. I did recall the couch toppled upside down directly in front of me, but already my memory of the flashed room had gone memetic. Figures crouched in the corners and among the debris, their features blurred but for the malicious stares from greedy eyes.

I shuffled forward, not daring to lift my foot for fear I might lose gravity again. Fixing my view lower, toward the floor directly in front of me, I snapped another picture. Okay, there was a path. I could avoid the couch and smashed end table by moving about forty-five degrees to my right. As I sidestepped, the sounds behind me and to my left became quieter; little creaks and moans, small taps of wood against wood, delicately stirred broken glass. Imagining Mercy airily traversing over the rubble, I quickened my pace.

I thought I felt the room open in in front of me, but my left shin bashed into something solid, and I screamed, then somewhat absurdly said, "I'm not feeling well, so I'm going back to my place."

I took three more pictures, one after the other. In the first flash, my route forward was clear, and I was most of the way across the room, but the coat rack was swinging down in front of the door, like the arm of a tollbooth. It clattered to the floor before I pressed the button for the second photo. In that next flash, the coats, skins emptied of their former bodies, were pooled at the door, and on top, Mercy's green jacket, and it twitched. It moved. The flash lasted for a fucking millisecond or whatever, but it moved. It turned. Maybe it was better to remain in the dark and walk into whatever it was I was going to walk into. That's how we get through most of our days and nights, right? We fumble heedlessly forward into the unseen future, a future guaranteed to one day cut us down. I shot one more photo anyway. I was almost to the door but all I could focus on was her green jacket and the face. There was that face again, the same one from the sleepover, that face made of folds, buttons, and stitch lines, and it had a frozen, ambered look, and it blamed me, and it wanted something from me, and that naked, unvarnished, violent-but-honest want was the most familiar and most horrible face one could ever see.

I refused to see any more of it. So, I plowed forward to the lone exit, and I muttered, "I want to go home, I want to go home…"

You're not in Kansas, Dorothy.

Wading into the coats, I sank ankle deep into their clutching mud eager to drag me down, to sink me. I turned the doorknob and fumbled for the dead bolt. Something coiled around and between my legs and it squeezed and it climbed over my knees, and even though I couldn't see it, that face was pressed against my left thigh and my skin itched with its lips worming voiceless threats and promises. My spine curled despite its metal scaffolding. My heart faltered, a dropped bass drum tumbling down a flight of stairs, and a stabbing chest pain ran down the length of my left arm. I couldn't breathe, or I couldn't breathe enough, and purple ink blots Rorschached in my vision. I was ebbing away.

Mercy, then behind me, possibly, above me, said, "I can give you a lift."

I opened the door, and the hallway light misted inside the apartment. I muscled out of the coat bog and lurched over the spindly coat rack, stumbling into the hallway. The hallway tilted, like a listing submarine, but my sputtering engine carried me away. I didn't hear her door close behind me.

Once outside, my chest pains and tightness subsided and my posture straightened, and I ran without thought or direction. I didn't stop running until I collapsed onto the greenery of scenic Prospect Terrace on Congdon Street. I skulked past the monument to Roger Williams and stood at the waist-high fence, the boundary of a precipice. Spread out in the distance, downtown Providence glowed and slept, and it didn't care what happened to me. It never did.

I left the fence eventually and curled up on a wooden bench under the canopy of a billowy oak tree. I woke early the next morning, slicked with dew. I still had her camera. *Oops, right?*

I didn't know what to do with what had happened at Mercy's apartment. What would you have done?

Me? Thanks for asking.

I tried to be normal. Scratch that. I attempted to crawl out of the haunted bottomless ditch I'd fallen into and climb back onto the road to wherever it was I was headed before Mercy's fateful return. *Yuck. Fuck fate.*

Prospect Park was a few blocks from Victor's (from my band *Fate is the* Antigone, remember him?) swanky apartment, but waking him up *rationalization* and begging for a ride back to my car or my shitty place, especially *for rapacity* the morning after I'd missed a rehearsal (oops) would've made me *and evangelical* out to be more of a fuck-up than I already was. He was a bandmate, *privileged* not a friend. Besides, I needed the walk to clear my head. (What a *chosen, for a* misleading bromide that is. "Clear my head" makes it sound like your *hand holding* mind is simply cluttered and only needs you to pick up your clothes *a weapon.* off the floor, wash and put away the dishes, maybe move some boxes of stuff you don't use but can't bear to throw away down into the basement. The reality is more like a mental Whac-A-Mole game: with a handy mallet you smash down the thoughts that keep popping up that you don't want popping up, and you whack and smash and whack until you're exhausted or numb, and either way, you give up.)

When I made it back to my apartment, mind uncleared, I ignored the blinking answering machine and I ate two bowls of cereal and then slept a full twenty-four hours, missing a bartending shift at the Paragon and another band rehearsal.

Victor woke me the next day with a phone call. He asked where I'd been in that aloof, I-don't-really-care-about-the-answer kind of tone. I told him I'd been sick, too sick to answer the phone. He said I'd missed the last two rehearsals and he left audioless space for me to apologize. I didn't. He said I wasn't reliable. Me, the grinder, the respected Susan

Lucci of the Providence music scene, was no longer reliable because I'd missed two lousy rehearsals (okay, maybe I'd missed a few more). He said that I was no longer in the band. I said, "You're doing this over the phone?" It was clearly meant to be a rhetorical statement-question that judged his lack of empathy. He miffed a clove-cigarette laugh and said he'd meet with me to do this, but he didn't want to catch whatever *illness* it was I had. I said, "Fuck you," and I said many other things with "fuck" in them after he hung up.

Although I'd been let go from bands before (well, just about all of them, really) I was so angry I cried. Anger crying is the ugliest crying and the least rational. In that least-rational state, I decided I was done with bands and I was done with Providence and re-done with Mercy. It was less me fleeing than I needed a change, and I needed a place to hole up for a while, to tend to myself and maybe save a little money while doing so.

I didn't tell anyone in Providence I was moving until the night before I left. I threw myself a bar-crawl dirge with a small group of friends. By the time I pixied into Tortilla Flats to end the night, faithful Walter was my last friend standing and politely trying to convince me it was time for him to get a cab. He stepped outside to call and smoke, and I sat at the bar alone, finishing my cerveza. When I rummaged through my jacket pockets looking for gum or a mint, I found the Polaroid photo that had cost me five bucks. Or a pain pill.

Walter led me out of the bar. "Are you okay? You gonna make it? Cab will be here in five. Let's get you outside, get you some air. Hey, what's that?"

"The photo of a rock star."

The night had pooled outside the bar. He glanced at the picture. "Was that last month, at AS220? Oh shit, your last show with us, yeah? I'm sorry about that." He went on, as he had earlier, about how that was no way to treat me and if it made me feel any better the new guitarist was shit and Walter was going to leave Antigone as soon as he had another landing spot. Walter did not look at the photo closely. If he had, he would've seen what I saw.

The creases in the leather, the zipper, the chrome buttons, and the shadow of the lapel impossibly swirled and fit together to make a face. Once I saw it, I couldn't unsee it. That fucking face was there. It was the same, but it was also different because it sort of looked like me. And I felt it staring from inside me.

In the cab I asked Walter to look at the photo again. He said it was too dark for him to see anything. When I smooshed the picture into his face and asked if he saw anything, he said, "Just you."

You felt it staring at you from the photo, or you felt it inside you and it was staring?

Walter helped me get my apartment door open. I hugged him and thanked him, and I took off my jacket and held it out toward him. I said, "I want you to have this."

He laughed. "What? Nah, man. Thank you, though."

"Everything must go. You get the jacket."

"You love that jacket. I've never seen you not in it. That jacket is you."

"I do. I did love it. Just fucking take it. I want you to take it from me." I draped the coat over his shoulder.

"Man, you're not dying. You'll be back." He tossed the coat to me. I wanted to cry because he thought I was drunk (which was true) and being maudlin and generous but I wasn't being generous. Walter, who'd been nothing but a solid friend, a good guy, did not deserve what I was trying to put on him. No one did.

I still tried to give it to him again. Walter refused. Eventually he jumped back into the waiting cab. I watched him drive away. He moved to North Carolina the following summer.

I left my jacket on the sidewalk. I let it go and it splatted, and maybe I tried stirring it to life with a hesitant toe in its water. I left the thing out there overnight and in the morning the jacket was gone and there was a puddle on the pavement in its place. (That's how I remember it anyway.)

That next day I brought all my packed-up shit to my mother's house in Beverly.

You stole my camera.

Can't say I was happy you tore the dresser out of the wall either. It was a conversation piece. Or to quote a famous filmic philosopher, it really tied the room together. So, yeah, during your freak-out you trashed my dresser and my apartment, but stealing my camera hurt. That was low. That was personal.

You're lucky I'm a forgiving person and lucky I remain a true friend. All I've ever wanted is to help you.

When I put the rock-star photo inside your snazzy leather jacket, I found a prescription bottle. I couldn't tell what the prescription was for. The label was ripped off and I couldn't open it and look inside while we were talking, not that I would've known what I was looking at. I'm guessing it was Percocet or maybe even oxycodone. Whatever it was couldn't have been good for your heart or your sleeping problems. I know you were in tremendous back pain, and I don't blame you if you were self-medicating. I'm guessing you didn't have good health insurance or any health insurance at that point.

You weren't moving so well, and you were pallid, drained, and slurring even before we drank at my place. It took a lot for me to come up to you after your Antigone show and I was truly happy to be hanging out with you again. But, if I can be frank, I was also scared by your battered and compromised condition, especially on the second night of your visit. I didn't know what to do, so I pretended your problems weren't that bad and would handle themselves.

I also probably should've been up front earlier about my having seen you play with most of your other bands along with my seeing you—from a remove—at your various places of employment. I worried it would've made me sound like a stalker.

And I wasn't. I let you _be_, and I was genuinely working up
the courage to say hey again, and I fooled myself into thinking
I was there for you as a kind of invisible safety net, or
something, should you need it. Man, ain't we a pair?

Maybe if we'd talked occasionally after some of your shows
and slowly rebuilt trust instead of our bingeing on a two-day
hangout/bender, the implosion in my apartment wouldn't have
happened. It makes sense now. There was so much pressure,
how could our reunion not have collapsed ruinously?

Personal demons aside, I am now impressed by how deftly
you've turned this whole thing into a vampire story. Plus, you
credit it as my suggestion! I'm touched. Truly. Your physical
ailments dovetail nicely with symptoms of visits from a folkloric
vampire. Hey, that's me! Yes, I'm coming to fictional terms with
my role, even warming up to the idea. I'm still waiting for some
sort of reveal or nod to my/Mercy's real name.

Your self-destruction and regular destruction of my property
aside, I liked the big scene in my basement. Ah, the vampire's
crypt, yes? I also dug the callback of my "Do you need a lift?"
line from earlier in the book.

There's a lot going on in this chapter. I won't detail all
my questions/issues because overall I think it works well enough
as-is. But, thoughts:

—Your recounting of the Providence music scene: There's no
way you were in that many bands, even over a fifteen-year
period. Plus, the rules and behavior of some of them were over-
the-top, though that in and of itself doesn't necessarily mean
it wasn't true. No shade to Providence, but it isn't exactly New
York or LA or even Seattle. I suppose Boston is close enough
geographically to create a co-scene. Still, would there have been

that many bands, that many talented or angry or lost or bored young people kicking around the city at that time? Maybe. Did you exaggerate the number of bands—and subsequent firings and dismissals—to externalize and emphasize your self-loathing, or to satirize your idealized punk scene and what it had become? Either way, it's entertaining. The danger is that it can read as less authentic, like the fantasy of someone who hasn't played in bands.

—Interpretations of your dead-of-night stagger through my darkened, suddenly evil apartment: First, the scene could be read as a metaphor for growing older. Stumbling around in the dark with inexplicable/existential threats behind you and within your path ahead including a closed door, and your heedless, bullish rush forward because having what's behind you catch and overwhelm you would be worse, knowing that someday—maybe today—there will be a final door you cannot open. Probably a stretch. I think a BETTER reading is specific to the career arc of a musician, especially within the context of the discussion of your dissatisfaction with music and my emboldening suggestion to give writing a shot. The old saw, particularly in music—though it applies to any artistic endeavor, given culture's thirstful lust for new/young voices—is that a band's "best" or most popular records are almost invariably produced within the early part of their career. There are exceptions to every rule, of course, but there's a sizable nugget of truth within the canard, and it correlates to your terror-walk through my apartment. Check it out: the new band/writer will plow recklessly though the darkened room, if not without fear, then putting that fear to use to absorb and ignore the stubbed toes and mashed noses accumulated on their way to finding an original, beautiful path out. With each stumble through concurrent rooms, the creator grows weary of the bumps and their barking shins and will stay upon the same path they'd worked so hard to forge and hesitate to take chances with other painful maybe even dangerous ways to escape. Or the creator obsessively returns to the same room over and over. Or, if the creator dares continue to explore new rooms and tread new paths, ones that threaten to become a maze, ones impossible to follow without having to absorb too much of the honest pain and difficulty of the experience, and the creator's listeners/readers—I will not use the word "consumers" as vampirically fitting as it might be—eventually balk, as they would rather remain on their favored path, the easier one to remember, the one they were originally led down.

—This dead-of-night scene as horror: Creepy for sure, especially the bit about my shifting from Hulk-smashing through the debris to lightly walking over it. You intimate I was floating, but I imagined me stretched out and insectlike, psychopomping my bulk in such an expert way that I weighed almost nothing. Chills, dude. Even though it's written in first person and the reader knows that at this point in the book there's no way you could die within the scene, and even though I know what happened, I was worried and scared for Punk Art. Horror at its core reminds us of the inevitability of death, even if it doesn't occur on the page. However, are you sort of maybe possibly taking the make-everyday-objects-and-scenarios-menacing thing a bit too far with floating dressers and jackets that become homunculi parasites? Yeah, when I state plainly the supernatural bits like that and without any story context it sounds silly, just as I could make so many other horror stories/movies sound silly

Doodle!

in a similar manner. *Sigh* Okay, I liked the uncanniness of you first seeing the dresser and then becoming obsessed with finding exactly where it was rooted to the wall. That's cool. It's weird and real at the same time. And, the following night, I liked the juxtaposition of your being scared precisely because the dresser is now *on* the floor. That bit works because the everyday, normal thing is now strange and off and creepy. And what happens next? Eh. Perhaps it comes down to personal taste, but I was more moved by the ambiguity of the dresser, of not knowing what the fuck was up with the dresser, than by it and other objects in the room gone floaty. Like I've told you before, I don't believe in the supernatural as it relates to ghosts or demons or beings, be they devils or gods. Despite my love of horror, I have a hard time suspending disbelief in fiction/movies too. I so desperately want to believe, but I cannot. Not for a lack of trying, either. I'm not expressing myself very well because there are plenty of books and movies with supernatural elements that scare and have scared the shit out of me, that bring me to a wait-a-minute precipice of belief. It's just the floating thing, man. I'm having a hard time connecting with it. But I'm thinking maybe the vampire me bombards you with a kind of pheromone that makes you more receptive and suggestive, makes you hallucinate. I like the idea of a naturalistic vampire, and pheromones messing with your head would be a cool callback to the classic trope of a vampire hypnotizing victims. Or, how about this: I like the idea of the vampire as some kind of transgression or transgressor from another dimension or something like that, something that can mess with space/time, can get quantum on you. I haven't fully worked that out, and maybe that's fine, we're not supposed to know, and maybe even the vampire/being straddling the multiverses or multiexistences doesn't know either. Why would the vamp know? I mean, think about it this way: Do you know the why or how of your own consciousness?

No, I'm not stoned, you asshole! Anyway, don't try to overexplain—like I am—either.

Hey, here's a suggestion. How about you cut to my POV for the first and only time in the novel during that scene, right after you wake up on the second night. You describe to the reader what is going on, and in doing so, depending on how you describe what's happening, you could still have the creepy floating stuff but leave it ambiguous as to whether it's truly happening. Find a way to leave us at that precipice. Stick with your POV until the moment the dresser rises again, then cut to my POV, keeping in mind you have already hinted that I've been draining the life-force from you, which is causing your heart palpitations, sleep apnea, chest pains, back issues, etc.

Okay, check this out from Mercy's POV:

There I am, lying in my bed. I've been asleep for hours, but also, at the same time, I'm returning to bed after having perched on your chest. I don't understand everything—I never have—but in this moment we are in two worlds of many.

You stand in front of the couch, shaking in air that has gotten thicker somehow, and shaking as you stare at the dresser that hovers above the floor

—and—

you are shouting at things that are not there because your brain is on fire and in this hallucinatory frenzy you rip the dresser from the wall and you gut it, spilling out the drawers.

You spin away from the levitating furniture, and I've never seen someone look so fundamentally frightened and lost

—and—

you are in a berserker's fury and you flip over the sofa and smash the lamp and scream unintelligibly.

I see it all

—and—

I hear it all.

I stretch and lope toward you on all fours, every inch of me a claw, a snarl, a fang, and also, I fill the room, I am the room, I am the world, and I'm enraged and rapturous and I will make this last forever

—and—

I'm in bed and I can't see anything, and I'm curled into a ball and I'm so small and I'm weeping because this will last forever.

Because you are in the same room with me and at such proximity—comparative to 1989 when I was sleeping an entire floor below you, or when I was underground, in my grave one hundred years prior—I am intoxicated and I am violence and I am possibility and I am blood in the water, no, I am blood in the air, the coagulating air

—and—

because you are in the same room with me and at such proximity I cannot move, cannot even open my eyes and I am soporific with you, and I am sick with you.

You try to leave, and I block your path at the door, and I wait, and the delicious fucking wait is too much, almost

—and—

I sense you leaving, and I want to say a single word that somehow means sorry, please, don't go, help me, it's not your fault, I wish it wasn't my fault, goodbye.

I wrap myself around your leg and I sift myself through your very essence. I shark within your cells, and I breathe you all in

—and—

I am losing you and the loss is as aching and delicious and bottomless and as addictive as the gain, as the replacing.

You open the door, stand at the precipice, break away, and leave

—and—

you open the door, stand at the precipice, break away, and leave.

I return to myself

—and—

I return to myself.

It feels like floating

—and—

it feels like falling.

MASOCHISM WORLD

(2014, with a few dribs and drabs about
the years since 2007 and before)

~~A chapter in which Art goes home again and it's better~~ I almost
trashed the whole book because of what happens at the end of
this chapter. I decided to leave this as written.

*Is there a monster at the
end of this chapter?*

TITLE: COAL SONG

```
(/) Slide Up  (\) Slide Down  (h) Hammer On  (p) Pull Off  (b) Bend (r) Release (v) Vibrato

Capo Fret 3

Stave 1: Repeat twice, second time through play the 'D' chord with hammer off an extra time

E|-----6-----6-6--6-6--6-6--6--6-6--6--6-6--6--6-6--6--6-6--6--6-6--5--5-3--5--5--
B|-----6-----6-6--6-6--6-6--6--6-6--6--6-6--6--6-6--6--6-6--6--6-6--6--6-6--6--6--
G|--------------------------------------------------------------5--5--5--5--5--
D|-----5-----5-3--5-3--5-3----------------------5--5-3--5--5-3--3--3--3--3--3--
A|-----6-----6-3--6-3--6-3--5--5-3--5--5-3--5--5-3--5--5-3--5--5-3------------
E|------------------------6-6-3--6--6-3--6--6-3--3--3-3--3--3-3-------------

Stave 2: Like above, second time through play 'D' chord with hammer off an extra time

E|--6--6--6-6--6--6-6--6--6-6--6--6-6--6--5--5-3--3--5--5-----
B|--6--6--6-6--6--6-6--6--6-6--6--6-6--6--6--6-6--6--6-6-----
G|--------------------------------------5--5--5--5--5-----
D|--5-5--5-5-----------------5--5--5-5--3--3-3--3--3-----
A|--6--6--6-5--5--5-5--5--5-5--5-----------------------
E|-------------6--6-6--5--3--3--3-3--3-----------------

Stave 3: Play 'D' for a measure on the second time through

E|--6--6--6-6--6--6-6--6--6-6--6--6-6--5--5-----
B|--6--6--6-6--6--6-6--6--6-6--6--6-6--6--6-----
G|--------------------------------------5--5-----
D|--5-5-----5--5-5--5-5-----5-----5-3--3-----
A|--5-5--5-6--6-5--5-5--5-6--5--5-----------
E|--3-3--6-----------3--3-6--6-3-----------
```

[Note: I can't write or read music, but I can use a guitar tablature generator.
I basically use the suspended chord shapes of C, G, Em, and D (not suspended),
moved them up to the third fret.]

Lyrics:

You see that
I jumped over the couch
You see that
I jumped over the couch

Get out the way
Go back to work
I've got a red and white
Get out the way
Go back to work
I've got a red and white

Coal song

Admittedly, I am not a strong lyricist. Though, if you were to hear the song performed, I think you'd agree the words somehow work. Mostly. And fine, I harvested the lyrics from a screaming toddler who Super Marioed around everyone's favorite box furniture store. (I wanted the Billy bookcase and all I came home with was a headache.) The kid had a binky in each hand, one red, one white. Sorry I demystified the song for you.

"Coal Song" is a Pallbearers Club original, and I work it into my sets. Despite the band name, I play solo now.

Looks like a devil's tail!

introduce myself?

Please allow me to rewind a little. After I moved back to my mother's house in August of 2007, I didn't pick up my guitar for eighteen months. I'd returned to a familiar place, but I was not, as they say, in a good place. To my eternal gratitude, Mom knew the living arrangements had to be tweaked so my prodigal return didn't in any way resemble a turning of the clock back twenty years. She relocated to the first floor and gave me the second. Aside from a common entrance (otherwise known as the front door) and my not having a full kitchen (though over the years I've added a mini refrigerator and microwave to what used to be my bedroom, which is now my hangout/rehearsal/writing space) we split the house into two mostly separate apartments. I got a job at Newbury Comics, a New England chain of alternative-chic stores that, in 2007, mainly sold CDs, DVDs, T-shirts, and some comics, where my sullenness could be read as an affectation.

My first days back in Beverly were the bleakest, so much so I prefer not to write about them, other than to say I survived. (Fine, I will write about them a little. There was no escaping that twenty years later I had returned home, utterly defeated. I knew I had been irrevocably changed, but I didn't know how changed. How much of me had Mercy consumed? Was I doomed to become something like her? Was I like her already and I didn't know it, couldn't recognize the transformation, because I was so radically different my now-thinking warped and changed everything I had thought previously? Each morning I conducted an Art Barbara systems analysis that was inconclusive because I felt different and I felt the same.)

You continually and stubbornly live in two worlds of many. You do it throughout the book.

Then day one at home became week one became month one, the days as wooden blocks that piled into a haphazard foundation from which I hoped to build. Maybe it's not much, but I have built a life, which is a terrible capitalist idea, isn't it? That we must manufacture our lives (strictly adhering to a consumer-culture standard) to give them meaning instead of simply living them.

Now seven years in Beverly later, was I happy? Content? Without fear of trapdoors and further transfiguration? Did I dwell on the unforeseen consequences of what happened with Mercy in Providence? No, no, no, and fuck yes. But, here in 2014, for the first time in my life, I was willing and able to be me, whoever that was, instead of striding toward some idealized version. Why? My not having to worry daily about making rent was certainly a factor that couldn't be underestimated. My consistently doing physical therapy to strengthen my core and back hasn't cured the pain but has kept it to a manageable low simmer on most days, which allowed me to become less reliant on painkillers. (Aside: I haven't

Less reliant doesn't mean "not reliant."

been as faithfully attuned to my heart—the physical one—thanks-no-thanks shitty and/or no health insurance. The last time I had my biannual echocardiogram to check the size and function of my potentially rascally aorta was 2009.)

So yeah, barring the unforeseen, I am not going to be kicked out of my apartment, and I feel better physically. However, I attribute the *novel* seven years of on-and-off-again writing of this ~~memoir~~, as frustrating and pride-swallowing and uncomfortable and impossible and improbable as it has been at times, to my current fatalistic (Mercy will be back at some point, but until then …) jouissance.

What's with all the French? One might observe that I never left,
because you kept me around by writing about me for seven years.

If you read the preceding passages and think, "Living with Mom isn't very punk, Art," or "I don't sympathize with Art because he's so passive," you can go fuck yourself.

Monsieur, that's not very jouissance-like.

When I eventually limped back to playing live music, I started with local open mics. Besides fearing I would see Mercy in the audience, the hardest part was overcoming my teenagery dread of running into ex-classmates. That happened less frequently than I had anticipated, mainly because the ones who remained local were married, had children, and were not frequenting the bars at which I performed. On the occasions when there were Beverly High alumni in the audience, most of whom (if I'm allowed to be gloriously mean and petty) had peaked as teenagers, socially if not physically (hello, polar-ice-cap receding hairlines), they remarked on my physical transformation. Like I said before, I do love my six-four height, Faustian-back-pain bargain be damned. I also had a scruffy, youth-culture-approved beard and carefree curling hair. When they said "Wow, look at you" or "You look great," it was meant in comparison to the willowy, zit-infested, stick-bug high school me, in comparison to their diminished and/or exaggerated memory of the high school Art. (How many versions of that poor kid are there? If only I could collect them all.)

Occasionally, post-performance a fellow grad would buy me a beer and I'd regale them with frothy tales of my slightly exaggerated hard-and-fast times as a musician. My accepting any-and-all-offered-free-beers policy (a sound policy) backfired one night when Eddie Patrick (Remember him? Former bully? Initial member of the original Pallbearers Club?) interrupted my spinning of tall tales to ex-classmate Kate and her husband, both of whom were in the French department at Endicott College, by clapping me on the back and saying, "Hey, it's 'The Undertaker.'"

I knew who it was without turning to look at him. The feeling lasted only (and dammit, I know I should avoid "only" as a writer, and there was nothing "only" about this) a moment, but I was a freshman again, sinking into that no-one-will-help-me trill of despair. That mewling fear quickly turned to anger. I stood up from the barstool and filled my chest with righteous air, an animal display, to show him what I had become. He couldn't see it. I could tell. He would never release the version of me he kept.

Who or what had you become?

A self-proclaimed *self-made* man (with help from his parents owning a chain of dairy farms), Eddie was a wildly successful hedge-fund manager, the type who played the shell game to his benefit, including his making (according to a scathing investigative piece in the now-defunct alternative weekly *Boston Phoenix*) north of $20 million during the housing crisis of 2008 by betting against the market, then cleaning up when prices bottomed out. He had a beachfront mansion in Beverly Farms (not that I was stalking him) worth $9.5 million (according to Zillow).

You're totally stalking him.

Eddie said, "Whoa, a big guy now," and his audience, two younger CrossFit bro dudes in slim-cut suits drinking low-carb beers laughed and chirped *Hey Spike, anything you say, Spike* support.

I said, "Bigger than some. How's it going, Eddie?" That fucking guy was a melted snow pile of avarice, full of rottenness and gunk, full of smug assuredness that everyone else in the world was there for his use or amusement. At least he looked like shit. Purple eye bags, a jowls starter kit, and hair too thin to even say it was thinning.

Clearly drunk, he said, "Fan-fucking-tastic, brother." Gross, right? Who says shit like that? He chucked my shoulder and joked about how I needed his permission to use the Pallbearers Club as a performing name, as he was once a founding member.

By this point Kate and her husband wisely fled. Eddie bought me two beers. I honestly don't know why I stayed. Eventually, during his bragging about myriad shady economic dealings and conquests, I extricated myself, claiming I had to pack up gear that had already been packed. I shrugged into my blue leather jacket, and Eddie made a crack about my being late for a motocross rally in the Liberty Tree Mall parking lot. I bumped into his arm, oil-spilling his drink onto his blazer and tie. He claimed I did it on purpose. I didn't disagree. I thanked him for the beers and tossed bar napkins at him. I left him grumbling and his Neolithic associates breathing through their mouths and unsure when the violence might finally start. I told Meg (the bar owner) I was leaving my stuff in the back room and would get it tomorrow, which was not unusual. Too buzzed to drive, too pissed to care to ask anyone for a ride, I walked the two miles home.

Before leaving, though, in a low moment, I keyed deep scratches into the driver's-side door of Eddie's car. It was a low moment because I guessed the BMW SUV was his. Oops.

Through sheer determination and persistence, the Pallbearers Club had semi-regular gigs at Mercy Tavern (I'm not making the name up, I swear) in neighboring Salem and the Copper Dog in Beverly. What set me apart from your typical nostalgia act of auto-tuned, drum-machine-accompanied, acoustic renderings of flower-power standards and soft rock "classics" (not that I'm judging) or shitty contemporary pop country (I am judging), was that I played electric and awash in distortion. The band was me, my electric guitar, and a mic. Well, I brought a PA, a mixer, an amp, a distortion pedal, and an iPad on a music stand with the lyrics and guitar tabs of about eighty songs I knew how to play, but no prerecorded loops, drums,

[handwritten margin note: I wonder if that applies to why you stayed at your old house.]

voice modulation, or other bullshit like that. I'm not saying I wasn't a nostalgia act, just a different kind. (Nostalgia is like the "Monkey's Paw" story; we want the long-gone thing from our previous lives back until we do and see what it has become, what it always had been.) I played for the subset of Generation Xers who yearned for the pre-fab, contrived edginess of '90s alternative rock while they drank wine and microbrewed IPAs. To further facilitate the *feel*, I performed a practiced and winking disdain-for-the-audience schtick between songs. Yeah, we Gen-Xers hated ourselves almost as much as we loved ourselves.

I cranked out loud, fast pop songs and I gave it my all every night, no matter the audience reaction. I knew given the platform/venue (whether it was an open mic in a pizza joint or playing covers for bar background music) it was uncool to publicly admit and display your unvarnished passion and that it was unseemly to try, to give the appearance of trying, particularly when by society's standards you were not and would never be successful/famous. But fuck it, I did it anyway, and on most nights, it felt right. Yeah, I missed the rush and the camaraderie of playing in a band. The shared-obsession thing used to get me out of bed most mornings. I didn't miss the inter-personal dramas, politics, hurt feelings, and the inevitable failures. Because the failures were shared, they felt amplified.

For my last show (October 2, 2014), Mercy Tavern was packed. Not because of me. I was not that delusional. October was Halloween season in Salem, and during that month tens of thousands of tourists poured into the town to kitschily celebrate the horrific, state-sanctioned deaths of nineteen innocent people. After setting up my equipment, I had a quick beer at the bar, then I strode (less athletically than the word implied) onto the stage (a minimally elevated square of plywood) wearing my blue leather moto jacket (purchased in early 2008; I admittedly look even more ridiculous in this jacket than the prior one, but that was the point of the purchase, and I like blue). There was a smattering of applause. I do get a few regulars at the shows; not people who follow me per se, but people who go to the same bar each week and I was the equivalent of their favorite booth or stool.

I strummed a ringing E chord, which turned a few heads in my direction, and I said, "I'm the Pallbearers Club," and I launched into a crowd-pleaser, "Luka" by Suzanne Vega, arranged at twice the tempo and using suspended chords with heavy distortion. Why a song about child abuse was a crowd-pleaser I couldn't say, but I had to give the people some of what they wanted. I played the usual '90s standards from Nirvana, Pixies, Belly, Neutral Milk Hotel, Sugar, Social Distortion's version of Johnny Cash's "Ring of Fire," and some deeper cuts, including Bob Mould's "I Hate Alternative Rock." After the Bob tune, I paused and told the bar crowd the title of the song. It elicited a few laughs, head nods, and smirks. Oh, you jaded Gen-Xers, acting as though some of you hadn't become some of the worst, most entitled assholes on the planet. At this point in the set, I had a full sweat going, so I shed my blue jacket and guzzled some water. Time for some banter.

"I'd ask how everyone's night is going, but I really don't care as long as you subscribe to the Pallbearers Club YouTube channel."

Some applause, laughs, and lots of shared *seriously?* looks.

Part of the joke was that I did have a channel. I created two-minute-and-thirty-two-second (the length of the song "New Day Rising," because in my meaningless world I must make everything mean something) mini documentaries for famous punk and new wave bands and forgotten local Boston and Providence heroes. Each band got the same egalitarian treatment. Offscreen I nasally narrated factoids, band highlights, and personal appreciations as well as critiques (I don't do hagiographies) over a montage of live performance clips. (As of the writing of this, I have 10,019 followers, not that I keep track.) A former bandmate reached out recently to ask if I'd be interested in doing a similarly themed podcast with her. I told her I'd think on it.

"I may not live to regret this, but any requests?" I asked.

A guy named Trace (one night we got to talking and found out that decades ago we both briefly worked at the United Shoe Factory before it closed), a regular at Mercy's, shouted from the nearest corner of the bar: "Oasis!"

I said, "Why do you hate yourself so much, Trace?"

He raised his glass to me, then shouted, "Smashing Pumpkins!"

I said, "Why do you hate everyone else here? Don't answer. It's rhetorical."

I played a quick set of '80s songs with the Ramones, Buzzcocks, Fine Young Cannibals, Mission of Burma, and Cyndi Lauper. While also sneaking in another original song called "Simpleton." G-D-C chords. Lyrics: I didn't know I was wrong / until you told me / you said I was wrong / then you showed me how / I had mistaken / the truth from your fiction / I guess I'm the simpleton / I'm your simpleton / I'll be your simpleton.

[handwritten margin note: Angst? Check. Self-loathing? Check. This could've been a '90s almost-hit.]

At the next break and every break after, the bar crowd got the hang of requesting Oasis and Smashing Pumpkins songs so I could pithily insult everyone. It was a fun night.

When I got home from the show, Mom was sitting on the front stoop smoking a cigarette. She had quit a month earlier and had quit six months before that.

It was a minor miracle Mom still owned the house. As much as she complained about the place and idly talked of selling, she was proud she had it. My moving back was good timing for her and had benefitted us both: I had a stable, cheap place to live, and because I helped with the monthly bills, including the remaining mortgage and real-estate tax, she was able to retire.

My parents came close to selling the place when they divorced in 1992, but Mom dug her heels in, wanting to stay. Dad begrudgingly relented. Less than two years later both were in serious relationships with other people. Mom was going to marry Larry, who had spent his adult life as a tech for National Grid on the natural-gas side. He helped Mom pay my father $5,000 (which represented their original down payment) so the house would be solely in her name. Larry was a good person, even if he thought I was a hopelessly slacking lounge-about, which, fine, wasn't true (not counting my bands, while in

Providence I generally worked sixty-hour weeks that weren't really weeks and more like a string theory of unrelenting days), but there were and are worse things to be. Larry treated Mom well. Tragically, five months before their scheduled wedding day, he died of a sudden heart attack at a work site. With the one-two punch of divorce and the United Shoe Plant closing, my father found (or re-found) religion. He somehow finagled Catholic back channels to officially, in the beady, weaselly eyes of the Church, annul his marriage to Mom. Her agreeing to the annulment, more than the ceremonial five grand (not that that wasn't a significant amount of money, particularly in the mid-'90s), was ultimately what got Mom the house for keeps. While Mom hasn't been a practicing Catholic for decades, the annulment remained a sore spot. Dad married a bouncing electron of a woman named Gretchen. She was a good person, even if she thought I was a hopelessly slacking lounge-about and, worse, a heathen, which, fine, because in the case of the latter, I was. She treated Dad well. She had some money squirreled away from her prior marriage to a real-estate developer, and in '98 they moved to a Christian gated community (not sure how it works, and I don't want to know) near Boca Raton, Florida. The two of them opened a hair salon called Curl Up and Dye. They've since opened two more salons on the southeast coast of Florida. Around the holidays (including their own birthdays and anniversary) they sent me über-religious cards with checks for $25, a photo of them tanned and on the beach, and neon yellow and pink adverts/coupons for their salons.

Mom stubbed out her cigarette on the top stair and groaned as she stood. She had just turned seventy, had recently allowed her short brown hair to go fully gray, and was generally in good shape aside from her arthritic knees. She asked if I needed any help carrying in my equipment.

I shook off the question and said, "I'm going to tell the landlord you're smoking on the stairs again. She'll throw you out on your ass."

Mom didn't address my why-are-you-still-smoking passive-aggressive jab. "You're home early. Must've been a good show."

"Yeah, it was. One of my best, actually." Purely a subjective statement, and any attendees were free to opine otherwise, but they would be wrong. No one knew better than I did when it was good (a rare, Halley's Comet kind of appearance) and when it was not so good. I didn't stick around on good nights because I didn't want to jinx it, even though it already had happened, and I didn't want to inadvertently hear someone shitting on the performance and thus ruin the vibe. (To still be so self-esteemedly reliant upon what other people thought of me never failed to make me feel worse. I couldn't and can't change that, try as I might.) I tended to stay at the bar after the not-so-good nights, a combo of penance and redo, hoping my hanging out and buying drinks and talking to people might leave everyone (including myself) with a better a memory of the evening.

Mom held the front door open, and I lugged my equipment to the second floor. I came back downstairs and sat with her at the kitchen table. The kitchen had been redone about twenty years ago, with all the work done by Mom and Larry. I wondered how often Mom sat in this room alone and thought, not about Larry but about the path that could've been. There was no need to update the still-functioning appliances, but some of the floor laminate was beat-up and the dingy white walls needed to be repainted. Painting the kitchen was something we both said we would help the other do, but that was still a future thing in our minds. It was nice to have a future thing.

We sat at opposite ends at the rigorously rectangular table. I drank water and Mom drank white wine. We had to remind ourselves to not be continually shocked at how old we were.

Mom asked me about the show because she knew I wanted to talk about it. I told her what songs I opened and closed with and the originals I played and what the crowd reactions were to those songs. Onstage or after, I never admitted I wrote the originals. If pressed, I credited the song to one of the bands I used to play with. Usually Rat Moat. I liked saying that band name.

Mom asked if either of my two briefly tenured girlfriends (since returning to Beverly) were in the audience.

I said, "Yeah, they were both there, dancing and cheering, and throwing roses at me."

"You think you're so funny."

A brief silence, acknowledging the glow of the evening was fading. I asked her about her day, her week, as recently we'd only seen each other in passing. She itemized her walks around the neighborhood and Lynch Park (including her terse confrontation with a man who didn't clean up after his Labradoodle), phone calls with her sister who lived in West Roxbury, dinner with one of her bank-teller friends who'd had a hard go of it lately. I diverted conversation away from the friend's hard go. Selfishly, I didn't want to hear about it, not then. So, I preemptively answered one of her usual questions about a gig.

I said, "No former classmates in the audience, tonight, which is always a plus."

"You're almost in your mid-forties, Art. You need to let those high school grudges go."

I laughed. "Says the person who still complains about when she was a freshman and her senior brother let his friends make fun of and embarrass her at a high school dance." It was kind of mean to bring that up, though I didn't do it to be mean. I took an odd sense of comfort from listening to a seventy-year-old (one who had lived a full life, a life blessed with a roof always over her head and loving, if not dwindling, family and friends, but a life certainly not free from upheaval, tragedy, loneliness, and disappointment) remembering the slights and cruelties of her youth with clarity and purpose.

"Well, that was an asshole thing to do. They were all assholes."

"They certainly were." I poured the rest of her wine bottle into my glass so that she wouldn't have to finish it alone.

"Whatever happened to that friend of yours? Mary? No, Mercy." She asked me like she didn't know her name, like she didn't ask me about her every six to eight months.

I said, "I don't know."

"Are you still working on your ~~memoir~~?" **novel**

"Oh yeah." Seven years and an untold number of rewrites. I never spent more than a week away from the manuscript. Some days I wrote one sentence and crossed out one hundred. Other days the ratio flipped. I started writing it because it felt like the only way to pick through the rubble of everything, and I didn't know what else to do. I discovered writing allowed me to turn off my yammering brain. Well, I didn't turn it off, more like I could trick my brain out of living and perseverating in the anxious now and the doomy what's-next. Even though the past was full of regret, ridiculousness, and fear, at least it had already happened. I knew what I would find, so I could control it, etch it out onto paper, and then I could do whatever the hell I wanted with it. I could examine the worst with a magnifying glass or bury it between the lines. And ultimately, I could destroy it if I wanted to. There were times when I fantasized about printing everything I'd written and burning it, turning all the ghosts to smoke.

"Where are you?" Mom asks.

"Huh? I'm here, in the kitchen?"

"No, in the book. What part of your life are you writing about now?"

"I'm up to ... right now, actually." I tapped a finger on the kitchen table.

"Oh wow, that's great. Does that mean you're done?"

"I don't think so."

"You can't write a ~~memoir~~ about things that haven't happened to **novel** you yet. It sounds like you're done to me."

"Doesn't feel like I'm done." I couldn't tell her that I was afraid to be done because for the seven years I'd been writing the book I hadn't seen Mercy. She hadn't come back. It was silly, but I wanted to believe my writing was a talisman, *the* talisman keeping Mercy away, keeping her from returning. Seven years was a long time. Not equal to my time in the Providence scene, but music has never been a talisman. Mercy had been there with me in Providence the whole time, hadn't she? Even if she wasn't at every show, she was at enough of them, and I'd bet my soul she went to every final show I'd had with each of my ill-fated bands. I knew the talisman thing was absurd, and correlation was not causation, but I also knew I wouldn't survive her next visit. Or worse, I wouldn't want to survive because of what I might then become. So, I would continue writing and rewriting the past. Forever if necessary.

Mom asked, "You don't have an ending planned?"

"I guess that's it. I'm not sure how to end it." I tried a joke. "Is that a funny thing to say about a ~~memoir~~?"

novel

"You'll figure it out. But you better make me look good when you write about me."

"I'm trying my best."

"Hey!"

"What? I didn't mean anything by that."

"Yeah, sure." She laughed ruefully, but it was the laugh of an opponent. I wondered if she was thinking something awful about me. We all think awful things about the ones we're closest to. She followed it up with "You were always so creative. I'm sure it's great because you're very talented at everything you do, and I can't wait to read it." She said it with such sincerity, I felt awful for thinking she was thinking awful things about me.

"Thank you. Yeah, we'll see."

"You could end the book with us chatting at the kitchen table. Airing grievances."

"Oh, is it that time now?"

"It's always that time. Hey, I'm on my third glass of wine." She adjusted herself in her chair, settling in. "Have you heard from your father lately?" His name was never spoken; simply "your father," with an emphasis on *your*, as though I were due some ownership or blame for who he was.

"No. Haven't talked to him in a while. Since late August, I think."

"That's because in the eyes of his church you don't exist, you never happened." Mom was in her glory, getting to be angry on my behalf.

"Ma, we're both busy—why do you still get so upset over the annulment thing? I don't believe in it, and you don't believe in it. It doesn't matter to me. So, whatever, right? Or do you believe in it? It's okay if you do. I get it." She grew up in a strict Catholic family, and while she hadn't been to a church in decades, she still prayed to Saint Anthony if she lost anything in the house.

"No, I don't believe in it, but it's not about what you or I believe. It's about what he believes. He'd rather wipe our marriage and your birth and baptism from existence so that he could get married again stain-free in his precious church. It's all about him, and it's not right."

What???
I didn't know you didn't exist, Art. Unclean!!!

I grumbled a kind of wishy-washy, what-are-you-going-to-do agreement. Because I wasn't ardent in co-condemnation, the rest of our conversation fizzled. I couldn't tell if she was disappointed that I was never as brutally honest as she was, never as angry, at least not in my direct expressions, and if I remained, in her eyes (as in mine), the sensitive child who wouldn't stick up for himself. I didn't blame her in the least for thinking I hadn't changed. That was the curse of being a parent: your child was forever who they once were, or at the very least the adult version of the child would be compared to the kid in whom the parent saw their own best and worst selves. The other half of the curse was that within the adult child's aging eyes the parent inevitably changed and became someone else, a person in whom the adult child saw their own best and worst selves.

My one glass of wine had already turned into a headache. I gave her a quick hug and tottered off upstairs with a large cup of water. Instead of bed, I plunked down at my writing desk and wrote about the show and my time in the kitchen with Mom. When I first sat down, I scribbled some thoughts into a notebook, something I didn't intend to include in the book.

But here it is anyway:

I wonder where we will be in another seven years. Will I still be writing this book? Will I still play live music? Will Mom still be who she is now? Will I? Will you? Will we have finally painted the kitchen? Will I still be living here? Will she be here? Will something terrible happen? When will something terrible happen? Is the worst always to come? The worst is always to come.

Sleep clouds in as I stare at the last sentence, wanting and unable to offset it with something more hopeful (and that's a failure, one of a million failures) but also, fuck it, my having written it down and acknowledging the truth of it will have to be hope enough. I let myself slump into my chair. I don't need to leave and retreat to my bedroom. I'm in the chair now and I'm in the chair in my head. Inside my head is a perfect replica of the house. I wander the hallway of this house. The hallway is quiet but not static, like everyone and everything the hallway is in the process of slowly decaying, and I realize this is what the hallway is like when no one is in it because I'm not in it now. Then I vapor down the stairs and into the dining room and I won't look at the latched basement door, and then I go to the kitchen and the light is off, but I see the outline of my blue jacket I left on the chair, and I'll have to move that tomorrow. Not because Mom would get upset. I don't want to make the living-arrangement boundaries we set more permeable, and that's how I feel right now, in this sleeping and not-sleeping state. Permeable. Then I leave the kitchen, not sure where I'm going next, but I am going and with intention, until I stir awake. And by that I mean I leave my head, which is disorienting. It's as though I've gone back in time to before I toured the house. I sit in my desk chair, and I still feel permeable, which means I'm not sure if I remain in the house in my head, and a flicker of fear and excitement at the thought that maybe I've always been in the house in my head. But no, this is happening. I am standing up now. There are the pressures and subtle physical sensations one cannot mentally replicate. I flicker out into the hallway, but I do not linger. I choose not to linger. I'm thirsty. No, I make the conscious decision to be thirsty, which, I think, means I'm trapped in both spaces; the real house and the head house. I walk downstairs and my back doesn't hurt despite my previously hunched-over sleeping position. My back is loose, and it feels good, great even, but I don't trust it. It's a too-good-to-last feeling. The same with my head. My head is too good to last. The earlier wine headache is gone, and the space behind my eyes is pressure-free and waiting to be filled. I am light and it feels dangerous, and I know there's danger somewhere, but I can't identify it yet, and I want to giggle at the absurdity and assuredness of it all. In the dining room, retracing steps that weren't stepped, I concentrate on the scratch and tickle of my bare feet on the rug to keep me rooted. I am so very thirsty, I decide, and my body obliges with dried, cracking lips, tightening throat, and a not-wholly-unpleasant quivering throughout my water-starved body. It's not unpleasant because my body knows our hungry-machine needs are at the precipice of being fulfilled. We are always at one precipice or another. In the kitchen now, and I see well enough to not have to turn on the light. My blue jacket is not draped over the kitchen chair, but our wineglasses are still on the table as though waiting for us to come back to pick up where we left off, to finish what was supposed to be finished. At the sink I turn on the tap and let the cold water run over and through my hand and wrist and then to fill a glass. I luxuriate in the sensation again because I'm still so permeable. I'll decide to worry about that after I decide I am no longer thirsty. I drink and I drink forever and the cold fills me until it doesn't. I am both recharged and thinning away, but then, an unbidden thought: *Mercy is in the basement again.* I drop the emptied glass and it clinks and clatters into the sink. Mercy has returned and she is in the basement again and that is why I am permeable. But that's not how I felt the last time I was with her and the other last time before that. There's no pain, and my heart isn't spasming, and, if anything, my heart has gone quiet, gone into hiding. Regardless, what am I going to do? I waver into the dining room and stare at the basement door. Mercy is somewhere below. In the house in my head, I don't dare go down into the basement. I am not permeable. I am here. Should I simply run away again? Get out of her range? Where would I go this time? And what about Mom? In her bedroom, in what was our TV room when I was a kid, Mom coughs. She coughs on cue, as though

I decided she should cough. I am not permeable. I am diffuse. I am in the air. I can reach without reaching. I can be at the basement door and back here in the mouth of the kitchen. I don't open the basement door even if the latch quivers to become unlatched. The metal hook vibrates and clinks as though my fingers tickle it. Inertia is a lie. With my hands at my side, I don't feel my side. Instead, I feel the latch and hold its thin, coiled tensile strength, and I lift then let it drop. I am diffuse. The latch is at rest. I don't run for the front door and to my car and then away, driving until I'm out of gas or out of road, and then on foot, walking until I'm forgotten. I wisp more than scuttle (I think I have done this before) the short journey to the TV room. The French doors are open. I don't go into the room, and I don't stand over her sleeping form like a mantid fiend. I hover, a cloud in the doorway. A crouched, kyphotic shape sits on my mother's chest. There isn't much light, but as the shape flexes and unflexes, adjusts, throbs like a heart, I see it is blue. It is a blue heart. I do not feel diffuse anymore. All of me has returned to here. It's a blue heart until it turns. It has a head and it has a face. A face I've seen twice before, but also I've never seen it before, but also I see it every day. Within its focused malevolence (am I mistaking focus for a cold disinterest, a witness who has seen the worst and the best and it knows which will always be remembered?) and hunger and despair, I'm allowed to wonder would Mom or anyone else see it is so clearly my face, or made from the same clay as my face? Its lips move in sync to my thoughts, to my worst thoughts. It turns away and I still feel its lips moving and whispering my whispers. I drift backward into the living room, letting the scene in her bedroom shrink and recede. I lay down on the couch and close my eyes to sleep and live forever, and it's—wonderful; I'm sorry and damn me but it is. I am not in my head and yet I do not feel the couch or anything else because I am diffuse and permeable. When I next open my eyes the blue jacket that is not a jacket has come back to me and pools on my chest. It rises and falls with my own breathing even though it doesn't feel like I'm breathing.

It doesn't feel like breathing. It feels like floating.

Since I wasn't in this chapter, I appreciate that it was relatively short. I also approve of your shitting on the bands that need to be shat upon.

Okay, I had to get the jokes out of the way first.

There's no good segue to the following:

I am so sorry about what happened to your mom. It kills me that you are—by the act of presenting this book as a memoir, not a novel, though it is a novel, the most novelest novel ever noveled—blaming yourself for her passing, and it is more than a little worrisome. I'm not good at expressing deep emotional truths—I'm not the writer!—but your mom was a good person, and you are also a good person even if you don't believe it. You are a good person in large part because she was. I hope you take solace in that.

Back to the story . . . this was a fun recap and you sounded, dare I say, like the happy Art—or happier Art—from the early sections of the book, with the notable exception of the Eddie-in-the-barroom confrontation. I don't blame you there. He was and is the worst.

Scratch that "happy" bit. I meant hopeful. Fuck happy.

I'm not sure if you need to include the two songs you wrote, but, you're the musician. I'm so vain I think that second song is about me.

We're deep into this novel now and I think I've pieced together more of the rules or whys of the supernatural/vampire element. You've made it abundantly clear that your assorted health issues are the result of my noshing. According to the Mercy Brown folklore, the victims almost exclusively wasted away via consumption/tuberculosis, but I'm okay with you switching it up. The supernatural works in mysterious ways. But, if only to satisfy my agnostic/skeptic self, I want more talk of nothing "supernatural" happening, and more than a "this was all a drug-and-painkiller-aided delusion." Maybe you should posit that you're now infected with an interdimensional or extradimensional virus/being whose very presence alters, blurs, or splinters reality.

Hey, I didn't pick up on it until I read through the last long paragraph a second time, but you switch to present tense after the kitchen-table bit. I think it works for your transformation scene. Or is it a reveal scene? Have you been that monster the entire time you were home, working on the book? Oooh, what if the book was what turned you into the monster? You always had the blue heart, the blue creeper inside, and writing about it, the act of discovering it, let it out into the world. I like that.

However, if we didn't already know this wasn't a memoir, present tense will make it feel even less memoiry—experimental memoirs/creative nonfiction notwithstanding. After ruminating on this while listening to glorious new punk bands who sound like old punk bands—Neighborhood Brats and Uzi—I have decided present-tense works, furthering the living-in-multiple-worlds theme; for you, fiction and truth are one, the past and present are one. They always have been one.

You've succeeded in bifurcating my perceptions. Reading this—and thinking deeply about it—has calved my head in two. Into two at least.

More story thoughts.

With the appearance of the blue parasite monster thingy, we have a pattern in . . . jackets? I know the jackets are fashion representations of who you and I were/are, etc. Given the chest-sitter has your face, or your resemblance, it's less a parasite than an externalized part of you/us—fine, I'll include myself, here—doing the life-sucking, life-eating. That the creature not only has a face like yours but lip-syncs your thoughts, makes it a part of you. An uncontrollable part. Or maybe you can control it but choose not to. You chose not to enter your mother's bedroom, and there was no thought of interfering or attempting to interfere on her behalf. This choice aspect is the scary part from the vampire's POV, isn't it? The vampire(s) here are not the inhuman equivalent of a wasp—or in this case a kind of life-force/spirit tapeworm—with solely the prospect of starvation/death being capable of frightening them. That's not what you're writing about here. You're attempting to make me and the original M. Brown, and now you, more empathetic by grappling with choice. Beyond the curse of having to live, if not forever, then for a fuckload of time, and what that might do to our minds, how do we justify our living off others? Your vampire must lie to herself about being a good friend—or in your case, being a good son— but still having to subsist off the loved one's, um, subsistence. Why is it always someone closest to us, someone we love? Why can't we choose someone else? Can we choose? Is our having no choice a lie, or the lie? When you believe you have no choice, it frees you from personal/societal responsibilities. Our choosing to have no choice ultimately makes ~~us vampires~~ more ~~human.~~ Or something like that.

Yeah, that stuff is cool to think about and all that, but this is still a novel, a story. And more pertinent to this story is the bit on page 204 where your mother blurted out a name different from Mercy. I was surprised you didn't comment or write about it at that point or at any point. Maybe you're in one of those forest-for-the-trees situations. Just because Mary is my real name doesn't mean you can't use it. I mean, fuck, you've used everything else, why not my first name?

For hundreds of pages the reader has been wondering if I am *the* Mercy Brown. Maybe at this point, they assume that, but I'd still bet your house that a part of them would be like, "Wait, wait, wait, the Rhode Island farmers already burnt Mercy's heart and consumed her ashes. How is she back?" Which is fun, in a way, that they would assume the cure worked. Sure, it's similar enough to the stake-in-the-heart stuff for someone to be culturally lulled into thinking drinking a heart-ash slushy killed the vamp dead. But in the world of this novel, if the heart cure worked, then why is Mercy still slam dancing around?

Therefore! I am not Mercy. Yeah?

I've been waiting for you to pivot to that, but you haven't. You haven't once wavered away from Mercy as Mercy in the text . . . until that little "Mary? No, Mercy" bit from your mom. Oh, man, when I read that I sat up in my coffin—come on, that was funny—but then you totally breezed by it, and a little too casually for the casual reveal. I kept waiting for you to point your authory, Nosferaturian fingers at it. But you didn't. Now, I think you included it in the novel subconsciously, and, man, for all the internalized spelunking you do, you need to listen to yourself closer.

Wouldn't it make more story sense that I am Mercy's sister, Mary? Mary was exhumed on the same gloomy day as her sister, but no one removed Mary's heart, or whatever was left of it. Mercy was cured. Mary wasn't. Think about it. Older brother Edwin still died after the exhumations and Mercy's heart roast.

Also, how did Mercy catch the wasting disease in the first place? Go back and reread the history paper you and I wrote. In my interview I, as Mercy, described my sister, MARY, sitting on my chest and going through the whole spectral vamp bit. You, Art, assumed and present it as Mercy's origin story, of how Mercy became a vampire. And THEN, prior to the sleepover, I go on to ramble about not knowing how I was made into a vampire. Maybe . . . it's because I wasn't Mercy, and I was MARY the whole time!

Everyone loves a good plot twist. The best twists may leave us dizzy while we recalibrate, but they are ultimately reassuring. The twist reinforces the rules of storytelling, and we take comfort because we misapply those rules, believing there are those plot/story gears in our own lives, gears that are tightened and greased and lovingly tended to. If only, right?

The Mary/Mercy twist as described above works. Mary still has her heart, and she fills it with your metaphorical blood, baby!

Not for nothing, it's possible I'm not Mercy or Mary and I'm Kathleen Blanchet, the not-quite-dead person you served at the first Pallbearers Club meeting, and I latched on to you without context, without reason beyond convenience—mine, not yours—and chance, and as I drained your heart, I filled your head with Mercy Brown. Real life works *that* way, but not stories, not novels. Not the ones we want to read anyway. Novels are lies. Great, big, wonderful lies.

I've said this multiple times before, but I am dreading the upcoming pages, the final pages, even though, at this point in the editing/critiquing, I know how it ends for all but the shouting. You have some shouting left to do.

I want to get the following in writing though:

If/when you/we publish this, you/we should consider including my notes. I give my blessing. In fact, I insist. What you've written is very cool, Art, and I can't say that strongly enough. You're a good writer and you tried, tried like fuck, but you need me to fill in some of the holes you left.

Just look at that deliciously ironic previous sentence! The vampire who steals life/soul from you is offering to then *add* to your book. Huh? That shit is gold, Art. You know you want it included. Ah, the jagged ouroboros of life.

You don't even have to include my name—fictitious or real—as a coauthor on the cover. I don't mind, and not what I'm looking for. Honestly and as always, I'm here to help you.

Look, just like how we wrote your history paper on poor Mercy Brown, we're collaborators. We always have been.

HARDLY GETTING OVER IT
(2014-2017)

I know you were too despondent to
leave a chapter title and summary, so
I added it for you.

~~A chapter in which acceptance is the price of freedom.~~
I know that's not as good as something Art would've written.
We should probably use what you wrote first, below.

The rest of this is an act of confession, contrition, self-flagellatory punishment, and just maybe a petty and glorious revenge. I am not and have never been above the latter. It might be all I've ever wanted.

At the writing of this, Mom has been dead for one year.

She had lung cancer. It was aggressive and didn't respond to treatment. Toward the end, she developed pneumonia, which was the phrase her doctor used. I asked, "Developed, like film?" I said it like I was angry at him, so angry I could punch a hole in his chest.

~~The infection killed her before the cancer could. And I know it's my fault.~~

~~I don't think I can write about this. I'm sorry.~~

I hated reading these lines. I wanted to burn them gone.

After (After what? After the night I saw it sitting on Mom's chest? After the night I didn't try to get it off her? After I didn't know if it had been feeding on her for part or the entirety of the time I'd been back home? After I still cowardly call it "it" and not "me"?), I threw away my blue jacket and I slept with my bedroom door closed and locked. Each morning when I woke the door was unlocked and ajar. One night I moved my dresser in front of the locked door. I had to take the drawers out first because it was too heavy to move otherwise. The dresser was back in its usual spot the next morning.

Mom's cough got worse. She lost weight. Her diagnosis was swift and irreparable. Irreversible.

I didn't know what to do. I tried staying awake while she slept, and I became a zombie—no, a ghoul. I became who I was.

I wanted to leave, to move out to keep her safe from me, from what was in me, but how could I have told her any of that? How could I have said, "Hey, I'm a weird kind of vampire (as opposed to the regular kind) and I haven't been doing it on purpose, but I've been feeding on you so it's my fault you're sick, and now that you have cancer, I'm going to get my own place and leave you alone"? It was already too late anyway. It was. (I must believe that. There is no other option.) As Mom became more ill, she asked me, as sheepish as a child admitting she was afraid of the dark, to sleep on the couch in the adjoining living room. It would make her feel better knowing I was close by, and I could leave the light on out there and read or work on my book while she slept, she didn't mind. I couldn't say no. I could not say no. (I must believe that. There is no other option.)

When she slept, her breathing was an excruciatingly wet sound, a foot being pulled out of pond muck, and each night the foot sank deeper. I stole that from her too. Now I must keep it forever.

In the morning I would ask her if she slept any better because I was supposed to ask. I already knew the answer. She said the nights were hard, and it felt like she slept with a mountain on her chest.

I cut down my hours at Newbury Comics to part-time so I could drive her into Boston for inpatient treatment. On the drives she thanked me. Said I was a good son. She asked if I remembered going into Boston for my many back appointments and the surgery, and she talked about how worried and scared she was for me, and she was even more worried when I returned home from the hospital. She would then talk about dropping me off at college and how worried and scared she was for me, then, too, but in a different way. She talked about the past on those drives, as though it was all we had.

When she was still able to live at home, her friends and my aunt stopped by a few times each week, bringing food and books and hats. I let Mom have her time with them alone. I didn't hover. I retreated upstairs, into my tower, so I wouldn't hear them be well-meaning and tell her she looked good and how strong she was. I still heard them say it all, though. And I cried when I heard Mom say she was trying, then a few weeks later she said she was tired, and then, eventually, she said, simply, "I'm ready."

On the nights it was just the two of us, we ate dinner together. She ate less and less with each meal. Then we watched TV until she fell asleep, which didn't take long. I would pull blankets over her, roll her onto her side without waking her, hoping she could breathe better.

We played gin rummy and cribbage at the kitchen table when she had the strength. She wanted to have the strength. In her final days, her eyes got big, the scleras turning yellow. They were hard to focus and hold still, she told me. I think she was covering up how desperately she wanted to see everything, even if it was just the kitchen walls that still needed to be painted. She said she was ready, but I knew she wasn't.

Some nights she rallied, found a hidden well of energy, and told jokes about wanting to smoke ten more packs of cigarettes and then she'd quit, jokes about her failing body, jokes about settling old scores and grievances from beyond the grave, jokes about where and how I would spread her cremated ashes. It was very important to her that she would be cremated. She asked, repeatedly, if I would do that for her. I answered yes, of course.

Every night (and on her last night, at the hospital) she tearily thanked me for being there.

Some nights we could look at each other when she said it.

I kept saying I was sorry. Mom, I'm so sorry.

She said it was all right, it was okay.

It wasn't.

* * *

For five months and twenty-nine days after she died, I left the house only to deal with probate lawyers, sell her car, and buy beer and occasional groceries. I still needed regular food, too, apparently. Not that I was eating much. I tried to waste away on my own. I became my own ghost, again. I've always been my own ghost (or my own ghoul, self-consuming, all-consuming). Like in the summer of '89, I haunted my own house, drifting around the first floor like I was broken, listening until I didn't hear any sounds I wanted to hear. There was nothing to hear.

Why did I never get or ask for help?

Who would help me?

Who would've possibly helped me?

What would their help look like?

Who would believe me?

Who would believe *in* me?

Who wouldn't say, "I believe that *you* believe this is happening"?

Sometimes I think about dying, despite how far away it now seems, despite its contiguity, and it brings temporary relief because I think, *At least then I won't have to worry about any of this.* This way in which I fantasize about dying is utterly ridiculous. I imagine it as akin to staying in bed all morning with my eyes closed, sometimes dozing, sometimes awake, and I'm able to see how people react to my passing, to see how the world shrugs and goes on without me. I invariably fast-forward to when everyone and everything that ever was is gone, except for me, because I'm still there to witness the sacred nothingness. Then, still in this fantasy, I come back to the now and I wake up, longing for a do-over armed with foreknowledge.

If I ever think about real dying (and I do and I have for as long as I can remember, usually at night and in bed, when dying feels close, as though it might be a tap on the shoulder, a whisper in an ear), I get scared. Quivering, whimpering scared. Overwhelmed. Even now. Even after everything that has happened to me and all that I've done.

I am trying to find help. I search the Internet for the living relatives of witnesses to Mercy Brown's exhumation, as though they have something to give to me, presuming they'd be willing to part with it. Same with historians, folklorists, and the gatherers of story, and I think they might come closest to giving me what I want or need. In the end I know they'll break my heart because they will approach the truth but not get all the way there. Those Internet searches don't last long, though, and then I randomly scroll through social media feeds and blogs of people I know or used to know and then total strangers and sometimes I pretend to be those other people, and it's a relief, and I imagine I'm like them, or like you: angry and sad, yes, but also dumbly hopeful.

Then I pretend that I'm helping everyone by taking and consuming their online confessions and their pain. I pretend I'm a different kind of monster.

What if the part you so achingly want to fix, change, banish, or destroy is the part that is fundamentally you?

I still don't know who can help me. So, I haven't asked anyone.

There's a part of me that thinks/hopes/wishes none of this is real. I haven't asked for help because I'm afraid to learn I could've been helping myself all along and I've wasted so much time, a lifetime, and I haven't asked for help because I'm trying my best and I don't want to know my best isn't good enough, will never be good enough, and I don't ask for help because help means coping with the terrible thing and I don't want to cope, to simply go on, and I childishly think coping hides the fact that there is no purpose and no reason for anything.

Fucking hell. The author is a monster. The ~~memoir~~ novel is a vampire, and it needs you to breathe life into its voice of the dead; like any book, it needs you to survive.

I wish I never fucking wrote any of this.

Yet here I am. And I have a new plan.

I will find Mercy.

Mom had a small bank teller's 401(k) I used to pay for cremation and settling her (and my) credit card debts. I probably should've used it to pay down the mortgage a little bit. Instead, I lived off it for almost two years. I quit the job at Newbury Comics. Besides being grief-stricken, depressed, existentially bereft (and vampiric, did I mention vampiric?), I worried that I might be unconsciously gnawing on or syphoning off my coworkers if I spent too much time around them. I didn't (and don't) know how this vampire thing totally worked. Yeah, the big feeds seemed to happen at night, when people were sleeping, but it's clear to me that Mercy chewed on me like I was bubble gum whenever we hung out together. Though, I have never been physically recharged or reinvigorated after a shift at work. Quite the opposite. And I feel like a beat-up person in their mid-forties. Or mid–four hundreds. Christ, can you even imagine living half that long and what that would do to your head, your spirit? No, I don't think you can. Our new advancing ages turn us all into cowards eventually.

How about a miximg straw? I loved chewing on them.

Anyway, I left the job because I didn't want to drain and sicken my punk or punk-adjacent comrades in black T-shirts, Doc Martens or Vans, hole-punched piercings, and sleeve tattoos. And I left because the store had long ceased to be a record store (sure, we sold some records, though vinyl collecting was now an exorbitantly pricey hipster niche pursuit), and had devolved into a pop-culture kitsch store; a Johnny Rotten on a coffee mug, Star Wars and Disney T-shirt and desk-calendar repository.

Besides, I needed more time to look for Mercy. My social media and White Pages search for her wasn't getting me anywhere.

To that end, I will drive to Rhode Island tomorrow.

It is a blah kind of early November afternoon in New England. Gray and Calvinist. But for the first time in almost a year, I have purpose. I make the ninety-minute drive to the College Hill area of Providence with every expectation I will find Mercy.

I cruise Benefit Street, working up the courage to ring her old

Present tense! Urgent! Sexy! You're driving by my old apartment right now!

basement apartment's buzzer. First, I scout the branching side streets for her orange Nissan, or any orange compact car. I find a blueberry muffin–sized Honda Fit that's a burnt orange. Close enough? I came prepared for long shots and maybes. In my hoodie's front kangaroo pocket, I have a stack of twenty stationery cards. I figure a well-made card (thicker stock, made from 100 percent compostable tree-free paper) would be less likely to be ignored or thrown away without being read than a flimsy, folded-up piece of paper. Stenciled on the front of each card is a brief Kurt Vonnegut quote of my choosing: "Hello babies. Welcome to earth." The card recipient then has the responsibility to be literate enough to know the rest of the famous text that follows about kindness. I wrote the following on the inside of each card. I only botched two that I'll recycle later.

Just "M," right?
Not Mercy.
Or MARY!

M—
We really need to talk.
Please. ▬▬▬▬▬ is
my cell. I'm back in
my old house in Beverly.
Art

Dude. You can't publish
your cell phone number.

I leave a card pinned under the Honda's windshield wiper. As I walk back to my car, the card rattles against the glass in an invisible breeze. It's like I'm making the note nervous by watching it. Should I leave a second one under the other wiper? No, my cards don't grow on trees, and they must be strategically rationed.

Like the twitching basement door latch from the scene with your mom?

Back in my own failed-inspection-twice vehicle, with the Fit out of sight, I reflexively check my phone for a text from Mercy, which is stupid, I know. There aren't any other orange compact cars parked in the neighborhood. I'm tempted to leave cards with random cars on the off chance she isn't driving an orange one anymore. If only I could dowse her car. (I love the word "dowse," and pledge to use it whenever I can.)

Obviously, she might not live here anymore, and even if she did, she could be working. I try to imagine the job she has: wedding photographer (that makes me smile), a photographer for dying newspapers (but an anti–Peter Parker, one who husked both Uncle Ben and Aunt May), or maybe her gig is totally random, like an archivist for one of the one zillion libraries in the area, or a conservationist accounting the yearly decline of barnacles growing on jetties, or writing term papers for college kids and ghostwriting online dating profiles, or a ride-share driver who leaves her fares with a backache or a cough. The latter is the least likely, I think. She's not that deliberate.

I can't tell if I'm insulted or interested.

I park and walk. Across the street college students sit on marble stairs adjacent to the yellow Shunned House. There are so many shunned houses, and I don't know why this one has sole claim to the name. The kids have sketch pads balanced on their packs, so I'm guessing they go to RISD. Maybe I'm self-conscious (duh), but I'm dressed like they are, or they're dressed like me (bootcut jeans, hoodie, black skully, chonky glasses; one has a thicker beard than I have but not patched with gray), and they watch me iceberg past. I'm the future natural disaster to be avoided (good luck with that, kids). One of them laughs as though all of this, everything, is funny. Maybe it is. The most cosmic of jokes and horrors. I have the urge to shout "Boo!" and scatter them like birds.

Two more blocks and here I am at the corner of Benefit and Bowen. The redbrick three-story house is scaffolded by fire escapes designed by an Escher wannabe. According to Zillow, the studio-apartment units are five hundred square feet and rent for one thousand bucks a month. I follow the slate gray of the foundation and curtained basement windows down Bowen and to the entrance. It's cold enough to see my breath. The outer door is locked. I buzz her apartment. No one answers. I wish I could tell you I feel or don't feel her presence. There's only a thrilling, hopeless uncertainty. The prevailing voice in my head asks variations on a theme of *Do you know what you're doing?* Not as insistent is a child's voice asking more directly *What if you don't find her?* and *What if you do?*

I buzz the apartment again, and nothing, so I tape a card to the door's window. I also tape a card to the apartment's locked mailbox.

Next, I go on a mini tour of Providence's music clubs and leave cards taped to windows and doors. I have plenty of cards left, so I pick out some bars and restaurants on Westminster and Thayer Streets and tuck the cards into unseen corners of their bay windows, and I drip a few on the sidewalk. Those cards are like lottery tickets, the one-in-a-gazillion chance that she'd find one. I Johnny Appleseed Providence until I have two cards left. Then I drive south to Exeter.

The Chestnut Hill Cemetery isn't hidden, isn't a lost place. Prior to arrival, I imagined parking on the shoulder of some winding, desolate road and then hiking along a secret overgrown path through a wooded glen, with the trees parting to reveal an ivy-and-mossed land of the dead, where few dare to tread.

What's up with the rhymes in the last few pages?

While its rectangular plot has been carved out of a sizable local forest, the cemetery sits on Route 102, which boasts a speed limit of forty miles per hour. A literal roadside attraction. So oddly disappointing, as though history and other people's suffering and deaths aren't living up to my poignant and creepy expectations. The Baptist church is a painted-white, U-shaped amalgam of buildings, slyly crouched and beckoning like a carnival huckster at the front of the lot. The church itself is another headstone or monument to the dead past within a flat plain of stones.

Not the usual description of a vampire being mortally afraid of God's house, but we'll work with it.

I turn my car right, onto a dried and rutted dirt road and pull over almost immediately. Mercy's grave is a few steps away and clustered within the family plot. Mary Olive is on Mercy's right, closest to the road. To Mercy's left is a scraggly tree and the headstones of her parents. Edwin's grave is there too.

Mercy's story has gained notoriety (if not popularity) in recent years. I didn't realize how much so. Granted,

The past is not dead.

it's only a week past Halloween, but I'm surprised to find so many trinkets (including, in case you can't make it out in the photo, coins, seashells, a black rose, a white rose with drops of red, and two Disney princess Band-Aids) left by . . . by whom? Fans? Curiosity-seekers? Believers? People who want their heart consumed too?

A metal bracing rings the base of the stone and runs up its back, as people have tipped the marker as well as chipped off pieces to keep as mementos. Mementos of what? Of a real vampire? If they really believed, wouldn't they be concerned they were inviting misery into their lives? Misery is coming for them regardless.

Unlike my other notecards, I place this one in a plastic sandwich baggie, then I lean it against the stone. That's not good enough, and with the added sail of plastic it might fly away in a breeze. I try pinning it under the small pumpkins, but some of those have already gone soft. Finally, I slide the card between the metal brace and the stone. That will have to do.

I have one card left and I leave it at her older sister Mary's grave, mainly because there are no Halloween-themed or gothy tchotchkes left at her stone. Not that I believe Mary knows what is happening in and around her grave, but I'd hate for her to be jealous of her younger sister's attention.   Yeah, sure.

Mary's grave isn't entirely forgotten though. At the base of the slate stone is a group of eight carnation flowers arranged in three rows: three pink, three white, two blue. They must've been left recently, given their fresh appearance. I think someone kept or took the ninth flower, likely a blue one. I put my card in the presumed-missing flower's spot. With rain in the forecast for the evening, I'm not sure how long this card will keep its form and message.

I return to my house, which is, if not a shunned one then ignored, but the Ignored House doesn't have the same echoey ring.

I haven't trashed the place. Sure, maybe it declines toward a certain feral state of anti-clean from time to time, but then I buckle down and swab what needs swabbing, and yeah, the windows should be washed, but who has time for that? And, fine, the basement is a disaster and it's where I piled boxes and plastic bins of Mom's clothes and other belongings, some of which were already dusty memories in unlabeled boxes I can't bring myself to open. I don't know what else to do with all her stuff and I empty-promise myself that one day soon I'll go through it all, figure out what I can donate or throw away and what, if anything, can be saved.

The glow of purpose from my Rhode Island tour dims considerably, so too my confidence in finding Mercy. I sneak into my own kitchen, not wanting to stir the echoes. I grab a beer from the fridge and plop down at the table in my seat, not Mom's. There is one new text waiting for me. It's clearly in response to a found note, but it's not from a Providence area code. A college student, or a professor? Maybe it's not from anyone in academia and someone who'd recently moved to the city. Whatever or whomever, I do not think it's from Mercy. The text is the last line of the Vonnegut quote from God Bless You, Mr. Rosewater. Good for them, even if they haven't read the book and plugged the quote into the ubiquitous online search engine. Maybe I should repeat this note-leaving exercise with other quotes from favorite books or song lyrics to share a little joy, momentarily connect with a stranger in a half-analog, unanticipated way? Then I remind myself I left those notes because I have been turned into a monster and I am trying to unbecome one by finding the one who made me.

Why not? That text sounds playful. I'm playful. But it wasn't me. Maybe.

The other note-sourced texts I receive over the next week are decidedly not rooted in Vonnegut's vision of kindness, or not in kindness toward me. One text lectures me to leave "M" alone. Another texter replies with a similar sentiment via a lowercase "creepy" and three puking emojis. One restaurant threatens me with banning because my note got wet and froze to the glass and had to be scraped off the bay window. Having worked in my fair share of restaurants, if I were suddenly saddled with having to go outside and scrape a window, I'd be salty too. I texted back: "Sorry.

My bad." Yes, the "my bad" is passive-aggressive. It is also a two-word symbolic representation of Art Barbara.

Two people texted me photos. One is of dogshit, likely generated from a large breed of dog, given the size of the pile on the sidewalk in front of the Strand (artfully composed, though). The other is of Mercy's grave. It's the headstone photo I included in the manuscript.

Click goes the digitized, avatarized sound of a phone's "shutter."

Three months pass and we're into March of 2017.

After bleary insomniac nights I spend my blearier hungover mornings scanning online obituaries in Beverly, Essex County, and Providence. I search for obituaries that are light on family detail, or any detail. I search for the name Kathleen Blanchet. I search for names using the initials KB. I search for names using the initials MB.

Mary Brown? I search for women who are roughly my age and of the ages of Kathleen and Mercy. Most afternoons and evenings I am a one-person Pallbearers Club. I have attended thirty-three wakes for people I do not know, have never met. I am generally able to avoid receiving lines because most of the wakes I attend do not have enough people to make one. If I'm asked how I knew the deceased, I say, simply, "An old friend." I sign registers using the name Art Barbara, which might as well be my real name now. None of the people I've seen have looked like Kathleen/Mercy but, just in case, I sneak a photo with my phone of the body or closed casket. I have no idea if finding Mercy's photographic proof works with digital cameras, as I've yet to see the blobs of color or anything out of the ordinary. Maybe it only works (if it works at all) with Polaroids, or specifically her camera. I haven't tested my phone camera's ability by taking a picture of myself. I'm afraid to confirm what I already know.

Before entering the small, sparsely attended services, I wonder about after. I wonder if I will begin to feel physically/psychologically better, nourished against my psychic will, a reluctant, resigned leech feeding on the unsuspecting grievers. Maybe that is what I want, or what the thing inside me wants. Of course, me and thing are the same, I can't lie to myself about that. Am I really going back to funeral homes to look for Mercy? Do I really think I will find her in this ludicrously scattershot way?

It doesn't appear that I'm feeding off the people around me. To my temporary relief, I do not feel better (in any of the possible ways) during or post wakes. I can't sleep despite all the beer I drown in when I come home, and I'm always exhausted the next day despite the gallons of tea I drink. My fingers and feet are going numb. I don't have health insurance. A doc-in-the-box clinician thinks I have multiple stenosis (a narrowing of the spinal canal, impinging and choking the nerves) in sites outside of my spinal fusion. She might be right, but I think parts of me are dead or dying already. Also, my heart has gone clunky, or clunkier, a puttering engine always threatening to stall one minute then a racing metronome the next. Maybe it's all the caffeine and beer, right? Maybe it's my congenital heart stomping out final warnings. Maybe I'm not feeding it what it needs.

It's April, and with Mom's IRA money all but gone, vampire or not, I need a job because I am not going to sell our house. Mom's house. It was and still is hers. I may not live here for long (certainly not forever), but I am not selling it now. It's too soon. I haven't even painted the kitchen yet. That needs to happen first.

I get a job driving a hearse at MacPherson's Funeral Home in Danvers. I tried Stephens Funeral Home first. Mr. Stephens retired ten years ago and sold his business to his nephew Charles. He wasn't hiring, but he and Mr. Stephens (from his retirement cottage in Virginia Beach) kindly found me a landing spot and put in a good word. During my interview, the implacable and silver-haired Roger MacPherson asked if we'd met before, said that I looked familiar to him. I played dumb and didn't tell him that I'd been to his establishment for three wakes in the prior two months.

It's a big and busy funeral parlor, so it's easy for me to keep to myself as much as possible. I don't interact with the bereaved beyond a quick introduction, tip of my cap, and I'm-sorry-for-your-loss. Because of my back issues I supervise and encourage the pallbearers as they load and unload the coffin to and from the hearse. I'm the kindly but distant, we've-seen-this-horror-movie-before tall and sad-faced driver. I like to think of my hearse and accoutrement as honest and proper stay-away-from-me messaging. So much so I'm not above grocery shopping in my regalia. When I'm inside the hearse, alone with the coffin, I take a picture with my phone and I may or may not have a conversation with the deceased on the drive to the cemetery, tell them about how many people showed up, how many people loved them.

When I come home from work, I watch TV, or I lie on the floor and listen to music at a volume that leaves my ears ringing. I listen to music like I did when I was seventeen years old, which means I imagine myself performing and singing the important words. I pretend I'm still seventeen even though I hated being seventeen; it's a default inner state I'm trapped in, that I clutch to and won't let go. I don't play much guitar anymore, because when I do there's an inexplicable sense of guilt and shame and the only way to wash that taste out of my mouth is to reread this stupid, incompetent manuscript. I tweak bits here and there, but I am no longer adding much. There isn't yet anything to add. How do I end this? How is anyone supposed to end this?

Still no sign of Mercy. <u>Even if she has never left.</u>

We get you're depressed and that it's a theme of the book—not that I enjoy being a metaphor for depression/anxiety—but average readers will have only so much patience for it.

Without premonition, precognition, certainly without warning, without rhyme, reason, pomp, circumstance, without any instinctual, vampy-sense tingling that this night is to be different from the others that preceded—and by the way, it's a warm, dry early evening in the <u>first week of June,</u> the kind that almost makes it worth living in New England, and the windows in my house are all open and a light breeze curls pages as I read this incomplete manuscript at the kitchen table

Why not say June 6, the anniversary of Mary Olive Brown's death?

and I think maybe I should sit outside because it's so freaking nice out, and yeah, I don't have any lawn chairs or anything like that but I could bring out one of the wooden kitchen chairs or sit on the back steps, leave the book inside—a car pulls up in front of my house. There's music (something up-tempo with a drummer desperate to keep impossible time) blaring from the car's stereo and it cuts out with the engine. The driver's door opens, slams shut, and maybe ten long seconds later, the doorbell rings.

I unfurl into my bipedal form and walk through the empty house, mere moments away from seeing Mercy (despite my earlier saying I had no special sense about the evening, once the doorbell rings, I know who it is). This is what I wanted. This is what I want. (Replace the periods with question marks as you wish.) But I'm not prepared for it. Why did I want this again? <u>Oh, right.</u>   *Have you explained your thinking on this? I don't think you have yet.*

The curtains in the dining room reach out as though to stop me, or to pat me on the back with a sarcastic *Yeah, good luck.* Sarcastic Curtains, were I ever to form a band again, would be a great bad-band name. A bad band is the only kind I ever wanted to be in.

I open the door.

<u>Mercy</u>, forever evergreen, stands on the front stoop, the storm door open and pinned behind her left leg. She says "Truce?" and throws a headless living shadow at me, its greedy arms flapping and wavering.   *You should've excitingly sleuthed or agency-ed out my location and uttered an '80s action-movie quip, then we could have an epic Final Boss battle.*

I didn't think an attack would happen so soon upon our reunion, but it is happening. I swallow a scream, but some of it kettle-whistles between my lips, and I squeeze my eyes shut, preparing to stoically absorb the apocalyptic assault. Whatever it is bounces off my chest with a brief jingle and puddles on my flip-flop-clad feet.

"Hey, um, it's your jacket. It won't bite."

I bend and pick up the black jacket by the scruff, the leather cracked and worn. After a quick visual, tactile, olfactory inspection, there's no question <u>it's my old jacket</u>, the same one I left (abandoned) on the street in front of my North Providence apartment, and it's gorgeous.   *Nah, guy, I bought it online and roughed it up a little.*

I mumble, "No way." I should be frightened and disturbed, but I'm neither. I'm honestly relieved. Mercy and I get to begin again, which means we're almost, finally, over. At least, that's the plan.

She asks, "What did you think it was?"

"A replica?"

"You're frightened of leather jacket replicas?"

"Pleather is terrifying."

"A few weeks after the blowout at my place, I went to your apartment," Mercy says, "and I found it on the sidewalk. I buzzed your room like ten times, but you didn't answer. So, I left and took it with me. Like you took my camera."

I won't say anything about her camera yet. It'll piss her off. It has taken me almost thirty years, but this latest, least-greatest version of Art might finally be on more equal verbal footing. I say, "This probably won't fit me anymore."

Her expression is eternal in its unreadableness. "Looks like it'll still fit. You might be surprised," she says. "Hey, don't take this the wrong way, but you look like you need a year or two of sleep."

"Gee, thanks. What can I say? I've been hit by the glacier called advancing middle age. You should try it sometime, O ageless one."

Meh, more like booze and pain pills are the name of that glacier.

"Yeah." Mercy pauses to let the unsaid words wreak havoc. "Well, I've always looked like I'm in advancing middle age."

We stare at each other. Or less a stare, more like a shared vigilance. She says, "Don't be in a rush to disagree with me about my appearance."

"You don't look middle-aged. You look the same as you always have." When I say it, the cowardly sun finishes slinking away into the night sky.

Her age remains stubbornly unidentifiable. A generational chameleon in jeans and a green field jacket, Mercy's hair is the same length, and her eyes are wide but not too big. The better to see me with.

"I'm not the same," she says. "I'm older, like you. We're all older, Art. Didn't you know that?"

"Older like me, huh? I feel one thousand years old."

"You'll have to get used to it."

"Is that how old you are?"

Mercy rolls her eyes so hard it's a wonder the momentum doesn't send her backward somersaulting down the front stairs. "Art?"

"Yeah?"

"I'm very sorry about your mom."

"Thank you." Tears threaten a flash flood, but I hold them back with anger and regret. I want to blurt out, *It was my fault, which means it was your fault too,* but I don't. And I don't ask her how she knows. If nothing else, I won't give her that satisfaction. She can have everything else.

"So, hey, do we have a truce or what?" she asks.

A truce implies a battle continues to wage. If so, it has been a decidedly one-way ass kicking. When I said I had a plan, my continued pummeling at her hands *is* the plan. Lose the battle and lose the war. What isn't a part of my plan is a truce.

Is she disappointed I'm not saying more? Is she impatient with me? I can't tell. I weigh the jacket in my hands but don't put it on. Maybe I'll try it on later tonight.

"Can I come in?"

I say, "Wait here a sec."

She remains on the stoop. I leave the door open and dash upstairs to my neglected music-studio-cum-writing-office in my childhood bedroom, and to the closet, my cryogenic chamber without the popsicled body parts, the same closet in which I used to hide my back brace. On the lone shelf above the row of empty clothes hangers is her Polaroid camera. It's dusty and hasn't been touched since my moving here in 2007. I want to smash it in front of her, see if that triggers an all-out offensive on her part, but that doesn't feel right. The truce talk has me rattled and sinking into my own quicksand. But when Mercy calls out, floating my name up the stairs, I get an idea. A wonderful, awful idea.

"Be right down," I say, and fuck it, since this might be it for me I sausage myself into the leather jacket. It fits. Almost. I love it and

Yeah, I found a note, like I "found" your Pallbearers Club flyer all those years ago.

I hate it. But it's way too tight on me to hide her camera within the lapel. I check the pocket and find <u>one of my Vonnegut notes</u> I left in Providence or in the graveyard. That she took this long to come to my house means something, but I'm not sure what. I repocket the note, peel out of the jacket, and drape it over one arm and over her camera like a deranged waiter. It's a look, and it'll have to do.

Back within the doorway I tell her, "Yeah, okay, a truce. And I can complete a ceremonial swap. I still have your camera—"

"Surprise, surprise. I figured you sold it."

"Sold it?"

"Yeah, for drugs."

I blink hard enough that my eyelids might as well clack together. What was that I thought earlier about our being on equal verbal footing? "The Polaroid-for-drugs market is a depressed one. Terrible value. Come on in. Let's get the camera. Don't mind the simultaneous emptiness and mess."

Mercy steps inside. I turn on a light and I lead her into the dining room, which is <u>the emptiness part I advertised</u>.

Empty except for the old wooden hutch buried in empty beer and whiskey bottles.

She says, "I love what you did with the room. I dig minimalism."

"The day after Mom died, I accidentally smashed the dining-room table. Repeatedly." After I smashed the table and stopped crying, I curled up on the floor and willed my breaths into the shallows where my heart could skim on the surface like a tossed rock before finally sinking. In my lowest moments, the ones buried beneath sedimentary layers of strata that have formed over my decades, I returned to this empty room and lay down on the floor, slowly, so as to not startle the emptiness, to not accidentally fill it with my presence, and I closed my eyes and dreamed of becoming permeable again, but this time I would disperse, dissolve, and dilute myself into nothing.

"I am sorry, Art. Truly." The way Mercy says it, does it mean more than commiseration with the grieving? Is she apologizing for making me into me?

"Thanks. I am too."

"So where is it? Or are you telling me you accidentally smashed the camera too?"

"No, it's in the basement." In a way, I am not lying because the camera will be in the basement once I bring it down there. I turn my back to her because I can't let her read me, not yet.

I don't walk the exaggerated wooden march of the schemer to the basement door, which is disconcertingly unlatched. Not sure why or how that is, as I always leave it latched. Earlier, less than an hour ago, when I was decidedly not permeable in the kitchen, I ignored my book to gape blankly across the dining-room vista to the basement door and its hooked latch. Believe me, I keep tabs on the latch, and it *was* hooked. Now I worry Mercy unlatched it, letting me know she is one hundred steps ahead of me.

You are always and eminently readable. Not necessarily a bad thing.

Mercy says, "Man, you left it in that damp-ass basement? You might as well have dumped it in the Shoe Pond."

"Don't worry, I kept it safe." Struck with a sudden superstitious urge, I relatch the basement door, eyeball it for a beat, then lift it away with a flick.

We walk down the softening wooden stairs for what could possibly be the last time, and I note, with gratitude and hope, that my heart announces its irregular presence with a clunk, a flutter, and a stitch in the center of my chest. The goddamned thing has always been a hopeless puppet eager for the ventriloquist to steal its life and secrets. Or maybe my heart can't be contained any longer and is trying to bust out, be like the cute, toothy embryonic xenomorph from *Alien* that, once free, will quickly grow up to be its own unstoppable monster.

Behind me, Mercy monologues about what mildew does to cameras, but I'm not listening, not really.

The ceiling is low, with skeletal beams, joists, and wire snarls exposed. The cement slab floor is gritty and cracked. Cobwebs greedily latch on to our arms, legs, and faces as we navigate past the boiler, the mini staircase to the rusted bulkhead, past Mom's stuff piled in a leaning tower of boxes, and to the floor-to-ceiling wooden shelves that are all but empty.

My head is an exhausted and resigned swimmer lost at sea. My heart continues its wounded spasms, caught on a fishing line. My numbed toes spark with needles of pain at their tips. It has already started or restarted. This is what I want to happen, what I've wanted to happen. This must be it now. We're in a basement again. I mean, we're subter-freaking-ranean! She can't resist who and what she is, not down here. She can't help herself. She has no choice. Like with me and Mom. That is the horror of us.

I wait and expect the hanging lightbulb above my head to wink out, or perhaps explode, showering me with glass and filament, or maybe I'll rise off the slab and smash into it, and I won't fight it. Mercy will finish me, turn me into a dried husk, lift me off the floor one last time, then grind me into dust, that sanctified disintegration, so that I might forever float forgotten in the air. She will consume me and destroy me and stop me from being a monster. I am ready. This is what I want.

But. My prior comparison to the *Alien* chest-birthing gives me a hey-dumbass-wait-a-minute pause. What if I am an embryo and haven't burst out of the metaphorical chest yet? What if I don't become the fuller monster until after I die, like Mercy did?

Mercy says, "Dude. What are you doing? You're starting to freak me the fuck out. Where's my camera?"

"Sorry. It's right here." With a shaky sleight of hand, I pretend to grab it off a corner of an empty shelf that I've mostly blocked from her view (I bet).

"Gimme gimme gimme."

I give it to her. With the camera out of my hands, swells of pins-and-needles numbness rise and fall. My chest constricts, flattening my heart and hostaging my breath. Mercy edges closer to me but I'm falling away, down a hole, a bottomless one, and this was and is my plan, but an instinctual terror implores me to return, to kick my legs and pinwheel my arms until I somehow cork up to the surface for one more chance, one more try, one more please.

Mercy shouts, "Aw, man, you said you kept it safe!" She furiously wipes dust away with a sleeve and blows repeatedly into the picture-eject slot. "Didn't even keep it in a box or anything? What the fuck. It better still work, or the truce is off." Muttering about my unconscionable negligence, she turns, walks away, and stomps up the basement stairs.

Wait. That's it? I'm still here. I'm not sinking toward the bottom of the bottomless well of souls. My palpitations and chest pains are gone. Numbness within my extremities subsides. I'm fucking fine. Goddammit.

I shout, "Hey! Where you going?" And goddamn me (again), I sound like the seventeen-year-old Art.

From the top of the stairs, she says, "Do you have any double-A batteries up here? This is an emergency."

I find her in the kitchen flipping through this manuscript.

"Hey, what's this?"

"A book." I toss my jacket onto the back of a chair and cross my hands in front of myself, as though she's seen me naked. I sink into a different kind of bottomless well. "It's a memoir. Just something I've been messing with. Off and on. It's not ready. Please don't look at any of it, not until it's finished."

"No shit." She restacks the flipped-through pages then backs away with hands raised. "Wow. A book, huh? What inspired that?" Her eyebrows arch and her mouth hangs open. I can't tell if she doesn't remember or is, again, fucking with me. "Wait, tell me later—first batteries. We must find batteries before the truce can be ratified."

We find a pack in one of the kitchen's utility drawers, buried under loose birthday candles, a roll of thread, Scotch tape, <u>empty prescription bottles</u>, two thermometers, and an assortment of pens. She pops the AAs into the Polaroid while I gather the manuscript and clutch it to my seated lap, and surprise, the camera works. I should qualify that statement by saying when she presses the shutter button, the flash flashes (albeit yellowed and weak, like the light it emits has gotten slower), and a photo slides out of the slot. I don't know if the

[handwritten margin note:] Those bottles weren't your mom's, as you imply.

photo develops properly, don't know if it displays me, or some form of me with her blobby is-it-a-thumbprint-or-astral-terror because she won't let me look at it. If she can't look at the book, then I can't look at the picture. She doesn't say that, but I know she's thinking it.

We sit at the kitchen table. I await some verdict on the photo or on me. One of my legs jitters up and down.

She says, "It works," and pockets the photo.

"Any of your proof in the photo?"

"I said it works. Barely." She inspects the camera. "It needs a new film pack, some tinkering, and some love, but don't we all." She smiles at the camera (not at me, an important distinction), satisfied.

I point my phone at her and take a picture. "My camera works too." I even deign to pass her the phone, show her the photo. No discoloration, not a pixel out of place in her don't-you-dare smirk.

"That's not the same. It's soulless." She swipes and deletes the picture. "But we have achieved a full truce, my puffy-eyed friend. Are you gonna offer me a drink or something?"

"Can I offer you a drink?"

"You can."

"What do you want to drink?"

"Water is fine."

After stowing my book above the fridge, I pour her a glass of water and grab me a beer. It's full night outside and somehow warmer, stickier, than it was earlier. And I'm confused. Warmer, stickier, and confused.

We talk and our shared time melts away. It could be ten years ago or almost thirty and we sound the same even if we aren't the same anymore. She asks if I'm playing in bands now and I tell her no. She brings up my YouTube channel, noticing it hasn't been updated in over a year. She says she's a fan even if she clicked the thumbs-down button on every episode to help keep me humble, yes, but also to stay true to her own punk roots. Nostalgia isn't punk, she tells me. Speaking of nostalgia, I tell her I drive a hearse for a big funeral home in Danvers. She tells me she's between jobs but has some money saved up. She doesn't specify what her old job was, and what her presumed new job would be. She says she's been thinking of fleeing Trumplandia and living abroad, becoming a permanent expat. I tell her that's a dreamy idea.

She says, "You can sell the house and go wherever you want."

"Yeah. Eventually, I guess."

"I get it. It must be so hard. Anyway, while you wallow—and you should be wallowing, by the way, and you wouldn't be you if you didn't—would you want me as a roomie while I figure my shit out?" She points the camera. "I won't step on your toes, get in your way. You'd be helping me out and I'll help you out too. Pay some rent."

Okay, this is more shocking than the truce bit. She is most definitely fucking with me (how often do I think and/or say that?). Is this off-the-cuff, or did she arrive planning to ask to live here?

Being around her has always negatively affected my health and literally curled my spine, but her two major feeds/attacks on me happened at night, when were both asleep in the same place. Within the folklore and my now-detailed personal experience, night and sleep and the consumption/consuming are conjoined. Her staying here while I'm sleeping in the house needs to happen, needs to be facilitated.

My destroy-the-me-monster-in-the-basement plan A didn't work. So now it's on to the decidedly nocturnal plan B. I say, "You're welcome to stay as long as you need."

She gavels the kitchen tabletop with an open hand. "Great. A pleasure, as always, Art. I'll be back tomorrow with my stuff. I'll leave it to you to decide where you want to put me." She gets up and walks out of the kitchen and out the front door.

After she drives away (her compact car is old and orange), I'm filled with the hope of anti-hope. To celebrate, I sausage into my leather jacket, drink my face off, and play guitar upstairs, the amp cranked to eleven.

* * *

I wake on the floor, fossilized next to my buzzing amp. Mercy rings the doorbell impatiently (the adverb here meaning her stabby finger continually depresses the button; the doorbell is equally as unhappy as I am). Fucking hell, the amp isn't buzzing; it's my hangover head.

I groan, as I haven't decided where she is going to stay briefly (the briefliest, one night, less than one night if it goes the way I want it to). And she is going to grill me about it. I could give her the upstairs, but I can't sleep downstairs, not in Mom's converted bedroom, I just can't, even though the thought of my being siphoned into oblivion in that same room has an undeniable tint of karmic justice. I can't put Mercy in Mom's old room either, certainly not on the same, decades-old pullout couch. That seems too fucked-up, even for me.

More doorbelling.

I stumble down the stairs and to the door. Cruel sunlight excoriates me. I say, "Kill me now, please."

"Good morning, sunshine." Mercy pushes past me with a duffel bag on one shoulder and her camera/laptop bag looped over the other. She dumps both in the empty dining room.

"Need any help? Please say no."

"There's a couple boxes of books and records in the truck cab, but they can wait. Put some shoes and pants on."

"I'm wearing shorts."

"*Art wears short shorts.* Like I said, put some pants on. And let's go."

"Where are we going?"

"To make a purchase. I knew you wouldn't be able to decide where I should sleep, so I did."

After splashing cold water on my face and, yes, putting on jeans, I slosh into the truck's cab and say, "Of course you rented an <u>orange one.</u>"

"It wasn't easy."

My knees are pinned against the dash because of the moving boxes behind my seat. Our first stop is the ubiquitous donut chain drive-thru, and she buys me a plain bagel and a cup of shitty tea.

Why not tell the readers that orange was my sister's favorite color? Or something to make me more relatable.

After my breakfast of non-champions, I almost become human. Mercy chides me for not drinking coffee like every other morally bankrupt person. I probably should've asked for a bottle of water, too, as I quiver with caffeine and dehydration.

Next stop: we pull into a famous international furniture superstore parking lot. Mercy tells me we're getting rid of the decades-old pullout couch downstairs and she's going to buy a futon. Sure, why not. At least the decision of the charade sleeping arrangements is made.

To sort of quote Camper Van Beethoven, I froggily sing, "*Take the vampires furniture shopping, take them furniture shopping*," as we pass through the automatic sliding doors.

"You can't make a stake with particleboard," she says. "We won't be long. I promise. I know exactly what I want. But would you be mad if I bought a little dresser too?"

Thirty-seven hours later, we are finally leaving the lot with the unassembled futon and dresser in the truck bed. Then Mercy says, *Stop being a whiny baby.* "Side trip," and pulls into the lot of the neighboring home-improvement box store (not the orange one, but the other one that spends less on political donations to hatemongers). As long as I can stay in the truck and nap, I agree to allowing Mercy to paint the wooden paneling in the living room-turned-bedroom, and yeah, sure, it'll brighten the space up, make it airy, and the painted paneling will look like clapboard, almost like a beach house. Mercy returns some untold time later with painting supplies, along with a screwdriver and pack of interchangeable screwheads, a toothy hacksaw, and a formidable drilling hammer. The latter two items have my full attention.

Back in the truck she waggles her eyebrows at me and says, "You're gonna have some fun with those."

"Wut?"

Back at the house, the home goods unloaded and not without great struggle and back pain, we stand in the living room/bedroom holding sweating glasses of lemonade.

Mercy says, "The futon and dresser were bad enough, there's no way you and I will be able to lug the pullout couch out of here. That sucker weighs a gazillion pounds."

"I can do it."

"No, you and your back can't." Mercy hands me the home-improvement bag, the one with the tools. "I need to return the truck," she says. "You can get started on taking the beast apart so we can move it in pieces out front. When is trash pickup?"

She leaves before I can lie an answer.

I am alone and I am confused. Utterly, wholly, starkly, gobsmackedly confused.

What is going on? What are we doing? What is this normal (whatever I mean by normal) house-making day, and why is it continuing to spool out into more normalness? Why is she and why are we pretending one of us is not going to finish destroying the other?

I come back to the word (her word) "truce." Truce does not mean the end of conflict. A truce is a pause, a respite, equal parts hope and cynicism. Truces end.

As I contemplate truces, armistices, peace treaties, and renewed hostilities, I drag the couch cushions and the lumpen sleeper mattress out front to the eroded curb, a blurry blacktop borderline where the sidewalk meets the street. I have no idea if the trash pickup will even take this. Next, with a box cutter, I slice away the upholstery, exposing a skeleton of wood, springs, and the metal frame of the pullout bed. I dissect the frame, surgically removing a few screws and bolts, but that's taking too long and, frankly, it's not very satisfying. Even though my back is a rusty hinge and threatens to lock up, I transform into a bloodthirsty Visigoth and I bash and hack the thing into pieces.

Surveying the rubbled aftermath, I think I get it. We're in a truce. And we'll be in one until we're not. *This was mean of me. We probably could've carried the couch outside, or even kept it in another room, but I needed a little eye for an eye.* * * *

You having to tear apart the sleeper couch was revenge for my destroyed dresser in Providence.

Our first night as roommates we split a late-night order of drunken noodles in the living room, which runs parallel to the dining room. A small TV set boulders within the cave of the inoperable fireplace. After eating I decline finishing our watch of an NBA Finals game played at the Oracle in Oakland. I say I want to work on my book a little and then get to bed because I have to wake up hearse-early tomorrow, and yeah, that's a term in the funeral biz, and whoa, my back and everything else is really sore and stiff and I know part of that is my fault because of how self-inflictedly hurt I was this morning after the all-night rock-out and beer binge that left me toadstooling on the floor next to the amp, and without any segue I offer an estimate of how many despair-filled steps we walked within the Dantean hell of the furniture store and then I added 25 percent to my steps total because of the trips in and out of the house I made transporting couch debris, and oh, the neighbor two doors down, the one with the dog, a hound mix that barks at leaves twitching in the wind and roams the streets until the sun goes down, unburdened by place or duty, that frigging dog already marked and re-marked the pile of couch, and I talk on and on and on and I can't stop talking because I'm the kind of bad excuse-maker-liar who makes it so obvious by <u>saying everything else</u> in the world possible except the truth or what it is I really want to say. Which, in this case, is fine, because I want Mercy to know I'm lying about something, and from that I want her to infer that I know she knows I'm lying, and from there, I want her to know I know something is indeed up or afoot, and that something is the quick end to the truce. The truce is up. I'm ready for it to be up, or over. I eventually stop talking to fill my mouth with ibuprofen and carbonated beverage. Mercy takes the opportunity to turn up the TV volume.

Hence all your rambly paragraphs.

I drag my calcifying carcass upstairs and collapse into bed. Despite being exhausted, I'm too excited and anticipatory to fall asleep. Each noise from the floor below is something creeping up the stairs to finally claim the overdue me. I tense up and my head fills with a banner-size, all-caps thought bubble: THIS IS IT. But this isn't it and, eventually, I fall asleep. The night passes without incident. My xylophone-toned phone alarm wakes me in the morning. Later, the hearse I drive feels permanent.

On our second night as roommates Mercy announces she will paint her room the next morning. The primer coat, anyway. I forgot about the paint she bought. I shrug and say, "Okay." I'm annoyed she uses the phrase "my room." She says, "I know your 'okay' really means, 'Hey, wow, thank you for the free home improvement labor, Mercy, because it'll help the value of the place when I sell it.'"

On our fifth night as roommates Mercy tells me the town's garbage pickup crew said they aren't allowed to take the couch and I'll have to transport it to the town dump during an oddly specific set of dumping hours that are more than a week away. There's no way I can fit the couch, even in disintegrated form, in my shitty little car. Maybe I could borrow the hearse for the dump run? (I'm kind of delighted by that idea.) Mercy also hands me a note, this one from the neighbor with the free-range dog. It (the note, not the dog) was taped to my front door, complaining about the mulched-couch eyesore, and they threatened to call the town on me. Mercy says she'd help me bring the pieces out back, buuuuut she is in the middle of touch-up paint work and didn't want to make a mess of things. Right. I lug the wood-and-metal and spongy cushions (which smell like dog piss) down the driveway and into the backyard and cover it all with a tarp while fantasizing about leaving a note on the neighbor's door that reads "You're an eyesore," and just maybe adding a hint of eau d'urine as well.

I wrote the note as a joke. I thought for sure you'd pick up on it, but then I felt bad and couldn't admit I wrote it.

On our tenth night as roommates Mercy tells me she has extra paint left over and since she did such a good job in *her* room, she asks if she can paint the kitchen. She says, "It needs a total gutting, to be honest," and then something about subway-tile backsplash and how the appliances are outdated and there's no pantry and zero cabinet space and if I really wanted to go whole hog, maybe knock out a wall, go more open-concept, and she DVRed a few episodes of a home improvement show she watches nonstop if I wanted to see what

So judgy of my hobby, wellness, and growth.

she had in mind. Perhaps sensing my lack of enthusiasm, she points out that, at the very least, she can paint over the nicotine stains on the walls, freshen things up a bit. And she might be able to add the backsplash herself. I say, "No, please don't."

On our sixteenth night as roommates Mercy tries to get me to watch one of those hokey paranormal reality TV shows. In this one, a fourteen-year-old girl was supposedly possessed. Episodes, for the moment, have been uploaded illegally on Vimeo and are bound to be taken down any moment, or, as Mercy speculates, it's a pre-publicity stunt to drum up interest in a DVD/Blu-ray release or a reboot. The show was filmed in Beverly a few years back. She can't believe I didn't watch when it originally aired and she launches into a feverish recap, including what happened to the poor family after the show, and how it was all unimaginably terrible, although, given the level of detail she provides, it's clear she can imagine the terribleness. Throughout the campfire retelling of the show's tragic aftermath, she is performatively unsettled (zealot eyes wet and shinning, hands clutched under her chin) and exhilarated (unbidden smiles, breathless half-laugh punctuations). I tell her that it rings a bell but, also, I was more than a little busy and preoccupied with my dying mother while the show aired. I add, "Sorry I couldn't join in the pop-cultural rubbernecking." Mercy slams her laptop closed, clearly exasperated with me. She says, "You act like your mother dying was your fault." Then she stops talking. What for most people would've been a comma is instead a period at the end of a single-sentence paragraph. I wait and she doesn't add *But it wasn't your fault.* It's the cruelest thing she's ever *not* said to me, even if it's not true. I seethe because she doesn't get to *not* say that and leave off her own responsibility link in that chain of horrific events. She smirks because she sees me boiling on the inside, threatening to diffuse into a scalding steam, threatening to go permeable, and now I'm thinking, always thinking, her final attack is coming. Maybe now. Please now.

On the twenty-fifth night as roommates I borrow the hearse after a Saturday-morning funeral. Instead of coming home and filling it with dump-bound couch bits, I drive it around Beverly all afternoon, passing by local institutions and old haunts, or where they used to be. The venerable Cabot Cinema continues to proudly perch at downtown's northern border. Local eateries Super Sub and Nick's Roast Beef remain traditional teen hangouts. The dilapidated, three-winged Beverly High School has been recently replaced on the same footprint with a singularly spacious, four-story-tall, state-of-the-art academic building attached to an equally behemoth athletics complex. On the more Art Barbara–specific leg of the tour, the beloved Record Rack is long gone from strip-malled Rantoul Street. Remember the night Mercy and I planned on breaking into a cemetery? Well, the tree I tried to use to climb down from the deathly pointy fence has been reduced to a chipped stump. I continue driving, neither to resurrect nor mourn the past but to bury it. To wit, I head north on Hale Street, the road hugging the rugged shoreline as my black car phantoms by Endicott College; a mile or so later is the obnoxiously and opulently quaint Pride's Crossing train station, and I enter Beverly Farms. Pronounced "the Faaahms," it is the rich (or more rich or most rich) neighborhood in town. I glide past the exclusive-to-Faaahms-residents West Beach and roll to a stop in front of Eddie Patrick's beachfront mansion. Can't say I've been invited to his house. Ever since the night I maybe-keyed Eddie's car after he crashed one of my Pallbearers Club shows, I've found myself periodically checking out his place on Google Maps and on real estate apps. Maybe once every month, or a few weeks. Certainly not every week. Why? Adolescent revenge fantasies, I suppose. Or revenge fantasies for the (proletariat) adolescent. (Oh, stop looking at me like that. Like you don't cyberstalk old high school acquaintances or enemies.) Now, beyond dusk but before dark, my hearse idles at the closed gate spanning across the drive, the grille's nose nearly touching iron, engine at a low growl. I wouldn't be able to climb that fencing, not without considerable help. I hope Eddie is home. An upstairs light flashes on. I can almost see him there, on the second floor, dressed in a non-ironic cardigan or a smoking jacket, his hair unburdened

Maybe. But driving to the dude's house is another level.

and freed from the exhaustion of pretending it is enough to cover his <u>balding pate</u>. Yeah, he sees me, and I waggle oh-hi-there fingers. *Send not to know for whom the hearse rolls, it rolls for thee, motherfucker!* His discovery of a waiting hearse is enough to momentarily unplug him from a barren inner landscape awash in inveterate narcissism, fatuousness, and cruelty. Eddie arches a villain's eyebrow and indulges in curiosity; contemplates a mystery outside the foulness of himself. He peers from his architectural opulence and wonders why a hearse crouches at the end of his fortified drive. Bringing his drooping face closer to the window but hiding his slacking, softening body behind a rolled curtain, he suffers a chill of promise and possibility. The heavy, off-time thudding of his heart flutters the bespoke cloth above his breast. Waves of exhaustion crash over him and the riptide sucks at the sand around his feet and ankles. He coughs, the kind that foretells of many more to come. The cough fogs the glass. He remembers a long-ago morning when an indifferent parent scolded him to cover his mouth after he had purposefully coughed on the kitchen window. The other less-indifferent parent added, with a familiar taint of sadism, that his soul will escape from his slack-jawed face if he isn't careful, and look, there's a piece of your soul there already on the glass, a piece you'll never get back, and the parent laughed and wiped the soul away, and Eddie clasped his hand over his mouth then, but later, when he was alone, and he was often alone, he spent hours breathing on and fogging the windows in his room, thinking if he did it enough he would see what his soul looked like, but also, he fretted about how much soul he was wasting and if it would grow back and how much did he have left, and he dreaded what would happen when he couldn't fog the glass anymore. This long-buried memory reveals his inevitable approaching death is as capricious as the strange hearse in front of his house and as transparently real as the glass inches from his face, glass that is no longer fogging as he breathes on it. He is breathing hard. And now Eddie is afraid. And maybe, just maybe, he feels me reaching across the expanse of his front yard and into his home and into him

After recently seeing Eddie at the press conference, you're overstating his follicle deficiencies.

and he feels me reaching and loosening and pulling at his fraying threads. When I fall back into myself, landing with a shudder that squeaks the hearse's shocks and wheels, an inexplicable and overwhelming panic erupts as bouts of uncontrollable, staccato laughter that threaten to turn to tears. I drive away from Eddie's house on unfamiliar winding roads that spool into the night.

On the thirty-seventh night as roommates Mercy surprises me with tickets to see Bob Mould at the Paradise in Boston. Because we get a late start heading into the city and finding parking anywhere near Commonwealth Ave is a nightmare, we miss the opening act. The place is packed and we salmon our way through the crowd without being too obnoxious about it, and we end up five rows of people from the front of the stage. Bob is great as always; all passion, energy, and integrity. For the hour and twenty minutes he performs, I'm a part of the crowd, a bobbing head in the shadowed sea, and I'm gifted the brief privilege of living in the sound outside my head. I don't wear earplugs and my ears will ring for days. On the ride home, I let my guard down and Mercy and I talk about music, the way we used to. It's warm and welcome, but there's a distinct, not unwholly pleasant tinge of sadness in the acknowledgment that this is how we used to be. Perhaps she is offering me a final moment of grace, and the end will come, if not tonight, then the next.

On the forty-second night as roommates I ask her if she's getting a job. She tells me to <u>mind my own business</u>.

On the fifty-first night as roommates Mercy asks when I'm going to start playing live music again. I tell her I don't think I am. Then she asks if I'm finished with my book. I tell her to <u>mind her own business</u>.

On the fifty-seventh night as roommates I drive the hearse back to the funeral home and I suddenly become convinced my own body is the reposed cargo. My body is not in a coffin. It rests atop the rows of chatty rollers. I position the rearview mirror down and away so I cannot look in the rear and so I cannot look at myself. I drive and I drive, deeper into the shrinking future. My body feeds off me just as I am feeding off it. We are our own parasite. We consume our secrets,

You discount how nagging and dadlike you asked me.

Alternately, I thought I was respectful in how I broached the subjects, the very opposite of nagging.

our thoughts, our memories, our identities. We consume everything and we are consumed by everything. As the hearse crests, dips, and swells within the road, the rollers shimmy and spin, and I have never been so frightened.

On the sixty-sixth night as roommates I can't sleep, which is not unusual. For the last two months plus I haven't been able to sleep for more than a few hours at a time. I lie in bed and my brain races with all that's happened and all that's supposed to happen but hasn't yet and I convince myself the next time I close my eyes will be my last, or the next time I open them I'll finally see her, or that part of her, squatting like a Sphinx on my chest, squeezing out the last bits of me. Some nights I go downstairs to the kitchen for a glass of water I don't need and then sulkily return to my room via the circuitous route, one that takes me by Mercy's room. She sleeps with the French doors closed and curtains pulled over the plate-glass windows. I do not linger.

Why are you always creepin'?

On the seventieth night as roommates Mercy returns from a day trip to Providence with her Polaroid camera repaired. She says it is finally working to her satisfaction, no thanks to me. "Say 'cheese.'" I reenact the famous Johnny Cash middle-finger photo. I lack the acoustic guitar hanging from my neck like it was there when I was born, and, frankly, the honest commitment to the gesture, given I'm a faded middle-aged wannabe punk in a mass-produced *Jaws* T-shirt, resigned to the slowest of deaths by vampirism. The cyclopean shutter opens with a white flash, another moment vaporized in a mini Oppenheimer glare. Maybe I am imagining things (again), but there is hunger as well as relief on Mercy's face as the photo of what was develops.

Aren't we all.

On our last night as roommates I stalk downstairs and into the dining room, my leather jacket looped over my shoulder. The dining room remains empty of furniture. It is less a neutral space than a nowhere space. Mercy is on the other side of the wall to my right, in the living room watching television. I am nowhere and I have spent recent days building up the desperation and courage to do what I am doing.

Mercy calls out, "You going out? If you think of it, pick up a bag of Hint of Lime tortilla chips. And medium salsa. Thanks, chum."

I could go through the kitchen and out the back door to my car and pick up chips and keep playing house for another night. But no. One way or another, this ends tonight.

I swerve right, dipping briefly into the living room. I glance at Mercy and ignore her tilted head and confused look, and then I turn left and push open the French doors into Mercy's bedroom.

"Hey, you won't find any chips in my room."

I haven't passed through the French-door boundary since I pulverized the couch and helped move her stuff in. The room is Spartanly furnished and clean. Even with the sun mostly down, the row of windows on the back wall (no longer partially blocked by the old sleeper sofa) and the white painted wooden paneling brighten up the space. Her futon is flush against the wall to my right and is iced with a yellow comforter. Next to the futon is a small nightstand fashioned from Tetrised wooden blocks. Atop the stand is an old mass-market paperback, cover-side down, and a squat bedside lamp with a blue shade. Against the windowed back wall is a blue plush chair (she picked that up last month when she said she had decided to stay here a bit longer), on which her green jacket is draped, and the only other piece of furniture, a four-drawer dresser, the same approximate size, color, and shape as the one she had in her Providence apartment. The dresser is elevated off the floor, its footings balanced on four unruly cairns of books. I shout, "Don't you keep chips under your dresser?"

She answers with, "Sometimes!"

This. This is why we're the best and wrong kind of friends. I don't think there's any question she's taunting me now. I wonder if all it would take for the dresser to timber to the floor would be a slight nudge. Maybe the haphazardly stacked books are for show and if I kick the books out from underneath, the dresser will hover in its

I'm embarrassed to admit how long it took me to get the dresser level.

elevated spot. (If/when this book is ever published, I wonder, will it hold up your wobbly legged couch or chair, will it be a doorstop or a bookend holding up the more beloved books, will you lend it to a friend to never see it again, will you donate it to a library or callously throw it into a donation bin, or will you leave it on a dusty shelf until you die and someone else then has to sort out what to do with it, as though the responsibility of the book was a curse to be passed on to the unsuspecting?) I'm sorely tempted to pull out one book. Just one, to see what happens. But I'll leave it be. I don't want to get a reputation as a <u>wanton furniture destroyer.</u>   *Well, the count is up to three pieces. That we know of.*

"Guy, what are you looking for?" Mercy asks. "Whatever it is, it's not in my room."

Wrong, Mercy. What I'm looking for is in your room. (This is me in my head now, by the way. It's where I'm safest and most dangerous.) *And I am going to take it. Once I do this, there will be no turning back. As absurd and risible as this act will seem, it will bring everything out in the open, and it will force your dastardly hand into reaching or flexing or crushing. And admitting. Mercy, just admit it.*

I snatch her green jacket off the blue chair, holding it away from my body like one might hold a hissing cobra, and I gunslinger into the living room.

Mercy pauses the streamed home-improvement show. "Eh, sorry, I don't want to go out. I'm too comfy and I want to see if this couple sells the house or stays. I've watched it before, but I don't remember what they do. Just the chips. Pretty please. With salsa on top."

I kneel in front of the hearth-bound television and sit back on my feet. My arthritic knees crunch and pop loud enough for Mercy to say, "Ow." I hold out both our jackets, one in each hand. They dangle slackly.

"Art. I said I'm not going—"

I say, "I know what you are and what you've done to me." I don't say it as me though. I say it through the left side of my mouth and in the imagined voice of my leather jacket (voice a little deeper and less nasally than my own, more heroic and competent-sounding; I've always been pretty good at doing voices). I puppet the jacket up and down as I speak, or as it speaks.

Then I voice Mercy's jacket, slightly higher pitched (but not in a mocking way), my mouth pursed to the right, if for no other reason than to give Mercy a clear visual cue that I am now speaking as her jacket. "Hey, that's crazy, man. I don't know what you're talking about."

My jacket says, "Stop it! No more lies. I know the truth and the charade ends tonight."

Then Mercy's jacket: "Fine. There can only be one."

Mercy's jacket loosens a barbaric yawp as I flutter it across my chest and smash it into the leather jacket, which shouts "Argh" and falls in slow motion to the floor with assorted impact and crashing sound effects. But you can't keep leather-jacket me down for long. It rises and counterattacks. I commit to this fight scene with the jackets entwining and grappling and I roll around on the floor throughout the epic battle, voicing an argument and quips between strikes and parries.

"I can't and won't live off other people's lives!"

"Pfft! Everyone does it!"

"No! For reals! It's unconscionable and intolerable!"

"Eh, it's not so bad! You get used to it!"

"I wouldn't be able to live with myself!"

"You're no fun! Give in to enjoying the sublime!"

"Kant says the sublime is not exterior and is a mental process!"

"Exactly!"

And back and forth and forth and back, and then, at the penultimate moment of the battle, Mercy's jacket says, "Hey look, your zipper is unzipped."

The naïve and sweetly gullible leather jacket looks down. Do not be fooled though, reader. This seeming momentary distraction, his inclination to trust, is purposeful. The jacket knows what he is doing. He chooses doom over the pyrrhic victory of continued parasitic existence. The green jacket billows open, exposing its greedy, leviathan maw, and engulfs the other, swallowing him whole.

I fall away from the jackets, settling into a splayed sitting position. I'm sweating and out of breath and I've wrenched my back.

"Does this mean you're not going out to get me chips?" Mercy asks.

"No chips."

"Okay, I'll bite. What's this all about?"

An eerily accurate portrayal of the evening thus far. And I still don't remember if the TV couple stayed or sold their house.

For over an hour I outline the evidence. Granted, it's a tad rambly and unorganized; Daniel Webster I am not. I use a whiteboard on an easel (I bought it a few years ago when I thought I might tutor SAT math as a side gig; I got as far as the whiteboard and an SAT prep book) and I divide the space into two columns with a red marker. One column is for circumstantial evidence (my various physical ailments and their onset or deterioration once Mercy started hanging out with me; her being so well versed in the Mercy Brown lore and helping to write my history paper on her; the blobby Polaroid photos) and supposition (her apparent agelessness, bands breaking up or kicking me out after she saw a show). The other column features my direct testimony and accounts of the sleepover night, her weeklong basement break-in after my back surgery, and the two nights at her apartment in Providence. Distilled, it sounds utterly ludicrous, and I'm leaving things out, important things. I was never a good public or extemporaneous speaker, never exceled in live, impromptu arguments where I invariably become instantly overwhelmed, angry, stupid, and loud, or I shut down and then hours and days later come up with the perfect things to say after having replayed and rehearsed the failed argument a billion times in my head.

Right, "helping."

During the presentation, I refer to my notes and this book. I don't think it's going as well as I hoped, and I would be better served to instead read the book out loud from page one, no matter how long that would take. This book is the case against Mercy (and the case against me), and this book describes how I feel and how I was and how I am, all two-hundred-plus messy and flawed but true

You're describing a novel, not a memoir. ⟋

pages of it. I can't possibly distill (nor do I want to) this into bite-size, digestible elevator-pitch data points or obvious <u>character arcs</u> and through lines that are easy to follow and swallow and are instantly disposable and forgettable.

I end my case with the part that's impossible, or more impossible, to talk about: what happened with Mom. Of course, what happened was that *I* happened, and after a few false starts and breakdowns, I stop trying to explain, and I read directly from the manuscript. When I finish, I say that the sole consolation (wrong word; there is no consolation) with my mother's death was her having chosen to be cremated so I don't have to worry about the possibility of her coming back and living or unliving. Though, clearly, I don't know how the transformation or transmogrifying part works, as <u>I haven't died yet</u>.

As far as you know.

Finally finished (but there's more to say, always more), I say, with my heart in my throat (replacing my missing uvula), "Well?"

Mercy's chin rests in one hand. The bored thinker's pose. "I wish I had those chips."

"This isn't a joke."

"I know it isn't. I'm sorry. It's just a bit much to take in."

[Later, I will think I should've said, "The truth, when laid out plainly, is always a bit much to take in," and I will wonder if saying that instead of nothing would have changed the winding course of our conversation, <u>which is to be our last.</u>]

When did you write this? It's like you're bending time/space and it's no biggie.

She glances at her jacket on the floor as though it will support her. "It kills me that you blame yourself for your mother's death and—and I just don't know what to say to that."

"Most people would say 'It wasn't your fault.'"

"I've said that. I've said that a thousand times."

"No, you haven't. Not once."

"Well, then. It wasn't your fault, Art. What else do you want me to say? And I didn't turn you into anything you weren't already."

"Wait. You admit to all this?" My voice quavers.

"Jesus, Art, no. Even if it were all true, I would never attack you like in your puppet show. I am, and always have been, your friend."

At least my jacket-performance intent was communicated clearly. I don't respond. A low-pressure front of quiet settles into the room. The air stills, waiting to be filled. I don't move and my edges grow fuzzy. There's a low drone in my ears, and then I hear her jacket rustle. Looking away from Mercy is probably a mistake but I do. Her jacket is on the floor, unmoving, but it lies too deflated, pressed too flatly to the floor, as though my much thicker leather jacket is no longer pinned underneath it.

Mercy says, "You know I don't believe in the supernatural, but to, um, respect all the thought you put into this"—she waves her arms in the air—"for the moment, and only for the moment, I won't refute any of it."

"You won't?"

"I won't. But—"

"What's the but?"

"The *but* is a question. Maybe two questions. Has anything you described previously happening to you when in my presence—"

"Or vicinity."

"Vicinity, sure. Has any of that happened in the two months since I moved in? Has anything at all strange happened?"

I blurt out "No," and then inwardly chide myself for not mentioning what I felt that first night of her return, when we were in the basement getting her camera. To be fair, I'm not sure what I experienced was because of Mercy or if I was too geeked up for something confrontationally big to happen. Ultimately, nothing happened, nothing compared to the something I wanted to happen, and nothing has happened since then, and fuck, I'm rattled. I say, "Well, I've been getting heart palpitations and extremity numbness."

"So," she holds the *o* long enough to pin me in place, "you weren't experiencing either of those symptoms—which are concerning by the way, please see a doctor—before I moved in?"

"Well, no, not exactly." I um and stutter through telling her about my driving to Eddie's house about a month ago with the hearse (but I don't tell her how last week I drove by his place again after getting off work) and what I did and felt there.

"So," the long *o* again (goddammit), "you felt weird and off when you were being weird and off while being a creeper out front of Eddie Patrick's house?"

"Yes. No, I mean, it was weirder than that. Stop pretending like you don't know."

Mercy holds up empty I'm-not-saying-I'm-just-saying hands, and I'm already angry, which means I'm losing, and not in the way I wanted to lose.

I say, "Whatever, fine, nothing, um, overt has happened since you've moved in. I can admit that. But that doesn't disprove everything that happened in the years, the fucking decades prior."

"I didn't say it did. Just establishing a baseline," Mercy says. "All of it—us being life-sucking vampires—could still be true, as you say. The universe—or this one, anyway—is a fucked-up place that seemingly makes up the rules as it goes, right? That's Kant, too, I think. Eh, who knows? I asked you the questions about what you've experienced lately, which we've established is essentially nothing, to point out the possibility that maybe we're in, like, remission now. Or, hey." She snaps her fingers. "Maybe we just got better, you know? Like getting over a nasty cold that hangs around for a while. I like that. We've recovered from some virus. A non-supernatural one. I can work with that."

She's laughing at me without laughing. I say, "We're not better. I'm not better."

Mercy stands up. "Give me the marker, please."

I toss it to her. She fumbles the catch. The first crack in the armor, maybe. She's careful to step over her jacket and not on it as she strolls to the whiteboard. Holding the marker like a rapier, she sighs as if to say, *Sorry but you're making me do this.*

She says, "I told you I wasn't going to refute any of this, so I will *not* point out that your connective-tissue disorder existed before you met me and that I do *not* have the power to change you on the cellular level. I

I wasn't laughing at you. I never did. Sometimes with, though.

will *not* remind you how high we both were the night I slept over your house, and you took a picture of me sleeping because you thought I looked like a dead woman—gee, thanks, by the way—and that my jacket had, um, a face." Mercy crosses out items one by one while *not* refuting. "I will *not* pretend I was there the times your bands broke up or gave you the heave-ho and I will *not* posit that you were struggling with alcohol and painkiller addiction and therefore likely not the most reliable bandmate. Further, I will *not* bring up the pills I found in your jacket and how blotto you were when you trashed my apartment. Hold this for a second." She hands me the marker and fishes a hand into her front jeans pocket. "I will accidentally take out my driver's license, but I will *not* force you look at the picture and date of birth and contemplate my agelessness." She pulls out a thin zippered wallet and removes her license. She holds it in the palm of her hand while looking away from me.

I peek. It's a Rhode Island license. The picture is hers, and whenever it was taken, she looks the same now. Her listed <u>date of birth is February 17, 1968.</u>   *Why not make it 1964? Then it would be*

I try to play it cool while I'm melting inside and say, "Three years *Mary Olive* older than me. I mean, *at least* three years older. And it needs to be *Brown's DOB* renewed."   *plus 100 years.*

"You're such a liar." She pulls the license away and inspects it. "Oh, wait. Dammit."

She returns the wallet to her pocket, and I give her back the marker. She continues, *not* telling me what I did and didn't see or feel or experience. She does *not* say that within the Mercy Brown lore, the vampire was dead and buried, or undead and buried, and wasn't walking around, as far as anyone knew. She ends by *not* pointing out that Mercy Brown's heart was burned, consumed, and cured.

Mercy has not succeeded in placing doubt where there isn't any, but I am drowning in hopelessness. Sure, there's a chance now that I've laid out everything in the open, she'll attack me later, when it's less confrontational, <u>when the time is of her choosing</u>, but given her response, it seems less and less likely to happen.

She says, "I can't believe this whole time I've been living here you were waiting for me to, what? Kill you by draining the life out of you? And! You want that to happen. Besides my escalating concern for your well-being, Art, I'm genuinely hurt that's what you think of me and think of us."

I ask, "Why did you choose me?" In a life that has always been too dependent upon what others thought and think of me, Mercy remains the one person whose opinion matters most. Even after everything, I crave her approval and rely on her to corroborate who I am. Who am I?

"Did I choose? Does anyone choose their friends? I will say, honestly, when I first saw you" (notice she doesn't say "when I first met you," because she first saw me when she was Kathleen Blanchet's corpse), "you looked like you needed a friend. But then we became friends naturally." She goes on about wanting to help me and blah-blah-blah and I can't listen anymore.

Okay, Columbo.

With the capped marker I tap the sole uncrossed-out item on the whiteboard. "What about your Polaroid pictures and the proof?"

"Come on, man, really? I put my thumb on the film before it developed. Easy sleight of hand."

I don't know why this upsets me more than the rest of non-refutation refutation, but it does. I say, "I can accept you did that for the old woman's picture. Remember? Then we tried to sneak into the cemetery?"

"Yeah, I remember."

"Okay, that blob looked like a thumbprint. But not the two pictures of me you gave me. No way. Those weren't thumbprints."

"What two pictures?"

I tell her: one from the summer of 1989 with me standing at the top of the basement stairs and the one at the music club she sold me for five bucks. I briefly describe each photo.

Mercy shrugs. "I don't remember what the basement one looked like, but I'm guessing it was too dark to get a good shot or the film got overexposed, and the club one, seeing a face in the folds of your jacket is like—like seeing a face in clouds or your breakfast cereal. It's there because you think it's there."

"Take a picture of me now, then."

"Really? The film is so expensive. I'm trying to save shots for special occasions."

"This is a special occasion."

Mercy shrugs, her shoulders getting right to the point. She says, "Fine," and goes to her room.

It has been almost three years since the night the new (or old) part of me ravened on my mother's chest. During that time, I've attempted to suppress the insuppressible, which is akin to trying to prevent my lungs from absorbing oxygen (although one can hold their breath, deny the oxygen, but one can only hold one's breath for so long). I am not claiming that I am not responsible for my actions because I can't control a process I do not understand. But now I am, for the first time, attempting to will my inscrutable vampiric inner motor to action.

I close my eyes and empty my lungs and, like I did the night after my last Pallbearers Club show, I build the house inside my head. But the one I build is not the now house. Maybe the house in my head is from three years ago, or maybe older, or from a different time altogether. There's something wrong with the head house, even if the dining room has a table again and the TV room's wooden panels are unpainted and the old pullout couch is where it always was. I am alone in the living room now and I am alone in the house in my head. My heart gongs in my chest. I am not permeable or diffuse and I want to leak into the adjoining empty dining room, puddle on the floor, and cry.

Mercy returns with her camera. "I shouldn't be indulging you with any of this, Art." How she says it is the opposite of what she means. Her *how* is saying *I thought you would never ask.* "What happens after I take a picture and you see nothing there besides yourself? Do you want the blue blob on the photo?" Mercy asks. "I could expose the pack before I shoot, but I don't want to ruin all the film. Anyway, watch me closely."

She lifts the camera to peer through the viewfinder, presses the shutter. Flash and whir. I watch closely, I do. The picture ejects and Mercy gently cradles it with one hand, a basket beneath the photo, fingers sequestered to the white plastic edges, careful to not touch the developing film. Then quick choreographed movement: she swivels, deposits the camera on the chair behind her, and switches hands holding the picture.

She says, "It'll take a few minutes to develop."

"I know." I watch the movie of her twitching hands.

"The newer film doesn't fully develop for, like, thirty minutes sometimes." She balances the picture on the tips of her fingers, showing off.

I ask, "How long has it been now?"

"I don't know. I wasn't timing it. I used to pocket pictures right away or stick them in my bag because sometimes it would make cool scratches and effects."

"When can I look?"

She peers at the photo, for the first time as far as I can tell. "All right, now if you want."

I hold out a hand. She drops the picture into my palm. The image of me standing in front of the fireplace is washed out but coming together, colors coalescing. There's a white blob above my head, though the longer I stare, it gains or grows a light-blue tint.

"Did you see me do it?" she asks.

"Do what?" I say, even though I know what she means.

"I pressed my thumb against the film, really quick, right when it came out. Did you see me?"

I did not see either of her thumbs scorpion out and press against the film. I ask, "How come there aren't any lines or swirls from your thumbprint?"

"I used the side of my thumb, not the pad."

"No. Your thumb never touched. I never saw your thumb touch."

"You didn't see it because I'm quick and I'm good. Years and years of practice," she says. "I can show you, teach you, if you want. You'll have to buy your own camera though."

I toss the photo at her. It dodges her torso and fighter-planes behind her, death spiraling onto a chair. I turn and walk out of the room, toward the front door. I don't know what I'm doing. I never have.

"Where are you going?"

"Out. To get some chips."

"No, you're not. Really? Art. Hey, you're upset. I know, and I'm sorry. Stay and let's talk some more, yeah?"

I say, "I won't be long," which is a lie, even if I don't yet know how much of a lie it is. I snatch my car keys hanging from the rack on the wall next to the front door.

"Don't you need your jacket?" she asks from the living room. She is not following me, not stopping me.

I open the door and pause for a moment. I say, "No. I don't think I do."

"You sure about that?"

"Yes."

I wait for her to say something else to stop me, to keep me. Nothing. Then I hear a rustle and a flourish, and I don't need the house in my head to know she picked up her green jacket off the floor.

She says, "Hey, where is your jacket? I didn't see you move it. Neat trick!" Your jacket was on the floor under mine. But I wanted you to come back to look for it. I wanted you to stay.

I drive through the town in my head. I don't have to build it. It has always been there.

I intend to drive aimlessly, but my car slots into the track previously forged by my hearse. And in no time (I perseverate on the expression "and in no time" and how wrong it is; everything pays a price in the currency of time) I am in Beverly Farms, the part of town that as a teen seemed as distant and out of reach as other continents. I pass few cars in the opposite direction and the quaintly opulent seaside center of town is as quiet as a memory. What time is it now? How long have I been driving? I don't have my phone with me and the clock in my car doesn't work.

An inversion of what is to be?
Who is still consuming whom?

Instead of continuing to the mouth of Eddie Patrick's driveway, I park in the nearly empty Beverly Farms train station parking lot. I climb out of the car and close the door as quietly as I can. More like I press my hip against the door until the lock clicks. I wear a black Ramones T-shirt and jeans, no jacket. There's a hint of fall in the air but I am not cold. My anger and confusion at how this night went, at how all the other nights before this one went, stokes the furnace and keeps me warm. I'm tired too. Tired of the compulsion to prove people (including Mercy, including imagined ones, including you, including myself) are wrong about me even when they're right. Or maybe I'm tired because I am reaching if not *the* end, then *an* end.

Why not a Hüskers tee? It's like you brought a piece of me with you.

For a half mile, I walk north on the tracks that split the wooded lots of million-dollar homes. I'm careful to step on the ties and not the crushed gravel between. No need to add more sounds to the evening; there's no telling how far those wavelengths travel. I turn right onto Beach Street, then left onto West Street. This is one of many alternate routes to Eddie's house I memorized from my online map searches. I would've preferred to park closer, either on the street or in the beach lot, but my car has a better chance of not being immediately towed from the train station.

I scuttle through the empty West Beach parking lot and onto the beach itself. My joints and muscles ache and my chest is knotted. Maybe Mercy took another chunk out of me earlier after all. To my right, about fifty yards away, a silhouetted pack of teens electron in the opposite direction. Are they finished with their night or just starting it? The strengthening ocean breeze carries snippets of chatter and laughter (carefree, commiserate, cruel; I always wonder). They couldn't possibly be laughing at me but sometimes it's too easy to travel backward in time. What if they are the children of my former classmates? I briefly imagine myself as the kind of ugly monster that had been locked away for a generation, and now I descend upon them, fangs bared and scything, reaping arms outstretched to extract revenge for the sins of their parents. That is, of course, not fair to them, but it's their lot, their doom. For a moment (still a price, a fee, in time),

I come closer until I am right behind them, on their heels that kick up sand and leave joyous, divoted prints for anyone to follow until the ocean will wipe them away as it will one day wipe away the Farms. There are four in their group. I hear their rabbit heartbeats and I smell their intoxicated and intoxicating breaths and they taste of salty, silly, beautiful hope and the vinegar tang of fear.

I pull away and fall to my hands and knees on the sand. I will not choose them, so I blot them from my mind. I wait for my own hitching breaths to recalibrate, to order themselves, then I stand. I could walk straight into the water and see how far I could swim. Maybe I'd make it to the wonderfully named Big Misery Island. It looks closer than it is. Instead, I scurry left, to where the sandy beach ends at an outcropping of seaweed-slimed rock. The wind is behind my back, urging me forward. I am fortunate the tide is out. If I keep to the rocks, I won't have to go in the water. The climb is treacherous and gothic in the indifferent moonlight until I step down onto sand again.

Weak sauce. You can't lay this one on me. You planned on going to Eddie's all along.

Why I am here? (It has taken me hundreds of pages to explain why I am here.) Despite my clunky reveal <u>Mercy didn't put a stop to me</u> and she didn't and wouldn't tell me why she chose me. Now I need and want to know if I can control it and if I can choose.

And, yeah, I choose Eddie. I will use him to learn what I can and can't do. I will use him to find out, finally, who I am. I will use him until there's nothing left and <u>there's no coming back</u>. I know it's wrong, even if he is a shit person by most people's metrics. But also, he's a shit person, so why shouldn't I? I'll answer: because to choose is to destroy (Mercy can never admit that to herself). I already know who I am, and I'm not that. Or I don't want to be that.

Are you talking about him or you?

As the ocean creeps back toward the shore it shapes and reshapes, I ping-pong on the questions of choice with the lamest and yet most compelling of reasons being *Well, might as well; I came all this way.* My body takes advantage of my distracted multiple minds and storms his beach.

About one hundred feet from the high-tide line is Eddie's obnoxious, none-shall-pass, six-foot-tall, stone-and-mortar seawall.

Staked in front of the wall is a large No Trespassing sign with novel-length text that reads, in part, that the private property legally extends to the waterline and if you are walking the beach do not walk on the sand. That fucking guy.

Interesting word choices.

I lift myself over the seawall and land on an incongruent patch of manicured grass. Twenty feet away is an in-ground pool with a slate-stone patio moating at the base of his Tudor-style house of too many gables. If there are security cameras (and I'm sure there are) I don't see them, which means, I decide, they won't see me. The motion-detecting floodlights do not turn on, as I move too smoothly for them. I move like I'm supposed to be there, like I'm inevitable. I ford the yard and patio to the house. The glass sliding doors to his white, open-concept kitchen are locked. I expect them to be locked. I walk around the house's perimeter until I find the open door. *Find* implies a search, though, when I know it will be there waiting for me. A side exit, a secret hobbit hole to his three-car garage, that's the door that opens at my command.

I close the door behind me and feel my way between a car and the nearest wall. I could key this car and then leave. Maybe that would be enough, would be a different kind of choice I can live with. Of course, I could key it after I sit with Eddie. I creep and edge forward, and I crouch in a corner used for garden-equipment storage. It's not the basement, but it will have to do. I don't close my eyes and I don't build his house inside my head.

And holy shit! That's it! The secret to control is loosening, disassociating from the illusion of control. Part of me pulls, stretches, then breaks away and enters the house. The rest of me stays behind.

Part of me flows through the house's interior as a chill, a draft of cold air, wisping through the antiseptic kitchen and then the vaulted-ceilinged, wainscoted dining room with its expansive baroque table that never once has been fully seated, and then through a maze of other rooms to the black-and-white marble foyer with an avaricious chandelier satelliting above a split staircase that foolishly insists one has a choice of direction.

Back in the garage, my eyes adjust to the light starvation, but I don't want to see. Within my cluttered nook, I find and quietly unroll a section of landscaping tarp.

The walls of the second and third floors are porous membranes that cannot contain this part of me, and I drift like time, and as I progress, the wood, drywall, fixtures, furniture, paintings, and family photos molder in my wake. Even if they are to be fixed or replaced, they would molder again because decay is the state of all things before me, during me, and after me.

I am gravid with exhaustion; the splitting and multiple existences drains me. I shakily pull the tarp over my body and head. It is dark enough and I am weighted down enough to easily imagine I am buried under the ground. The tarp will keep weeds and grass from growing over me.

The part of me I feared was never there, the part of me I feared was always there solidifies, and now on all fours, I ascend to a turreted bedroom on the top floor. The door is closed. The door is open. The door has always been open. Welcome to Dracula's castle?

Under the tarp I can't see anything. I wrap my arms around my legs and I'm curling, shrinking, and I cry because I don't want to do this, I don't want to be here anymore, and I'm afraid this will last forever.

Part of me finds Eddie alone in the polluted sea of his king-sized bed. I am permeable. I fill the room. I am the room. I am the world. This is the mantra. This is the prayer. The bedroom responds, the yellow walls mood-ring into other colors, curtains raspberry their tongues, the nightstand and lamp and furniture tilts, lifts, and bows to me, and his bedspread ripples, then swells like a thunderstorm cloud. Eddie stirs and moans but does not wake. I want him to open his eyes, so he can see me as I rush forward as unformed muscle and sinew. I bound onto the bed and onto him.

Lightning discharges within the middle of my chest. The blast of electrical current gnarls my fingers and arcs out excruciatingly from between my shoulder blades. I gasp and sink into the cold, fathomless waters of agony and torment. My left leg spasms against the garage wall and kicks over a shovel. Dying stars alight in my vision. This isn't how it was supposed to be. No, this is how it is supposed to be.

Part of me is a gargoyle on Eddie's chest; a squat, hunched figure of molten stone pinning him to the mattress. His mouth opens and closes, and for once, nothing comes out. There's a distant clang from the garage but I ignore what it might mean. I am so close, but I strain to withhold for one more aching moment to savor the vista, the yawning chasm of hunger about to be fulfilled. I could live here forever and forget everything else and be nothing else other than the vessel. But no, I'm greedy and I'm a monster and I want more. I send tendrils and protuberances to pry open Eddie's eyelids. He will see this, and I will see him see this. The cold shock of me touching his skin wakes him. He grunts and flops under my weight and I make myself heavier. His animal eyes turn and wheel and focus. I wonder what he sees, what he can possibly see, until I see it; the widening of the eyes (which stay open on their own now), then within his mind-blanking terror, a brief, twitching relaxation of the lids before the brows arch. Recognition. I try to speak, to say, "Hello, Eddie," but I cannot. My mouth fishes open and closed, and my lips undulate but no sound comes out as I spout a lifetime's litany of grudges and disappointments and how they are rooted in and represented by Eddie and all the other Eddies of the world, which, even now, I know isn't wholly true. Doubt and anger begin to shrink me, as they always have, and in this same room in another universe I allow this part of me to recede away to nothing. But here, now, I don't, and I hover my terrible face (an amalgam of all my terrible faces) a whisker's length from the un-fogged window glass of Eddie, and I will steal his breath and I will eat his withered, tainted, unsure heart, and I will feed until there's nothing left of him but clay and dust. And oh, I feed. And it feels like floating.

The pain in my chest mercifully ebbs, though I can't tell if that's because my heart has given up. I'm afraid to listen and feel for it. With my right hand clutching my chest, holding it together, I mount my feet, shuffle across the garage's back wall, and enter Eddie's house. I follow the trail that has been left. The trip to Eddie's bedroom is a journey across the desert of me and it takes decades, all my previous decades, to traverse. I see everything I've done and been and forgotten. If I was never quite happy and if I didn't know who I was and if I was never able to identify the formless yearning for something unattainable, there's solace in who I am not and there's solace in my continuously and infinitely halving the distance toward a bittersweet, wondrously, longingly inexplicable truth. Gabba gabba hey, right? When I finally

Damn right!

arrive at Eddie's bedroom, I might be too late. The bedroom is dark and fuzzy, which might be a me-and-my-shrinking-corona-of-vision problem. My chest is full of shrapnel. I sway and limp to his bedside on feet that are fully numbed. I am winding down, but I still have a few ticks left. I bet. Eddie's aging face is graying and wrinkled. So is mine. I don't need a mirror to know that. I don't like seeing the part of me curled atop Eddie's chest and, sorry, I will not tell you who or what I see. I'm keeping that for me too. I say, "I could stand here until I can't stand anymore and watch you shrivel up, you fucker." I wearily climb onto the bed that's as soft as a marsh and I crawl onto Eddie's chest and part of me tantrums and howls and beats its mighty fists against me as I reclaim it. No one likes a whiner, right? Eddie's face has gone a splotchy, puffy purplish red. A hiss splits his lips when I shift my weight. I say, "You will be visited by three other spirits," just to fuck with him a little more. I roll off Eddie's chest and bed. He coughs and retches and gasps for air. Whole but still split in a way I'll have to learn to live with, I mosey out of the bedroom a hero or antihero to no one,

Fucking mosey. You crack me up.

myself included, and that's okay by me. By the time I get to the garage, Eddie stops coughing and switches to shouting out hysterical threats and entreaties to God-sanctioned vengeance. As if. But before I'm smote, I hustle out the garage's side door, into the floodlit yard, across the grass, and over the fence (not very gracefully) to the beach. And I don't hear Eddie anymore. There's only the wind and waves.

So, hey, remember when Mom asked about how I would end this book?

Well, I'm ending it now, by choice, with me walking on the beach. Maybe I'll just walk for a while, up the coast, see how far I get. No more crossing the old desert sands, at least not now. I've had enough of that and, frankly, I'm fucking exhausted.

Like all stories, this is one about failure and temporary victory. What makes this one different (good, bad, or indifferent, and all shades between) is this book contains me. Well, it holds the parts of me, big meaty chunks of me, that I've named Art Barbara. In the pages and between the covers is who I am and, eventually, as it will be for all of us, the *who I am* statement will turn to past tense.

But what about ME? What are you going to do about me….???? [handwritten marginalia]

Hey, so this book is like my casket, yeah? Maybe it's morbid to think of this book, or any book, as a coffin, but hang with me for one more moment or two (despite the cost).

A book is a coffin because it holds a body, sometimes more than one, and we readers are there to witness, mourn, and celebrate. I like the idea of people (Yes, you. Hi, there!), no matter how small the number, lifting and carrying this casket for a time, honoring it with their attention, experience, memory, and melancholic wonder at what was, at what might be. When you put it down, when you stop carrying it, you'll move on, like you must. And who knows, perhaps years later a snippet of the book's memory will unexpectedly alight and linger; a memory of a time and place and of the person you once were, if you allow it.

Thank you for volunteering to carry me to the end. And welcome to the Pallbearers Club.

I've written and rewritten and crumpled and recrumpled so many notes regarding this last chapter. I didn't get through any of them without crying. Stupid crying. So, I'm going to just plow ahead with this one and not stop to make it pretty. I'll write down everything I want to, even if maybe I shouldn't.

I'm sorry, but I don't think what you wrote should be the end of this book. Never mind that it strikes me as a wee bit sentimental, certainly and surprisingly more so than you ever were in life. Unless you were keeping that deep, dark secret from me all this time. Possible, I suppose. More to the point, the end you wrote is not the end, not the real end, even if it's the one you wanted.

When we publish this, I won't cut or edit your ending—I made a promise I wouldn't rewrite your stuff—but we're going to include my notes, all of them. I do feel bad that I have the last word, or I'm taking the last word. If I was a bigger person, maybe I wouldn't need to.

I'm not a hundred percent clear on how and when this manuscript was finished and then printed out. Let's work out the timeline. I didn't find the book until after the cops came by the house to tell me they'd found your body. You'd been missing for more than two days at that point. After the cops left, I drifted upstairs in shock, and I don't know why, but I was afraid/freaked out. It was like that instant blast of grief was too much to handle, so I had to convert some of it to irrational fear, or the not-so-irrational fear of being alone. It took all I had to work up the courage to go into your music/writing room area. The printed-out, neatly stacked manuscript was on your desk.

The night you stormed out of the house, I stayed up as

late as I could, like a nervous parent waiting for you to come home. I fell asleep eventually, and then later, God knows what time, I heard you come in through the front door and shut it quietly, and then you pattered up the creaking stairs, and man, I was so relieved. You came back. I was convinced that you wouldn't. But the next morning, you and your car were gone again, so at the time, I assumed I'd dreamed your late-night return.

Here's where I'm at: I think you came home to write and print the ending, the section about our last night together, and then you went to Eddie's, or went back to Eddie's. Based on what I know now, it's possible you went to Eddie's first then came back home to finish the book and then went back to his place. Whatever. You coming back home, that's when you had to have written the rest of this. Because how else would you know it would be our last night? Fuck, even I am now thinking like this is a memoir and not a novel. How you wrote about the jacket puppet fight and your whiteboard presentation to me and how it was our last conversation has me shook because it's true. And if that's true, maybe the rest of this is true.

I wish I knew beforehand you weren't coming back. I wasn't ready.

Eddie's gardener found your body in the garage under a tarp. I know you weren't in pieces but, goddammit, I instantly imagined you like the old pullout couch that's still out back in your yard. According to the coroner's report, you'd been dead for two days. Until the report was released, there were rampant rumors in the press about you having OD'd or died by carbon dioxide poisoning or autoerotic asphyxiation—ha! Sorry,

I'm joking on that one—a joke I know would've made you mortified. Fuck, I miss you.

For a few weeks people freaked the fuck out and you became Beverly's new bogeyman, especially after the cops found your car and searched it and in the trunk was some of the stuff we'd bought on my move-in day: rope, the hacksaw, and the hammer. Not a good look for you and your Eddie-intentions. Sorry, my bad? As a gag, I stuck that stuff in your trunk the day after we were done using them thinking you'd find it and you would've been like what the fuck, but I guess you don't open your trunk, like, ever, and I totally forgot about it. Why didn't you ever open your trunk, Art? I tried telling the cops that it was just stuff we used during my move-in and bedroom remodel. I didn't tell them I'd dumped it there as a joke because things would've become way more complicated than they needed to be. As it was, they searched the house and confiscated your phone and iPad, which they still haven't returned. I made sure they didn't get their grubby fascist hands on your laptop or this manuscript though. I had to protect you and protect our book. I did that for you, at least. And I will do one more thing for you/us too. Besides making sure the book gets published.

Man, if you could've seen snivelly old Eddie at the press conference he ran from his front yard. He was shit-scared and raving about having been poisoned and that you were part of a larger commie/anarchist/antifa conspiracy against him. He did look like shit on camera , but purposeful, exaggerated shit. Like someone painted purple eye bags under his eyes and powdered his face. He had a nasty cough, though. A frog throat, in that when he coughed, you could imagine literal frogs spewing out.

The day after the presser he checked into a hospital and reportedly he had a drug-resistant strain of pneumonia. Again, apparently, it got dicey for him. But, eh, he's home from the hospital now. So I'm told. I have a nagging feeling he might have a relapse.

When your tox screen came back—no drugs, clean, surprisingly—along with the full coroner's report, the cause of death was a catastrophically ruptured aorta. Is there any other kind of aorta rupturing? I won't shame you here, now, about how you were supposed to be monitoring and taking care of your heart, however one does such a thing. I can't help but think that it didn't have to happen or didn't have to happen this way.

What are the odds of your heart grenading in Eddie's garage, though, right? Has to be at least 3 to 1.

Sorry, I have to joke, or I won't be able to finish this. The hard part is still coming.

The reality of the timing of your heart attack doesn't work as fiction because people will think it contrived. Though, maybe not, since this is about you being a vampire and fulfilling your—ugh—fate of eventually being buried, and then coming back fully, vampirically blossomed. But you're not coming back. That's the part that sucks. No vampire pun intended?

Goddammit, Art.

All your mom's money—what little is left—and the house is in probate, so I helped your dad pay for your plot and your burial. I couldn't find any living will of yours and I wasn't going to show anyone this manuscript, not yet anyway, not until it was ready. I know your mom was cremated, but it wasn't wholly clear to me if you wanted to be cremated too. Sure, given the implication(s) of your choice in the last chapter, you probably wanted to be cremated so you wouldn't "come back." A novel is hardly a living will, though. I didn't want to guess at something like that, so when your dad insisted that you be buried, I didn't fight him. Burials and ceremonies are for the living anyway. And yeah, I was being a little selfish here too. I wanted you buried. I planned on seeing you again.

I won't put you through the details of who and how many people came to your wake and funeral. Suffice to say, it was a healthy crowd. The services were nice, tasteful, and the speculation about what you were doing at Eddie's was kept to a minimum among the attendees. I made a playlist of your favorite songs that played on low, murmur volume during the wake. Your dad picked out a plot at St. Mary's Cemetery.

I'm sitting in your room as I write this. I'm not going to stay in your house much longer. Not sure why that feels important enough to write down.

Okay, I think we're here, Art. Here's the end-end. Maybe not the one you wanted, but the one this book needs.

(I'm going to employ your parenthesis in this last section, and one long paragraph, both stylistic tics in your honor.)

Earlier (which seems like an incongruous word to choose, because I'm referring to late night, late-late night, as in earlier it was late and now it is early, almost dawn as I scribble this, and this is why I'm not a writer because I'd get bogged down in the details no one else cares about), I snuck into St. Mary's Cemetery. The sneaking wasn't difficult. Yeah, there's a formidable wrought-iron gate (hungry for your shorts) blocking motor-vehicle access, but it was flanked by a shrimpy stone fence, about waist high. I'm not as spry as I used to be, but me and my bigger shoulder bag (I splurged for a new one) had no trouble scaling the wall. The cemetery was a big one, though, and the lengthiest part of the evening was the walk to and from your grave. It was cloudy, dark, and chilly with full-on autumn temps; I could see my breath. Can you make smoke rings with cold breath? I tried to (I'm representing within the text that I was avoiding thinking about what I had to do next) and failed; no rings, only ghosts. After about ten minutes I was deep enough into the cemetery that I couldn't see Brimbal Ave and the giant gas station and convenience mart across from the entrance, and I couldn't see any neighboring homes. There was only a rolling carpet of grass and stone markers and large oak and fir trees dutifully lining and protecting the outer perimeter. If not for the paved car and walking paths, I could imagine I was anywhere else and anytime else. Maybe even Chestnut Hill Cemetery in Exeter, Rhode Island, more than a century ago. (Ooooh, right? Is this me being truthful or playful and fulfilling wish fulfillment? I mean, this isn't necessarily a confession of my being Mercy or Mary. I could still be anyone or anything else and I'm just trying to put the cherry on top of the sundae. Or story.) Eventually (er, sorry, I forgot where you were laid to rest, but cut me some slack. It was dark and the place is a fucking unorganized maze, and maybe I enjoyed the walk, wanted to make the pre-part last a little bit longer because when the end happened, that was it; it wasn't happening again), I found your grave, covered with a fresh lumpen roll of sod. Three bouquets of flowers piled at the head of the grave. One of them was from me. I wanted to say something, but I didn't know what to say, so let my actions talk. I unslung my bag and rabbited the camera out of the hat. I crept close and

took a picture of your grave, the flowers in center focus.
I wasn't worried about anyone seeing the camera flash or
hearing the whir. Careful to not touch the developing film with
my thumb (I promise I was careful, but it's not a guarantee, is
it?), I balanced the photo atop a thatch of taller grass strong
enough to hold it up. Next out from the bag of tricks (or
treats) was a camper's hand shovel. I removed the flowers and
placed them to the side. I expertly (if I do say so myself) pried
up the edges of the sod and rolled it up. Now, fuck me, I
wasn't going to dig all the way down to you. Instead, I became
permeable, like you described, and I did so quickly. I thinned
and fogged out from where I was, so it was like I was there
and somewhere else, the multiple places bent and folded over
each other so I could be in all the places, all the theres.
I filled the gaps between the dirt (as there are gaps between
everything) and made more gaps. I expanded and kept
expanding until the dirt and earth moved away. If you were
watching it might've looked like the earth was being vomited up
and out, but that's not how it really happened, and by now
I would hope you've learned you can't fully trust your perceptions
around me. Years and years of practice, my friend. You would've
learned and you would've been better than me at it, I think.
Shit, you were already, um, permeating, without knowing. When
we were in my apartment in Providence, that floating dresser
bit was all you. Not me. I swear. You were so hyped up or
something, the minute you walked in my place, the dresser went
right up. I know, right? I don't know how you couldn't feel that
charge in the air, the splitting and meeting of places and times.
But again, I've had oodles of practice. Anyway, moving all the
grave dirt was a tiring activity, but I would be replenishing soon

enough. Next from the bag was my cell phone and the hacksaw. (Or fine, a hacksaw. It wasn't the same one. The cops kept the other.) I turned on the phone's flashlight and balanced it at the hole's edge so it spotlighted your casket. I climbed down into the grave and its choking chemical smell. So gross. The top half of your coffin was already open (I helped choose one that had an upper and lower lid. The one-lidded ones are a giant pain in the ass). I was crying this whole time, Art. I want you to know that. I'm making this sound way easier than it was because I don't want to linger here any more than I have to. Jesus, your face. Should I tell you what you looked like? I was reminded of one of the earliest chapters of this book when you attended and saw "Kathleen Blanchet" in her coffin, or when you saw me, and went on about her/me being your first dead person and it didn't seem real, etc. Well, it was real. Me seeing you was real too. So, your waxy, dead face staring up at me is the other bookend of the book. Yet even though I knew better, better than most, it didn't seem real. With the top of your head haloed by thin, curling vines, you seemed shrunken, almost kid-size. Clean-shaven and all, you were back to being the Art I first met. Oh, by the way, I lost the funerary clothing battle, as your dad had you buried in a suit. I know, I tried. I pushed aside the suit jacket flaps and popped off your shirt buttons, and holy shit, you had on a Hüsker T-shirt underneath the dress shirt, the one I gave to Mr. Stephens's nephew. Fuck. (I had to stop there for a minute and hold my face.) I said, "Sorry," and tore the shirt down the middle and exposed your zippered chest. I leaned away from you and sat back up. I needed to take a break and inhale a few breaths filtered by the collar of my shirt. A yellowish-brown fluid pooled under your neck and shoulders, and good on you, Art. Your body was rejecting, pushing out (or creating more gaps between things) the embalming fluid. I had dared hope that would be the case, but I wasn't sure if you were strong enough (for lack of a better phrase) yet. I wasn't sure if your heart would be tainted. Fucking cremations and modern industry-standard embalming are why it is now so hard, almost impossible, to make someone like us, to keep us going. I don't know this for sure, but my theory is if the heart was part of the embalming process, then that was it, there was no coming back from that. But my friend! With you, the coroner removed your tattered, exploded heart, and after the exam he dumped it back into your body but without reattaching it to arteries or anything like that. Why would he? So later, when your body's veins were pumped with the dead juice, none of it got pumped into your heart. Maybe that's fucked logic, I don't know. Based on my experience and many failed experiments, it feels right to me. Maybe I'm wrong. Maybe it's just super fucking hard to make one of us and there's no rhyme or reason to the why of me, you, or the why of anyone. Okay, the pre-hard part was me reopening your chest, but it wasn't as difficult (in terms of physical effort and exertion) as I feared. It was a matter of sawing through the sutures and not flesh. Not really. I expected to find your lungs and heart like a heap of campfire firewood, randomly piled, but they weren't. While not in their exact anatomical spots, they'd already started creeping and snailing back into place. It was kind of cool. I was tempted to wait and watch, see them slug into place. But I couldn't take my eyes off your heart. Your magnificent heart. It glistened and it swelled with a dark-red, almost purple blood. It was the most beautiful heart I'd ever seen, Art. No lie. Had you been re-visiting Eddie? Noshing on randos who came to the cemetery or night-calling at a house close by? (And here we are. We're at the hardest part. But like I said earlier, I did this for you, Art. You made it clear that you chose not to come back. And I won't lie to you now, Art, I did this for me too.) I needed both hands and was careful to not squeeze while at the same time pulling. The tug of war was brief, and your body lifted, leaned toward me as I pulled, and I stared at your face the whole time, waiting for your eyelids to flutter open, and they did, but then your body let the heart go with a slick, detached pop. Your body settled back into the coffin, your eyes closed, and I hopped out of the grave. I forgot to mention I'd already set up a ceramic bowl atop a burning pyre of sticks and leaves. I placed the heart inside the bowl and sprayed it with olive oil (I know, aerosol cooking spray isn't good for anyone, but there was a limit to what I could and wanted to carry in my pack). With a burning twig I ignited the heart. It burned quickly and with a somber light show that I wish I'd recorded with my phone. When your heart was ash, I poured wine (plain water?!? Pfft) into the bowl. And I drank. I won't wax poetic about the taste (unavoidably smoky, but with a perfect layer of sweetness) and my gourmand palate and the rush (swallowing supernovas) or anything like that. No one likes a braggart, but this was the culmination of a lot of work on my part, and your heart was the best one I've ever had, certainly the longest one in coming/making. So, I savored. Once finished (I tried to make it last, but it was over too soon, always too soon; ah, the eternal lament), I packed up. I'm embarrassed to say I almost forgot about the Polaroid picture. That would've been a disaster.

Within the photo was a lovely, the loveliest, blue orb above your grave. The color was full and bold, and the shape was boundaryless and morphing and reaching and nebulous and, well, pulchritudinous, and it welled in me a tsunami of grief and gratitude. I wanted to keep the picture, put it in a pocket so it would always be with me, but I couldn't. That would be me being too greedy and not honorable. I sent the photo spinning down into the grave. I didn't watch it leaf its way down, but I assume it nestled where it belonged, inside your emptied chest. Then I left the graveyard and drove back to your house. I sat in the kitchen with a bottle of wine. I reminisced and remembered and toasted you, my friend, then I moseyed (as you say) up to your room to write this.

How about one final toast to you, my dearest friend.

For you, Art, I will be the monster you wanted and needed me to be.

Salut.

ACKNOWLEDGMENTS

For the historical details of Mercy (and Mary) Brown's stories I used the referenced *Providence Journal* newspaper articles and Michael E. Bell's wonderful book *Food for the Dead: On the Trail of New England's Vampires*. There are scores of Internet resources about Mercy as well, but from what I could tell, they all cited Michael's comprehensive book.

Thank you, Lisa, Cole, and Emma, as always, for being understanding and supportive. A huge chunk of this book was written while we were in the teeth of pandemic lockdown (I finished a first draft almost to the day of my second vaccination shot in mid-April 2021), and there was no way I would've been sane enough to write this book without them. Extra thanks to Emma for drawing the floating vampire dresser.

To be clear, Art Barbara is and isn't me. Well, fine, he's mostly me. But! The other characters in the book are fictional characters. Thank you, Mom and Dad, for allowing me to continually fictionalize you both in ways big and small. I love and admire you more than you could know.

Thank you, John Langan for always being the ear that listens, and the friend on which I can lean. I still owe you a terrible fictionalization. It's coming.

Thank you to friends and first readers Stephen Barbara, Lydia Gittins, and Sarah Langan. Your feedback and encouragement were invaluable.

The teams at William Morrow and Titan Books went above and beyond with this book, helping it to be and look the best it could be. Thank you to my editor Jennifer Brehl, who got me to wrestle this unruly thing into shape (I cut about thirty pages from the draft I'd turned in). Thank you, the tireless team of editors, copyeditors, designers, and marketing/publicity (and sorry, the next book will be easier to deal with. I mostly promise?): Nate Lanman, Mumtaz Mustafa, David Palmer, Pam Barricklow, Rachelle Mandik, Leah Carlson-Stanisic, Andrew DiCecco, Miranda Ruoff, Elina Cohen, Ryan Shepard, and Camille Collins.

Thank you, friends and family for the encouragement and support. Extra thanks to Michael Coulombe for coming with me on the visit to Mercy's grave. I wasn't too afraid to go by myself, I swear.

Thank you to all the musicians mentioned in the book who helped me to get through high school and beyond, and who continue to inspire me. Extra thanks to Andy Falkous who helped with some of the gear talk.

Special thanks to Rachel Autumn Deering for designing the rocking flyer.

Thank you, kind reader. And bless your delicious heart.